Kissing in the Dark

WENDY LINDSTROM

Winner of the Romance Writers of America's
prestigious RITA Award

Books by Wendy Lindstrom

Shades of Honor
The Longing
Lips That Touch Mine
Kissing in the Dark
Sleigh of Hope
The Grayson Brothers boxed set

rustic studio
PUBLISHING

Originally published by Leisure Books
Copyright © 2005 Wendy Lindstrom
Digital edition published by Wendy Lindstrom
Copyright © 2012 Wendy Lindstrom
Second edition published by Rustic Studio Publishing
Copyright © 2013 Wendy Lindstrom

ISBN: 1939263107
ISBN 13: 9781939263100

Cover design by Kim Killion of Hot DAMN! Designs

Publishers interested in foreign-language translation or other subsidiary rights should contact the author at www.wendylindstrom.com.

Chapter One

Fredonia, New York
June 1879

The tangy scent of soaps and spices made Duke sneeze as he entered Brown & Shepherd's store. He grunted in pain and he clapped a hand over his aching shoulder.

Wayne Archer looked up from the package of medicine he was delivering to the store. The stocky apothecary propped his fists on the counter and eyed Duke with suspicion. "Are you ill, Sheriff?"

"Morning, Archer." Duke ignored the man's question. Archer didn't care about Duke's health. He wanted to get elected sheriff in November. Six men were running for the position against Duke, who had been the sheriff of Chautauqua County since he was twenty-three years old. Five of the seven candidates could handle the position. Duke was one of them. Wayne Archer wasn't.

Duke stepped away from the soaps and spices and greeted the store owner, Agatha Brown, a kind, elderly widow he'd known since he was a boy.

"You're too late for licorice sticks," she said. "I sold the last one yesterday afternoon to your niece, Rebecca."

"That qualifies as a crime, Mrs. Brown." He'd been buying or begging licorice sticks from her since he was old enough to ask for them, and he was still one of her best customers.

"My next shipment will arrive tomorrow. Will that keep me out of jail?" she asked.

"This time," he said sternly.

Her laugh lit her eyes and transformed her somber demeanor into that of a softer, more youthful-looking woman. Agatha Brown was six years older than Duke's mother, and could make some man a good companion, but Duke suspected she would choose to remain a widow. He'd been a boy when her husband died, and he barely remembered the man, but Agatha had never forgotten him. She seemed content to live with his memory and to run their store on Main Street in the Village of Fredonia.

"What are you looking for?" she asked.

"Something to relieve a headache." His nagging shoulder pain was bringing it on, but the last thing he would do was announce that fact to Archer. Which was why he wasn't buying the powder in Archer's apothecary: Archer would use the information to sway the voters.

Mrs. Brown pointed to the opposite wall of the store. "Top shelf on the left."

"Thank you." The pine floorboards sounded hollow beneath his boot heels as he wove his way past a rack of ready-made clothing. Heavily laden shelves sagged beneath tins of food, and wooden bins overflowed with everything from shovels and rakes to bolts of fabric. Brown & Shepherd's carried anything a man or woman could need.

But as Duke surveyed the medicines, he felt a sharp poke in his ribs.

"Grayson." Archer scowled at him. "For being a sheriff, you're sadly unobservant." He jerked his chin toward a boy who was examining a lady's comb and brush set. "That young man is attempting to fill his pockets."

The boy took a fancy lady's brush from the oak box and slipped it inside his shirt.

Duke's heart sank. He hated this part of his job.

The boy cast a furtive glance at Mrs. Brown, who was dusting trinkets then ducked outside.

Duke ignored Archer's snide look, and quietly followed the boy. A few paces outside the store, he brought his hand down on the boy's thin shoulder. "Hold up, young man."

The boy yelped and spun to face him. The movement jerked Duke's arm and sent a hot spear of pain into his shoulder socket. Damnation! His shoulder was so torn up he couldn't even detain a child.

The skinny, long-limbed youth stared at him, dark eyes wide with fear as they locked on the silver sheriff's badge pinned to Duke's leather vest.

"I'm Sheriff Grayson," Duke said. "You didn't pay for that hair brush you're hiding under your shirt."

The boy's gaze darted to either side, as if he were deciding whether or not to run.

"I'd rather not handcuff you, but I will if you try to run off on me."

"I'll put it back," the boy said, his voice cracking into a fear-filled falsetto.

"Looks like you could use the brush."

The boy lowered his eyes and raked bony fingers through his mop of brown hair. "It's not for me."

"Are you stealing it for your girl?"

"I don't have a girl."

"For your mother then?"

"No, sir."

Duke rubbed his aching shoulder, cursing the nagging pain that had made his life miserable for the past month.

The boy's Adam's apple dipped on a nervous swallow. "Are you taking me to jail?"

Jail wouldn't teach him anything of value. "I'm taking you home so I can talk to your father."

"I don't have a father."

No surprise there, Duke thought, but checked his unfair judgment. "We'll talk to your mother then."

"My mother's dead." The boy's voice was so heavy with grief that Duke's chest tightened in sympathy.

"How are you getting along without parents?"

"I've got Faith."

"You'll need more than faith and those light fingers to get by, son. Where are you sleeping?"

The boy turned away. "At home."

Duke gripped the boy's shoulder and spun him back around to face him. "I'm sorry about your parents and whatever troubles you're having, but when I ask you a question I expect a straight answer."

"I gave you one, sir." The boy pointed down Water Street. "I live at the old Colburn place with my older sister Faith and our aunts. We moved in three weeks ago."

Duke had heard that somebody bought the mill, but he hadn't stopped to officially welcome the owners to town yet. "Is your sister planning to reopen the grist mill?" he asked, believing it impossible for a woman to do so.

"No, sir." The boy squinted as a bright flood of June sunshine washed across the plank and brick buildings on Main Street. "She's a healer. So are my aunts."

"Healers?"

"Yes, sir. They grow herbs and mix tonics and salves that help people."

The warning twinge that tightened Duke's gut was as unwelcome as Archer's earlier probing. He did not need another problem right now, not with the election coming up, not while his wretched shoulder was making his life miserable.

The boy pulled the hair brush from beneath his shirt and handed it over. "I'd like to return this. I don't want my sister to know what I did."

His earnest plea moved Duke, but being soft on the boy wouldn't serve the young man. "You should have considered that before you walked out of the store without paying for it. Come on," he said, nudging him down Main Street. "Let's see if your sister can heal your bent for stealing."

"Sir, my sister is... she'll... I'd rather go to jail than tell her what I did."

That was the point in taking the boy home with the stolen item. Shame would be more effective than fear to keep him from repeating the act.

"What's your name?" Duke asked, keeping his hand on the boy's shoulder and guiding him down Water Street.

"Adam Dearborn." The boy's body jerked as if he'd been stuck with a needle. "I mean, it's Adam... um... dang it all." He hung his head.

"Something wrong, Adam?"

"No, sir."

"All right, let's meet this sister of yours and figure out what to do about your crime."

"I'm not a criminal."

"You took something from a store without paying for it. That's theft, and theft is a crime punishable by law."

Adam dragged his feet, his shame so acute Duke pitied him. He knew from his own experience how miserable Adam felt right now, but the boy needed to learn the same harsh life lesson Duke had learned at the age of eight from his own father. The burning shame he'd felt that evening nearly twenty-three years ago had been seared into his conscience, and he'd never forgotten his father's admonishment that honorable men never lie, cheat, or steal. Ever.

Adam would learn that lesson today.

"How old are you, Adam?"

"Just turned thirteen."

"You're old enough to work then."

The boy nodded. "I've been working in our greenhouse since I was four."

They turned down Mill Street, a tiny lane connecting Water and Eagle Streets.

"Tell me more about this greenhouse of your sister's."

"Faith grows herbs and stuff for healing."

"But what does she heal?"

The boy shrugged. "Everything, I guess, or people wouldn't buy our tonics and balms."

Suspicion tightened Duke's gut. He did not need some crazy woman selling snake oil and promising miracle cures to his unsuspecting friends and neighbors.

Adam stopped in front of Colburn's former mill, a three-story gambrel-roofed building with a towering brick smokestack, and a one-story stone addition attached at the rear. To the left of the huge grist building stood a plank structure that once housed the bales of hay and straw that Colburn had sold. And beyond that was the horse barn, right where it had always been. But Duke's gut insisted something was different. And his gut was never wrong.

He'd been inside the cavernous building often enough to know that the interior light was too negligible to successfully contain a greenhouse. The water was plentiful, though. The Canadaway Creek was a ready source of power for the many businesses built along its banks as the gristmill was.

"Sheriff Grayson?" Adam bit his lip. "I'd rather go to jail."

"I'm not offering that choice. Is your sister here?" At Adam's resolute nod, Duke ushered him inside.

The first thing to strike Duke was the sunlight streaming through new, large windows that lined three of the four walls. That's what had looked different about the building when he'd eyed the exterior. The lower floor of the building was filled with windows and flooded in sunlight.

The smell of fresh soil mingled with the astringent scent of herbs and an indefinable floral fragrance. The thriving profusion of plants and flowers told him that Adam's sister knew what she was doing. Maybe the woman was just concocting a few harmless homemade remedies that would save other women the tedious task. Maybe he was overreacting because of his own worries about the upcoming election.

This was his eighth year as sheriff, and he had every confidence that he would keep his position—as long as he could get his shoulder healed. Just one rumor that he couldn't do his job could change the outcome of the election and end his hard-won tenure as sheriff.

From the back of the greenhouse a child laughed and women's voices tittered. A softer female voice drew his attention to the front of the building. The woman had her back to him, but her quiet singing was laced with such sadness, Duke felt he was trespassing on a private moment.

Adam stayed by the door and hung his head. "That's my sister."

Faith, Duke remembered. She was watering plants, gently touching the green leaves and inspecting the buds.

"Please don't be mean to her, Sheriff. Faith taught me not to steal. She would never steal anything. Not even if she was starving."

Shocked by the boy's plea, Duke eyed Adam. "Why would I mistreat your sister for something you did?"

"Because she's responsible for me."

"No, son, *you* are responsible for you. And you're responsible for your actions."

"Yes, sir."

"Why did you take this?" Duke asked, lifting the fancy brush.

The boy ducked his head and his ears turned red. "Faith misses our mother real bad. I thought a new brush might make her happy again."

That simple declaration sliced through Duke. He'd heard the sadness in Faith's voice as she sang, and could understand why the boy wanted to make her happy. It was hard for an adult to acknowledge that depth of grief, but far more difficult for a child to witness it in someone he loved and needed. No wonder the boy seemed lost and afraid.

Adam's sister turned toward them with the watering can clutched in her hand, and every thought in Duke's mind dissolved into silence. She was as exotic as the plants she tended.

Her arched dark eyebrows drew together as she spotted him and Adam. She set the watering can on a flat of green plants then moved her slender, lithe body gently but hurriedly in their direction, pushing aside plant vines and leaves that congested the narrow row between the wooden flats. With every lift of her arm, the worn blue fabric of her shirtwaist tightened across her full breasts and tiny waist.

"What's happened?" she asked, stopping before him with fear in her almond shaped eyes.

Duke could only stare in mute appreciation. From the age of eight, he'd made it a policy not to exaggerate or lie, not even to himself. And he could honestly say he'd never seen a more beautiful woman than the one standing in front of him. Her oval face was slightly squared at the jaw and softly rounded at the chin. Her parted lips were lush and made for kissing, her eyes a deep whiskey brown that made him thirst for a drink. She was tall, and he would only have to dip his chin to kiss her forehead or to bury his face in those thick waves of dark, chocolate brown hair.

"Sheriff? Has something happened?" she asked, tiny worry lines marring her forehead, drawing his attention to the bronze tint of her skin. Her voice was smoky, or perhaps slightly hoarse from a cold or singing, but it sounded sultry and sexy to him.

"I had some trouble in town," Adam blurted.

"What sort of trouble?"

Adam's chin dropped to his chest. "I stole something from Brown & Shepherd's store." He peered up at her, his own almond-shaped eyes full of remorse. "I wanted to give you a birthday present to make you feel better."

She brought slender fingers to her chest, drawing Duke's gaze to her nicely rounded breasts. "Oh, Adam, I don't need a present."

"You deserve to have your own brush," Adam said with a touch of defiance that surprised Duke. "You shouldn't have to borrow from Aunt Tansy"

Color flooded the crests of her cheekbones, but she swept her brother into her arms. "Your character and reputation are far more important than me having my own hair brush."

Adam's face grew crimson, and he pulled away as if embarrassed to be hugged in front of Duke. Or maybe it was shame that made his face turn red, Duke couldn't tell. He was struggling with his own embarrassment for gawking at Faith like a schoolboy.

"I wanted to return the brush," Adam said, "but the sheriff said I had to bring it to you."

Duke expected to see condemnation in Faith's eyes, but he saw surprise and confusion. "I felt he would learn more from his family than any punishment I could give him," he said. He handed the fancy brush to her. "This is yours."

"I... I'll pay for this," she said, but Duke could tell she didn't want the brush. She turned to Adam. "Go to the house and get our money jar." As soon as Adam sprinted from the greenhouse, she faced Duke again. "I'd rather return this and save my money for more necessary items."

It struck him then that Faith and her family were not only grieving but also having money troubles.

"Maybe we can work out a better solution."

Wariness stole the warmth from her eyes. "I'll pay for it."

Adam hurried back into the greenhouse with an old quart jar that held a few paltry coins in the bottom. Faith upended the jar and spilled the coins into her palm. She held them out to Duke, her cool look saying she wasn't open to other solutions.

"I hope this is enough," she said.

It stung to have his integrity questioned, but she was new to town and didn't know that he would eat dirt before doing anything dishonest or indecent. He'd pay for the brush himself, but it wouldn't serve Adam if someone else paid for his bad decision. Adam needed to learn a lesson about taking responsibility, a lesson that would serve him well as he became a man.

And Faith needed to learn that Duke was worthy of her trust.

"Adam meant for the brush to be a gift," he said. "Why not let him work off his debt in the store? I'm sure Mrs. Brown will welcome his help, and that way Adam can give you the gift with a clear conscience."

"I'll do it." Adam lifted his skinny chest like a soldier bravely facing battle. "I'll apologize to Mrs. Brown and work extra hard to make up for stealing from her."

"Mrs. Brown isn't likely to allow you in her store, Adam." Faith shook her head. "You can make your apology when you take this money to her."

Duke suspected those were her last coins, and he couldn't let her use them for Adam's mistake. "This is Adam's debt. Let him pay it," he insisted. The boy wanted and needed to make restitution.

Before Faith could answer, a small brown-haired girl whooped and darted between them. She threw her arms around Faith's skirt and hugged her legs.

"Mama, Aunt Iris said she's gonna plant me with the onions if I pester her anymore!"

Duke's heartbeat faltered. During his covert admiration of the woman, he hadn't considered Faith's personal life, that she might have a child, that she might be married, that his own growing anticipation of making a personal call on her was out of line.

"This is my daughter, Cora," she said, brushing the girl's curls out of her lively green eyes.

Cora pointed to the badge on his chest. "What's that?" Before he could answer, she gawked at his revolver. "Is that a gun? Do you shoot people?" She was a slip of a girl with skinny arms and legs, and a cute little mouth that spewed questions faster than Duke could answer them. Her curiosity made her bold, and she tried to touch the gleaming metal cuffs hanging from Duke's gun belt.

He stepped back, removing the gun from her reach. "Careful, missy," he said. "Guns are dangerous. Never touch one. Not for any reason. Not ever."

"Cora Rose, mind your manners," Faith said, laying her hand on Cora's head and gently chastising the girl.

"What are those?" she asked, undaunted.

"Handcuffs."

"What are they for?"

Duke glanced at Faith, who gave him an apologetic look. "She's four," she said, as if that would explain Cora's curiosity. For Duke, who had six nephews and two nieces, it explained everything. A four-year-old's questions could wear a person down faster than an interrogation by the United States military.

He reached to unhook the cuffs, but the move shot a fierce spike of pain into his shoulder socket. He bit his lip to stop an agonized curse from slipping out then forced himself to pull the cuffs from the clasp on his leather belt. His shoulder throbbed as he squatted and showed her how to work the cuffs. "If you go quietly, you might be able to cuff your Aunt Iris to a fat plant," he suggested, hoping the child would scamper out of earshot. He didn't want her to hear his conversation with Faith and Adam.

Cora giggled and charged toward the back of the greenhouse.

"Consider your handcuffs lost," Faith said. "She'll bury them someplace, and we'll never find them again."

As he stood, he eased out a breath, letting the pain ebb from his shoulder and the hope of courting Faith ebb from his mind. Faith was married. Nothing to do but accept it, take care of the business with Adam then leave. Adam seemed to be a considerate boy, but he needed a man's guiding hand. Much as Duke didn't want to meet Faith's husband, he felt it his duty to inform him of Adam's mistake and hope the man could provide the guidance and influence the boy needed.

But he stole one final moment to admire Faith—a woman he wanted to know more about.

With a resigned sigh, he nodded toward the open door of the greenhouse. "Is your husband at home today?"

Her lashes lowered. "I'm a widow, Sheriff Grayson."

Surprise, relief, and a deep sympathy rushed through him. She couldn't be more than twenty-five or so. To be widowed in old age was a sad thing, but to lose a spouse at such a young age was tragic. She had lost not only her husband but her mother as well. No wonder her sultry voice was laced with pain.

Duke understood grief. He'd lost his father over a decade ago, but the pain would never go away.

The realization that she was hurting and having hard times, too, shifted Duke's direction like a compass needle seeking North. He'd never been able to turn away someone in need— especially a woman in need—and he sure wouldn't turn away the gorgeous widow with the sultry voice and those beautiful whiskey eyes.

Chapter Two

F aith didn't want her not-so-innocent little brother party to her lies, so she touched Adam's shoulder and nodded for him to leave. "Go see that Cora doesn't lose the sheriff's handcuffs," she said.

"Yes, ma'am." Adam headed toward the back of the greenhouse, leaving Faith with Sheriff Grayson—a man she did not want to be alone with.

His powerful body was overwhelming, but it was the close inspection the ruggedly handsome sheriff was giving her that completely unnerved her. If she wasn't careful with this man, he would see through her thin veil of pretense to the hard, ugly truth no one could know.

"I'm sorry about your loss, Mrs....?"

"Dearbo—oh... oh my, how rude of me not to have introduced myself." She stuck out her trembling hand. "I'm Faith Wilkins." A necessary lie. "Pleased to make your acquaintance, Sheriff Grayson."

"Likewise." He closed his long, warm fingers around her hand, making her stomach flutter. "I'm sorry about your tragic loss."

She pulled free of his firm grip and curled her fingers into her palms, hiding her green fingernails. "Are you in pain, Sheriff?" she asked, noticing that he'd been rubbing his shoulder.

He lowered his hand as if she'd caught him revealing an unpardonable weakness. "Just a sore muscle," he said, but she suspected it would take far more than muscle pain to bother an obviously strong man like the sheriff.

He surveyed the greenhouse then returned his scrutiny to her. "What exactly do you do here, Mrs. Wilkins?"

"I grow herbs, vegetables, and flowers."

"Adam tells me you're a healer."

"Adam is a boy who overstates the importance of things. I make healing balms and teas from my plants. Simple as that, Sheriff. If you'd care to sample them firsthand, I have a balm that might ease the pain in your shoulder." The sooner she could appease his curiosity the sooner he would leave. And the sooner her heart would stop hammering in her chest.

She headed to a small counter in the north corner of the greenhouse. He followed then watched while she opened a large glass jar and scooped out a spoonful of yellowish balm.

"Gads, is that chicken fat?" he asked, his voice laced with disgust.

She laughed. "It's a mix of resins and oils." She lifted the gluey-looking balm to her nose, and inhaled. "I add herbs, and salicin, which is harvested from the buds of poplar trees—part of the willow family."

"I know trees," he stated bluntly, as if she'd insulted his intelligence. "I own a sawmill with my brothers."

Her cheeks burned. "Forgive me. I'm used to teaching Adam and Cora this way"

"I'm not offended. I'm curious to see what you do here." He gestured toward the balm. "You made this, I presume?"

She nodded. "The salicin and herbs reduce pain, fever, congestion, and inflammation. The balm even smells good." She put the spoon beneath his nose. "It's not bay rum, but it smells better than an onion pack."

His mouth quirked up on one side. The slight lifting of his lips surprised her and made him seem less formidable. Their gazes met over the spoon. He openly inspected her, but unlike most of the men who'd crossed her path, there was nothing lecherous in the sheriff's eyes; he seemed to appreciate her boldness, as if there weren't many people who would dare to shove something beneath his nose. Her nerves had made her careless. She hadn't meant to challenge him. But apparently she had, and apparently he'd liked it.

She plopped the small glob of ointment into a jar and handed it to him. "Two or three applications should ease your muscle pain. After you rub it into your shoulder, you'll feel a soothing warmth in that area."

"What if it doesn't work?" He braced his large, long-fingered hand on the counter. "Will I get my money back?"

"You haven't paid me anything."

"I intend to."

"I'll refuse it. This is the only way I can thank you for being so kind to Adam today."

"I wasn't being kind."

"The way you treated him was more than fair. In my book, that's being kind."

"I would have done the same for any boy."

"But you did it for my brother, and that's what matters to me. Please, take the balm."

"What other treatments do you offer?"

He seemed sincere, but she sensed he was digging for something. The pleasantly warm day suddenly felt close and hot with this giant of a man leaning on her counter asking too many questions.

"It would depend on the severity of your problem. But I would first suggest that you see a doctor." She closed the jar of balm and placed it back on the self.

"I've seen the doctor. He says there's nothing to be done for my shoulder but to rest it."

"Then it is more than a sore muscle?"

His lip quirked up again. "You have a knack for recalling details. I could use your help when questioning suspects."

She'd hoped to put him off with her nosy question, but instead of urging him out the door, she'd invited his closer observation. "Forgive me for taking up your time." She stepped around the counter and called toward the back of the greenhouse, "Adam! Come up here, and bring Cora and the handcuffs with you."

Adam swept Cora into his arms, pushed through a maze of plants, and deposited the girl a few feet from the sheriff.

"Cora, give the sheriff his handcuffs," Faith said then frowned as Cora duck-walked across the plank floor. "Why are you walking so oddly?"

Cora leaned back on her heels, pressed her brown gingham dress to her knees, and lifted the toes of her tiny brown shoes. "I hooked 'em on my own self."

The metal handcuffs were locked around Cora's skinny ankles. A quiet chuckle rumbled in the sheriff's chest, his thick-lashed eyes crinkling at the outside edges as he looked down at her.

Cora squatted, grabbed the chain between her ankles, and grinned up at him. "Aunt Iris says to keep these on me until I get married."

With her hands between her ankles, and her knobby knees jutting upward, Cora looked like a little brown frog. Her stockings were twisted around her ankles, her hair in wild disarray, but Faith could not have adored her more.

Nor could the sheriff, if the tender look in his eyes meant anything.

"She reminds me of my niece Rebecca at that age," he said. "Too smart, too curious, and a smile so bright she could melt a heart of ice." He sighed and shook his head. "Rebecca turned thirteen last week."

With Cora's rosy face beaming up at them, Faith understood the sheriff's melancholy. She wanted Cora to stay an innocent, if precocious, little girl forever.

Faith spied her Aunt Iris around the corner, and cringed as Iris lunged from behind a cluster of lemongrass to tickle Cora's ribs.

"There you are, you little imp!"

Cora screeched with laughter and threw herself against the sheriff's legs.

Iris, who had crouched to grab Cora's ribs, took her time looking up the long length of the sheriff's body. By the time her frank, appraising eyes lifted to his face, Faith's own cheeks were burning with embarrassment.

"Mercy..." Iris said, rising to her feet with a fluid grace Faith envied. Iris carried her mother's Japanese blood in her veins, and men paid exorbitant amounts of money to bed the rare onyx-haired beauty. Faith knew little about Iris or how she had come to be in America. She was seven months older than Faith, but Iris had seen too much to pretend an innocence she'd shed long ago.

"Is there a woman waiting at home for you, Sheriff?" Iris asked, extending her hand to him.

Faith's jaw dropped, but the sheriff smiled and lifted Iris's hand to his lips as if too-bold women propositioned him every day. "I'm afraid so, ma'am. My mother is expecting me home for supper." His gaze lingered on her silky black hair and the pretty Oriental tilt of her eyes, and Faith knew Iris was as novel to the sheriff as she'd been to Faith when first arriving at the brothel eleven years ago. Iris said a small colony of Japanese people had come to America in 1869, but Faith still hadn't seen another man or woman like her. Apparently, the sheriff hadn't either.

Iris laughed the way she talked, without reservation. Her exotic eyes sparkled like black diamonds as she assessed the sheriff. "Not only handsome but charming." She winked a thick- lashed eye at Faith. "Marry this man."

"For heaven's sake, Aunt Iris!" Novel or not, Faith wanted to shoo the woman out the door. They couldn't afford to have their reputations questioned. Drawing a breath to calm herself, Faith gave the sheriff a wobbly smile. "This is my aunt, Iris... um..." Dear God, she hadn't given thought to a last name for her aunts. They had never used last names at the brothel, and they had flown from that life in such a rush of terror, they had never discussed taking last names.

"Wilde with an 'e'," Iris said, mischief twinkling in her eyes. "Miss Iris Wilde, not to be confused with a wild Iris."

The sheriff laughed.

"Are you getting married, Mama?" Cora asked, looking up at Faith with hopeful eyes.

Faith wanted to turn green and disappear among the plants. "See what you've started?" she said to Iris.

Iris gave the sheriff a friendly wink. "My niece is so shy she'll never get herself a suitor or a marriage proposal. I'm just letting you know she's looking for a husband."

Faith choked on her outrage.

Iris ignored her warning look and pouted her lips at the sheriff. "I was hoping to beg your assistance for a few minutes. Adam is our man about the place, but he doesn't know about gas lines yet."

Faith tried again to convey a message with her eyes, silently warning Iris to clamp her red lips shut. "As soon as the sheriff removes these cuffs from Cora's legs, he and Adam have business in town. I'll hire a man to take care of the gas line." She lifted Cora into her arms and forced herself to face the sheriff. "I apologize for wasting so much of your time."

"It's not a waste of time to welcome new residents," he said. "I'll look at that gas line as soon as I free this little frog girl from her chain."

Cora giggled and lifted her feet, asking six questions in the time it took him to unlock the cuffs.

"The cuffs are made of steel," he said, answering her first question. "Because steel is strong. I put them on bad people so they can't get away. Yes, my shoulder hurts. Yes, I'll come play again. And no, I'm not marrying your mother today"

For the first time since the sheriff arrived, Faith willingly met his eyes. "I'm impressed."

He shrugged his wide shoulders. "Lots of practice. I have six nephews and two nieces."

"Any unmarried brothers?" Iris asked.

"Two older, one younger, all married," he said. "I'm the last man standing."

"Not for long, Sheriff." Iris linked her arm with his and turned him toward the back of the greenhouse.

Faith stared openmouthed at her aunt's swinging backside, wondering if Iris was matchmaking for her, or worse yet, if the ex-prostitute was angling for the handsome sheriff herself.

Chapter Three

Duke rolled up his shirtsleeves then showed Adam how to hook the gas pipe to the old boiler. The boy seemed interested in learning, but there wasn't room for him to help connect the gas line to the burner beneath the metal tub. Colburn had tried using natural gas eight years earlier, but the supply from his gas well on Mill Street was insufficient to power the grist mill. So, like other business owners, he'd diverted a feeder stream from the creek and used water and steam for power.

Colburn must have needed the water reservoir for his grist mill, but Duke couldn't understand why Faith would want to heat this enormous bin of water. The deep, rectangular vessel had to be nearly eight feet long and four feet wide, and the copper had aged to an ugly greenish black.

Puzzled, Duke squeezed his aching shoulders between the cold stone wall and the tub. By the time he finished the back-wrenching work, his shoulder throbbed so painfully he wanted to knock back a quart of whiskey and sleep until the dang thing healed.

After Adam fetched a cake of soap, Duke rubbed water on it then applied a soapy lather to the gas pipe connections to see if any bubbles developed.

"How often should I check for leaks?" the boy asked, like a man, even as he shoved his mop of hair out of his eyes like a school boy.

"A couple times a day for the next day or two. If you can't see any bubbles in the soap, you can assume the connections are secure."

Adam nodded, and Duke struggled to his feet, realizing the boy was missing school. "Why aren't you in school today?"

"There's only two weeks left of the year, sir."

"Well, if you were in school, Adam, you wouldn't have been in Mrs. Brown's store, and you wouldn't have gotten yourself in trouble."

"I was running an errand for Faith. She needed some cheesecloth."

"I want you to go to school next week."

Adam lowered his chin. "Yes, sir."

Iris strode into the stone room and flirtatiously brushed dust off Duke's shirtsleeve. "Finished already?" she asked.

Her boldness surprised him as much as her appearance had, and it seemed to fluster Faith who had followed her into the room. "I just need to light the burner and I'll be done here." He'd traveled some during his years as sheriff, but had never seen anyone like Iris, or any woman as beautiful as Faith.

Iris clasped her hands in front of her. "Let us repay you by sending a few herbs home to your mother. Or perhaps you'd rather choose a few for yourself? We grow special herbs for men," she said with a saucy wink. "Ginseng and passionflower—"

"Basil!" Faith blurted, crowding Iris away from him. "We grow basil and valerian and aconite." Pink stained her cheeks, but she didn't spare Iris a glance. "We grow healing herbs like comfrey, chamomile, feverfew; that sort of thing. But your mother would probably prefer cooking herbs like chives, basil, or bay leaf."

"I wouldn't know one from the other," Duke said, looking through the doorway at the rows of flats covering the greenhouse, "but I'd like to look around." And he would enjoy the pretty widow's fetching blushes while he found out a little more about her unusual business.

"Clean your hands and wait out front, Adam," Faith said. "We'll be out in a moment."

After Duke lit the burners for the tub and boiler, he stepped into the greenhouse with Faith.

"This is comfrey," she said, lifting a large, hairy leaf on a plant about three feet tall. She stroked her fingertip over a purple bell-shaped flower adorning the plant, and it sent a ripple of warmth down Duke's spine. He hadn't felt the stroke of a woman's fingers across his flesh in a very long time. His choice. He had friends who would welcome an intimate visit from him; but after years of watching his brothers flirt and joke with their wives, he just couldn't stomach the hollow feeling that followed him home after a late-night visit to one of his lady friends.

"We use the root in tea to help reduce inflammation and to heal broken bones," Faith said. She moved to a neighboring plant about a foot tall with strap-like leaves that she didn't touch. "This is autumn crocus. The seeds are used to treat gout and rheumatism, but all parts of the plant are poisonous."

Alarm bells went off in his head. "Then why would you give it to a person? Aren't you afraid of accidentally killing somebody?"

She faced him squarely. "I know my herbs, Sheriff Grayson. I have over one hundred varieties in my greenhouse, thirty of which are highly toxic but of immense value. I know how to use them for safe and effective treatments of minor ailments, but I don't pretend to be a doctor."

He watched Cora dump a bucket of soil into a mound on the greenhouse floor, and his gut tightened with worry. "Aren't you afraid to have these poisonous plants around your daughter?"

Instead of answering, she lifted her slender fingers and beckoned Cora. The child leapt to her feet and ran to her side.

"Sheriff Grayson wants to see our dangerous plants, Cora. Will you show him which herbs are poisonous?"

"That's aloe," the child said, pointing to a green plant with long, tapering stems that reached up from the soil like grasping fingers.

Duke reached out to touch the fleshy stems, but Cora pushed his hand away.

"Don't ever touch them!" she said dramatically. "You could get poison on your fingers and rub it in your eyes and go blind. Or you could get it in your mouth and die."

"I didn't realize aloe was poisonous."

"It's good for healing burns and minor wounds," Faith said, "but it's a violent purge if you ingest it. To Cora, anything that could hurt her is off limits. That means no touching."

Duke nodded then gave Cora a little bow. "Thank you for protecting me."

"You're welcome," she said, so sincerely that Duke bit his lip to stop a grin. "I'll show you more, but you can't touch them."

"I won't," he promised then followed the little imp as she dashed from one dangerous plant to the next. "How do you know which ones are bad?"

She pointed to a red ribbon tied to a stick in the corner of the flat where the herb was planted. "Mama marks them with a bright cloth. That's foxglove, and it's very bad because it's marked with red."

"What if somebody came in here and stole all your ribbons?" he asked, hoping his question wouldn't offend Faith, who stood protectively beside her daughter. "How would you know the good plants from the bad plants?"

Cora wrinkled her nose as if he were a pitifully stupid man. "I would look at their leaves or their flowers."

"What if someone like me came in and got confused? I don't know much about plants. What if I can't tell if it's foxglove or a snapdragon?"

"Then don't touch it."

He laughed at her refreshingly honest and simple answer. Faith's lips twitched, but she didn't gloat. "Since you're such a smart lady," he said to Cora, "perhaps you can tell me the name of that plant over there with the blue eyes and brown handkerchief that's watching us."

The little girl pivoted on her heels and looked behind her. "That's not a plant!" she said with a giggle. "That's my aunt Tansy hiding behind the fennel."

"Oh," he said in a whisper. "Why is she hiding from us?"

"Because she don't like you."

"Cora!" Faith gasped and laughed at the same time, blushing dark pink as she spoke to Duke. "I believe your badge has made Aunt Tansy wary." She turned and gestured for the woman to come out.

Tansy stepped into the row and offered a nervous smile. Her hands flitted to her throat, and Duke thought of a butterfly. She'd tied her kerchief on her head, leaving the tail ends sticking up like antennae, and she seemed breathless and alert, as if the slightest move would make her fly away.

"Good morning," he said with a polite nod.

Her vivid blue gaze flitted from him to Cora to Faith as if searching for a place to land.

"Aunt Tansy, this is Sheriff Grayson," Faith said, but he sensed her reservation in introducing them.

"G-good mornin', Sheriff."

Her soft southern drawl surprised him. He would guess the blonde to be in her forties, but he could never tell with women because they were sneaky about concealing their age with face creams and hair dyes. But no herb or balm could change Tansy's demure southern drawl or camouflage Iris's dramatic Oriental looks.

Faith's aunts could not be related.

Faith tapped her palm against a bushy green plant that looked like a weed to him. "You may as well come out, too, Aunt Dahlia."

To his surprise, another woman with red pouty lips stepped from behind the bush. She looked Tansy's age, but was shorter and more buxom, her hair and eyes dark brown. Maybe this one was related to Faith, but not the other two.

"Hello, Sheriff." Dahlia bobbed her head. "Iris was right about you being handsome," she said then surprised him further by reaching behind the bush and tugging a fourth woman into sight. "This is Aster," she said.

There was no doubt that Aster was the oldest, and she had the air of one in charge. Though she was Faith's height, she had white hair, a solid build, and wide shoulders.

She stood like a soldier and met his eyes without a shred of shame that she'd been caught peeking at him. "We're glad you stopped by, Sheriff. It's good to know our niece has a man to depend on."

"Oh, for pity's sake!" Faith scowled at the women and slipped her hand into the crook of Duke's elbow. "My aunts will take up your entire day if you don't escape now." She pressed her lips together and steered him to the front corner of the greenhouse, where she'd set up a counter and shelves to make a small store of sorts. "Don't forget your balm," she said, snagging the jar off the counter as they passed. She thrust it into his hand then hurried them outside to where Adam waited in the warm sunshine.

"How can those women be your aunts?" Duke asked, wanting to hear her explain it to his satisfaction.

"I used to ask my mother the same thing," Faith replied brightly, "but she assured me they were." She pushed the hair out of Adam's eyes, putting an end to the discussion if not Duke's suspicion. "Come straight home from the store," she said to the boy. "You need a haircut. And don't forget my cheesecloth this time."

He lowered his chin. "I won't."

Faith turned a warm smile on Duke that made him wish they were spending the evening together. But she'd dodged his question and he wanted an answer.

She spoke before he could pursue it, however. "Thank you for your kindness today, Sheriff. Please let me know how else I can repay you."

He hooked his thumb in his gun belt. "If this balm relieves the ache in my shoulder, I'll be in *your* debt, Mrs. Wilkins. I'll let you know how well it works." He wanted her to know that he would be back, that he would be watching her, and that he was interested in more than her business.

"Consider it an even exchange, Sheriff." She kept her smile in place, but his gut insisted there was something secretive about her, something odd about her business and her aunts.

Maybe the boy could answer some of his questions. He clapped his hand on Adam's shoulder and turned the boy toward town. "Well, young man, let's go settle your debt with Mrs. Brown."

⇐⊹ ⊹⇒

The minute the two males were gone, Faith rushed into the greenhouse. Her aunts were gathered near a flat of peppermint-scented geraniums, tittering and whispering. She didn't even want to imagine what they were talking about, but their outrageous behavior must stop before the sheriff guessed the truth about them—and herself.

She made sure Cora was occupied with her pail and hand spade and safely out of earshot before she confronted her aunts. "What were you ladies thinking?" she asked, certain they had just forfeited their one chance to build a safe and decent life for themselves.

"That the sheriff is the most handsome man I've ever met," Tansy said, placing her long, artist's fingers over her heart.

"The sheriff isn't interested in a woman ten years his senior," Aster countered in her blunt fashion.

Faith gritted her teeth. "The only thing the sheriff will be interested in is evicting us from his town."

"The sheriff loved our flirting," Iris said.

"Well, I didn't. I was terrified one of you would go too far and—" She bit her lip to stop her rush of words, but tears welled up in her eyes.

"Oh, dahlin', don't do that." Tansy grasped Faith's hands. "There's no need to worry."

"This is our only chance," Faith whispered, choked by her emotions. "We have to be careful not to tarnish our reputations."

"We know that, child." Tansy parked her hand on her narrow waist. "We only teased the sheriff a bit." She nodded toward the corner where Cora was plowing a stick through soil. "Not one of us will do a single thing to ruin that little girl's future."

Her aunts adored Cora and Adam, and Faith wanted to believe they would behave themselves, but she feared the women had spent too many years working in a brothel to be able to conform to polite society.

"Faith, you were so tense you were making the sheriff suspicious." Iris grinned with satisfaction. "I just flirted a bit to get him to hook up the gas line."

"I could have hired a man to do that."

"With what?" Iris asked. "We each contributed every penny we owned to make the move to Fredonia and set up our business. Other than the few coins in your jar, not one of us has a penny to our name."

"All the more reason for us to mind our manners and present ourselves as decent, respectable women," Faith insisted.

"Being respectable isn't going to put food on our table. The only way we're going to eat this week," Iris said, "is to get some paying customers into that soaking tub."

"No." Faith pressed her palms to her nervous stomach. "I don't think it's a good idea to open a bathhouse."

"Selling herbs won't earn enough to feed us," Iris insisted. "Our stock in trade is our ability to make men feel good."

"That's exactly what worries me! You know what people will think when they hear we're giving herbal baths and massages."

"My growling stomach doesn't much care," Aster said, her white eyebrows dipped in a scowl. "I vote for Iris's plan."

"Me, too." Dahlia patted the small paunch beneath her large breasts. "Maybe we weren't respected while working at the brothel, but at least we ate well."

Tansy nodded. "What harm can come of giving herbal baths, as long as our patrons wear bathing garments and we don't give any massages in private?"

"The harm is that one false move, or one nasty rumor, could tear our reputations to shreds, and it's a risk we can't afford to take," Faith said. "We've only been here three weeks. Let's wait a while and see how we do selling herbs."

"We could afford to wait if one of us had a husband who could provide for us." Iris arched one ebony eyebrow at Faith. "Maybe *you* should have flirted with the sheriff."

"He wouldn't want a woman like me."

A sly smile tipped Iris's lips. "Oh, he wants you."

Faith heaved an exasperated sigh. "I meant that he wouldn't want to marry a woman with my past."

"None of us will get a marriage proposal if we don't get some men in the door," Dahlia said. "Believe me, Faith, they won't come to buy herbs. The only way to get male patrons is to make them feel good."

"And in turn," Iris added, "they will make us feel good, which is my first requirement. The second is that the man is handsome. The third is that he's—"

"Who cares about feeling good?" Aster asked. "I'd be happy with a man who has money and a comfortable home."

Tansy hugged her arms to her waist. "I would love to hear a man sing again."

"Bah." Dahlia patted her buxom cleavage. "Give me a man who's willing to put his money right here, and I'd spend an hour or two with him."

Faith threw up her hands and stared at the women. "You are incorrigible! You're all addicted to men."

"Not addicted," Aster said, "just in need. We need money, and we can only get it from the men in town. Without that bath, we're going to starve." Aster widened her stance and crossed her arms over her chest. "When was the last time we ate a decent meal?"

It had been at least a month. The week before they left Syracuse they had barely slept, much less eaten a decent meal. But their goal had been to stay alive and to get out of town before Judge Stone returned and stripped them of everything they owned. Faith and her aunts had pooled their money and hired a local livery owner to secretly transport the contents of their greenhouse to Fredonia. In addition to paying his enormous fee, Faith had to buy the grist mill and pay a carpenter to install the huge windows in the first floor. They were broke, out of food, and out of options.

"All right," she said, heaving a defeated sigh. "I suppose we have no other choice. But you four must promise to be on your best behavior."

"Fine," Iris said, "but don't you forget your part of our bargain. You promised to use your pretty face to get a marriage proposal from a man who can protect us from Judge Stone."

"Surely you don't expect me to marry one of those men who proposed to me?" Faith shuddered, remembering the rangy, leather-faced man who'd caught her in the yard while they were first moving plants into the greenhouse. He had kindly carried in several flats of herbs, but he was twice her age and dense as a brick. A young store owner had offered her credit if she would allow him to court her, but his intense interest in the bodice of her dress sent her from the store empty-handed.

"Dahlin', I wouldn't let you cross the street with either of those men," Tansy said, "but I'd push you straight into the marriage bed with that handsome sheriff."

"Are you insane? The last person I want snooping around here is a lawman."

"But who better to have defending our lives than the sheriff?" Iris gave her a bold wink. "Can you imagine having a man like him in your bed?"

Yes, she could. In one short visit she'd noticed too much about the handsome sheriff. He was a take-charge man, a man in control of himself, a sharp-eyed investigator aware of everything around him. His dark eyes had sized her up within seconds of their introduction. His smile said he liked what he saw, but she sensed a fierce resolve in him that scared her to death.

Chapter Four

Adam was glad the sheriff had hooked up the gas line for them, but the man should have kept his big mouth shut: He should have put Adam in jail, or let him pay his debt privately instead of upsetting Faith.

As they headed toward Water Street, Adam stole glances at him. The sheriff's hands were huge, with big knuckles that could knock a person's teeth out with one punch. Adam's own knobby, long-fingered hands would never be as big or strong as the sheriff's. The man was a giant. His arms bulged with so much muscle they were bigger around than Adam's legs.

"I'll drop this at my office before we visit Mrs. Brown," the sheriff said, lifting the jar of balm that Faith had given him.

Adam didn't know if the sheriff might throw it out, but it had taken a long time and a lot of work for him and Faith to make that balm. If the sheriff was just going to waste it, he was going to ask for it back. "You should use it, sir."

"You think it will help then?"

Adam nodded. "The salicin and herbs work good on sore muscles."

"So you know a bit about herbs?"

"Yes, sir." Adam lengthened his stride, but was unable to match the sheriff's long gait. "I know almost as much as Faith does. She's been teaching me since I was Cora's age."

"Did your mother grow herbs too?"

"No, sir. She grew roses."

"How did Faith learn about herbs?"

"Books. She says that's the best way to learn about things."

The sheriff angled his Stetson to shade his eyes from the sun. "You enjoy reading?"

"Yes, sir." Adam squinted up at him. "We read every night after supper."

"We?"

"Faith and I read to Cora."

"Would your sister let me come by some evening and listen?"

"No, sir. Faith dislikes men." And Adam didn't want the sheriff around spying on him or upsetting Faith.

The sheriff raised his eyebrows. "That must have made her husband uncomfortable."

Adam looked at his feet and called himself an empty-headed idiot. He wasn't supposed to talk about Faith's husband. His big mouth could ruin everything if he wasn't careful.

"Something wrong, son?"

"No, sir. I was... I was thinking that Cora might tell you a story, but it'll be so crazy you won't understand it. The last story she told was about a flying snake named Lester who gave Cora a ride over a rainbow and turned them both into butterflies so they could live in my mother's rosebush." He glanced up to see if the sheriff had that squinty suspicious look on his face, hoping his story had smoothed over his mistake. The sheriff's grin relieved him. "I told Faith that Cora must have eaten jimsonweed. It makes a person hallucinate."

"You don't ever eat those type of plants, do you?"

"No, sir," Adam said between clenched teeth. He hated that everyone always thought the worst of him.

"Good." The sheriff clapped his big hand on Adam's shoulder and drew him to a stop in front of the barbershop on Water Street.

A man even taller than the sheriff stepped into the rutted street to meet them. "Where have you been hiding?" the man asked. "I've been by your office twice this morning."

"I've been training my new deputy" The sheriff patted Adam's shoulder.

Although he was joking, a thrill rushed through Adam. He couldn't even imagine what it would feel like to be a strong, respected lawman.

"This is Adam Dearborn," the sheriff said. "Adam's sister bought Colburn's mill and is opening a greenhouse business. Adam, this is my oldest brother, Radford."

The man was taller and leaner, his hair darker and his eyes lighter, but he and the sheriff looked like brothers. "Pleasure to meet you, Mr. Grayson," Adam said.

To his surprise, Mr. Grayson reached out and shook his hand. "You're the youngest deputy I've ever met, Mr. Dearborn."

Adam tried to smile, but it hurt too much, knowing a position like the sheriff's was beyond his reach. He shook Mr. Grayson's hand then stepped away while the men talked.

Women blushed and smiled as they passed by, especially at the sheriff, but he and his brother just nodded in their friendly way and kept talking about timber.

Adam leaned against the warm red bricks of the two-story building, wondering how it felt to be greeted like that. The sheriff's brother had been nice to him, but that was because Adam was with the sheriff. If he'd been alone, the man wouldn't have noticed him at all. No one ever noticed a prostitute's bastard. And for Adam, it had been safer to be unseen.

When the sheriff finished talking with his brother, Adam crossed Main Street with him then walked a block down Temple Street, the one that cut between the parks. Adam was proud that he was remembering the street names and learning his way around his new hometown.

They entered a brick building with two square towers on the front, and he wondered if the sheriff locked criminals in the towers but didn't dare ask. Inside they passed a small room with iron bars on the door. It looked dark and cold there, and Adam was suddenly glad the sheriff hadn't locked him up.

At the next room, a note had been tacked to the door. The sheriff pulled it free and unlocked the door. A huge wooden desk squatted in the middle of the office, with papers scattered over its surface. The sheriff read the note, laid it on the mess on his desk, and plunked the jar of balm on top of it. "Looks like I've got a busy afternoon," he said.

"What is all that stuff?" Adam asked.

"Arrest warrants. Complaints. Tax notices. Town meeting notes. Court papers." The sheriff shrugged. "The usual." Adam wrinkled his nose, and the sheriff laughed. "I couldn't agree more. Give me a couple of bank robbers to chase any day."

Adam gawked. "You chase bank robbers?"

The sheriff laughed. "Only twice."

"Gosh."

"I was jesting with you, son. I dislike the paperwork for my job, but I don't want any robberies of any kind in my county."

"Yes, sir." Adam hung his head and followed the sheriff back outside.

As they crossed the wide grassy Common, Sheriff Grayson nodded to the men they passed, and lifted his Stetson to the ladies. Adam imagined himself Duke's son, a prince walking beside a king, instead of an unwanted bastard scurrying out of the way so he wouldn't soil anybody's clothing.

He was so busy admiring the sheriff's badge as they entered Brown & Shepherd's store, he ran into a man with a chest as hard as a brick wall. His eyes flashed upward, and he saw that he'd run into the sheriff's brother. "Sorry, sir," he said, quickly stepping aside.

Mr. Grayson gave him a pleasant nod, but Adam barely noticed. Standing beside the man was the most beautiful girl he had ever seen. She was as tall as he was, and she looked straight into his eyes, smiling with such warmth that he felt as if she'd hugged him.

Girls never smiled at him. Not ever. In Syracuse he'd rarely left the yard of the brothel or explored outside his own neighborhood, but when he had, everyone knew he didn't belong near them. They would lift their noses or turn away, pretending not to see him. He didn't belong there, and he knew it.

"This is my daughter, Rebecca," Mr. Grayson said, putting his arm around the girl. They both had dark hair, but Rebecca's brown eyes were shades darker than her father's, and her smile was much friendlier. "Rebecca, this is Adam Dearborn, who has just moved in at the old Colburn place."

"Why, that's just down the street from us." Her smile widened, and she extended her hand. "Welcome to Fredonia, Adam."

His name had never sounded so important. He'd never felt his heart bang in his chest so hard, not even the time one of Iris's johns had caught him peeking in the brothel window. He raked his hair out of his eyes and reached to shake her pretty white hand.

"Pleased to meet you," he said, but his voice cracked and it sounded like he'd said, *Pleased to MEET you.*

Rebecca laughed, but it was a warm sound, and she gave his hand a secret squeeze.

Her father drew her away. "We need to get home before your mother accuses us of dallying all morning."

She nudged him in the ribs. "You're just rushing me home because you want me to help you clean the livery."

"You're getting too smart for me." A smile made her father look much friendlier, but it was the love in his eyes that jolted Adam. His own father would never look at him like that. He didn't know the man. Didn't know his name. Didn't even know if he was alive. Didn't care either.

"It was nice to meet you, Adam."

He nodded to Rebecca then curled his trembling fingers into his palm, wanting to trap the tingling sensation and keep it with him forever.

"I'll see you two at supper," the sheriff said to Rebecca and her father.

Rebecca waved good-bye to the sheriff, but her big brown eyes were looking right at Adam as she stepped outside with her father.

The sheriff's lips quirked up. "Looks like my niece intends to be your friend."

Girls like Rebecca didn't befriend boys like Adam. He opened his mouth to tell the sheriff that, but realized for the first time since coming to Fredonia, no one knew he was a prostitute's kid. They only knew he was Faith's brother, and she was a respectable widow running a respectable business.

He could be like everyone else here. He could have friends, play ball, go swimming in the lake in the summertime. And someday, maybe he could even have a secret sweetheart like Rebecca.

The possibilities made his heart leap. A newfound sense of freedom filled him with hope.

"Come on, son, it's time to make your apology to Mrs. Brown."

The sheriff could have punched him with his big fist and hurt him less than the sudden regret twisting Adam's gut. How could he have been so stupid as to steal a brush? Thieves weren't any more welcome in a town like this than prostitutes or their children.

"Sheriff Grayson?"

The sheriff turned back, his dark eyebrow arched in question. "Thank you for not telling your brother what I did."

"This business is between you and Mrs. Brown. It doesn't concern my brother."

"I won't... I swear I won't do anything like this again," Adam said, fumbling for words, wanting to undo his mistake. All he wanted now was to make himself over into a man like the sheriff, a man worthy of a girl like Rebecca Grayson.

Chapter Five

At six o'clock in the evening, Duke left his deputy Sam Wade in charge and walked down Water Street toward home. The sun cast a golden sheen across the huge windows of Faith Wilkins's new greenhouse, and he wondered how he could have overlooked such an obvious change in the building.

He shook his head, cursing his shoulder. Like a nagging toothache, the pain was distracting him to the point of madness. The doctor said to rest it and let it heal, but how long would that take? It had been a month since he'd tangled with Arthur Covey and injured his shoulder. He clenched his hand around the small jar of balm, hoping it would work as well as Faith and Adam claimed. Because if it didn't, his career was in trouble.

Maybe he should stop by the greenhouse again to check on the gas line. His feet slowed, but his brain ordered him to quit making excuses and keep walking. Radford and Evelyn were expecting him and his mother for supper. And he had chores waiting after that.

Lowering his tense shoulders, he crossed the bridge over Canadaway Creek then lengthened his stride and headed out on Liberty Street.

In less than five minutes, he approached their house and livery, a place that felt like home to him. Duke lived with his mother in her house just beyond Evelyn's apple orchard, but they both spent many evenings at Radford and Evelyn's house, carrying on a tradition that began with Evelyn's and Duke's parents.

His mother and father had been close friends with Evelyn's parents, William and Mary Tucker, and the four of them raised their children as one family. Duke and his brothers and Evelyn had tromped from their house to hers, exploring every tree, creek, and stone in between. When Evelyn's mother died, Duke's mother opened her loving arms to the girl. Evelyn's father treated Duke and his brothers like his own sons. William and Radford even went through the war together, and came home with a deeper bond between them, both men forever changed from their experience. Evelyn had planned to marry Duke's brother Kyle, but her heart chose Radford. That upheaval had shaken the foundation of their family, but they'd held on.

Evelyn's parents, and his own beloved father, were now buried in a shared family plot behind Evelyn's home. Those left behind had grown closer despite all the heartache.

Duke and his brothers owned their father's sawmill now, each of them contributing what they could to keep the business healthy. Kyle and Boyd ran the mill full time. Radford owned the livery, but dedicated two days a week to their sawmill business. When Duke wasn't busy with his duties as sheriff, he gladly spent his time working with his brothers. He loved the smell of fresh cut wood and sawdust, and the hard, honest work, but he was relieved he didn't have to go there this evening. He wanted to sit on Radford and Evelyn's porch, drink a glass of cold tea, and give his throbbing shoulder a chance to settle down.

The livery sat back from the road with a small paddock behind it where Evelyn trained her horses. A sprawling oak stood in the front yard and shaded the deep porch on their two-story home. A long fieldstone fence girded their property, and was a favorite hiding place for their sons William and Joshua.

As Duke had come to expect, his nephews popped up from behind the fence like well-trained soldiers, aiming their sticks and shooting at him a dozen times before he could grab for his carefully unloaded revolver. He would never draw it from his holster, of course. Not ever. Not even knowing he'd meticulously cleared the cartridges from the chamber.

With a loud groan, he clutched his chest and fell to his knees.

The boys let out a victory whoop. Seven-year-old William planted his hands on the fence and vaulted over, followed by four-year-old Joshua, whose chubby, little boy body forced him to claw his way over the stones.

Duke fell on his good side, let the jar roll away from him then put his hand over his revolver and turned so the boys couldn't pounce on his sore shoulder.

William ran toward him then stretched out his skinny frame and flew through the air like a gangly bird. He landed hard on Duke's chest, wrenching the shoulder in spite of Duke's effort to protect it. Gads, that hurt! Joshua barreled across the spring grass and tumbled onto Duke's head. The two boys grunted and tussled and tugged until Duke surrendered.

They rolled off then ordered him to get up and get moving. He scooped up his jar of balm then marched to their prison, which was behind the railings of the front porch. Their eyes flashed with excitement, and it struck him that jail was just a game for his nephews, as it had been for Duke and his brothers at that tender age. But it wasn't a game for a boy like Adam Dearborn. The boy's tense, drawn face when he'd seen the barred cell earlier said he knew jail was a looming possibility for his ultimate future.

But not if Duke could prevent it. Adam was an intelligent boy in need of a firm guiding hand.

Radford was lounging in a chair with his feet propped on the handrail, grinning like a happy, satisfied man. "It's nice to see the rascals clobbering someone else for a change," he said.

Duke leaned his hips against the handrail and rubbed his shoulder. "Sometimes I think that's the only reason you invite me over."

Radford's grin deepened. "Nonsense. I like having my brothers around. That's why I'm inviting Boyd and Claire to supper tomorrow and asking Kyle and Amelia to come by the night after."

Duke's snort drew a laugh from their mother, who was sitting on the porch holding Radford's seven-month-old daughter Hannah, a dark-haired beauty who was drooling and chewing on her fingers.

"Uncle Duke, come wrestle," Joshua said, tugging on Duke's leg.

"Let him be, son." Radford hauled Joshua onto his lap and tickled him into a wild giggle. "You boys go wash your hands. We'll be eating soon."

Joshua squirmed free and charged into the house, bumping into his mother's legs and nearly upsetting the tray in her hands. Evelyn stood with the door open and looked straight at Duke.

He lifted his hands. "I'm not responsible for Joshua's mad dash into the house."

"What mad dash?" Evelyn carried her tray of drinks on to the porch. "If the boys aren't running, they're sleeping."

"Or yelling and fighting," Rebecca said, carrying a heaping platter of fried chicken and plump biscuits outside.

"You have no right to talk about bad behavior, young lady, after buying Mrs. Brown's last licorice stick and leaving me without a single one," Duke said.

Rebecca set the platter on a low table in the center of a group of chairs. "The early bird gets the licorice." She leaned over and gave him a loud, smacking kiss on the cheek.

"And the pretty girl gets the new boy in town." He hooked his arm around her waist and pulled her into a one-armed hug. "I see you're not saving that pretty smile for your daddy and your uncles anymore."

Her cheeks flamed, and she shot an embarrassed look at her father.

Instead of smiling, Radford wore a puzzled look, as if Rebecca's shiny black hair had just turned orange.

Evelyn poked Duke's ribs and pulled Rebecca free. "Don't start on her. She gets enough grief from her two brothers." She brushed Rebecca's thick braid behind her shoulder. "Would you bring the plates out?"

With a look of gratitude, Rebecca raced inside.

Duke scowled at Evelyn. "You ruined a perfectly good bout of teasing," he complained.

She looked unmoved. "I know what it's like to be outnumbered by nasty little boys."

"I was never little."

She laughed and picked up the jar of balm. "What is this?"

"Love balm. I rub it on a woman and she falls madly in love with me."

She plunked the jar down beside him. "What a waste. Every woman in town already loves you."

"Not the pretty widow who made this balm," he said, nodding at the jar. "One Faith Wilkins just opened a greenhouse in Colburn's old gristmill. I stopped in to... welcome her to town, and for some reason that made her nervous."

"Maybe she's hiding a criminal in her house," William said—so sincerely Duke didn't dare laugh at his nephew.

"I worried about that, too, Will, so I went right inside her greenhouse and looked around. Didn't find a thing but herbs and flowers in there."

"Maybe she's a witch," the seven-year-old whispered, wide eyes blinking.

"You know, she did have a big cauldron in the greenhouse. She didn't seem like a witch, though, and she's awfully pretty."

William's nose scrunched. "Oh. Well, witches have boils and warts and—"

"William, tell your brother and sister to come eat." His mother gave him a gentle nudge toward the door then went to sit by Duke's mother. "I can't imagine why your barging into her greenhouse would have made the lady nervous," she said to Duke.

"I didn't barge in," he replied, crossing the porch and seating himself opposite her.

Radford followed, and Joshua, William, and Rebecca hurried outside. Everyone sat at the table and started eating.

Evelyn bit into a biscuit, but her green eyes sparkled with mischief.

Duke lowered his chicken leg. "What?"

His brother's wife chewed like she had all evening to enjoy that one bite.

"What?" he prodded. He knew that look in her eyes. The last time she'd directed it at him, she'd hung his boots from the top of her oak tree. She was half his weight, and had climbed to the very top of the tree where the limbs were as skinny as toothpicks. He'd nearly broken his neck retrieving them.

Evelyn ignored him. "Mother, would you like to go with me tomorrow to welcome Faith Wilkins to town?"

"Of course," Duke's mother said, making him groan. He wanted to warn her to stay away, but his mother was short and sassy and the last woman he would cross. "I'll take a jar of preserves to welcome her."

"And I'll take a plate of the cookies I just baked." Evelyn hooked her arm around her daughter's shoulders. "Sweetheart, would you watch the children tomorrow while I go meet this pretty widow who has snared your uncle's interest?"

Like mother like daughter; Rebecca's eyes sparkled. "Of course, Mama. I owe Uncle Duke a favor."

He flicked a biscuit crumb at Evelyn. "You're ruining my niece."

"I'm teaching her that turnabout is fair play"

Radford tossed his napkin onto his plate and leaned back in his chair. "Save your breath, Duke. When the ladies set their minds to something, the boys and I clear out."

Evelyn patted Radford's thigh. "You poor, mistreated man."

He sighed dramatically and looked down into her upturned face. "To think I'll spend the rest of my life being treated like this..." He trailed off, the warm look in his eyes saying everything. He was a man in love, a man in awe of all he had.

Duke had witnessed their private exchanges many times during the eight years of their marriage, and the intensity of their passion made him yearn for what they had. Kyle had found that passion with Amelia. Boyd had found it with Claire.

But what made that passion ignite and burn between two people was still a mystery to Duke.

Chapter Six

A fter lunch, Faith was in the bathhouse pumping water into the tub when three women walked through the open greenhouse door, chatting gaily and bearing... gifts? Surely not. The oldest and shortest of the three spotted Cora playing by the door and gave her a friendly wave.

"Let's hope they're customers," Faith said to Iris, who'd been helping her fill the bathtub. She brushed drops of water off the long apron covering her dress then headed toward the front of the greenhouse with Iris, giving them her warmest smile. "May I help you ladies?"

"I'm Nancy Grayson, and these are my daughters-in-law Evelyn and Claire," the older woman said, giving Faith a jar of preserves, but her gaze was riveted on Iris. Faith was used to the surprised, intrigued stares cast at Iris, but it made her sad each time it happened. Iris was exotic and beautiful, a rare bird that drew attention with every move. Iris didn't seem to mind the looks, but she must: she was a woman disconnected from her family and her people, too different to blend in anywhere.

"My son, Sheriff Grayson, said you opened a greenhouse, but I wasn't expecting anything this grand," Mrs. Grayson continued, shifting her gaze to the plants as if she realized she'd been gawking.

Faith's stomach plummeted. Had Sheriff Grayson sent them to spy on her? Or had he sent them here to look her over? She'd seen the spark of interest in his eyes yesterday. And maybe Iris had fanned that spark. Blast the woman! She should have never told the sheriff Faith was looking for a husband. They'd planted that ridiculous notion in Faith's own head too, and now she was acting like a suspicious goose.

But she wished she looked better. She smoothed her skirt, sopping wet at the hem from working in the bathhouse then hid her hands behind her back because her fingernails were green from pinching stems all morning.

The two younger women were of nearly the same height and dressed in neat, pressed frocks. Evelyn was dark-haired, and Claire was blond, and both were beautiful.

Nancy Grayson's too-direct gaze made Faith want to shy away, but the remarkable youthful energy that radiated from the woman was surprisingly familiar. The sheriff possessed that same directness and intensity.

The blond woman, Claire, handed Faith a deep pot. "I thought you might appreciate not having to cook this evening. I hope you like venison stew."

Faith would gladly toil over a stove if she had money to buy food.

"And I brought a treat for after supper," Evelyn said, giving a plate of cookies to Cora.

Cora scrambled to her feet and gawked at the mound of oatmeal cookies. "Can I eat one, Mama?"

To refuse the cookies would be rude, and to refuse Cora a treat would be unkind. But Faith hesitated to accept their gifts not knowing the ladies' motives.

"Of course you can eat a cookie." Iris lifted the heavy pot from Faith's hands and held it beneath her nose. "Smells divine," she said then winked at Faith. "Let's not wait for supper. Let's eat it right now."

Her teasing made the three women laugh. "Thank you, ladies," Faith said, striving to appear as relaxed as the Grayson women even as worry flooded her mind. "This is my aunt, Iris... Wilde," she said, silently cursing Iris for blabbing the name in front of the sheriff and locking them into using it.

"There are four of us here with that last name, so call me Iris."

The younger ladies nodded politely, but Nancy took a bold, sweeping look around the greenhouse. "What is all this?"

"Let me put this on the counter," Iris said, "then Faith and I will show you what we're growing here."

"I'll show 'em!" Cora declared, rushing up with a half-eaten cookie in her hand. She looked up at Evelyn Grayson. "You make good cookies."

The simple, sincere statement filled the brunette's eyes with tenderness. She opened her hand to Cora. "What should we see first?" she asked.

Cora led Evelyn to a flat of chives that were poking through the soil. "We're gonna eat those when they get bigger," she said.

Faith followed, feeling proud of Cora's knowledge, but she gently took over, wanting the Grayson ladies to see how much her greenhouse had to offer. While Cora charmed them, Faith and Iris answered Nancy's questions about their business. Iris's good behavior relieved Faith, but Nancy's avid curiosity made her stomach queasy.

"Quite impressive," the woman said, touching and sniffing everything until Cora scolded her and warned her she could go blind. Nancy chuckled, but she continued asking questions in a forthright manner that convinced Faith the sheriff had sent his mother to snoop.

Faith showed them the herbs, vegetables, and flowers then guided the ladies to the front counter where she kept her jars, bags, and tins of herbs and balms.

Aster and Tansy were working near the counter, preparing a flat of baby tomato plants for transplanting to their garden. Faith wasn't sure she could trust her aunts to behave, but they had to begin settling into their new town. "Come meet these lovely ladies," she suggested to her aunts.

The pair washed their hands in a bucket of water then dried them on their aprons as they walked to the counter.

"This is Evelyn and Claire Grayson, the sheriff's sisters-in-law," Faith introduced. "And his mother, Nancy."

Cora puffed up with importance. "Aunt Iris says Mama's going to marry the sheriff."

Faith nearly choked, but Nancy Grayson laughed.

"Who brought those delicious cookies?" Aster asked.

It allowed Faith a moment to recover. Living her life behind a brothel and learning everything from books had filled her head with knowledge of trees and herbs and flowers. She could name every muscle in the body, but she didn't know how to navigate through an ordinary conversation.

"Evelyn baked them," Nancy said. "Claire made the stew. You'll soon see why I'm glad my sons married these gals."

Aster nudged Faith's arm. "Marry the sheriff so we can claim our place at this woman's supper table."

Faith wanted to clap her hand over her aunt's mouth, but the Grayson women laughed. Nancy and Aster exchanged a look of frank appreciation. Aster had a harder, grittier edge than Nancy, but they were two of a kind with their plainspoken manner.

Iris handed Nancy a small jar of lavender oil. "Let us return your gifts by giving you a peek at the other side of our business."

Faith shook her head, but Iris ignored her and upended an empty metal pail. "Tansy, round up a couple more buckets for the ladies."

Tansy hurried off in a swish of skirts.

"Iris, we've kept the ladies too long already," Faith said, warning Iris not to cause trouble like she had with Sheriff Grayson. "I'm sure they have to get back to their families."

"Oh, I hope not." Iris clasped her hands in front of her like an excited girl. "Say you'll stay for a few minutes and let us treat you to something special."

"You'll love it," Aster added, nodding for Nancy to sit on the bucket.

"All right. Why not?" Nancy Grayson sat her small, slightly plump body on the pail. "What do I do now?"

"Close your eyes," Iris ordered, moving to stand behind her.

Faith wrung her hands. "Aunt Iris, please."

"To be surprised at my age is an immense pleasure," Nancy said. "Let her be." With that, she shut her eyes, and Faith shut her mouth.

"This is best done with oil and herbs, but you can still enjoy it this way." Iris pushed the pads of her thumbs into the flesh between Nancy's shoulder blades. "There is an art to massage," Iris explained, her voice smooth and mesmerizing as she rubbed slow, small circles on Nancy's back.

The woman's shoulders lowered and her head sagged forward. "I'm gaining a new appreciation for art," she said.

Evelyn and Claire exchanged a sisterly grin, as if seeing a side of their mother-in-law they hadn't known.

Iris worked Nancy's trapezius muscle between her thumb and index finger, relaxing the muscle one delicate pinch at a time. Tansy returned with Dahlia, each of them carrying a bucket. Faith introduced Dahlia to the ladies, but Nancy could barely open her eyes to greet her.

She moaned and hunched her back like a cat. "This old body hasn't known so much pleasure since my husband was alive."

Evelyn and Claire laughed, and Faith couldn't stop her smile. Like Aster, Nancy Grayson's candor was growing on her.

Tansy overturned a bucket in front of Evelyn. "I'm good at this too."

Evelyn held out her hands as if to ward her off. "I'm happy to watch my mother-in-law melt off that pail."

Tansy caught Evelyn's hand and peered at her palm. "Lord, child, how did you get these calluses?"

"Taking care of a livery full of horses."

Cora's eyes goggled. "You have horses?"

"Twelve of them."

"Can I see 'em?"

"If it's all right with your mother."

"We'll talk about it later, honey." Faith put her hand on Cora's tiny shoulder, her silent way of telling the child to hush, that she was being ill-mannered or inappropriate.

Tansy opened a jar on the counter. "I have something that will make your hands as soft as a baby's behind," she said, scooping cream onto her fingers then slathering it on Evelyn's hand. "It's honey, lanolin, almond oil, and wax."

"It smells wonderful," Evelyn said.

"It is, dahlin', now sit down and let me do this properly."

Like an obedient child, Evelyn sat on the pail.

"We mix mint and lavender in to make it smell good," Tansy said.

"It's lovely" Evelyn glanced at her sister-in-law. "You don't know what you're missing, Claire."

The other woman shook her head. "My aching feet are jealous."

"Not for long." Dahlia slid a pail behind Claire. "That cream will soften your feet and soothe the ache, too."

Claire gasped and laughed in the same breath. "I was teasing."

Dahlia dipped her fingers into the jar and scooped out a dollop of cream. She gestured for Claire to sit. "Let me show you how to apply it, so you can teach your husband how to pleasure you."

Claire laughed. "Believe me, my husband knows all about that."

Faith's aunts all grinned like the four lusty prostitutes they were, and Nancy glanced at her daughter-in-law. "The only pleasure I get comes from a hot stove or holding my grandchildren. It's been ages since anything has felt good enough to make me moan, so sit on that pail and let this lovely woman rub your feet while I enjoy myself for a spell."

Cora patted Faith's leg. "Why does she want to moan, Mama?"

Heat burned up Faith's neck, and Nancy ducked her head.

With a hoot of laughter, Claire sat on the pail, hiked her dress to her knees, and stuck out her foot. "Cora, do you know how to unlace shoes?"

"Mama showed me how," the child said, and joyfully helped remove Claire's shoes and stockings.

Dahlia slathered cream over Claire's slender foot and began kneading her toes. Cora sat knees-bent, heels-out on the floor beside Dahlia, rubbing Claire's other foot.

Nancy hunched her back. "Iris, you must come live with me," she said.

Warm laughter filled the greenhouse, and Faith let herself relax for the first time since moving to Fredonia. Maybe her aunts weren't too outrageous. Their naughty sense of humor had won over the Grayson women. And maybe Nancy, Evelyn, and Claire would tell their friends about her business.

Maybe everything would work out after all.

"You all look so different," Evelyn said, eyeing Faith's aunts. "It's hard to believe you're sisters."

Faith's stomach plummeted.

"It's a remarkable story," Dahlia said, calmly reaching over to guide Cora's hand. "Slide your thumbs around her ankle bone like this." After she demonstrated, the woman lifted an amazingly serene face to Evelyn. "We all share the same father."

Faith scoured her mind for a way to change the subject, wishing they'd taken time to think this through and invent a new history for themselves.

"Our father was a big, handsome, American-born German," Dahlia said in the mystical sounding voice she used when telling a tale to Cora. "There wasn't a woman alive who could resis—"

"Aunt Dahlia, the ladies can't possibly be interested in... all that. It's a painfully long history," Faith said, doing her best to dissuade them from pursuing the topic. "Dahlia could waste half a day trying to explain it all."

Nancy fairly purred as she closed her eyes. "Take all the time you like, Miss Wilde."

Dahlia's lips twitched. "As I was saying, we share the same father, but—"

"The sheriff's here!" Cora leapt to her feet and ran to greet him.

Faith's day went from bad to disastrous. The sheriff hadn't taken five steps inside the greenhouse before his eyes widened and he jerked to a halt. He looked from Claire, barefoot with her dress hiked to her knees, to his mother, who sat with her back hunched and her head hanging, to Evelyn, who lounged cross-legged on her pail like a queen getting a manicure.

Evelyn waved him over. "Pull up a pail, Duke. You're just in time to hear what promises to be an interesting history of the Wilde women."

The instant the words left Evelyn's mouth, Faith's aunts howled with laughter.

Under less worrisome circumstances, Faith would have appreciated the wild women pun, but to flaunt their past as if they were beyond the bounds of social etiquette was foolish. And that is exactly what Iris had done when she came up with that suggestive last name.

"Can I play with your handcuffs?" Cora asked, poking at the sheriff's thigh.

He pulled the cuffs off his belt without looking away from his mother. "What is going on here?" he asked.

Nancy half-raised her eyelids. "I'm having one of the best moments of my life. Now sit down and let Dahlia finish her story about how these lovely ladies came to be sisters."

Faith scooted around a flat of wintergreen and stopped before him. She tried her best to get things on her own terms once more: "I assume you're here to report on Adam's first day at the store, so why don't we go outside and talk?"

⚬⚬

Duke heard Faith's request. But, after walking in here and finding his respectable mother and sisters-in-law looking intoxicated, he wasn't budging from this spot even if Faith promised to lead him to her bed. He was going to stand right here beside this flat of smelly green stuff until he figured out exactly what was going on. His mother looked drugged out of her head. Had these crazy women fed her some of that jimsonweed Adam mentioned?

Duke nodded to Dahlia—at least, he believed the buxom woman was Dahlia—who was rubbing Claire's feet. "Don't let me interrupt," he said.

Dahlia turned her attention to manipulating Claire's toes in a way that made his own toes jealous. "I was saying that the five of us had the same father."

His mother's head lifted. "Five?"

Dahlia nodded. "The four of us and Rose, Faith's mother."

"Rose? Oh, of course." Duke's mother's lips pursed as if she were holding back a smile while listening to one of her grandchildren spin a wild tale, but she waved her fingers for Dahlia to continue.

Duke shifted his gaze between his mother, who was an excellent judge of character, and Faith, whose scowl said she didn't like Dahlia sharing this information.

"Papa first saw Rose's mother, Violet, dashing through a field of wildflowers," Dahlia said. "She was running away from her dreadful parents."

Faith closed her eyes and pinched the bridge of her nose.

"Papa said Violet was a beauty beyond compare, and claimed she inspired him to lus—love—um, to marry her and plant flowers."

Duke's mother's hoot startled him.

"They named their first child Rose." Dahlia rested Claire's foot in her lap and sat back on her heels. "For some reason Violet left Papa before they could plant any more flowers."

Duke watched Faith brush Cora's hair off her forehead. "Sweetheart, go see if you can find that plate of cookies," she suggested.

"Can I eat one?"

"Yes, but wash your hands first."

When Cora dashed down a plant-shrouded aisle, and out of earshot, Faith blocked Duke's view of Dahlia. "I'd like to talk with you. Would you step outside with me?" she asked him.

"Of course," he said, "as soon as your aunt finishes her story."

A sick look washed across Faith's face, and she lowered her lashes.

"What happened to his daughter Rose?" he asked, prodding Dahlia to continue.

"She remained with Papa, which encouraged him to find a new wife fast."

Duke frowned. "Wasn't he still married to Violet?"

"He surely was, but he married his neighbor's spinster daughter anyhow, and added Aster to his garden."

Duke saw the soldier-like woman with white hair lift her snowy eyebrows as if this was news to her, but she didn't comment.

"For some reason Aster's mother took Aster and went back to her father's house, leaving Papa alone with Rose. Papa saw no reason to stop planting flowers, so he moved to Georgia and promptly added a wealthy southern belle to his arrangement."

"Oh, Dahlia! Honestly," Faith exclaimed, her face flushing crimson. "This is more than these poor ladies need to know."

But it was nowhere near enough for Duke—or for his mother, if her now-keen gaze was any indication of her interest.

"Well, it's the truth." Dahlia stood and wiped her hands on her apron. "Papa was married to three women at the same time. But the problem was diminished when Tansy's mother died during childbirth."

The blond woman gasped, her hands flitting to her throat, reminding Duke that Tansy was the butterfly of their group. Aster was the white-haired soldier, Iris the Japanese flirt, and Dahlia was the one with the cantaloupes on her chest. Crude, but it was the only way he could keep these women straight.

Dahlia planted her hands on her ample hips. "You didn't know Papa was a bigamist?"

Tansy squinted. "A what?"

"A three-timing rat," Aster said with an odd gleam in her eyes. "But the story gets worse. You see, Dahlia's mother was the robust Italian kitchen maid who worked for Tansy's mother."

Even Duke felt his eyebrows lift with this revelation, but Dahlia just laughed and straightened her apron. "Aster is teasing you ladies. My mama was Italian, but I would call her voluptuous rather than robust. Papa met her in New York City... at the theater. When Tansy's mother died, Papa was much improved in the pocket, so he packed up Rose and Tansy, and moved to the city. While he was establishing himself as a businessman, Aster was delivered to his doorstep with a letter saying her mother had been killed in a carriage accident."

Aster cast a mean squint at Dahlia. "This, of course, left him free to marry your mother."

"Not quite. He was still married to his first wife, Violet. But Papa met Mama that very evening." Dahlia's eyes softened and her voice lowered. "She was at the theater with her father, and she got so excited during the performance, she dropped her fan over the balcony. It hit Papa on the head."

Iris's hoot of laughter snapped everyone's attention to her. She clapped her hands over her mouth, but another squawk of laughter slipped from her throat as she stepped away from Duke's mother. "I... I remember Papa telling that story," she said, pushing her shiny black hair out of her eyes.

"Well, that was the only thing humorous about him meeting that woman," Tansy said. "She was a viper after she married Papa."

"Truly wicked," Aster agreed, her voice filled with sympathy that was contradicted by the gloating look in her eyes. "Dahlia's mother left Papa with another child and an empty pocket then got her wealthy father to buy her a divorce."

"Who's telling this story?" Dahlia asked irritably.

For some reason these women were taunting each other, and Duke's attention sharpened as he searched their faces and words for clues.

"Dahlia!" Faith caught the woman's elbow. "We've only just met these ladies, and this story is... inappropriate."

Dahlia drew in her breath, lifting a good-sized bosom in the process. "There's not much left to tell anyhow. Papa already had three girls he couldn't take care of, so he hired a soft-spoken Oriental woman as a nursemaid and promptly forgot his vow to stop planting flowers. His new Japanese wife added Iris to the garden then died with Papa shortly thereafter in an explosion aboard a steamer."

"Good heavens! Can this be true?" Claire asked, her shoe dangling forgotten from her fingers.

Duke nearly laughed aloud. Of course it wasn't true. These women were actresses of the finest caliber. And he wanted to know what they were covering up with their acting skills.

Everyone looked at Faith, but her jaw was clenched and her stony gaze was fixed on Dahlia.

"Not entirely," Dahlia said with a dismissive wave of her hand. "I can't remember every detail, so I decorated the cake a little bit. It would have been a lifeless and sad story otherwise."

"It's tragic." Evelyn pressed her hand to her heart.

Duke grimaced. Leave it to the ever-compassionate Evelyn not to see past a mountain of blarney, and that's surely what this all was.

Her concern must have nudged Dahlia's conscience, because the woman heaved a sigh and shook her head. "I was teasing my sisters a bit just now, because the truth is we spent our childhood away from each other. Rose set up a house in Syra... Saratoga, and one by one we found her and transplanted ourselves to her garden." She flipped her palms up and grinned like a pleased child. "But wasn't the first version more exciting?"

Duke was just working up a line of questions when his mother burst into laughter and clapped her hands like an enthusiastic fan at a rousing performance. "I'm taking you women home with me."

Iris joined in the applause. "Well done, Dahlia."

Dahlia curtsied to Evelyn, Claire, and his mother then boldly winked at Duke over her shoulder. "Welcome to the Evergreen House, where we treat our female guests to a healing massage with our special herbs and balms while entertaining them with fabulous stories." She stepped back and hooked her arm around Faith's shoulders. "My niece here is so worried that the ladies in town won't buy our herbs and special treatments, she can barely sleep at night."

"That's absolutely true," Tansy said, all aflutter. "Why just last night—"

"We decided to offer one free massage to every lady in town," Faith declared, not batting a lash for cutting in on her aunt. "Mrs. Grayson, we would be in your debt if you would pass word of our business to your lady friends."

So that's what these women were up to. Duke ground his teeth. They were swindling his family into promoting their business.

"Of course," his mother said in her usual obliging way. She got to her feet and grasped Iris's hands. "The girls and I will be happy to promote your business to every woman we know, and I'll be your best customer. You are truly an artist, and well worth whatever price you're charging."

"Not a penny, Mrs. Grayson. Consider it our gift to thank you for such a warm welcome."

"We are the ones who received the warm welcome." Duke's mother patted Iris's hands, but spoke to all of the women. "Thank you for a wonderful afternoon."

Duke waited until his mother left with Evelyn and Claire then he took Faith firmly by the elbow. "Let's have that private talk now, Mrs. Wilkins."

Chapter Seven

Duke guided Faith outside, away from her daughter and out of earshot of the outlandish women she called her aunts. He'd wager his badge, or a win in the next election, that the women weren't related to each other at all, much less related to Faith.

He folded his arms across his chest and leaned against the vertical board and batten wall of the building. "I stopped to make sure the gas line was secure, but that was some story your aunt just told."

Faith fiddled with her apron, aligning the two large pockets with her hip bones then smoothing the dark green fabric over her flat stomach. "Aunt Dahlia has a flare for drama."

So did Faith. Her casual tugging and smoothing of her apron made him vividly aware of what lay beneath the fabric of her dress.

"Dahlia was just entertaining our guests."

"Your guests were my mother and my sisters-in-law, decent people who don't deserve to be manipulated."

Her head jerked up. "Manipulated?"

"Misled, if you prefer."

Her eyes sparked with anger. "In what way, Sheriff?"

"Dahlia's story is leaky as a sieve."

"Because she was shamelessly embellishing her past, which she confessed to your mother. Storytelling is a great pastime in my family, but I can't see any reason for her silly story to upset you. Dahlia admitted she was 'decorating the cake'."

He lifted his eyebrows. "Then you're saying those women aren't your aunts?"

"I've already answered that question, and the answer hasn't changed."

He eyed her for a moment and decided she would defend those crazy women as fiercely as she would defend Cora—and Adam, who was walking down the street toward them.

"Your brother is nearly here." He nodded in the boy's direction.

Faith looked peeved. "Adam and I have to finish our planting, so if you'll excuse me."

"One more question." He thumbed toward the greenhouse. "What else are you selling here? What are those special services you and your aunts offer?"

Faith's scowl deepened. "Healing massages."

"What exactly is a 'healing massage'?"

"It's the practice of manipulating muscle while applying healing herbs and oils to a sore or injured area of the body."

"Will you be offering this service to men?"

Her eyes sparked with anger and she refused to answer.

"How do you intend to apply oils and balms without asking your patrons to remove their clothing?"

She tried to step around him, but he caught her elbow and stopped her from opening the door.

"Mrs. Wilkins, I'm responsible for what goes on in this town, and I want to know what manner of business you're running. How will you and your aunts provide these massages?"

"With our clothes on!" She tried to jerk her elbow free, but he held fast.

"Let go of my sister!" Adam pushed between them, shielding Faith with his skinny body. His chest heaved and his fists clenched at his sides. "Leave her alone. She didn't do anything to you."

Duke yanked his hand away as if he'd touched a hot poker, ashamed that he'd been gripping her so tightly. He was used to apprehending men. He would never handle a woman roughly. But he couldn't allow anything, including Faith's pretty face, to stand in the way of doing his duty. He'd taken an oath and he would uphold it regardless of the cost.

"All right, son." He nodded to acknowledge the boy's anger, but spoke to Faith. "I hadn't meant to insult you, or to hurt you."

She put her hands on Adam's shoulders and turned him to face her. "I need to talk with the sheriff." Adam opened his mouth, and she shook her head to silence him. "Go check on Cora while I have a final word with him. When I finish here, I want to get the rest of the cabbage planted."

Adam glared at Duke. "You better not hurt her," he said then stormed inside and slammed the door.

Duke felt a mix of admiration and concern for the boy. Adam was justified in his anger, and right to defend his sister, but if he wasn't careful, he could be heading down a path that would put him on the wrong side of the law.

"I'm sorry I pushed you." Duke rolled his aching shoulder and released a sigh of regret. "Adam told me you dislike men. I guess I haven't helped improve your opinion of us."

A startled look crossed her face. "I never... I dislike being bullied is all."

"I hadn't meant to bully you. But it's my job to look out for the residents in my town."

"I know that." She rubbed her elbow and met his eyes with an openness that shocked him. "I'm one of those residents too,

Sheriff. My aunts and I are struggling to build a new life here. If my business doesn't thrive, I can't support my family. I'm out of money, and I'm mourning someone I love, but despite being desperate and so scared I can hardly take a full breath, I've never once considered performing the crude services you've unfairly accused me of selling."

A slap across the face couldn't have been more effective in snapping him out of his single-minded pursuit of information. Shame snaked through his gut as he looked through the greenhouse window. Adam stood amidst the mass of greenery, watching them. The plants were stretching upward, alive and healthy, proof that Faith was selling herbs. No harm had come from the balm she had given him, or from the massage Iris gave his mother, or from the existence of Faith's greenhouse.

Chagrined, he blew out a breath. "This is a peculiar business you've opened, and I won't deny being skeptical about what you're doing here, but I had no right to insult you, and no intention of doing so. I'm sorry."

"Sheriff Grayson, everything I do here is with the intention of helping people improve their health. How can that be bad?"

He didn't question her sincerity, but his gut insisted there was something about these women that would bite him the minute he turned his back.

"Did my balm help your shoulder?" she asked.

"For a few hours."

"But your shoulder is growing worse, isn't it?"

It was, but he wouldn't admit it.

"I can see that it is, Sheriff. Your grimace gave you away when you took your handcuffs off your belt for Cora."

"I'm fine."

"Lift your arm then."

"What?"

"Lift your arm above your head."

He stared at her, liking the challenge in her eyes, but confused by her odd request.

"You can't do it, can you?"

He didn't know because he hadn't tried. It hurt too bad just maneuvering his arm into his shirtsleeve.

"I can fix your shoulder for you," she said, with a confidence that surprised him.

"How do you propose to do that?" His own doctor hadn't been able to repair the injury or ease the pain, and he strongly doubted Faith could do so.

"Herbal massage."

"I'm not interested in Iris's massage."

"I'll do it."

"You?"

Her chin dipped once in a decisive nod. "I'll make an exception and treat your shoulder, only to prove that I can make it better."

It would be no hardship having the pretty widow massage his shoulder, but he could, and would, resist his base desire. He'd been sheriff for a long time and had faced life and death situations that taught him how to ignore distractions. If this worked out like he expected, he could get some answers to his questions and prove her healing massage was just a ruse, saving his friends and family from discovering this for themselves. With elections coming up, he couldn't afford to let anything unsavory take root in this town.

"All right, Mrs. Wilkins, when do we start?"

"Now, if you like—but with one stipulation," she said. "If I succeed in restoring your shoulder, you must publicly acknowledge that my business is legitimate."

"If you succeed to my satisfaction, I'll gladly make a public statement. But I have a condition, too. I pay for my treatment."

He could see a calculating look creep into her eyes. "Would you consider paying me with lumber?"

He lifted an eyebrow, wondering what she was angling for.

"I need to put up walls in the building we're living in."

"I'll donate the lumber."

She shook her head. "I can't accept anything from... I can't accept a donation."

From him, she'd been about to say. Did she think a donation would leave her in his debt? "My brothers and I donate lumber to several causes."

"I'm not a cause, Sheriff. I insist on paying for it by fixing your shoulder."

"Let's get started then."

Duke followed Faith to the back of the greenhouse and sat on a long, wooden table. She retrieved his cuffs from Cora then sent her daughter outside with Adam and two of her *aunts* to finish planting their vegetable garden behind the cavernous building they called their home.

"You'll have to remove your shirt, Sheriff."

His gut clenched, even as he felt an instant stirring of desire. No respectable woman would ask a man to bare his torso in a public place, and he was so taken aback, and so taken with the thought of her hands touching him, that he couldn't decide whether to chastise her or welcome her invitation.

"I know what I'm doing, Sheriff. I've been studying botany and anatomy and forms of healing since I was old enough to read. I'm a widow, not an innocent. I'm capable of tending to your shoulder without compromising my morals or damaging my reputation. But if you're too uncomfortable with this arrangement—"

"It wasn't my discomfort I was worried about," he said then gritted his teeth and struggled out of his shirt.

Her cheeks flushed as she tied a long length of linen toga-style around his torso, leaving his injured shoulder exposed. She poured a sweet-smelling oil into her cupped palm, rubbed her hands together then moved behind him. "This is almond oil mixed with arnica." She smoothed her warm palms up his back and over the crest of his shoulder. "The massage will relax your muscles, and the herb will soothe the ache."

Relax him? Her touch snapped his body to attention. His stomach muscles quivered and his thighs tensed. His heart thudded so hard it vibrated his rib cage. He was reacting to her stroking hands like a boy experiencing his first romantic moment with a lady.

Her thumbs traced the sore muscles beneath his shoulder blade, and he willed his body to settle down. She moved her fingers upward along his spine then pinched lightly across the crest of his shoulder. The tension in his neck melted by degrees as she worked downward to the muscles in his upper arm. He could hear Iris and Aster talking as they worked together in the greenhouse, and Faith's soft breathing near his ear as she leaned over him. A hint of flowers and mint and almond teased his nose, and he wondered if the nice smell was the oil or Faith. Her touch was innocent and pleasing, but his aroused body leapt at every sweep of her palms over his skin. A man would have to be dead, or completely in love with another woman, not to be aroused by Faith's stimulating fingers.

"Lie down, Sheriff."

"Do what?" he asked, astonished at her boldness and at his eagerness to do whatever she desired.

"I'm going to stretch your muscles." Her soft hands pressed him toward the table. "I can't do it with you sitting."

He yielded to her touch and lay on his back, wanting to see how far she would take this *massage*. The table was several inches wider than his shoulders, but his heels hung off the end.

She clasped his wrist, but her fingers didn't come close to encircling it. "Your muscles are so tight they're restricting your movement." She cupped her other hand beneath his elbow. "I'm going to lift your arm above your head and exert pressure. Tell me when you can't bear it."

She was going to kill him. He braced for the pain, knowing it was going to hurt, but when she raised his arm, his breath exploded outward through his clenched teeth. It felt as if she'd driven a spike into his shoulder socket.

She lowered his arm an inch, which blessedly allowed the pain to ebb. "Your shoulder will get worse if you don't move it," she said. "You need to stretch your muscles or they'll weaken and shrink around the joint. It's already happening."

That flew in the face of his doctor's orders. "Doc Milton said to rest it."

"With all due respect, I disagree with his advice." She lowered his arm to the table. "If you won't allow me to stretch the muscles, I can't fix your shoulder. That means our agreement is off."

"How will wrenching on my already sore shoulder help it improve?" After hearing Dahlia's outlandish tale, and feeling the blinding pain Faith had caused him by raising his arm, he was more than suspect of her healing skills.

"I had a... friend who injured his shoulder and it ended up frozen like yours is getting. His doctor said the only fix was to stretch or tear the muscles to free up the arm then keep the muscles stretched until they healed, otherwise the arm would remain useless. Your doctor should know that."

Well, he obviously didn't or he wouldn't have told Duke to rest his shoulder. Doc Milton had doctored his family for as long as Duke could remember. Duke should listen to him, especially since he didn't want his sore muscles stretched or torn. But he couldn't. He had to yield to his gut, which insisted he needed to keep an eye on Faith and her aunts. He needed to be here, inside the greenhouse, participating in these massages they were offering. In all fairness, Faith did seem confident in her knowledge, and hardly the type of woman to swindle anyone, but her aunts with their bent for telling tales were another story. And his shoulder wasn't improving on its own.

So he would stay, for whatever good it might do him. Without a doubt, Faith and her aunts would behave in his presence, but he would ask one of his friends, someone like Anna Levens who could be trusted to partake of Faith's services and keep him informed. One negative word from Anna, and he would shut them down at the first sign of wrongdoing.

He lifted his wrist to Faith's waiting hand. "All right, Mrs. Wilkins, work your magic."

"Are you sure?" she asked. "My friend said the doctor's treatment was excruciatingly painful."

"But it worked?"

She nodded. "It can take months, though."

"Then we'd better get started."

———

Faith had half-hoped the sheriff would take his questions and suspicions and his too-male body and leave her greenhouse. He'd been imposing with his shirt on, but when he'd exposed his broad, muscled torso, her stomach had done a crazy dip that left her breathless.

Her breathing was still so shallow she felt lightheaded. But now that she had an opportunity to win the sheriff's support, she couldn't back down. She had to show some of the same starch and wit her aunts displayed. Dahlia had been brilliant to say they were here to serve the ladies in town. That was a perfectly reputable way to earn an income. The ladies would receive great pleasure from spending their husbands' money, and as long as Faith could bear touching the sheriff's bare body, she would eventually get his muscles stretched and his shoulder healed. Then he would have to give them his public approval.

"Have you changed your mind about treating me?" he asked.

"I was giving you a chance to run."

"And miss out on such excruciating... pleasure?"

Her puff of laughter surprised her as much as his humor had. "I'm amazed, Sheriff. You're capable of making a joke."

"And you're capable of laughing." His lips lifted in a half-smile. "You have a nice laugh, Mrs. Wilkins."

"And you have a pleasing sense of humor," she replied, but her bravado failed her and she lowered her lashes. Her aunts would have made the statement while looking him in the eye, but he was too handsome, and too overwhelming up close, and she was unskilled at flirting.

She slipped her fingers around his manly wrist and felt his hard pulse and warm skin beneath her fingertips. When he turned his palm up and clasped her hand, she flinched then flushed because she was acting like a skittish, naive girl.

"We've started off on the wrong foot, Mrs. Wilkins. Maybe we can start over?"

"I don't intend to make this more painful just because you judged me unfairly"

His laugh echoed in the stone room. "I hadn't thought of that," he said, his eyes filled with warmth. "Just don't forget I'm the one with the badge and the gun."

Lo! The man had been handsome when scowling, but when he laughed, he was spectacular. Full, smiling lips set perfectly in his strong, sturdy face, and his warm, sparkling eyes looked at her in a way that made her stomach go light and fluttery.

"I was joking." He winked, and her heart kicked so hard she feared he could hear it thump against her chest. "How about starting over. Can we do that?"

She'd rather run for the hills before he broke her heart. No woman could look in this man's eyes and not fall in love. To save herself, she swung her attention to his shoulder. "If you'll put aside your suspicions and judge me by my actions."

"Fair enough."

"Then brace yourself, Sheriff, because you're not going to like what I'm going to do to you."

His scowl and grunts conveyed his pain. Sweat beaded his forehead as she bent his arm at the elbow and rotated his forearm away from his body. After stretching the deltoid and triceps muscles, she straightened his arm and slowly pushed upward, forcing his tight, unwilling muscles to stretch or tear—whatever it took to free the arm. "You'll need to do this twice a day," she said, holding his arm in a forced stretch. "And you need to force it a little further each time you do it."

"I'd rather shoot myself," he said, his teeth clamped, his jaw muscles bulging.

"Only a minute more." She held his arm steady then lowered it a half inch at a time, pausing each time he puffed out a pain-filled breath.

"Gads! It's worse bringing my arm back down."

"That's because your muscles are contracting after a hard stretch."

"I'm tempted to yield to Dr. Milton's advice."

"You're free to do as you wish, but that's what got you into this situation." She lowered his arm to rest on the table beside him. "If I were you, I'd arrest him for giving bad advice that's causing you pain and suffering."

He rubbed his injured shoulder. "I certainly have grounds to press charges."

"Sit up and let me rub some balm into your shoulder."

He swung his long legs over the edge of the table and hung his head as if he'd just engaged in an exhausting battle. "I'll never be able to stretch like this on my own."

"You'll have to. Coming here once a day won't be enough."

"Then I'm afraid you're going to be seeing me twice a day, Mrs. Wilkins, because I need this shoulder fixed."

She suspected he simply wanted to do more snooping, but she kept her thoughts to herself and smoothed the balm over his shoulder. She massaged gently, wanting to relax his muscles and ease the tension in his neck and shoulders.

"I can't believe those are the same hands that were torturing me only a moment ago," he said.

She smiled and worked the pads of her thumbs into his sore muscles. 'Let that be a warning not to cross me."

He laughed, and the linen slipped down his arm. A deep valley cut down the center of his back, with hard ridges rising up on either side of his spine. Sinew and muscle shifted beneath her kneading fingers. His skin was warm and smooth, and suddenly it was no longer the sheriff's back she was treating; she was touching the body of a strong, handsome man who could joke and laugh and look at her with warmth in his eyes.

Faith's stomach tingled with awareness, and she jerked her hands away as if his skin scalded her fingertips.

"You've successfully survived your first treatment, Sheriff," she said.

He stood and faced her. The linen hung at his waist, and her gaze riveted on his broad chest. Curly dark hair swept over bulging muscle that bunched and flexed as he reached for his shirt. He slipped it over his sore left arm then his right then shrugged it into place.

"What time would you like me to come by this evening?" He tugged the linen from his waist and tossed it on the table. "I can't stretch without your help," he reminded her.

She picked up the towel and scrubbed the balm and oils off her hands. "Nine o'clock would be best for me, if it's not too late for you. I like to put Cora to bed myself, and I'd rather do this when she's not here."

"I have plenty of chores to keep me busy until then, so nine o'clock is fine—unless I'm needed somewhere. A sheriff is never officially unavailable. If I'm not here by quarter after, I won't be coming."

"All right." She fiddled with the linen to divert her eyes while he buttoned his shirt. The sight of him should not leave her as breathless as an innocent girl; she was far from innocent. She and Iris had massaged men's bare torsos at the brothel, but not one of them was as handsome or intriguing as the sheriff. She had quickly culled out the nasty, groping men, and gained a small group of regular and somewhat respectful customers. That's how she'd met Jarvis Powell, and though he'd paid her a small fortune, he'd left her soul impoverished.

Still, Faith hadn't worked as a prostitute. She'd lived out back in a one-room, one-bed shack with Adam and Cora. Faith's mother had lived there, too, but spent most of her time sleeping, or in the brothel earning money. And except for buying books and plants, Faith had saved every dime she earned, vowing to help her mother escape the place and buy their dream house with a porch and a rose garden.

But her mother's death had left Faith to pursue that dream alone. Now it seemed the only way she could give Adam and Cora a comfortable home was to use the skills she learned at the brothel. So here she was, this time treating women—and one man—who would appreciate her skill, but not understand the value of it.

She could accept that, if she had to. What she couldn't accept was her natural but foolish attraction to the sheriff. He was too smart, too curious about her business and her past. A man like him would dig until he got to the truth. And when he found it, she was afraid he would evict her and her family from his town faster than she could open her mouth to beg for mercy.

Chapter Eight

"Why are we going to church?" Cora asked, as Faith stopped in the sun-washed Common.

Adam flicked his fingers across the top of her head. "Because we want people to like us."

Faith exchanged a glance with her aunts, who had altered their old dresses to appear respectable enough for church. They had even donned bonnets, but their usually vivacious faces were pinched with discomfort. Faith suspected it had been years since any of them set foot in a church. She had been herself once, and it was the worst moment of her life. But Adam was right. If they didn't attend church, they would be ostracized from the community.

It sure seemed like every person in Fredonia was gathered in town this morning. The streets surrounding the Common were lined with carriages and nickering horses. Large families gathered and greeted friends as each made their way inside one of the three churches near the twin parks. Faith eyed the brick buildings with their arched windows and tall spires, and had no idea which church to enter.

"Look, Mama!" Cora pointed. "There's the sheriff!"

There he was indeed, his tall, broad-shouldered body clothed in a well-cut black suit that enhanced his dark good looks.

Last night he hadn't shown up for his shoulder treatment. Faith didn't know if his job had called him away, or if he'd changed his mind about having her restore his shoulder. Whatever his reason for not visiting, she didn't want to discover the answer in front of his family or his admiring lady friends.

Several young women were twirling their parasols, vying for his attention, but he only nodded pleasantly and strode toward the church. How could he be so unaffected by those pretty women? Even from where she was standing, Faith could see that some of them were lovely. Was the man immune to a woman's charms?

"It could benefit us to go to the same church the Grayson family attends," Iris said, her cheeks flushed from all the stares she was receiving. Tansy, Aster, and Dahlia nodded in agreement.

They were right, but Faith waited for the sheriff to enter the church before she led them across the Common and followed him inside.

After being in the bright morning sunshine, she found the interior of the church depressingly dim. The building smelled of musty books and beeswax and a cloying mix of colognes. Why worship God in a dark building when he'd given them this beautiful morning to enjoy? Why not stand in the fresh air beneath the maple trees in the Common to sing praises?

Faith stood at the back of the church, scanning the full pews, wondering where they would sit. Would they be asked to leave if there wasn't room for them?

"Good morning, Mrs. Wilkins."

The sheriff's voice startled her, and she glanced up into his warm brown eyes. A flock of flutter-birds took flight inside her stomach. Her mother had told her when she was a small child that her stomach was a world of its own, complete with sky and sea and tiny flutter-birds that were upset by any nervous shift in the wind; and Faith had believed it for the longest time. Even now she couldn't shake the appropriate image of birds beating their wings in her stomach, because that was exactly how it felt.

"Good morning, Sheriff Grayson!" Cora said brightly.

Faith laid her fingers over the child's mouth. "Hush, sweetie."

"Good morning," he whispered then reached up and pulled the cap off Adam's head, revealing Adam's new haircut. "No hats in church," he said.

"Yes, sir," Adam agreed quietly then tucked his brown cap under his arm.

The sheriff looked less threatening without his gun, but he was too handsome and far more dangerous to her heart in his suit and tie. He gestured with his chin. "My mother is making room in her pew for you ladies."

Faith looked over a sea of people to where Nancy Grayson waved her glove-encased hand at them. The sheriff escorted them to her pew, but didn't sit with them. He guided Adam to the back of the church to stand with a large group of men, three of whom shared a remarkable resemblance to the sheriff.

"Those are my sons," Nancy whispered, stepping aside so Faith could enter the pew.

Faith lifted Cora onto her hip then stepped in behind Iris. As she sat, she nodded to Evelyn and Claire and another woman about their age with hair the color of a burnished chestnut.

"That's my daughter-in-law Amelia," Nancy whispered, settling beside Faith. "She married my son Kyle, who's in back with Duke."

Faith looked toward the sheriff and the men beside him. There was no doubt those four tall, handsome men were brothers. She turned to greet Amelia, and received a warm smile in return. Amelia was as pretty as Evelyn and Claire, but the three women were as different in looks as each season. Amelia was autumn at its peak color, with her brown eyes and gorgeous hair of reds, golds, and browns. Evelyn's sable hair was black as a winter night, and her gemstone eyes sparkled like holiday ornaments. Blond-haired, blue-eyed Claire reminded Faith of a summer field of wheat under an endless blue sky.

Nancy Grayson was no season at all. She was mother earth, and this family drew their sustenance from her.

"This is my granddaughter Rebecca." Nancy slipped her arm around a cute, dark-haired girl about Adam's age. "She's Radford and Evelyn's oldest."

The girl nodded politely, but a blast from a pipe organ buried her soft greeting. The sound filled the church and vibrated in Faith's chest. The congregation surged to its feet en masse. Faith and her aunts hurried to follow suit.

Cora put her hands over her ears. "What's that noise?"

Faith lifted the child onto her hip. "It's an organ," she whispered quickly, hoping no one realized Cora didn't recognize the sound. Faith had only heard it once herself, but she would never forget that powerful blast that had swept the breath from her.

Six weeks ago on a chilly Sunday morning Judge Stone had shown up at the brothel and demanded the deed to the property. Her mother had argued fiercely and tried to push him out of her home, but that had caused her own fall over the second floor railing. Stone had walked out, leaving them to get a doctor, but they hadn't known any doctors. So Faith and Dahlia had rushed into a church several blocks away, their cries for help buried in the blast of the church organ and impassioned singing. When the song ended and their pleas could be heard, a kind doctor in the congregation had gone to the brothel with them, but the fall had injured her mother's head too severely, and she died twelve hours later.

Faith had known few acts of kindness from strangers, and she would forever remember the bespectacled doctor and his sincere sorrow that he couldn't save her mother.

Thinking back, she'd assumed she would now hate the sound of the organ, but the vibrating pipes filled the church with such majesty, her lips parted on a sigh. Awestruck, Faith listened, captivated by the impassioned people around her lifting and blending their voices in song. The glorious music flooded her with a sense of rightness. They would come to church on Sunday mornings just like the other respectable residents of Fredonia. And someday, she might even have a husband who would love her, who would stand at the back of the church with their sons, waiting to escort her to their safe, love-filled home.

When the song ended, Faith sat in the pew with Cora on her lap, vowing she wouldn't be weak like her mother, a woman condemned for her tawdry profession. Her mother had provided food and a dry place to sleep for Faith and the children, but precious little of her time. She'd dreamed of a better life, of marrying a man she loved, of giving her children a real home, but she'd spent thirty years as a prostitute and died in her brothel.

The sad truth was that Faith's mother could have moved to a new town and kept her past a secret like Faith was doing. Men would have lined up to propose marriage to the unequaled beauty. But Rose had lacked the courage, or the desire, to change her life. And that's why Faith hated her.

But she loved her for so many other reasons, it wrung her heart.

That conflict gnawed at Faith's conscience each day of her life, feeding her anger, increasing her guilt. Some days she wanted to forget everything—the brothel, Jarvis, even her mother. Other days she ached for one of her mother's hard, apologetic hugs.

Cora's breathing slowed, and Faith held her close as the little girl fell asleep. They would build a good life here, she vowed. They would plant their dreams in this rich farming soil of upstate New York and nourish them with firm conviction, courage, and love.

Here, in the ashes of her mother's life, she would plant her dreams and they would bloom like fireweed.

Certainty swept through her, and the church no longer felt dim and airless. The space felt sacred, the pastor's words inspiring and uplifting. Faith listened with her eyes closed and her heart open, drinking in the nourishing words she'd been so long denied.

When the service ended, her heart overflowed with hope as she followed the Graysons outside into the bright June sunshine. She wanted to linger in the Common, to deepen her acquaintance with the people who would become part of her garden, but an outraged shout from across the park drew everyone's attention toward Main Street.

"That man's stealing my horse!"

Before Faith could understand what was happening, Sheriff Grayson sprinted past her, jaw set, suit coat flapping as he raced across the small park, followed by his brothers and several other men.

The accused man leapt onto the horse and dug his spurred heels into its flanks. A collective gasp burst from the crowd as he wheeled the horse toward the sheriff and tried to run him down. Instead, the sheriff side-stepped the mare, reached up with one hand, and hauled the rider off the horse. The man hit the ground hard and rolled away from the rearing animal.

Faith held her breath, fearing those sharp hooves would crash down on the thief, or worse yet, slash the sheriff's head and shoulders. But one of the sheriff's brothers caught the reins and led the frightened horse away from the tussle.

As the man on the ground pushed to his knees, the sheriff planted his boot against the seat of thief's pants and shoved him face down on the grass. And before the man could push himself to his elbows, Sheriff Grayson pinned him to the ground with a knee to his back.

"Stay put, Covey."

"Go to hell."

The man called Covey struggled and cursed, but the sheriff braced one hand on the back of Covey's head, pressing his face into the spring grass. "You're under arrest," he said.

With his free hand, the sheriff fumbled beneath his suit coat, but Covey surprised him, slamming his elbow into the sheriff's ribs.

A husky man pushed through the crowd and headed toward the scuffle, and Faith willed him to hurry.

"Archer!" Another of the sheriff's brothers stepped forward and blocked the man's way. "Stay out of it."

Faith gaped in disbelief. Covey was thrashing like a rabid dog, kicking his boot heels up and using his spurs like small knives. She couldn't tell if he was hitting his mark, but the sheriff's suit coat was ripped in several places and he'd lost his hold on the man.

Covey leapt to his feet and bolted into the crowd. Several women screamed as the sheriff tore after the thief.

Archer pushed forward, but the sheriff's brother grabbed his arm and stopped him. "Duke will handle this."

"Damn it, Boyd, unhand me!" Archer struggled against Boyd Grayson's unrelenting grip. "That thief is getting away!"

The sheriff tackled Covey near the huge water fountain.

Boyd grinned. "No, he's not."

The sheriff and Covey were so tangled up that Faith couldn't tell who was winning the fight, but she was on Archer's side; somebody needed to step in and lend a hand.

Covey reared up and slammed his elbow into the sheriff's sore shoulder. The sheriff's pain-filled grunt could be heard across the Common, but unbelievably, no one moved to help him. Faith's jaw dropped. What was wrong with these people? Why on earth weren't his brothers helping? There had to be forty men in the park, but they were just standing there watching while that horrid thief swung his elbows and fists like hammers.

With a low growl, the sheriff grabbed Covey's wrist and wrenched the man's arm behind his back. Covey cursed and struggled, but the sheriff out-muscled the horse thief and bound his hands with a pair of black suspenders he'd pulled from beneath his coat. Only then did Faith realize the sheriff was without his gun and handcuffs.

When he finally pulled the man to his feet, the sheriff was breathing hard and dripping sweat. Faith knew the extent of his shoulder injury and could imagine the wrenching pain he must be in. But he kept his jaw clenched and propelled the horse thief through the crowd. Nobody said a word until the sheriff pushed Covey inside the brick building on the corner of Temple Street.

"He's taking him to jail," Adam said, his face lit with excitement as he pointed to the building that Faith hoped to never visit. "Did you see the sheriff pull that man off that horse?"

She sure had seen it, and it scared her sideways. Even injured, the sheriff wasn't a man to cross.

Everyone began speaking at once, filling the Common with enough noise to startle the birds out of the maple trees.

"He did it with one hand," Adam continued with awe. "Those men didn't even have to help him."

Faith was trembling so badly she couldn't bear Cora's weight another moment. She set the child down on the bright green lawn then led her and Adam to where their aunts and the sheriff's sisters-in-law were gathered around Nancy.

"Of course these things terrify me," Nancy was saying. "Duke says it's senseless for me to worry about him, but a mother will worry to her grave."

"Surely his brothers or one of those other men could have helped him," Tansy insisted, apparently as appalled over their lack of action as Faith was.

"They know Duke can do his job, and they respected him by not getting in his way."

"But that man was beating him!" Faith said, her outrage revealing two things she did not want to know: The sheriff's job was too dangerous, and she was far too concerned about him for her own good.

"I know," Nancy said, the tremor in her voice belying her brave front. "Believe me, if the situation had turned ugly, his brothers were right there ready to step in."

If it turned ugly? Faith's heart was still banging in her chest. How much uglier would it need to get before the man's own brothers would step in and help?

Chapter Nine

I t took Duke two hours to get Covey settled and the horse owner calmed down, and by the time his deputy Sam Wade arrived to guard the prisoner, Duke's shoulder hurt, the pain almost beyond bearing. And doubt tormented him.

If he hadn't yanked Covey to the ground and stunned the man, Covey would have thrown him off like a bothersome blanket. When he'd broken loose and bolted into the crowd, Duke feared his brothers and the townsmen would have to bring down the horse thief. This was his responsibility. He'd taken an oath to protect the area residents, and he couldn't do that with only one healthy arm.

Sick with worry and pain, he struggled to greet people cordially as he made his way to Faith's greenhouse. When he found the door unlocked and Faith inside alone, he sagged with relief.

"I know it's Sunday, and that you're obviously closed for business," he said, startling a gasp from her, "but I'm prepared to pay any price you ask if you'll fix my shoulder."

She pressed her hand to her chest and leaned against a flat of leafy green plants. "Why didn't those men help you in that fight?" she asked, her face pale. "Your own brother kept a man from helping."

"I didn't need help," he said. Thank God. But next time...

"Surely they could have saved you from getting kicked and... and oh gracious, did Covey cut you with his spurs? You must be in terrible pain."

"I'm not cut, but I was hoping for a massage with some of that balm you gave me."

"It should give you some relief," she agreed. She crossed to the shelves and retrieved a jar of balm.

"Where is everybody?" Duke asked, joining her at the counter.

"Adam's playing out back. Cora's napping, and my aunts are in the house. I just came in to pick some herbs to make soup for lunch."

"Should I come back later?" he asked, praying she wouldn't ask him to. His back was cramping, and his neck muscles were growing so tight he could barely turn his head.

"I'd rather do it now while Cora is sleeping."

"Thank you," he said then clamped his teeth against another back spasm.

She eyed him closely. "I think you need more than a massage, Sheriff." She gathered an armful of linens and headed toward the back of the greenhouse. "I have a bold suggestion, but you have to promise not to arrest me for making it."

He smiled, appreciating a bit of lightness in an otherwise dark morning. "I promise not to arrest you."

"All right then. I'm going to mix a tea that will relax you."

"I can't see why I would arrest you unless you add some of those poisonous herbs you grow."

"If I did that, you'd be dead, and I'd get off scot-free," she said with an easy laugh that soothed him.

He lowered his aching shoulders and followed her to the small stone room at the back of the greenhouse where he'd hooked up the gas line for her tub. She set the linens on a chair beside the tub which was large enough for six adults. Then she uncapped a jar and poured purplish liquid into the tub. The scent of lavender wafted through the room.

She capped the jar and set it on a nearby stand. "While I'm brewing your tea, you can remove your clothes and settle yourself in the bath."

She couldn't have surprised him more if she'd kissed him.

She scooped out a bucket of bath water and sat it on a low table beside a dish of soap shavings. "Everyone must wash from nose-to-toes then rinse off before getting into the bath. When you're clean, tie one of the linens around your hips before you get in, so I can bring in your tea."

Maybe Covey's hard elbow to the temple had jarred his brain.

"A warm soak in an herbal bath will soothe your muscles, Sheriff," she continued, straightening the linens. "We empty and clean the tub once a week, so I can assure you the water is fresh. The tea will relax you and help reduce inflammation. If you'd rather just have a massage, I'm happy to accommodate you, although it won't be as effective without the herbal bath."

"You want me to get into that tub of perfume water?"

"And submerge yourself to your chin for fifteen minutes. I'll be back in a little while with your tea." She left the room and pulled the door closed behind her.

The thought of dousing himself with lavender appalled him, but the muscle spasm wrenching his back made the decision for him. He struggled out of his soiled suit, scuffed shoes, and sweaty undergarments then scrubbed himself nose-to-toes with the soap and water she had provided. After rinsing clean, he tied a long strip of linen around his hips.

An overturned crate and an old wooden trunk sat on the floor, forming steps beside the tub. Duke climbed them gingerly, testing his weight on them then stepped into the water—and realized too late it was deeper than it looked. And hot. He went under face first and came up like a roaring geyser.

"Geeawwwd!"

He stood on his toes on some sort of metal grate, trying to keep his already toasted privates from burning to cinders.

"Are you in the bath?" Faith called from the other side of the door.

"Bath? Ha! It's a soup pot."

She opened the door, but her beautiful smile froze when she saw him standing in the middle of the tub. "Is it that hot?" she asked, rushing forward to dip her hand in the water. She swished her fingers through the scented liquid and sighed. "Why, it can't be much warmer than you are."

"Believe me, it's a lot hotter than the boys appreciate."

Her face flushed and she turned away. "I'll cool it some." She set his tea on the table then lifted the long iron pump handle. She pumped it twice and cold water gushed from a fat spigot into the tub.

"You'll need to sit to benefit from the bath."

"And blister my behind? No thank you." Despite the metal grate that kept his feet several inches above the bottom of the tub, the water was much warmer near the burner.

"For someone who can pull a man off his horse and wrestle him into submission one-handed, you're ridiculously sensitive to a little warm water."

"Why don't you step in here and see how it feels?"

Her lips parted, and he thought he heard her gasp. She was flustered. Did his bold talk offend her? Was it his bare chest that had her acting so shaky? Or did she feel his attraction to her? Heat flushed through him. He'd come here out of desperation, so he could relieve his shoulder pain and get his mind back on his job, but his head filled with thoughts of Faith.

"I spent twenty minutes in the bath before church," she said, her bodice straining to contain her breasts as she worked the pump handle. "It felt perfectly lovely to me."

A vivid image of her glistening wet body caused his own to react. Sergeant and the boys might be poached, but they were wide awake and ready for action. The linen toweling did a poor job of concealing his lust, so he clasped his hands in front of his hips while she worked the pump handle and drove him crazy.

She stopped pumping and unbuttoned her cuffs. "Will you treat Covey like you did Adam, and have him work for the horse owner to right his wrong?"

"No. This is his third offense."

She pushed her sleeves to her elbows and submerged her hands in the bath water, moving slowly around the tub, swishing her hands around. "This ought to make the temperature more comfortable."

The temperature of the water, maybe, but her swirling hands and jiggling breasts were bringing his desire to a slow simmer. Duke tried to distract her by pointing to a linen bag floating near the spigot. "What's in that sack?" he asked.

"Chamomile, lavender, agrimony and mugwort, with a liberal dose of almond oil. The herbs relieve stiff muscles and aching joints. The oil softens and soothes the skin. The warm water relaxes you. The oils also help keep the tub from rusting." She lifted her hands out of the water. "That should be more than comfortable, Sheriff. Please sit down."

Good idea. His aroused body was too exposed in the clinging wet linen. He lowered himself cautiously until he was submerged to his neck.

"Are you sitting or floating?" she asked.

"Floating." And aching in every way possible.

She leaned down and picked up a short-legged metal step stool, causing the fabric of her shirtwaist to pull tight across her breasts. Long-limbed and lithe, her movements were as graceful as a dancer's, and he couldn't look away. Her slender fingers circled one of the sturdy round legs of the stool, and his mind went crazy remembering the feel of her fingers massaging his back and sliding over his skin, and he couldn't help imagining her hands touching him in other places.

"Sit on this. I'll get your tea and a towel to put behind your neck." She dropped the stool into the water and turned away.

Getting splashed in the face was startling but deserved. He grabbed the submerged stool and dragged it under his bare bottom, feeling both excited and ridiculous in her big steamy bath.

"Pull it away from the edge so you're forced to lean back," she said, placing the cup of tea on the stand near him. "You need to keep your shoulders submerged."

He scooted the stool out several inches and leaned back against the side of the tub. She rolled one of the linens and tucked it behind his head. "It must have taken you a week to fill this tub."

"Four hours of constant pumping, but we share the duty between the five of us so it's not so bad. Now drink your tea and relax. I'll come back in fifteen minutes."

"Stay." He caught her hand to keep her from leaving. "If you can, that is. If you're not too busy."

"I think you'd be the first to note that it's improper for me to be in here with you."

"It will be more improper if I fall asleep and drown in your bathtub, Mrs. Wilkins."

"Which is highly unlikely. But you're the sheriff," she added. She picked up the stack of linens, sat on the chair, and parked the towels in her lap. "What's going to happen to that man who stole the horse?" she asked.

He sipped his tea and found it surprisingly pleasant. "He's going to jail." Why was she talking about Covey, for Pete's sake?

"That's sad. He looked young."

"He's twenty-three, and he's been a troublemaker since childhood. He's had ample opportunity to change his ways. Covey chose his path, and it's led him straight to prison. And it's about time."

"I take it you've dealt with him before?"

"Many times. Five weeks ago Covey walked out of Taylor Hotel and stole a horse belonging to one of the guests. When I caught him in the act, he ran the horse at me like he did today in the park. I made the mistake of grabbing the horse's bridle instead of Covey. When the horse reared, it jerked my arm up and wrenched my shoulder. Covey got away with the horse, which he promptly sold."

"And you got a nasty shoulder injury."

"Doesn't feel so bad at the moment."

She smiled. "I told you the bath would help."

"Maybe it's your pretty smile that's making me feel better."

Why not enjoy his visits? He was attracted to her, and he could keep his duty separate from his personal business with Faith. And just to make sure he didn't get preoccupied and miss something, he would make that call on Anna Levens and ask her to visit the greenhouse.

Faith's lashes swooped down to cover her eyes.

"I meant to compliment you, not embarrass you."

She straightened the stack of linens on her lap, and asked, "What made you want to be a sheriff?"

So much for compliments. "I wanted to redeem myself in my father's eyes."

Her lashes swept upward, her face lit with interest.

"It's true," he said, wanting to take their conversation to a personal level, admitting and accepting that he couldn't resist her shy smile and pretty whiskey-colored eyes. He flexed his shoulders in the warm water, enjoying the heat that had nearly cooked his bacon earlier. "I was eight years old when I committed my first and last crime. I stole a reel of fishing line from Brown & Shepherd's store."

"Well, that explains why you went easy on Adam."

"Mrs. Brown has had more wayward boys working in her store to pay their debts than any store owner in town. I wasn't the first boy to work off my mistake. I'd wager that Adam won't be the last."

"Did the sheriff make you work to pay for what you took?"

"My father did. He told me nothing can justify lying, cheating, or stealing. I promised him I'd live an honorable life from that day on, and I went right to the sheriff's office and volunteered to be his deputy"

She smiled as if she appreciated his boyhood sincerity.

"The sheriff was kind enough not to laugh at me. He let me run errands for him when I wasn't in school or working at my dad's sawmill. When I turned fourteen, he had me sit as guard on weekends. Mostly I guarded an empty cell, or sometimes a local drunk who'd gotten tossed out of a saloon. I spent most nights reading law books. I got my deputy's badge when I turned seventeen."

"Your father allowed this?"

"I had spent nine years running errands for the sheriff, babysitting drunks, and studying law to get that badge. Dad knew how much I wanted to wear it."

"But that badge put you in danger."

"The sheriff kept me away from the nasty side of the job until I was nineteen. I helped him track down a bank robber. We put the man in jail, and I earned the sheriff's respect. When he took a job in Buffalo four years later, he pushed me to run for the sheriff's job. I won the election."

"That must have been a proud day for your dad."

"It would have been, but he didn't live long enough to see me pin on my sheriff's badge."

She brought her hand to her chest. "Forgive me. I didn't realize."

Her compassion warmed him. Having lost her husband and mother, she must understand how the loss of his father tortured him.

"Dad died knowing I was fulfilling my promise to live an honorable life. I think that was enough for him."

"I'm sure it was," she said, but her eyes filled with sadness. "You can leave the bath now, Sheriff."

As he inched himself out of the water, her gaze dropped from his shoulders to his chest to his waist. He took his time, wanting her to look, wanting to know if she felt the vibrations traveling between them, because for all his good intentions, he wanted to do more than investigate her business.

When his hips cleared the water, she vaulted from the chair and put her back to him. Laying two thick towels over the table, she asked, "Do you mind waiting to dress? It'll make it easier to massage your back."

He wouldn't mind at all. He'd like nothing better than to help her out of her clothes and into the tub with him. "Maybe you should stretch my shoulder, too."

She looked at him from the corner of her eye. "I would recommend it, but it's up to you."

Forcing his sore muscles to stretch was the last thing he wanted, but he couldn't wait for his shoulder to improve on its own. Resigned, he sat on the table. "Let's get it over with."

"You'll have to lie on your back," Faith said then turned herself away while he did so. When she turned back, she opened another linen and draped it over Duke's hips and legs.

The sheriff glanced down and back up. "What's that for?"

"I don't want you catching a chill," she explained. But she was the one shivering. Gracious, she had to get away from this half-naked warrior. "Sheriff, I... I think Iris can do a better job with your shoulder," she said.

"I don't want Iris."

"But she's better at—"

He wrapped his long fingers around her wrist. "I want you."

She looked down at his handsome, water-speckled face, and couldn't force another word from her throat.

"My name is Duke."

He spoke softly, but she heard the command behind his words, and saw the hunger in his eyes. This man wanted more than a massage.

"May I call you Faith?" he asked.

Her flutter-birds beat their wings in panic. He was flat on his back, but the sheriff could easily overpower her. He could make her life miserable, run her out of town even, but it wasn't his strength or position she was afraid of—it was her sense of being out of control, of being governed by her body rather than her brain. She should never have offered to treat his shoulder.

"May I?" he prodded.

"It's inappropriate, Sheriff. We're just partners in healing your shoulder."

"I like the partners part."

There was nothing to do but get this over with as quickly as possible. She slipped her fingers around his wrist and lifted his arm at the elbow to form a right angle. "I need to stretch your muscles while they're warm and relaxed."

He sighed and closed his eyes. "All right. I'm as ready as I'll ever be."

She worked silently and slowly, wincing when he grunted, biting her lip when she saw perspiration bead on his forehead, battling her own tears when the corners of his eyes grew moist from pain. She rotated his forearm to the side, and returned it slowly. Then she straightened his arm and lifted it above his head, pressing and pushing his stiff muscles to stretch until neither of them could bear it a moment longer. With her breath held, she lowered his arm in tiny increments, sighing with relief when she finally laid his arm to rest beside him.

His broad chest shuddered as he exhaled, but his eyes remained closed and he didn't move.

She spooned balm into her hand and warmed it in her palms before smoothing the thick ointment over the front of his shoulder. With gentle strokes, she rubbed it down his biceps muscle to his elbow and forearm. The tension in his body ebbed slowly away, his breathing growing less ragged as she walked her fingertips across his muscles.

"Roll over, Sheriff, and I'll do your back."

He didn't say a word, didn't open his eyes, didn't even argue about his name. He just rolled onto his good arm and over onto his stomach, twisting the linen around his waist—and leaving his firm buttocks in full view of her greedy eyes.

Did he realize...? Had he done this on purpose?

Faith whisked a linen off the dwindling stack, snapped it open, and draped it over the enticing distraction. He wasn't the first undressed male she'd seen, but he was by far the most affecting. Her hands were sweating!

"Something wrong?" he asked, his voice muffled in the scrunched linens.

"I'm getting more balm," she said, but her heart pounded so hard her voice quaked. Would he feel her trembling?

She slathered the ointment over his broad back and forced her thoughts to the methodical process of weeding her garden, one section at a time, one plant at a time. She kneaded his muscles and imagined her hands working the soil. The scent of herbs, oils, and resins rose from the bath and his damp skin. She pressed the heels of her palms at the base of his spine and pushed them up his back as if she were creating furrows for seeding.

He moaned low in his throat.

She hesitated. "Did that hurt you?"

"It felt even better than the bath."

A smile tugged her lips. "I knew you'd like it."

"This or the bath?"

"The bath."

"I did. But your hands feel better."

She had no idea how to respond without encouraging or offending him, so she kept silent.

"Where did you learn to do this?"

"In my garden," she said, uncertain if his question was sincere interest or intentional probing. "Working muscles is similar to working the soil. Planting and weeding take patience and practice. After a while your hands learn what to do without needing instruction from your brain."

"Thank goodness you're not a blacksmith who manipulates iron with fire and hammers."

His analogy made her laugh. "Do your brothers have your unique sense of humor?"

"Unique?"

"Teasing. A bit cryptic. Sometimes a tad odd."

His lips quirked. "I preferred unique."

"Then you shouldn't have asked me to clarify."

He chuckled. "We're as different from each other as a willow is from a poplar or an aspen or a cottonwood. Same family, very different trees."

She leaned on the heels of her palms and moved them up his back. "You and your brothers look remarkably alike."

"Trees are trees. Men are men. The difference is in their grain. My oldest brother Radford is a deep thinker and peaceful man. But he's the only man I'd ever steer clear of. When he came home from the war, you could look in his eyes and feel tortured by the pain he was carrying. He wouldn't even pick up a gun to go hunting with us. Still won't, and it's been fifteen years. But he's not so jumpy since he married Evelyn."

Faith nodded. "She has a way of making a person feel like a friend the minute you meet her."

"She does, but she was engaged to my brother Kyle when she fell in love with Radford."

"Oh, dear, what a horrid situation for them and your family!"

"It was tough. Kyle was so enraged when Evelyn broke their engagement, he tore into Radford. By the time Boyd and I got to the livery, Radford was so out of his mind he nearly killed Kyle. He—" The sheriff lifted his head. "If this is boring you, I can stop."

"No. I'm intrigued. Really," she insisted. And she was.

"Then please don't stop working on that muscle. It's just beginning to un-cramp."

She hadn't realized she'd stopped massaging his back. Amazing, but his story had shifted her mind away from touching his bare skin. "I'll massage as long as you talk." She pressed her thumbs into the hard latissimus dorsi muscle and used deep, slow strokes to release the tension.

"Best offer I've had in years," he said with a sigh.

She massaged for several seconds then paused. "Moaning doesn't count as talking."

His lip quirked up.

"Let me put a cool towel around your shoulders while you finish your story." She worked the pump and soaked one of the remaining linens then wrung the excess water into the tub. "Brace yourself," she said then draped it over his shoulders.

He sucked in his breath. "Gads, woman! The shock just stopped my heart."

She choked back a laugh. "Are you going to finish your story, or should I stop massaging your back and let you get dressed?"

"It's not a pretty story."

"I wasn't expecting one."

"All right. When Radford realized what he'd done to Kyle, he fell apart. He couldn't eat or sleep. He had nightmares that woke the house. One night it scared Rebecca so badly that she ran out of the house in her nightdress and bare feet. It was winter, and she was only four."

"Wait a minute. How can... Evelyn and Radford weren't married yet."

"Another woman gave birth to Rebecca shortly after Radford was mustered out of his regiment. Apparently she didn't want a baby or a husband, so she left Rebecca with Radford and disappeared."

"That poor little girl."

"Rebecca found a loving mother in Evelyn. There's always been a special bond between the two of them."

"I noticed that in church this morning. They're both so pretty and have such lovely hair, I thought they were mother and daughter."

"They are."

No two words could have touched Faith more deeply. Tears blurred her eyes, and she looked toward the ceiling and blinked to keep them from dropping onto his back.

"If it wasn't for Evelyn and Rebecca, I don't think Radford would have pulled himself back from the past."

Faith swallowed her sadness. "War would scar any man."

"And leave some men so tortured they have to fight another war to get their life back. Radford had to do that when he came home."

"Did Kyle ever forgive him?" she asked.

"Kyle is as stubborn as they come, but yes, after stewing a while, he forgave Radford."

"So Kyle's a stubborn but forgiving man?"

"And the rock in our family. He kept our sawmill running and held everything together when my dad died."

"For some reason I see *you* in that position."

He peered at her from the corner of his eye. "Kyle was the boss. I was the peacekeeper. My younger brother Boyd was the one who made us laugh. Even when we wanted to pound him—and Kyle always wanted to pound him—Boyd could make us laugh. He still does."

"Hmm... I'm beginning to understand your analogy about trees and their grain. Your mother raised a deep-thinker, a rock, a jester, and a peacekeeper. Sounds like she had her hands full."

He laughed. "Which is exactly why my father made me promise to keep the peace and hold our family together."

"Which makes me more irritated that your brothers didn't help you today, or at least allow that other man to step in."

"That other man was Wayne Archer and he was looking to earn himself some votes for the upcoming election for sheriff."

"He's running against you?" she asked in surprise.

"And would have liked nothing better than to prove me incompetent in front of all those people watching. My brothers showed great restraint and respect by letting me handle that situation alone."

"I hadn't thought... I'm sorry I judged them without knowing the politics involved."

"Does that mean you were concerned about me?" he asked, rolling onto his back.

Panic kept her gaze locked on his face. God only knew if that towel was still covering him. "I would be concerned about anyone in a fight."

He gripped her balm-soaked fingers. "Can I call on you this evening?"

"I... of course, Sheriff. I can give you another treatment at nine o'clock if the time suits you."

He rocked upward and swung his legs off the table then slid off and stood beside her. "I'm not asking for a shoulder treatment, Faith. My call would be personal, to allow us time to become better acquainted."

Oh, no... Iris would be ecstatic, but Faith was terrified. She could never tell where this man was going with his questions and those private looks that were growing more heated by the minute; but worse, she had no idea how she would respond, because one smile from him could melt her kneecaps. And was that towel still hooked around his waist?

He squeezed her hands. "I would like to court you."

"Oh... I don't think that would be a good idea."

"Did I misunderstand Iris when she said you were looking for a husband?"

She shook her head. She longed for a noble, handsome, and tender man with strong, protective arms to welcome Adam and

Cora, and keep them safe. She wanted a man like the sheriff to hold her against his warm body and love her, but she wasn't worthy of a man like him. "I'm not sure we would suit."

"Let's find out." He dipped his head and pressed his warm, firm lips to hers.

She felt as if she kissed the sun. His hot mouth melted her. The birds in her stomach scattered sideways then swept upward en masse to fly in a frenzied circle that left her breathless and dizzy.

His arms encircled her, his heart pounding against her palms, a low moan vibrating in his throat as he deepened the kiss. She'd heard that same intimate sound when massaging his back, when her hands gave him pleasure. To hear it now while he was kissing her, while he held her against his hard, naked chest thrilled and frightened her. He was too big, too strong, too... umm... gentle... and tender. His tongue delved into her mouth, slow and insistent, sparking a fire deep in her belly.

He broke the kiss with a shaky outrush of breath, gazing down at her with stormy eyes. "I'd say we suit just fine."

She gazed up at him with her fists bunched against his chest and her body quaking, lost in the heat of his gaze.

"You can give me your answer this evening." He pressed a polite kiss to her lips then stepped away.

Dazed and too weak-kneed to move, Faith leaned against the table. There was a fine line between arrogance and self-confidence, and this strong, proud man walked dead center of that line.

He hooked his thumbs beneath the linen that was thankfully anchored around his waist, and paused with a roguish smile on his face. "I'm about to shuck this towel. Don't suppose you'd like to stay and help me dress?"

With a gasp, Faith fled the room, at war with the rash, reckless part of her that would like nothing better.

Chapter Ten

Faith's stomach was full for the first time in weeks. A man from the Taylor Hotel had delivered a large roast beef with bowls of potatoes, vegetables, and two apple pies, along with a note from the sheriff thanking her for generously opening her business for him.

"That meal had to cost the sheriff a fortune," Dahlia said, stacking clean plates back in the wooden crate the hotel had shipped them in.

Faith had expected to trade her services for lumber, but after eating like paupers for the last month, this unexpected meal was a blessing. Cora and Adam had eaten with such unabashed joy it had moved her to tears. They were so full from their meal, they flopped on their pallets at the far end of the building and hadn't moved since. Adam was engrossed in a book, but Cora was lying on her back thumping her heels against the wall, waiting for Faith to finish washing dishes and come read her a story.

Yet, Faith desperately needed to talk to Aster, the most levelheaded of her aunts, and to Iris, who could negotiate her way around any situation. She rinsed a bowl and handed it to Tansy.

"I need a few minutes alone with Iris and Aster," she said. "Would you and Dahlia tell Cora a story, and keep Adam settled with his book until I finish here?"

Tansy put the bowl in the crate of dishes that Adam would return to the Taylor Hotel tomorrow. "Of course, dahlin'. The way my back aches, you won't have to ask twice." She dropped her towel on their makeshift counter then nudged Dahlia. "Let these gals finish the dishes while we concoct a story for Cora."

"It'll be a trial to relax for a while, but I'll manage," Dahlia agreed. She tossed her towel over the edge of the crate, and followed Tansy to their cluster of straw pallets at the back of the building.

Their little family had set up a makeshift kitchen in one corner of the building, using planks atop flour barrels for counters, and large tin pans for dish tubs. The only furniture they'd brought with them was Faith's mother's mahogany kitchen table, which had been the center of their family gatherings for as long as Faith could remember. They'd left the chairs in favor of flats of herbs that would better serve their new business; flour barrels and solid planks worked suitably well for table seating.

"What's wrong?" Aster asked, her face pinched with worry.

Faith dried her hands on her apron. "Have you ever been married?"

Aster's white eyebrows whisked upward. The ebony arches above Iris's eyes lifted, too, but neither woman spoke.

"Mama said stormy weather drove each of you to her door, but she never said what kind of storm it was."

"Does it matter?" Aster asked.

"Yes." Faith sighed. "I need to know who you were before you met Mama."

"Honey, I'm not even sure I can remember," Aster said.

"What was your name? Before you became one of Mama's flowers."

Aster braced her hand on the counter, a towel bunched beneath her fingers. "Marian. And I was no different than any other hardworking farm girl, but I hated that life and my father's heavy fists and my mother's pathetic mewling. By my sixteenth birthday, I couldn't stomach one more day of their endless drama, so I left and began my own life. Four years later I found your mother and my first real family."

"So, you never married?"

"No. I lost that opportunity decades ago. And I haven't been particularly fond of the men I've known, so the point is moot."

"How about you, Aunt Iris? Have you ever been married?"

"My mixed blood didn't allow me to fit into any man's world. I was too Japanese."

"Were you born in Japan?"

"Right here in America," she said. "My father was a commodore in the U.S. Navy, and a son of a wealthy banker from New York City. He was already married thirty years when he sailed his ship into Tokyo and met my mother. He smuggled her onto his ship and brought her to New York and made her his mistress. She conceived me on the ship during the crossing."

Faith pressed her hand to her chest. "How dreadful. Forgive me for asking something so personal."

Iris waved away the apology. "He cared deeply for my mother and provided very well for her until he died. But his estate went to his wife and children. My mother was forced to find herself another provider. Unfortunately, that man preferred her daughter Akiko."

"Oh, Iris..." Faith's eyes misted and she wanted to kick herself. "How unkind I've been to ask such intimate questions of you and Aster."

Iris shrugged. "Life is intimate even when you don't want it to be. Sometimes you enjoy that. Sometimes you simply bear it. Either way you've got to live each day the best you can."

"Your life hasn't been much easier," Aster added.

Faith nodded because it was true, and because she was too choked up to speak. Her aunts hadn't just lost their homes, they'd lost their names and the very cores of who they were.

"Don't fret over this," Iris said. "When I found your mother's house and met Aster and Tansy and Dahlia, I gladly became Iris—a beautiful flower that grows in the wild."

Faith blinked the moisture from her eyes. "All this time I thought you'd chosen it from the Iliad. Iris, the goddess of the rainbow."

Iris hooted in amusement. "I like that." She cocked her chin and feigned a thoughtful pose. "Goddess of the rainbow. Yes, that's lovely. Tonight I'll be a sultry hue of violet. Tomorrow I'll be—"

"A wilted flower just like the rest of us," Aster said in her too-frank manner.

"You're not wilted flowers," Faith insisted. "You can take back your real names and start over here."

Aster shook her head. "I've been Aster for so long I couldn't answer to anything else."

"Same for me," Iris said. "Besides, I think I enjoy being a rainbow goddess."

Despite their sad stories, Faith smiled. "You're still so young, Aunt Iris, does it bother you that you never married?"

"I'm too fond of men to ever settle for just one."

A tad of panic shot through Faith. "But you will now. Right?" Iris's silence increased Faith's heartbeat. "You all agreed to look for a husband here."

"And we'll look as promised," Aster said.

"That doesn't mean we'll find a man willing to marry us," Iris added.

"You can't pin your hopes on me."

"We have to, Faith. You know that," Aster said. "What man is going to want to marry an ex-prostitute?"

"Or a woman who looks Japanese?"

"You're kind, beautiful women, and you deserve love."

"So do you, dear. Much more than us. You're young, and have everything to look forward to."

"With that handsome sheriff," Iris said with a wink.

"You should have never told him I was looking for a husband. Now he wants to court me."

"He does?" Aster asked, incredulous.

"Wonderful!" Iris clapped her hands. "Say yes."

"I can't say yes."

"Of course you can. You must!" Aster said. "The man just sent us a meal fit for a king."

Faith tugged her apron ties loose. "What if he learns the truth about us? What then?"

"All the more reason to marry him quickly, so it's too late for him to change his mind."

But it wouldn't be too late for him to hate her, and that's what she couldn't bear. Sheriff Grayson was the kind of man she could fall in love with. To gain his affection and possibly his love, only to lose it when he learned the truth, would be devastating. "I can't do it. It's underhanded and... the sheriff is too respectable for me."

"No one is perfect, Faith, not even the sheriff." Iris sighed dramatically. "But he sure looks perfect, and just think of the benefits of having that dream man in your bed, kissing in the dark, feeling those strong arms—"

"For pity's sake!" Grasping at her last thread of patience, Faith yanked off her apron. "This isn't just about sharing a bed with a man. I'll have to live with him, and have his children, and...how will I ever look him in the eyes if I don't tell him the truth? He deserves better than my lies."

"Men will want you, but mark my words," Iris warned, "they won't offer marriage if they know where you came from."

"You need to think of the children," Aster added. "The sheriff adores Cora. You can see he'd be a good father to her. And he was more than fair to Adam over that incident with the hair brush."

"I know. That's because he's a kind, honorable man." Faith blew out a breath. "But will he be so kind if he learns the truth?"

"No one can know for certain," Aster said. "That's why you need to guard the truth. It's *your* past, not his. It should be your choice whether or not to share it with him."

"If our courting leads to marriage, and he discovers the truth too late, he will never forgive my deceit."

"Bah." Aster crossed her arms over her chest as if the answer was obvious and the conversation unnecessary. "You're worrying about something that may never happen. And if he does learn the truth, the sheriff is an intelligent and fair man. He's also a man who can provide for you and the children."

Iris put her arm around Faith's shoulders. "Honey, I think half your nerves come from being attracted to him," she said, her voice surprisingly gentle.

Faith's face heated. Had she been that transparent? What woman wouldn't be attracted to a man like Sheriff Grayson? *Duke* Grayson.

"If I were in your shoes I would savor every minute of that man's attention," Iris continued. "And I'd do my best to get him to marry me. The alternative to marrying the sheriff could be far less desirable, you know."

"I know." She only had to think of the men who had frequented the brothel or called at her greenhouse.

"Courting him doesn't mean you have to marry him," Iris continued. "But it could make him more accepting of our business, and help establish us in the community."

Faith tossed her apron into the crate on the floor. "It could help immensely to be in the sheriff's favor. But our hopes could also come crashing down on our heads if he has a change of heart."

"Then don't let him have a change of heart."

Faith looked to Aster, the honorary mother of their misfit family. "What do you think?"

"I think he's the one man who can protect us," she said quietly. "If we need him to."

Chapter Eleven

Night had fallen by the time Duke entered the earthy-smelling greenhouse. A lantern burned on the counter in the front of the building, and another shone from the stone room in the back where he found Faith waiting for him beside the tub. She stood as he entered the room, and dazzled him with a smile.

"My answer is yes," she said.

Her smile and her words stunned him. Was she saying yes to him? To courting? He'd been prepared to hear the word no. Or to have her avoid his question altogether. "Yes?" he asked, needing her confirmation.

She clasped her hands in front of her hips, her beautiful smile wobbling. "If you still desire to court me, I'd... I would be honored to accept your suit."

If he still desired her? He nearly laughed. She worked hard, she was intelligent, and so beautiful it was a struggle to keep his hands off her. Yes, he definitely desired her.

He returned her smile. "I still want to court you."

"Then I shall call you Duke in private."

"That's considerable progress from this morning."

Her lips tilted, enhancing her smile, but her lashes swept down to conceal her eyes.

He watched her changing facial expressions with appreciation. She looked nervous and embarrassed and, if he wasn't mistaking the tiny tremor in her chin, a little scared.

"Faith?"

She raised her lashes.

"I'm glad you said yes. But if you're not sure, if you have any reservations—"

"None, Sheriff." Her cheeks flushed. "I mean Duke."

"I can change my name if you don't care for it."

A breathy laugh sailed past her lips. "You have a fine, strong name," she said with sincerity. "It's just awkward for me to be so... intimate with you."

"Maybe this will help us get better acquainted." He brushed his lips across hers to seal their agreement. "I'm honored to be your suitor."

Her lashes swooped down like a shield. Did she know that her emotions shone in her eyes? Was this a habit of hers to hide her thoughts? And why the need to hide them?

He eased away. "Why do you do that?" he asked quietly.

"Do what?" She whisked her gaze to his face.

"You hide your eyes from me."

"I don't," she said, but down went her lashes.

"You wield your eyelashes like a woman wields her fan. You give me a glimpse of your beauty then steal it away in the next second. A glimpse here, a peek there. It's an art for sure, but it can tease a man to the point of losing control." Her eyes flew open, and he chuckled. "I got your message, Faith. I won't lose control."

Down went her lashes again, the black crescents emphasizing her pink cheeks.

"There you go again, peeking and hiding."

"Oh, my." She pressed her palms to her flushed cheeks. "What a dreadful habit."

There was an endearing quality to her shyness, but it would drive him crazy to forever witness her emotions in snatches and glimpses. "Your husband never mentioned this to you?"

She lowered her hands and averted her face. "He was away frequently."

"Why? That is, if you don't mind my asking."

She dipped her fingers into the tub. "His father was a planter, and my husband took their plants to the market. The water temperature feels fine now. I would recommend another soak before we try to stretch your muscles."

"Do you miss him?"

Her hand went still in the water. "We didn't have a close relationship," she admitted softly.

"Then I can only believe the man was a fool."

"I was the fool." She turned and looked straight into his eyes for the first time. "Thank you for that wonderful meal you had delivered this evening. I've never received such a thoughtful or meaningful gift."

Until today, he'd never given one. He'd given plenty of fancy and expensive gifts to women, but never something as simple or valued as a good meal. "I couldn't have made it through the day without the treatment you gave me this morning. Thank you for your kindness."

Down went her lashes yet again, but they flashed up an instant later, as if she realized she was indulging her habit. "You should get in the bath now."

He nodded and waited for her to leave the room before he undressed. After shucking his clothes, he wrapped his hips in a towel then sat on the edge of the tub and dunked his foot into the water. He wasn't trusting her to protect his assets.

The water felt comfortably warm, so he pushed off the edge of the tub and submerged himself completely. Underwater, he stretched out. His left shoulder screamed with pain as he forced his arm away from his side, but he couldn't raise his fist higher than his neck. He rolled his body in the water like one of the logs they cleaned in the gorge behind the sawmill. The heated, scented liquid swirled around his aching body. He could do without the herbs and oils, but the water felt good. As the tension in his back eased, he released his breath and sank to the bottom of the tub. When he broke the surface, Faith was standing beside the tub, smiling.

"Cora loves blowing bubbles in the water too."

He slicked his hair back one-handed. "I need to own this tub."

"That's why I bought the place," she said. "I wanted to buy Mr. Colburn's house across the street, too, but I couldn't afford it."

"I thought it was odd that his house was still for sale."

"I'm hoping it stays that way until I can afford to buy it. Of course, that will be five or ten years from now." She handed him the metal stool, and waited while he tucked it beneath him. "I brought you some tea."

"Thank you," he said, accepting the cup.

She moved to the door. "I'll come back in fifteen minutes."

"Do you have to go?" He held the cup near his dripping chin. "If you can spare the time, I'd appreciate the company."

Her answer was to sit on the table and fold her hands in her lap.

"Thank you," he said. He sipped the hot tea then rested the cup on the edge of the tub. "I'm glad you could see me tonight. I'm taking Covey to Mayville tomorrow, and won't be back for a week."

"I've not heard of Mayville, but it must be far from here if you'll be away so long."

"Just under twenty-five miles. I have a meeting there, and I make several stops along the way to check in with my undersheriff and our deputies."

"I thought Sam Wade was your deputy."

"He's my only paid deputy. My other deputies are men who volunteer to act in a legal capacity for their towns. They handle small issues but wire when they need me. Otherwise, I visit them every couple of months."

"Sounds like you spend a lot of time out of town."

"Not really." He filled his mouth with tea and studied her as he swallowed. "Did it bother you that your husband spent so much time away?"

"No." Her lashes twitched, but amazingly she didn't hide her eyes. "I stayed with my mother and my aunts."

"Where was your father?"

"I don't know." She looked down and fiddled with the linens beside her. "Mama said he ran off after I was born, and only came back long enough to sire Adam. After that, he disappeared and broke my mother's heart."

"Is this one of those stories like your aunts invent?" he asked, feeling as skeptical of this story as he'd been of Dahlia's outlandish tale.

"Adam and I share the same father, although we've never met the man. I suspect he's in prison, but my mother never talked about him. That's the truth."

He finished his tea, and set the cup on the stand. "What was your mother like?"

She sighed and shifted her gaze to the stone wall behind his head. "In a word, she was sad. My aunts could make her laugh, but her eyes were always filled with heartache. The only time she seemed at peace was when she tended her roses. She loved them and planted them all around our house. You could smell roses in the air all summer." Her gaze dropped to his. "In the winter, she wore rose perfume and planted rosebush clippings in our greenhouse."

"Was Rose a name she gave herself?" he asked, wanting to know more about the woman.

"Her name was Celia Rose, and she was as beautiful as the roses she grew."

"I wish she were still here for you," he said quietly, knowing Faith's pain would ebb but never leave completely.

She acknowledged his comment with a small nod, but the sadness in her face made him want to hold her against his chest and comfort her. Not that he'd be able to restrict himself to that noble impulse for more than a minute, but he'd try.

"I lost my father thirteen years ago to a disease that sucked the life out of him." Duke could usually talk about his father, but not about his death, which was why it surprised him that he was confessing to Faith. "When I was a boy, my dad was strong and had a laugh that filled the house. By the time I turned seventeen, he couldn't even feed himself. He died before I turned eighteen."

"I'm so sorry," she said, her voice barely above a whisper. "How awful for you and your family"

They fell silent, and he searched her eyes for whatever she was hiding from him. Maybe it was only heartache.

"It's growing late." She stood and shook open a large towel. "We should treat your shoulder now."

Did she know it was too painful for him to converse during his treatment? Is that why she was standing beside the tub with a towel in her arms? He wanted to linger in the bath and talk to her, but her drawn face and dark eyes suggested she needed sleep.

He stood and took the towel she handed to him, but purposely caught her hands in the folds of soft cotton. Standing in the tub made him several inches taller than her. "Why don't we skip my treatment tonight? I'll leave so you can enjoy the bath before going to bed."

She gazed up at him, her eyes startled and uncertain. "You need your treatment."

"I'll stretch when I get home," he argued.

"It won't be enough."

"I was afraid you were going to say that."

She smiled. "Get out of the tub, Sheriff. I promise I'll be gentle."

"I thought you were going to call me Duke."

Her lips parted, and all he could think about was kissing her. He had to taste her.

Her lashes swooped down then up, her gaze clashing with his. "Get out of the tub, Duke."

The tremble in her voice undid him. He tugged her toward his mouth and leaned down to kiss her, knowing his need for her would consume him. He just didn't give a damn.

⭤ ⭤

Instantly Faith's good intentions to take care of Duke's shoulder and protect her heart were splintered to flinders. She should shoo him out the door for taking such liberty with her, for standing in her tub like a king, stark naked but for a skimpy towel around his hips, kissing her like she was one of his harem. But her heart skipped a beat and her eyes fell closed and she forgot everything but the feel of his hard chest, the taste of his mouth, the low moan she knew meant pleasure... for him... for her.... His touch was soft, as was his tongue that pressed to part her lips; not pushing, not assaulting or demanding, just there, asking, wanting... her.

Against all doubts, and filled with a hope she'd never known, she parted her lips and allowed the kiss to deepen. Her stomach lifted and her legs trembled, and she thought of his tender tone when she'd told him he could be her suitor. She'd have been a fool to turn this man down, to forfeit a chance to win his affection that promised to be stalwart, true and... physically pleasurable.

He moved his hands to her waist, caressing her, drawing her toward him, making every nerve in her body grow taut with desire.

She fought her need to lean into his embrace. It was wild and abandoned to kiss like this. What would he, a man used to courting respectable women, think of her wanton response?

Was she more her mother's daughter than she'd thought? With a gasp of denial, she pushed away from him. She wouldn't be like that. Not ever.

He stared in surprise then snapped to attention as if he realized how inappropriate their kiss had been. But she was the one at fault. Water soaked through the front of her dress and she trembled as she backed away.

He finger-combed his dripping hair with his right hand, the act so natural and male it captivated her. "Guess we'd better get my shoulder stretched," he said.

Faith nodded and turned away, fearing he would see her unbridled lust and figure out where she'd come from. She'd made a mistake with Jarvis, and she wasn't going to repeat it with the sheriff no matter how wanton his kisses made her.

Her hands shook as she spread towels on the table. Duke sprawled his big body on top of them, acting as if nothing had happened, but Faith wasn't that good of an actress. She avoided his eyes and hurried him through his treatment. When she finished, he caught her hand to keep her from moving away.

"Will the water ruin your dress?" he asked, sitting up to face her.

She nearly laughed at the absurdity. Here he was worried about ruining her dress when she was worried about ruining her reputation. "It'll be fine."

"Will you?"

She ducked her face, embarrassed. "I hadn't meant to... you caught me off guard."

He hooked his warm finger beneath her chin and lifted until she was looking at him. "I know. I hadn't meant to kiss you either, but I couldn't resist. It was the best moment of my day" His lips quirked. "What was yours?"

The kiss for sure, but it was also her worst moment. How could she have let herself go like that?

He tilted his head, looking askance at her, his eyes encouraging her to answer.

"Hearing the organ in church was the best—" She couldn't lie and say *moment*, because that belonged to Duke and the thrilling kiss he'd just given her, so she said instead, "It was beautiful."

"So is your smile, Faith." And then he silenced all her protestations with a tender, lingering, almost chaste kiss.

Chapter Twelve

"Stupid, stupid, stupid!"

Adam kicked a round stone the size of a plum ahead of him as he walked down Liberty Street toward the small school in Laona. He didn't know why he had to go school. There were only two weeks left. At breakfast, Faith had said the sheriff would be out of town this week, so the man wouldn't even be around to check up on him.

He batted the stone with the side of his foot. It was stupid to go for the last two weeks. If he wouldn't fit in at the beginning of the year, how was he supposed to fit in now? The children would stare at him, and whisper about him like they had when he'd tried to go to school in Syracuse.

He kicked the rock so hard it ricocheted off the stone fence guarding somebody's front yard.

"Adam?"

He jerked his head up to see Rebecca Grayson sitting on the fence.

"Good morning," she said, sliding off the pile of stones and walking toward him. "Are you heading to school?"

He nodded, not trusting his changing voice to stay steady while his heart banged around in his chest. Did she live in that huge house? Did those horses in the paddock behind the barn belong to her family?

"Can we walk with you?" she asked.

He had no idea who "we" were, but he nodded and stuffed his hands into his pockets.

Rebecca turned toward the house. "Hurry up, William, or I'm leaving without you!" she yelled.

A boy about half Adam's age pounded down the porch steps then raced across the yard. "Beat you there!" he said, and raced down the rutted road ahead of them.

"William, you better watch you don't get run over by Mr. Carlson's horse," Rebecca shouted at his back, but the boy didn't appear to hear.

"Want me to get him for you?" Adam asked, knowing he could run the boy down.

"No, my brother will just pester us to death if he walks with us. Besides, he knows I can catch him if I want to." She flashed a sweet smile that made Adam's stomach grow tight. She angled the toe of her shoe behind the stone he'd been kicking and rolled it ahead of them. "Come on. We can't be late or Mr. MacEnroy will switch us."

No man would switch Rebecca while Adam was around, but he wasn't daring enough to tell her that. He followed her down the street and gave the stone a solid kick.

Rebecca skipped ahead and kicked it several feet. "My mother says you live with your sister." she said.

He nodded, wishing his voice wasn't so wobbly that it terrified him to talk.

She waited for him to catch up. "Don't you have a mother and father?" she asked.

He shook his head, surprised that her question didn't offend him. It didn't feel like she was being nosy or judging him. "I didn't know my father. My mother died six weeks ago." The less he said, the less it hurt, and the less chance that his voice would squawk.

"I'm sorry, Adam. My dad says I'm too curious and I ask too many questions sometimes."

The unexpected kindness in her eyes made his throat ache. He hadn't talked to anyone about his mother. Faith had always been the one to take care of him. His mother had been more like a grandmother to him, like she was with Cora. He lowered his chin and kicked the stone. "It's all right. My sister is more like my mother anyhow."

"Really?"

He nodded.

"I'm glad you're going to my school," Rebecca said, scampering along beside him to bat at the stone. "We can walk together if you want."

"Sure." He wiped his sweaty palms on his trousers, and took his turn kicking the stone ahead of them. Maybe going to school wouldn't be all bad.

While he and Rebecca took turns flicking the stone with their feet, he stole quick looks at her. Her shiny black hair bounced against her back in long, loose spirals that hung to her waist. Her eyebrows were black as coal, and her dimples flashed when she smiled at him, which was nearly every time he looked up. He liked her dimples and her smile, but he liked the friendliness in her eyes even better.

"Oh, no," she said, slowing to a standstill in the road. He looked up and followed her gaze to where several children gathered in front of a white schoolhouse. "Melissa Archer just waved to us."

"Is that bad?"

"She's a worse gossip than her mother, and she's mean to William and the younger children."

"Why?"

"Because she can get away with it." With a sigh, Rebecca kicked the stone to the side of the road. "Let's leave it here so we can kick it on the way home. Come on. We'll try to sneak past her," she said then caught his elbow and tugged him into the school yard.

Adam would rather wait for the bell to ring and dash inside to the first empty chair he could find. But he would walk through fire before letting Rebecca know he was afraid.

"Rebecca!" Melissa Archer caught Rebecca's arm and stopped them. "You nearly walked right past me."

"Sorry, Melissa. I was talking with my new friend Adam Dearborn," she said, making Adam sound as important as President Hayes. Rebecca introduced him to the girl and her brother Nicholas, both husky children about his own age with wheat blond hair.

He nodded to them, but when Melissa extended her hand as if she were a fine lady and he her suitor, Adam didn't know whether to kiss it, shake it, or laugh in her haughty little face.

Rebecca whacked Melissa's hand down. "For Pete's sake, just say hello."

Melissa's face turned as pink as the ribbon in her blond hair, and she jutted out her chin. "I was just going to welcome you to school and tell you that there's an empty seat at my desk if you want to sit with me."

Adam's heart plummeted. He wanted to sit with Rebecca.

"He's going to sit with me," Rebecca said, causing Melissa to glare at her, and Nicholas to scowl at him.

Nicholas Archer outweighed Adam by at least thirty pounds, and Adam had no desire to test the strength of Nicholas's hefty arms. The boys in his old neighborhood had given him a healthy respect for big muscles and hard knuckles.

Melissa lifted her nose and turned away as if Rebecca didn't exist. "I'm the best student in my grade," she said to Adam. "Mr. MacEnroy will favor you if you sit with me."

He didn't care about pleasing the dumb teacher, and he didn't want to be anywhere near Melissa Archer or her scowling brother. "I already promised ReBECca," he said, cringing at the squawk of his voice.

Nicholas laughed, and Adam curled his fingers into his palms, wanting to cram his knuckles into the boy's mouth.

"Go ahead then," Melissa spat. "Sit with Rebecca. I don't want to sit with a boy who can't even talk." She tried to shove past him, but Adam didn't step aside quickly enough, and she tripped over his foot. He caught her elbows to save her a fall, but she kicked her hard shoe into his shin. "Let go of me!"

Nicholas shoved Melissa away from Adam. "Quit acting like an idiot, Melissa."

"Don't touch me." She raked her fingernails across her brother's neck, leaving a trail of red scratches. Nicholas bared his teeth and lunged at her.

Adam stepped between the pair and batted Nicholas's hands down. "Don't hit her," he said, his voice far calmer than he felt inside. It wasn't right to hit a girl, and it was worse to stand aside and allow someone else to do so.

Nicholas shot him a look of surprise just as Melissa kicked Adam in the shin again. "Don't you dare hit my brother!" she hissed.

Rebecca shoved Melissa and knocked her to the ground on her backside. "Don't you dare kick my friend!"

"What in blazes is going on here?" a thunderous voice demanded.

When Adam saw the stocky, balding teacher bearing down on them, he knew what was coming. He would get blamed for causing trouble. He always did.

Melissa burst into tears and struggled to her feet. "This boy hit my brother, and Rebecca shoved me."

Rebecca gasped in outrage. "Adam didn't hit anybody, Mr. MacEnroy."

"Silence!" He turned to the boys and girls who'd gathered to watch. "Get inside, all of you." As they beat a path for the door, MacEnroy turned his steely gaze on Adam. "Who are you, young man, and what are you doing in my school yard?"

"This is Adam Dearborn," Rebecca said, "and he's new to town."

MacEnroy leveled a fierce scowl at Rebecca, which made Adam want to slug the man. "I was not addressing you, young lady."

"Yes, sir."

"Sheriff Grayson ordered me to come to school today," Adam said, hoping the sheriff's name would put the fear of God into the man.

But MacEnroy's lips pinched. "Ah, you're one of those boys I'll need to keep my eye on."

One of those boys. Adam had heard that comment so many times, he should be able to ignore it by now. But the insult cut through him like a dull hunting knife, ripping and tearing at his gut, making him want to slam his fists into every stinking person who'd ever insulted him.

"That's right," Adam said, knowing there would be consequences for being disrespectful, but he was too angry to care. "The sheriff wanted to teach me a lesson so he sentenced me to two weeks in your classroom."

A laugh burst from Rebecca, and she clapped a hand over her mouth. Melissa gasped, and Nicholas bit his lip.

MacEnroy's face turned beet red. He stabbed his finger toward the school. "Rebecca Grayson, get to your desk this instant. Melissa and Nicholas, go with her." Rebecca cast a rebellious look of admiration at Adam then dashed into the school behind the Archers.

Adam stood in the yard alone, facing MacEnroy, expecting at any minute to feel the man's hard backhand. MacEnroy straightened his shoulders and unclamped his jaw. "So you like being a wiseacre, do you, Adam?"

Adam knew not to answer that question.

"If you're such a wise young man, who invented the steamboat?"

"Robert Fulton, sir."

MacEnroy's eyebrow quirked as if Adam's knowledge surprised him. "And the year of the invention?"

"1807."

"I'm impressed," he said, but he didn't look impressed at all. He looked furious. "How many feet are in a mile, Adam?"

"Five thousand two hundred eighty"

"What city is our state capital?"

"Albany, sir."

"And what mountain ranges can be found in New York State?"

"The Appalachian Highlands, the Catskill Mountains, and the Adirondack Mountains."

"Well, since you're such a bright and witty young man, I'll have you teach class for the day."

A flood of heat seared Adam's body and scorched his ears. He would answer any question MacEnroy asked, but he couldn't stand in front of the class and talk. His voice would squawk like a chicken. He couldn't go up there.

"Come along." MacEnroy clasped the back of Adam's neck and herded him toward the door.

Adam wasn't going inside. The instant MacEnroy released him, he would sprint away. He would tell Faith that MacEnroy kicked him out of school for being disobedient. Faith would be angry, but she would let him off the hook until the new school year began. Sheriff Grayson wouldn't be pleased, but facing the sheriff was better than facing a room full of children who were only going to laugh at him.

MacEnroy jerked Adam to attention outside the schoolhouse. "You find yourself a seat inside and keep that wise mouth of yours shut while I'm instructing class. Do you understand?"

"Yes, sir."

With that MacEnroy yanked open the door and shoved Adam inside ahead of him. While the teacher strode to the front of the classroom, Adam eased into the one and only empty chair in the room—right next to Melissa Archer.

"You'll be sorry," she hissed.

He already was. This would be his first and last day in this wretched place. He wasn't coming back. He could learn more from books anyhow.

He sank low in his chair and looked for Rebecca, wanting to signal that he wasn't coming back after their lunch break. He sighted her two desks away, smiling at him like he was the most handsome and daring man on earth.

Chapter Thirteen

Saturday evening Faith stood outside the bathhouse door, listening to Claire Grayson and her friend Anna Levens laugh uproariously as they frolicked in the tub with three other women. The three lived with Anna in a home Claire and Boyd Grayson provided to women who were desperate for a refuge from heavy-handed husbands. Claire said she and Anna had opened the home five years ago after Anna's husband Larry Levens was sent to prison for murdering two men.

Faith didn't have to ask if Anna had been one of those beaten women. If the scar on Anna's shoulder wasn't proof enough, the wariness in her eyes was. The woman was petite and pretty, and so sweet Faith couldn't imagine any man wanting to hurt her. But apparently her husband had beaten her unmercifully and even threatened to kill her. Thank God the beast was in prison.

The bruises on the other women who were staying with Anna broke Faith's heart. The bath had brought the ladies so much pleasure, Faith had invited them back for a second complimentary treatment.

The Grayson women had done such an amazing job of promoting her business, the female residents of Fredonia swarmed into Faith's greenhouse. Some came to buy herbs and salves and teas, but she suspected most of them came to get a look at Iris. The more adventurous ladies accepted their complimentary bath and massage. Afterward, they raved with such enthusiasm, the customers poured through the door faster than Faith could service them. She and her aunts worked from morning to night, and still they had to ask several ladies to return the following week.

Dr. Milton and the apothecary owner, Wayne Archer, had stopped in to caution Faith about giving the ladies harmful treatments and selling toxic herbs. Faith had listened politely, but Aster and Dahlia marched the snobbish men right out the door in front of several customers. Faith had feared the women would follow the men out, but they'd only laughed and applauded.

Several other men had stopped in during the week, pretending to want herbs or flowers, but they never left without stating their desire to court Faith or one of her aunts. Dahlia refused all offers without considering them. Iris flirted and left the men guessing. Aster and Tansy said they were too busy now and asked the men to stop back in a month or so. It was a relief for Faith to tell the men that she had accepted the sheriff's suit. He hadn't returned from his trip to Mayville, but Faith thought about him constantly, about his shoulder, about his kisses. Every minute she wasn't working or thinking about work, she would think about Duke and wonder if he would kiss her again.

She carved out time to take her meals with Cora and Adam, and to read with them at bedtime. But each night she had fallen asleep beside them, exhausted, with a few pennies added to her money jar.

Tonight, though, she was so fatigued she could barely manage to massage oil into the ladies' backs. When she finished, Claire and her friends gave her a warm hug before leaving the greenhouse.

"Go on in," Aster said. "We'll clean up and be in shortly"

"Bless you, Aster." Faith pumped the faucet handle, washed her hands, and dried them on her apron as she hurried to the house where Cora and Adam lay on their pallets reading.

Thank goodness tomorrow was Sunday. Fully dressed, she flopped down between them and gave them both a hug. "I love you two. Thank you for being so helpful this week."

Cora hooked her arms around Faith's neck and plastered her cheek with an exuberant kiss. "I miss you, Mama."

She kissed Cora then leaned to kiss Adam.

Braced on his elbows, Adam ducked his head and focused on his book.

His avoidance made Faith's heart bleed. She hadn't even had time to ask him about his first week in school. She tweaked his side. "Does that look mean you're getting too old for my hugs and kisses?"

He lifted his head, leaned over and pecked her on the cheek. "You look awful."

"Thank you," she said with laugh. "I feel awful."

"Want me to tell you a story tonight?" Cora offered.

"That would be wonderful, sweetheart." Faith's eyes were so blurred from fatigue, she doubted she'd be able to read a single sentence.

Cora sat up and studiously placed the book they were reading in her lap, as if she were going to read it. Faith stretched out on her stomach between them and warned herself not to fall asleep.

"Once upon a time there was a girl who was so small she could dance on the top of a thimble," Cora said, imitating Dahlia's best storytelling voice.

Faith grinned into the pillow.

"The little girl was beautiful, and she was the best dancer in the whole world. But she was very, very sad," Cora went on, lowering her voice to sound ominous.

"Why was she sad?" Faith asked.

"Because she didn't have a daddy."

A spear of pain shot through Faith's chest. Cora had started asking why she didn't have a daddy, but Faith had been skirting the question because she honestly didn't know how to answer. She knew how painful it was to wonder about a father who was absent, but Cora would never understand the truth. And Faith would never tell her.

"One day," Cora continued, "the little girl caught a beautiful pony, and when he let her ride on his back, she went looking for her daddy..."

Two strong hands settled on Faith's shoulders, startling her from her somber thoughts. She peeked up to see Adam sitting beside her, his long fingers gently kneading her tense shoulder muscles. For all his acting tough and disinterested in her affection, Adam was a tender, thoughtful boy who needed her love as desperately as she needed his. The two of them had spent years together living with fear and loneliness, having only each other for company during those long evenings and miserable nights while their mother worked the brothel. They'd cried together and laughed together. And Faith had mothered Adam from the day of his birth. He was her brother by blood, her son by possession, and she loved him as fiercely as she loved Cora.

"Adam, that is absolute heaven."

Cora paused. "Do you want me to rub your back too?" she asked, her desire to please shining in her eyes.

"No, sweetheart. I want to hear about the tiny girl and her pony. What did she name her pony?"

"Dandelion."

"That's not a pony name," Adam said.

"It is too," Cora insisted. "Her pony has white fluffy spots on him that look like dandelion puffs."

Adam's laugh cracked into a falsetto, which set them all off, and Faith basked in their shared moment of happiness. They'd been so heartbroken over her mother's death, and so panic- stricken afterward in their rush to escape Judge Stone, they hadn't shared a family moment like this in nearly two months. Cora hadn't noticed the upheaval so much, but Adam bore the weight of needing to be a man while still a boy. Faith lifted her hand and stroked her fingers over Adam's bony knuckles. He paused, a question in his eyes. Her own misted, and she gave him a smile that said she loved him. The needy boy in him returned her smile.

Adam's tender consideration and Cora's sweet little voice warmed Faith, and she closed her eyes to savor the moment.

She woke at dawn the next morning, still dressed and aching in every muscle.

Cora and Adam were burrowed in their blankets, but they had lain a blanket over her. They took care of her that way. But they shouldn't have to. Knowing she'd fallen asleep on them made her eyes flood with tears.

The cavernous building was silent as Faith pulled the blanket off and laid it over Adam, who'd sacrificed it to keep her warm. Her aunts slept a few feet away on their own pallets, looking as exhausted as she felt.

Faith quietly left the pallet she shared with Cora then gathered clean clothes and slipped out to the greenhouse. In the bathhouse she lit a lantern, lowered the wick, and shed her dress and petticoats. Shivering in the predawn coolness, she scrubbed herself clean, rinsed then draped a towel on the edge of the steaming tub. Sighing, she lowered her body into the soothing hot water. How could the sheriff not like the water this warm? It felt divine to her, and it was her only comfort.

Tugging the metal stool beneath her, she leaned back and rested her head on the rolled-up towel. No matter what happened, she wasn't leaving the bath for at least an hour.

The soft airy hiss of the gas burner beneath the tub was her only company. An occasional drop of condensation fell from the cold iron faucet into the water with a quiet blip. The light scent of lavender, chamomile, and almond oil wafted from the bath. Goosebumps speckled her flesh, and her nipples puckered in the steamy air. She shivered with a soul-deep loneliness she'd felt since childhood.

From the age of five, she'd spent most of her time alone with her books in a one-room shack behind the brothel. As she grew older, she'd played in the greenhouse surrounded by plants that became her only friends.

At two o'clock each day, Faith and her mother and aunts had shared their main meal in the brothel kitchen—the only room Faith was allowed to enter in the big house until she started giving massages. Faith loved that hour of laughter and attention, and the two hours afterward when she and her mother would go to the greenhouse to tend her mother's roses.

But when the clock struck five, Faith's happiness changed to dread. Her mother would fix a sandwich for Faith's supper and see her safely back inside their shack. Before going to work, she would remind Faith about the bell hanging from a string in the corner of the room that she was to ring only in an emergency. The rope ran between the brothel and the shack with a bell at each end, and her mother used it to check on her. She would tug her end, making the bell at Faith's end ring. Faith would tug back to ring that she was fine. But if Faith rang the bell without her mother's prompting, it meant she had an emergency.

She was five years old the first time her mother left her alone during the evening. Faith rang the bell because she was lonely and frightened. Her mother raced into the shack with two of her aunts, fearing that one of the male customers had strayed out back. When her mother realized there was no emergency, she grew furious and slapped Faith. Then she broke into tears and sank to her knees, rocking her child in her arms and promising they would have a real home someday with a big porch and lots of roses.

It was winter, and her mother tucked a blanket around Faith then stoked the stove before going back to the brothel to continue an endless night of work. Faith huddled alone on her pallet in the silent room, nibbling her sandwich, her hand clinging to the bellrope, desperate to pull it, knowing she didn't dare.

She'd been twelve when Adam was born, and she learned how to care for an infant. Her mother made frequent visits to the shack to feed him, but seemed unable to give him anything more than her mother's milk. So Faith had been the one to give Adam the love he needed. The two of them clung to each other, spending years alone in that shack, day after day, night after night, waiting like prisoners for their mother to come and dole out their daily sustenance.

Her mother had wanted to protect them from the ugliness of her life, but in doing so she'd kept herself away from them, depriving them of her mothering and love, and imprisoning them in a world they didn't understand.

And that's why Faith hated her. She could bear her mother's neglect. But Adam and Faith had needed the woman in their lives more than three hours a day. Was it too much to ask for a mother's love? For a little of her attention and time?

That would have been enough for Faith. That's all she herself had wanted from her mother.

And that's what Adam and Cora needed from Faith. But her debts and expenses were pulling her away, stealing her time and forcing her to make choices as destructive as her mother's had been. Faith couldn't bear another day of seeing Adam and Cora's desperate faces as she dragged herself inside and fell asleep without tucking them in.

She needed help.

She needed love.

She buried her face in her hands, lost and alone as she'd been all her life. Her anguished sob echoed off the stones, and she couldn't hold back the deep sorrow wrenching her heart. She wept for her mother and her aunts who'd been stripped of their innocence and driven into a soulless life of prostitution; and for Adam and Cora, two beautiful children who were deserving of a better life than they'd been given; and for herself, because she was paying for the sins of her mother. And because she was repeating them.

⟞⟞ ⟝⟝

Duke rushed to the bathhouse with his revolver gripped in his hand and his heart pounding. Faith stood in the huge tub, her face in her hands, her glistening body convulsing with hard, wrenching sobs.

He looked around the small stone room and saw nothing wrong, no fire, no man lurking in the shadows, just Faith alone and weeping. The greenhouse was empty and silent. The only sound was her broken sobs, which he'd heard on his approach.

"Faith?"

She sucked in a breath and whirled toward the door, her face soaked with tears and misery, her breasts peeping through her wet hair.

"Are you all right?" he asked.

She blinked in shock. A second later, she shrieked and sank into the water. "What are you doing here?"

He holstered his gun. "I thought you had a fire in here."

"What?"

"I just got into town and saw a glow through one of your windows while I was heading home. I thought the gas burner had started a fire, or that somebody was snooping around in your greenhouse."

"It's five-thirty in the morning."

"Which is exactly why I was suspicious."

She snatched the towel off the ledge and dragged it beneath the water. "It's just me and my lantern, so you can leave."

He gave her a consoling look. "Nobody with a heart could witness those wracking sobs and walk away."

She turned her back and lowered her chin. "I'm fine," she said, but her voice came out in a shaky whisper.

"You're not fine."

She swiped her fingers beneath her eyes, telling him she was struggling to hide more tears. The lantern cast a golden glow across her wet skin and the rippling water that blessedly hid her body from him. After glimpsing her breasts, he was relieved he couldn't see into the water. She needed comfort now, not a sexual proposition. And that's what he'd want to give her if she unveiled the rest of her beautiful body. He wasn't a cad, just a man who was fiercely attracted to her.

"Wrap that towel around you so I can come over there." Her tears wrung his heart, but he wasn't going near that tub until she was covered, because he'd had her on his mind all the livelong, boring, tedious week he'd been away, and to stumble upon this feast for his eyes was torture. Just knowing she was unclothed, her skin slick with water, drove him crazy.

"Go away."

"And leave you alone in the dark, crying your heart out? I can't, Faith. I'm coming over there, so you'd better cover yourself."

He took one step, but she lifted the sopping towel and threw it at him. It hit him in the chest with a wet splat and landed on his boots. "That badge on your chest doesn't give you the right to trespass on my privacy, Sheriff. Now get out."

Her accusation stunned him. "Do you think I'd use my badge to take advantage of you?" he asked, feeling the warm water soak through his shirt.

"Men who have a badge or political title can get away with that. The law doesn't apply to them."

"Do you honestly believe that?"

"I don't believe it, Sheriff. I know it."

He stared at her, insulted to the core. But she wasn't being vicious; she was sincere. She really believed all lawmen were cut of the same cloth, that they used their power to manipulate people. Some did, he knew, and that sickened him. But he would turn his revolver on himself before abusing his position.

She crouched in the tub with her arms crossed over her chest, her shoulders and hands peeping above the water. Her hair floated around her in long black strands. But her puffy eyes were dark pools of despair as she returned his stare. Suddenly he realized how vulnerable and scared she must feel, and that somebody from the law had put that fear in her eyes.

"For whatever happened to make you believe I'd manipulate or harm you, I'm sorry. And I'm sorry I disturbed you, but I'm truly relieved to know you're safe." He backed out of the room and pulled the door closed to keep her safe from any unsuspecting passerby who might jump to his same stupid conclusion that the building was on fire.

The only thing burning was Faith's conviction that she couldn't trust him.

Chapter Fourteen

F aith spotted the sheriff at the back of the church, standing with his brothers and nephews. She was sitting with his mother and sisters-in-law, but he seemed oblivious to her presence.

Her accusation this morning had been unfair. She hadn't meant to hurt him, but she had. And she felt awful about it, because she knew in her heart Duke Grayson was a man of fierce integrity. The opposite of Judge Stone.

She practiced her apology during the long service, but afterward, when she stepped outside and saw him standing in the Common talking to Wayne Archer and a stocky, bald man, her hopes fell.

She pulled Aster aside. "Will you take Cora and Adam home? I need to talk to the sheriff, and I have no idea how long I'll have to wait." But she would wait as long as it took, because she couldn't let him walk away.

"Take all the time you need." Aster chucked Cora under the chin. "Did I ever tell you how my hair got white?"

Cora shook her head, rapt.

"I'll tell you all about it on the way home."

Faith saw Adam cast a nervous look at the sheriff; then he followed Aster into the crowd.

Tansy, Iris, and Dahlia had joined a group of men and women near the park fountain. Two of the women were customers at the greenhouse. Iris, with her shiny black hair and ivory skin, stood out like an orchid in a field of dandelions, but she was smart and had a playful sense of humor that made people like and accept her. The way men were looking at her, Faith didn't believe for one minute the woman had never received a marriage proposal. Iris just didn't want marriage.

Faith didn't blame her. Marriage was a scary business. One bad investment could ruin your whole life. Anna Levens was proof of that.

Not wanting to interrupt Duke, Faith waited on the fringe of his gathering and tried to catch his eye. His chin was down while he was listening to the bald man talk, but then he nodded and looked up—right into her eyes.

Her heart jolted, but he acted nonchalant as he clapped the short man on the shoulder. "I'll take care of it," he said then stepped away from the men.

She laced her fingers in front of her to keep from fidgeting. "Would you consider walking me home?" she asked when he came to her side.

"I think it would be a good idea." He gestured for her to precede him through the crowd, but Faith slipped her hand into the crook of his elbow, wanting to show those gathered in the park that she and the sheriff were courting. Maybe then he wouldn't change his mind about doing so.

He glanced at her in surprise, but escorted her through the park without comment. When they headed down Water Street, Faith slowed their pace.

"I owe you an apology Duke," For the first time it felt right using his name, because her apology was meant for the man behind the badge. "I'm sorry I insulted your integrity this morning."

He stopped to face her. "Faith, if you really believe what you said then I think we should reconsider courting."

"I meant it, but not for you. You're a better man than I accused you of being."

"So are many of the lawmen I know."

"My comment was unfair, but not completely unfounded. Some lawmen do use their power to intimidate and manipulate others." Judge Stone had.

"I know." He sighed and rolled his shoulder. "And you obviously know one of those men."

It wasn't a question, but even if it had been, she wouldn't answer. "I felt compromised this morning, but I know you're not like those unscrupulous men," she said, hoping to smooth over her earlier offense.

"How do you know?" he asked. "Who says I'm not corrupt?"

Years of guarding her virtue from the men who frequented her mother's brothel intuitively told her that Duke Grayson wasn't like them. He didn't lie, cheat, or steal, and he wasn't corrupt. He was the furthest thing from.

"Your mother told me you weren't." She smiled, hoping to dissolve his anger and welcome back the warmth that had been building between them before she'd insulted him.

Humor sparked in his eyes then faded. "What upset you this morning? It drove me crazy to leave you like that."

She turned away and resumed walking. He kept pace beside her, and she hooked her hand in the crook of his elbow again. "I was thinking about my mother."

"I haven't asked, but have you been without her long?"

His gentle query about her mother's death made her eyes mist. "Seven weeks," she said, but it seemed like she'd been without her mother all her life.

"Even after thirteen years it's hard," he said thoughtfully.

She nodded. Especially when your grief was all mixed up with guilt and love and hate.

"Sounds like you could use a day away from everything," he said.

"I could use a day of uninterrupted sleep," she answered truthfully. "My greenhouse has been swarming with women all week."

"That's what my mother said this morning when I went home to change."

"She came in twice this week," Faith remarked, feeling a sincere fondness for Nancy Grayson. "I think she was serious about being Iris's best customer."

"All her life she's sacrificed for my father and us boys, and now for her grandchildren. She deserves to treat herself to a massage when she wants one. And you deserve a day of enjoyment. I have an idea for our first official outing." They turned left onto Mill Street, but he stopped before they reached the greenhouse. Light shadows underscored his eyes, as if he needed sleep, but his gaze was alert and sincere. "That is, if you're certain you want me to court you."

"I'm certain," she said. She not only wanted him to court her, but to marry her, because she needed to be a better mother to Adam and Cora, and Duke could help her do that. He was a man she could respect and possibly learn to love. She was a woman who would spend the rest of her life trying to bring him happiness. Many marriages were built on far less.

Chapter Fifteen

F aith had never been to a circus, so Duke was taking her and the children to see the show before Van Amburgh moved his act to Mayville in the morning. They rode the street rail from Fredonia to Dunkirk then watched the circus animals parade down Central Avenue to attract people to the afternoon performance.

"Is it over already?" Cora asked, her voice filled with disappointment as the last caged lion passed by.

"This is only the parade, princess. We're going to the circus now," Duke said. As they walked to the fairgrounds, he patiently answered Cora's endless stream of questions then paid their admission.

Faith suspected Adam was staying away from Duke because of the incident with the hair brush, but Cora hadn't detached herself from Duke's side since he met them at the greenhouse.

He took them to see the sideshows first. Cora's eyes bugged at the snake lady. The woman sat in a cage playing with an enormous snake that Faith feared would haunt her nightmares, but all of the acts were performed to music that incited everything from fear to excitement.

Adam was enthralled with the sword swallower, and forgot himself so completely, he blurted out that he'd sneaked into the circus in Syracuse right before they moved. "But they didn't have a sword swallower," he said, not realizing his mistake.

Faith's stomach clenched. "You mean the circus in Saratoga," she said, praying Duke was as interested in the sword swallower as he appeared. "I'd better not hear of you doing anything like that again, Adam."

He threw a desperate glance at her, and she was sorry to see his joy melt away.

She tried to smile at Duke, but her lips were too stiff to be convincing. "This is my favorite show so far."

"Mine too," he said casually. Too casually. She looked away so he wouldn't ask questions she couldn't answer.

When the act finished, they circled the grounds. Duke bought them pork sandwiches for a late lunch then treated them to ice cream.

"Thank you," Adam said, but he kept his head down while he ate. Cora licked her spoon and savored her ice cream with such pleasure, Faith admitted to Duke that they'd never had the frozen treat before. "My mother couldn't afford admission to events like the circus." At least that's what her mother had led them to believe. But when Faith found her mother's guest book, she'd also found a surprising amount of money. Between her mother's stash, her own savings, and her aunts' combined money, they had been able to escape Syracuse. What Faith couldn't understand was, why her mother had stayed. Why, when she had some savings, hadn't she escaped like Faith and her aunts had after her death?

Cora stopped eating. "Grandma said we're going to have a real home someday with a big porch and lots of roses around it."

Faith had heard that litany all her life, but it had been an empty promise. She had accepted that years ago, but it hurt that Cora was innocent enough to believe it. And it hurt that they had gone without so much when her mother had money hidden away.

Duke pulled a white, folded handkerchief from his pocket and swiped a drip of ice cream off Cora's chin.

"I'm going to have a pony at our house," the little girl added.

That simple declaration made Faith want marriage more than anything. She wanted a man who could make some of their dreams come true because, God help her, she couldn't do it on her own.

Cora stuck her tongue out to lick the ice cream bowl, but Faith took it from her. Cora's expression fell. "I couldn't get the rest with my spoon," she complained.

Faith looked at the bowl, but it was empty. She tilted it so Cora could see inside. "Honey, it's gone."

"Here," Adam said, offering his last bite to Cora, who snapped it up like a turtle.

"Have either of you had peanut brittle?" Duke asked.

"Yes, sir." Adam ducked his head again, and Faith squinted at him. Why was he acting so nervous?

"Let's go get a sack of it for you to take home."

"Can we get some for Aunt Iris and Aunt Tansy and Aunt Aster and Aunt Dahlia too?" Cora asked.

Duke's laugh washed over Faith. She could get used to that deep, warm sound. He slapped his thighs and got to his feet. "Come on, princess, I'll buy some for everyone."

Faith returned their bowls to the ice cream vendor then hooked her arm around Adam's shoulder, lingering behind Duke and Cora. "What's wrong with you today?" she asked.

"Nothing."

Which meant it was serious. "Are you feeling all right?"

"I'm fine."

Which meant he wasn't. "I'm getting the feeling that you don't like Sheriff Grayson."

"He doesn't like me."

She tugged him to a stop. "He's been kind to you from the moment you met him."

"He thinks I'm a criminal."

She laughed. "Adam, the sheriff knows the difference between a boy who takes a hair brush without paying for it, and a man who robs a bank or kills someone."

"He told me stealing is theft, and that theft is a crime punishable by law. That means he thinks I'm a criminal."

Duke couldn't be that literal. Could he? "It means he was trying to teach you a lesson and make you understand that what you did was wrong. Just like sneaking into a circus without paying." She squeezed his shoulder. "I know why you did those things, Adam, but it's wrong."

"I know. And I'm sorry about taking the brush because I like Mrs. Brown."

"From what I hear, she likes you too."

"I paid off my bill yesterday, but she wants me to work after school a couple of days a week."

He said it like it was unimportant, but Faith could hear the pride in his voice. "I'm not surprised, Adam. You're a strong, smart boy who deserves a job where you can earn a little money for yourself."

Hope filled his eyes. "You mean I can work there?"

"I think I can spare you two days a week."

A crooked grin broke across his face. "Really?"

Duke had stopped just ahead to wait for them. She gave him a smile, but lingered with Adam. She needed his help at the greenhouse, but she knew he needed the job at the store. "Yes, you can work the store—and I'm very proud of you," she said then basked in his quick hug.

That's when Faith saw Judge Stone in the crowd. "Adam, get Cora," she whispered, faint from fear.

"What?" He pulled away, confused.

She couldn't move. Couldn't breathe. "Go, Adam." The white-bearded, husky judge was heading right for them.

Instead of running, Adam gave Duke a frantic wave.

Duke swept Cora into his arms and rushed to Faith's side. He passed Cora to Adam then gripped Faith's arm. "What's wrong?"

Judge Stone was thirty feet away, threading his way through the crowd, and she couldn't move, not even to draw a breath.

Duke gave her a gentle shake. "Are you all right?"

She sucked in a breath and began breathing so quickly it made her lightheaded. He guided her to a bench where she collapsed in a trembling, gasping, terrified mess.

"Sheriff Grayson!" the judge called jovially, his voice as smooth as molasses. "Good to see you out and about." The white-haired man thrust his hand toward Duke.

It wasn't Stone! Merciful God, it wasn't him. It wasn't the corrupt judge with the grating voice that haunted her nightmares. This man was a friend of Duke's.

Faith sagged against the back of the bench. How could she have been so careless? She'd nearly given herself away!

The man arched a white eyebrow. "Should I find a doctor?"

She waved off his offer with shaky fingers. "I just... I had a spasm in my back." She gave the man a tremulous smile. "I'll be fine in a minute."

But she knew she would never be fine as long as she was looking over her shoulder for Judge Stone. It horrified her that she'd been unable to act, that she'd been too frightened to grab Adam and Cora and run. If it had been Stone, she would be in his clutches by now.

Duke introduced her to Judge Barker, who resembled Stone in size and coloring, but in no other way. Judge Barker was a kind gentleman with compassionate eyes and warmth in his voice. He invited Duke and Faith to his upcoming lawn party then stepped aside with Duke to speak quietly for a few minutes.

Duke returned to her side alone. "Are you sure you're all right?"

She clasped his strong hand, immensely grateful to have him with her. She may have been frozen with fear, but Duke would have protected her and the children.

"Should I take you home?" he asked.

She shook her head. She couldn't spoil the day for Adam and Cora, "Let's go watch the show."

Her legs quaked as they crossed the fairground and found a seat in the stands. Adam and Cora were quickly captivated by the tumblers and jugglers. The equestrian act followed, with trick riders who rode standing on their horses' backs.

"Evelyn and Rebecca can do that," Duke said to Adam and Cora. "I'll take you by sometime to watch them ride."

"Can I ride a pony too?" Cora asked.

"If your mother says it's all right."

Faith put her fingers over Cora's mouth before the girl could ask. "We'll talk about it later. Watch the show, sweetheart."

Adam and Cora shifted their attention back to the show where a clown was getting chased by a bull. The clown threw his floppy hat in the air and leapt over a barrel, making Adam grin, and sending Cora into a fit of giggles. Faith exchanged a look with Duke, needing his solid presence and the security he gave her.

"Sorry about the pony" he mouthed.

"You're spoiling her," she mouthed back.

He smiled. "I can't resist."

She felt her own lips twist. "I know."

"I can't resist you either, Faith."

She watched the tip of his tongue caress his teeth as he finished mouthing her name, and she remembered the thrilling feel of his mouth and tongue when he kissed her in the bathhouse—and she wanted more. She lifted her gaze to his deep brown eyes that had gone from warm to smoldering.

"I'm glad you said yes today," he said quietly.

"Me too." She was glad for many reasons. Cora and Adam needed the treat. She needed to see them happy. And she needed to see Duke as a mate and a father, and as a man who could love and protect them.

While the circus went on around them, Faith and Duke studied each other, their gazes straying from mouth to eye to mouth again, until Faith was aching for his kiss. She liked what she saw, and wished they were alone in her bathhouse.

Adam's burst of laughter not only startled her, it shocked her. Cora giggled wildly at two clowns in the ring, pretending to be boxers, taking wild swings at each other, pummeling each other's red noses, stumbling, falling, and popping back up like puppies. The crowd roared with laughter, but it was hearing Adam's laugh that was Faith's most treasured moment of the day.

＝◁┼▷＝

Six o'clock that evening, Duke returned Faith and the children home. He couldn't have been more tired if he'd chased Arthur Covey across three counties, but the joy on Faith's face made the ache in his shoulder and the exhaustion in his body worthwhile. Cora darted inside the building they were living in, with the bulging sack of peanut brittle he hadn't been able to resist buying her.

"Look what we got, Aunt Iris!" she called.

"Thank you for taking us to the circus, sir." Adam bobbed his head at Duke then stepped inside. Duke expected the boy to keep going, especially since Adam had seen MacEnroy and Wayne Archer talking to him in the park after church that morning, but the boy turned back. "The ice cream was the best thing I've ever eaten." He scooted inside then, leaving Duke alone with Faith.

She looked tired, but far happier than she'd been that morning. "I've never been to a circus," she said. "I'm glad my first time was with you."

He wished her first time making love could have been with him, but it was too late for that, so he would gladly be her last. All day he'd kept his conversation mild for the children, not allowing his gaze to rove her body, but he remembered how she looked in the bath that morning, dripping wet and beautiful, the more so for her tears.

Cora skidded to a stop in the open doorway. "Thank you, Sheriff Grayson, for taking me on a train ride and to the circus and for getting me a pork sandwich and ice cream and peanut brittle, and for the ride on the elephant and..." She scrunched her face and thought for a moment. "And for letting me sit on your shoulders to see the clowns ride the ponies."

He laughed because she was such a little blabbermouth, and because her enthusiasm and the awe in her eyes was so real.

"You're welcome, princess. It was the best day I've had in a long time," he said, wanting more days like this, more time with Faith and her family, and hopefully more time alone with Faith in her bathhouse.

Iris stood behind Cora in the doorway. "I just made a pot of vegetable soup, Sheriff. It won't be your best meal, but you're welcome to stay for supper."

A look of horror replaced the smile on Faith's face. "I'm not eating," she said. "I mean, I thought I would treat your shoulder now."

Before Duke could answer, Iris pushed the door wide open. "This man took you to the circus today. The least we can do is feed him his supper—even if it isn't much."

Duke didn't want to make their meal any lighter by eating part of it, but Faith, who looked ill, stepped inside and left the door open for him. He stepped in behind her and understood immediately why Faith didn't want him here. The room was barren, and the only piece of furniture was the table.

Iris waved him toward makeshift benches, unashamed. "Pull up a barrel, Sheriff, and make yourself at home."

Faith gasped, her embarrassment so acute it moved him to pity, not because of the condition of her home, but because her poverty shamed her so deeply.

"You can sit with me on my board, Sheriff Grayson," Cora said without a drop of concern as she galloped to the table.

Duke lifted the little girl onto the wide board laid across two flour barrels. "Did you design this bench?" he asked, wanting to ease Faith's discomfort.

"Adam made it," Cora said.

Duke nodded to Aster, Tansy, and Dahlia as he swung his legs over the plank and sat down. He bounced on the board. "Good choice of wood, son. Nice and solid. I chose pine slabs from my dad's sawmill for my first tree stand."

"What's that?" the boy asked, looking confused as he sat on a barrel at the end of the table.

"It's a little platform you put in a tree. You nail a few boards together and secure it in a tree so you can sit up there and watch for deer." Duke accepted a bowl of soup from Iris. "Thank you," he said, purposely keeping his eyes off Faith while placing the full bowl in front of him. "I was your age when I made my first tree stand," he said to Adam. "It was dead winter, and I was sitting in that stand when I heard this cracking noise. I couldn't figure out what it was. Just then I spotted a brown bear twenty feet away walking right toward me. I thought he was snapping twigs beneath the snow."

Adam's spoon paused halfway to his mouth. "Did you shoot him?"

Duke shook his head and dipped his spoon into his soup. "That cracking noise was coming from the boards I was sitting on. They snapped in half and I fell. When I hit the ground, my rifle discharged and blew the stand right out of the tree."

Adam laughed, and Duke congratulated himself for the small achievement. Faith's aunts were smiling, but he still wouldn't allow himself to look at Faith. He took a bite of his soup. It was tasty but meatless, and he was certain the lack of meat wasn't from choice. Maybe this is why Iris had encouraged him to stay, so he could see how poorly they were living. Maybe he wasn't the only one making judgments. Iris didn't strike him as a woman who would seek sympathy or charity. Maybe she just wanted to see if he was the kind of man who could love a woman who had nothing but herself to offer.

"Did the bear get you?" Cora asked, her eyes bugging with fear.

"Naw," he said. "The gunshot scared him away. But I remembered to use a good, thick piece of hardwood after that."

"I saw a bear behind our house once," Adam said. "He was trying to crawl in our window. When I asked what he was doing, he said he was looking for Cora."

Duke felt his mouth quirk, but Adam took a spoonful of soup with a straight face.

"That's *me*." Cora tapped her spoon against her chest. "He was coming to see me."

Adam backhanded his mouth, and Duke suspected the boy was wiping away a smile. "The bear said he wanted to take you for a ride, Cora, but I told him you would only ride ponies."

Cora looked at Duke, her eyes wide and serious. "Would the bear bite me if I rode him?"

Thankfully he'd played these games with Rebecca and his nephews, so he answered with care. "A real bear probably would, so I wouldn't be too friendly with one. But a storybook bear might give you a ride on his back." He shrugged. "It's probably safer to ride a pony."

"I'm going to ride my pony to church someday," she said, her voice so wistful he wanted to go right to Radford and Evelyn's livery and buy her that pony she longed for.

He looked at Faith and saw that same desire reflected in her face. She lowered her lashes and dipped her spoon in her soup bowl.

"Is a bear bigger than a pony?" Cora asked.

"I think it weighs more," Adam answered, and the meal progressed with Cora asking questions and making them forget they were eating meatless soup and sitting on barrels and planks.

When they finished, Faith kissed the top of Cora's head. "Sheriff Grayson and I are going to the greenhouse so I can put some balm on his shoulder. Help clear the table, and maybe Aunt Dahlia will read with you until I come back."

Duke followed Faith outside, but stopped her near the door. "You don't have to bother with my shoulder tonight. You must be exhausted."

"It's been a week since I've stretched your muscles."

"I've been doing it myself."

"Are you getting the same amount of stretch?"

"No."

"Then we'd better do it tonight before we lose the progress we made last week."

Even though he'd been stretching each night until he howled from pain, he could feel the muscles tightening up again. Faith's treatment might have felt like torture, but he'd started seeing some results before he'd left for Mayville.

They crossed the yard and entered the humid world of her greenhouse. When she reached for a stack of linens on the shelf, he caught her hand. "I'll skip the bath tonight." He couldn't strip and soak in that tub without craving her in there with him, naked and willing to do all the things that had circled his mind all week.

"Are you sure?"

"Absolutely," he said then followed her back to the bathhouse. He sat on the table and removed his shirt, but his eyes shifted to the bath and he thought of Faith standing in the tub, dripping wet with her dark-nippled breasts peeping through the wet loose strands of her waist-length hair, and those deep gulping sobs wracking her body. He wanted to take her in his arms and protect her from everything that had ever hurt her.

She stood behind him, slathering an herb-scented oil over his shoulders and back. "I can do this better when you're lying down."

He stretched out on the towels she'd spread on the table. They were both silent, listening to the condensation drip off the water faucet while she massaged the muscles in his neck and shoulders. Sighing, he forced his thoughts from all the sensual ways he wanted to hold and kiss her, and remembered Adam's scuffle with the Archer children last week. He debated telling her. She had more worries than she deserved, but she was Adam's guardian and should be aware of a situation that could grow worse if not dealt with.

"Has Adam mentioned having any trouble at school?" he asked, hoping the boy had told her.

Her fingers clamped on his shoulders. "No. Why?"

"It seems he got in a scuffle with a couple other children last week." Duke pushed to his elbows and turned so he could see her. "One of those men I was talking with after church this morning was

Ike MacEnroy, Adam's teacher. MacEnroy broke up a commotion in the school yard last Monday, and said Adam was disrespectful to him."

"He's never been disrespectful to anyone, including me."

"I'm repeating what MacEnroy told me," he said. "He didn't seem that upset over the incident, and I suspect the man admires Adam's intelligence. Archer was the one demanding that I punish Adam for attacking his children, Melissa and Nicholas."

Faith gasped. "Adam would never attack a person unless they were threatening to harm one of us."

Duke couldn't picture Adam attacking anyone either. Especially if unprovoked. Those scratch marks on Nicholas's neck didn't come from Adam. "Archer's story is one-sided. Since Adam hasn't told you about this, don't mention it to him just yet. I want to confirm the story with my niece Rebecca, who was also involved then I'll talk to Adam."

Faith leaned her hip against the table. "So this is why Adam avoided you today." She buried her face in her hands. "What next? I can't handle another problem."

She looked exhausted. And scared. Duke pushed to his hip and swung his legs off the table so he was sitting. He put his arms around her and made her sit beside him. "Let me handle it with Adam. I'll be fair. You know that."

She sighed and lowered her forehead to his shoulder. "I could get used to having you around."

And he could get used to holding her in his arms. He liked the feel of her body against him, the warmth of her breath on his bare chest. He stroked his fingertips over her back, and she melted against him. He knew how good it felt to have the tension rubbed from his sore body, and he wanted to give her that pleasure. With light pressure, he kneaded the muscles in her neck and down between her shoulder blades.

"Mmm... that's nice," she said, relaxing her breasts into his chest, and sending a fire bolt of lust burning through him. He could make her feel so much better if she would get in that tub with him, if she would let him make love to her.

He wanted to keep her in his arms, but she deserved better than his selfish fondling. "Lie down and let me rub your back."

"I'm supposed to be doing that for you right now," she said, her voice so slow and dreamy it kicked his lust up another notch.

"But you need it more than I do." He kissed her forehead. "Lie down."

"I won't get back up if I do."

It was easy to angle his shoulders and pull her down onto the table with him. He lay on his back on the cool wood, with her lying on her side, half on his stomach, staring down at him with shock in her eyes. She braced her hand on his bare chest.

"What are you doing?"

"Making it easier to rub your back," he answered, demonstrating by rubbing his palm down her spine.

She lay against him, her knee braced on his thigh, her breasts pressed to his chest, her mouth inches from his, and her eyes full of suspicion. "I think you're taking liberties with me because I let you kiss me."

Her accusation stung. "I think someone in your past made you distrustful of men, and I'd like to beat the heck out of whoever did it. I won't deny having a hundred thoughts about making love to you on this table and in that bathtub, but I won't force you into anything, Faith. Not ever."

She perched against his side, looking ready to bolt.

"You're fully clothed, and so am I in every way that counts."

"We're not married."

"We're courting."

"And unchaperoned."

"A widow doesn't need a chaperone," he countered.

"Because she knows where this situation can take her."

"It won't." He held her chin and forced her to look in his eyes. "You can trust me."

"Then let me up."

He sighed and lifted her off him, bringing them both back to a sitting position.

He expected her to move away, but she stood and faced him. "I trust you," she said softly. "But I'm afraid we'll get carried away again and I can't... It's improper for us to... I like your kisses too much."

Her confession warmed him. He slipped his arms around her waist and pulled her between his knees. "It was my fault that we got carried away. I won't let it happen again."

Down went her lashes, and she leaned her forehead against his chest. "Duke?" He liked the sleepy softness of her voice. "I changed my mind about the sword swallower being the best show."

He'd forgotten the circus.

"The clowns were the best."

He stroked her back, pleased that the clowns had made Cora and Adam laugh, but even more pleased that they'd made Faith forget her troubles for a while.

"Thank you for taking us to the circus today," she said.

"I should be thanking you," he replied sincerely. "This is the best day I've had in... I don't know how long."

She lifted her head. "Truly?"

"Truly," he said, liking the way her gaze roved across his face and lowered to his mouth. Their eyes met, and his heart pounded while he waited for her to decide on their next step. Would she kiss him or torture him by starting his shoulder treatment?

Her lips parted and she lifted her mouth to his. The kiss was soft, tentative, lingering, and it drove him wild and made him want to take it slower and deeper until they were naked and making love. But he clenched his fists and ordered his body to settle down, letting her decide where the kiss would lead, knowing it wouldn't lead far enough, but craving every second of what she was giving him.

Faith thought her heart would explode from the pressure building inside it. She had never initiated a kiss before, but oh! She liked kissing this man.

Three men at the brothel had stolen kisses, once when she was thirteen, twice when she was eighteen; and Jarvis had romanced her into accepting his kisses then misled and pressured her into forfeiting her virginity. Never had she felt free to pursue a man at her own exploratory pace. She liked being able to take her time now, to feel the texture of Duke's lips with the tip of her tongue, to hold her mouth an inch from his and feel his warm breath caress her lips.

His hard chest muscles bunched beneath her palms, both exciting and scaring her. He could easily take what he wanted, and his shaky breathing and dark, intense eyes said he wanted more than her kiss. But she drank in the masculine beauty of his face, feeling a deep urge to give him more.

He nibbled at her lips, drawing her mouth to his, softly at first then deeper and slower, sweeping his tongue into her mouth in a seductive rhythm that melted her against his hard body. The birds in her stomach soared to the sky and dove to the sea in a mad, repetitive rush that stole her breath. Her nipples hardened and she longed for the caress of his hands in all the places he was making her ache. But she forced herself to break the kiss. Widow or not, he would expect her to retain some shred of respectability, which she *must* do at all cost.

He closed his eyes and rested his forehead against hers, his arms encircling but not imprisoning her. "Thank you," he whispered.

"For the kiss?" she asked, as shaken and breathless as he appeared.

"For stopping before you drove me insane." He opened his eyes and winked at her.

Nothing could have pleased her more than that teasing wink. To know he could enjoy kissing her like this, and could stop without growing petulant or angry as Jarvis had, told her everything she needed to know about Duke Grayson. He was a man worthy of a better woman than a prostitute's daughter, but Faith was going to claim him for herself. And she would do whatever it took to make sure he never regretted it.

Chapter Sixteen

Faith was in the house folding clothes with Iris when someone knocked on the door.

"If that's Adam or Cora clowning with us, I'll hang them on the clothesline," Iris said, heading to the door.

Faith smiled and shook her head. If it was one of the children, Iris would wrangle a kiss or a hug from them before sending them back to play. For all her starch, Iris was a softie.

When she opened the door, a man nearly as tall and wide-shouldered as Duke stood on the doorstep, looking like an overgrown farm boy in denim jeans and a blue cambric shirt. He wasn't catch-your-breath handsome like Duke or his brothers, but his boyish good looks brought a spark to Iris's eyes that put Faith on guard.

"Well, well, well." Iris smiled and leaned against the door frame. "Are you lost, farm boy?"

His gaze swept down her body and back to her face in a slow, seductive appraisal that said he'd rather be inspecting Iris with his big hands. Faith and Iris were used to being ogled, and at the brothel they knew exactly why the oglers came knocking. But this handsome, overgrown farm boy wasn't looking to buy anything; he was here to sell. To Iris.

He braced his muscled forearm against the door frame and gave her a wolfish smile. "I've been waiting all my life to knock on a door and find you on the other side." he said.

In all the years Faith had known Iris, no man had ever left her speechless. Until now. Until this stranger brazenly leaned in her door with that honest face and those blue eyes that declared Iris his even before asking her name.

He tilted his head. "Are you not telling me your name for any particular reason?"

Iris lifted her chin, but Faith could see her aunt was rattled. "I'm Iris Wilde—with an 'e'."

He chuckled, "Well, Iris Wilde with an 'e', are you married?"

"I've never found a man worth marrying."

"Well, you've found him now, Miss Wilde. I'm Patrick Lyons. I suppose you'll want to be courted before we marry?"

Faith nearly gasped aloud. What a rascal!

But Iris seemed to like his too-forward outrageous manner, because she laughed. "Mr. Lyons, what are you delivering to my door other than blarney?"

He glanced at Faith then leaned closer. "It's Pat, or Patrick, if you prefer. I have a delivery for Faith Wilkins."

Faith lowered her lashes, embarrassed that she'd been shamelessly eavesdropping. But with that heated introduction, how could she not?

"Oh... of course," Iris said, but Faith heard the disappointment in her voice. She obviously liked the man and enjoyed his flirting. Too much, by Faith's measure. Iris had promised to behave herself, but that promise had flown on the wind the minute Patrick Lyons had come knocking.

Faith waited for someone to speak to her, but the odd silence made her lift her head. Both Iris and Patrick were gone.

Ridiculously curious, she went to the door. To her shock, a wagon stacked five feet high with lumber was being backed toward the house by a team of the biggest horses she'd ever seen. When the driver stopped the wagon near the door, she ducked back inside.

Patrick came in carrying an armload of planks, followed by Iris, who was swinging her hips like she used to do at the brothel.

"Afternoon, ma'am," Patrick said with a nod at Faith. "Mind if I use this empty corner?"

"I'm Mrs. Wilkins, and I didn't order lumber," Faith said.

"Pleasure to meet you, Mrs. Wilkins, but Sheriff Grayson said to deliver it here."

"You know the sheriff?"

"He and his brothers are my best friends." Patrick nodded to the corner. "Mind if I put this down before I strain something important?"

Iris laughed. "Go ahead. That corner has been lacking something from the day we moved in."

He gave her a crooked grin. "I like you, Iris Wilde with an 'e'."

"Likewise, Mr. Lyons." She gave him a flirtatious smile that made Faith's heart hammer with fear. What on earth was Iris thinking? Flirting with a stranger, especially a man who knew the sheriff, was appallingly inappropriate.

Another similarly dressed man carried in an armload of fresh-smelling wood. He stood three inches shorter than Patrick, who Faith estimated at nearly six feet, and was lean with sinewy forearms and a weathered face that suggested he was at least forty.

"This is Cyrus Darling," Patrick said, pausing to introduce him to Faith and Iris.

The man set down the wood then tipped his cap to greet them.

"Pleased to meet you, Mr. Darling," Faith said.

Iris gave a pleasant nod, but a smile broke across her red lips and she winked at Faith. "I can just hear Tansy greeting Mr. Daaahlin'."

"Awful name for a man to be stuck with," Cyrus said, "but I've owned it for forty-five years and suppose I can survive a few more years of taunts and grins." The man radiated kindness and a quiet serenity that told Faith he was not only comfortable being alone, he preferred it.

"Why, Mista Daaahlin' sounds like a perfectly handy name to me," Iris said, mimicking Tansy's southern drawl, and horrifying Faith. "Cyrus, dahlin', thank you for carrying in that wood. If I were your wife, dahlin', I'd tell you to forget the wood and give me some sugar."

Pat's hoot, and Cyrus's chuckle, interrupted Iris's performance, but Faith stewed. Her aunt had promised to act like a lady, but here she was flirting like a prostitute with not one but *two* men!

"Thank you, Miss Wilde," Cyrus said. "That sweet southern touch makes it a handy name indeed. Guess I need a southern gal who can appreciate it."

"Then you must meet Tansy." Iris headed for the door, but turned back, her dark eyes lit with mischief. "Mr. Darling, do you sing by chance?"

Patrick's laughter boomed through the building, and he clapped a hand on Cyrus's shoulder. "I'd be careful how you answer that, Cyrus. That's one of those tricky female questions that can trip a man right into marriage."

"I've avoided marriage this many years, I don't see how my worst vice could hook me into it."

Iris clasped her hands together in front of her chest. "Mista Dahlin', if singing is your worst vice, Tansy is going to adore you." With a laugh, she ducked outside leaving Faith with two strangers and a fury she could barely control.

"Faith isn't going to like this," Adam said, holding a stud in place while Duke nailed it into the wall.

"I don't suppose she will." Duke had meant to stop and tell Faith his plan after the lumber was delivered and it was too late for her to argue with him. But he'd gotten tied up with Henry Oakley, a local farmer who'd been swindled by a wily salesman who'd asked him to sign a receipt for his employer. The receipt was rigged so that Henry's signature appeared on the bottom page, which happened to be a note for a hundred dollars—enough to buy a team of horses, a house, and feed a family for years.

Adam moved his hands lower on the stud so Duke could continue nailing it into the wall. "She won't like all these people in here seeing how we live. You saw how upset she was when Aunt Iris asked you to stay for supper last night."

He'd noticed all right. She'd been near tears until Adam teased Cora about the bear climbing in her window. Faith would be furious to find him in her house putting up walls. He couldn't imagine what she would do when she found him here with his brothers and some of their mill hands.

"Any idea how I can keep myself out of hot water?"

"She'll just singe your ears some. If she's really upset, she'll act disappointed and start crying. That's the worst."

"I think I'd rather get my ears singed," Duke said.

"Me too."

"Looks like we're both in hot water then." And he'd best take care of his business with Adam before Faith came in from the greenhouse. "She knows about your scuffle at school last week."

Shock flashed in Adam's eyes, but he didn't try to defend himself.

"I talked to Rebecca, and she told me what happened. Sometimes trouble finds us even when we're minding our own business."

"Melissa ARCHER is a troublemaker," Adam said, his voice squawking.

So was her father Wayne, but Duke kept the information to himself. "Rebecca says you walk her to school and back, but you don't attend. Where have you been going each day while your sister thinks you're in school?"

Adam cast a nervous glance at Radford who was working close by. "To the gorge."

Duke drove the last nail home and reached for another stud. "So you've been lying each day about going to school, dawdling in the gorge while your sister does your work in the greenhouse."

"I can't go back or I'll end up in a real fight," he said, defending his actions. "Nicholas doesn't like it that I'm friends with Rebecca."

Duke set his hammer down. "I don't like it that my niece is friends with a boy who would lie to his own sister."

Adam's face drained of color, and Duke knew he'd gotten the boy's attention. He disliked being harsh, but Faith's brother needed to develop his character to a higher standard.

"You're a smart boy, Adam. You could teach Rebecca all kinds of useful things from those books you read. Rebecca is a good, honest girl, and she's been raised to speak only the truth and to accept the consequences. I wouldn't want you to influence her to start lying."

"I'd never do that."

"Rebecca admires you, and she may think it's all right for her to stretch the truth like you've been doing."

Adam's cheeks flamed and, near tears, he faced the wall.

Duke put his hand on Adam's shoulder, sorry to embarrass the boy, but knowing he'd done the right thing. "Everyone deserves a chance to prove himself, Adam. Since this is the last week of school, I want you to stay home and help your sister when you're not working at the store."

"Yes, sir," the boy said, his youthful jaw clenched.

"You owe her an apology."

"I know."

"All right then. I'm trusting you to be a good friend to Rebecca."

The boy shot a worried look at Radford, who'd moved to work on the opposite side of the room. "Did Rebecca get in trouble because of me?"

"Her father wasn't pleased, but he didn't punish her for trying to right a wrong." Duke made a big show of squaring up the stud to let Adam know the lecture was over. Then he said, "Steady this while I drive in this first nail."

<hr/>

Faith was the last one to leave the greenhouse for the evening. The place had been teeming with customers when she sought Iris earlier, so her aunt had avoided her thus far. But their workday was over, and Faith was going to have a talk with her aunt.

Outside, she massaged her lower back and gazed with longing at the Colburn house across the street. How lovely it would be to sit in a real parlor on a sofa instead of planks and barrels.

The staccato sound of hammers whacking wood echoed through the neighborhood as she walked to the barren building she was living in. She'd heard the muted sound from inside the greenhouse, but didn't realize until reaching her front door that the banging was coming from her own house. Startled, she opened the door and stared in shock.

Eight men carrying hammers, saws, and nails swarmed like carpenter ants from the front door to the back, framing up walls as fast as they could measure and saw the boards. Adam worked with

Duke. Iris and Tansy flitted around like butterflies, pouring and serving beverages to the men. Cora, in a green pinafore, helped.

Duke shouldn't have sent the lumber so soon. She hadn't earned it yet. He'd never mentioned bringing his family and crew to work on her house, or even his intention of doing so. If he had, she would have told him no. She could never pay for this. And she hated for these people to see her family camped out in a vacant building like a band of gypsies.

If Iris had instigated this, Faith would strangle her. She waved from the doorway, wanting a word with her outrageous aunt, but Iris was too busy flirting with Patrick to notice.

"Faith!" Evelyn Grayson beckoned her to the kitchen corner where she and Amelia were working at Faith's makeshift counter. "I'm afraid we've taken over your kitchen, and borrowed some plates from that crate," Evelyn said cheerfully.

Heaping plates of food covered Faith's plank counters. Had they known she couldn't feed these men? That she couldn't offer anything but cold glasses of water? Were they here to make sure their husbands didn't go without supper?

Faith looked at her dented metal dishpans and the mountain of pots and plates stacked in crates on the floor, and her face burned. She forced herself to face the ladies. "How kind of you to bring supper." Several plates were laden with quartered potatoes that looked as if they'd been cooked in the same pot as the thick slabs of roast pork. The aroma made Faith's mouth water. "I'm afraid I have nothing to contribute. I can't even offer you ladies a chair, because I don't have one." Aster and Dahlia had moved the table aside, and tucked the barrels and planks underneath to keep them out of the way. Now they were piling their pallets and blankets on top of the table in an embarrassing heap.

"Well, you just moved to town." Evelyn placed fat, cooked carrots on the plates. "It makes perfect sense that you dedicated your time and efforts to your business first. I don't know of a place that can compare to your Evergreen House."

Her greenhouse was special, with its hearty plants and unique herbs, and the pleasure of her bathhouse was unmatched by any business in the area, but that didn't lessen Faith's embarrassment over her makeshift furnishings.

"Everyone has raved about the bath," Amelia said with a warm smile. "My mother-in-law and I are hoping to schedule a visit later this week, and I honestly can't wait."

"That will give me an opportunity to repay you for bringing all this lovely food," Faith replied.

"Absolutely not!" Amelia and Evelyn said in unison. Evelyn pushed a plate into Faith's hands. "Neighbors help each other. Now eat. You look tired and hungry. I'll tell the men to stop for supper."

She left Faith standing with Amelia, whose eyes were filled with compassion. "I used to teach in Laona several years ago," she said. "My stipend was so scant it took me three months to afford fabric for a dress. I lived in a tiny room attached to the schoolhouse, and my worldly possessions consisted of a dry sink, a too-small stove, one rickety table, and an old bed. There's no reason for you to feel ashamed of this building, Faith. It may be empty of furnishings at the moment, but it will make a fine home."

Faith lowered her lashes to hide the tears in her eyes. She cursed her weakness, but she was tired and overwhelmed by the warm welcome from the Graysons. "Thank you," she whispered, hoping Amelia heard her appreciation through the banging hammers.

Amelia patted her shoulder. "I'll take a plate to your daughter. Maybe she can convince this little one inside of me to be a girl. I'm due in December with my third child," she said, rubbing her flat stomach. "Marshall is six, and Lucas is three. Kyle and I adore our sons, but I'm feeling outnumbered and would love to have girl."

Amelia's confession warmed Faith. "I'll pray that December brings you an easy delivery and a healthy girl," she said.

"Thank you, and please add a prayer that my morning sickness ends soon."

Faith laughed. "Ginger might help. You may still get sick, but it will settle your stomach. I'll give you some roots before you leave," she said, relieved she could offer something in return. "Simmer three or four thin slices of the root in a pint of water for about twenty minutes then sip it a little at a time throughout the day."

"I'll have Kyle purchase some from you before we leave."

"Absolutely not," Faith argued. "I'll *give* you the roots."

"Thank you." Amelia squeezed Faith's hand, and her warm acceptance allowed Faith a necessary measure of pride.

When Amelia walked away, Faith picked up a plate of food and leaned against the wall to eat before she fainted from hunger. Across the room, Cora's face beamed with importance as she toted a full water glass to Duke's brother Boyd, who knelt on one knee and pressed his hand to his heart, looking like a prince as he accepted Cora's gift. He was playing with the child, flirting with her, his smile so charming Faith would have swooned if he'd directed it at her.

But Cora blabbed and picked sawdust off his shirt as if he were her pet dog.

Boyd shrugged at his brothers as if to say he'd lost his touch. Kyle's laughter boomed through the building, and his teeth flashed in the light of several lanterns. He was handsome like Duke. And clearly in love with his wife. He slipped his arm around Amelia and placed his palm over her belly as if assuring himself his lady and baby were all right. The gesture was tender and intimate and so loving, Faith wondered if anyone else noticed it.

Evelyn and Radford had, and it seemed to please them. They also exchanged a heated look of love and desire, and it could have broiled the roast pork Evelyn was offering her husband.

Yes, these Grayson men were handsome, lusty creatures. They were cut from the same block of stone. Of course, the Creator had used a finer tool to chisel Evelyn's husband Radford and his brother Boyd. These two were slimmer in build, with finer features—not more handsome than Duke or Kyle, just more polished. Duke and his brother Kyle were rough-cut, with wider, muscular builds, and slightly rugged features that lent Duke a dangerous edge to his scowl and a heart-stopping intensity when his eyes locked on hers.

Like when he'd kissed her in the bathhouse.

Like now, when he stood across an entire room and caressed her with his gaze.

He wore denim pants and a green cotton shirt with the sleeves rolled up his thick forearms. A hammer hung from his hip instead of a gun, but she felt power and danger radiating from him nonetheless. He started toward her.

The plank floorboards vibrated beneath the heavy tread of his boots as he crossed the room, and she could barely swallow the piece of pork she'd been chewing. She tried to calm herself and clear the desire that was clouding her thinking. She wanted this man, not just the security he could give her; she'd known for certain when he'd given her that playful wink while they were in the bathhouse. He was a good man, a kind and generous man to bring the lumber and put up her walls for her. But regardless of their heated kissing match in the bathhouse, or the seductive promise in his eyes as he strode toward her on those long, powerful legs, she was going to take him to task for doing all this without consulting her.

He stopped in front of her and dipped his mouth to her ear. "I missed you today," he said then boldly nibbled her earlobe with his warm lips.

She melted like grease on a griddle; hot in the center, sizzling on the edges.

He lifted his head and smiled with his eyes. "I suppose you're going to flay me for this?"

"To pieces," she said, "just as soon as I get my breath back."

His chuckle was so intimate, so unforgivably seductive, she couldn't decide whether to kick him or lean into his hot, hard body and be consumed by his fire.

Chapter Seventeen

The hours and days spun by too fast for Faith to find time to really sit down and talk to Iris. She woke before dawn, worked until dusk in the greenhouse then spent the evenings feeding Duke's family and crew.

Duke played seductive games with her while he and the men worked on her house. The Grayson women brought food and a neighborly friendship Faith had never known. The ladies society delivered curtains, and one woman donated parlor furniture she was replacing. Another woman donated paint and rolls of wallpaper from her husband's store. Several women had received complimentary massages from Faith and her aunts, and were happy to contribute what they could to make Faith's house a home.

Faith stood in her makeshift kitchen, proudly dishing up a hearty beef stew she'd made for supper. The meal had diminished her meager earnings but contributed to her pride. Claire and Anna brought three warm loaves of bread and two blueberry pies to complete the meal.

Faith handed a bowl of stew to Claire, who carried it to her husband. Intrigued by their relationship, Faith lowered the ladle in the pot and watched them. Claire Grayson playfully lifted a spoonful of stew to her husband's gorgeous mouth. Boyd devoured her with his eyes as he accepted her offering, and Faith could see that he didn't just lust after his beautiful wife, he loved her deeply and passionately, and didn't care who could see it. Radford and Kyle were the same way with their wives.

Faith's life had provided endless examples of lust, but not one example of love, so when Claire returned to the kitchen Faith longed to ask her what marriage was like. But she also feared the question might be too personal, and that asking would reveal too much about herself.

Dahlia placed a stack of pie plates on the counter next to Claire. "How can you breathe with your husband's gaze gobbling you up like a dish of cream?" she asked.

Claire smiled. "I gave up breathing the moment I met him."

"You mean after you shot his window out," Anna commented with a soft laugh. The woman's shy, hesitant manner made Faith feel protective of her. She seemed afraid to relax, as if she was always waiting and watching for some unseen danger.

"Is that true?" Dahlia asked.

"I'm afraid so. Boyd owned a noisy tavern across the street from my boarding house, which we now live in," Claire said. "His wretched saloon was ruining my business, so I dragged my grandmother's revolver outside in hopes of convincing him to shut the place down. I accidentally shot out his window."

"And when that didn't work," Anna added, "she led a band of temperance women against him."

Dahlia lifted her water glass in a toast. "I'd be proud to call you my sister."

Claire's smile faded. "It was a bad idea, Dahlia. I wanted to protect my business, and stop men from beating their wives and children, but I caused more harm than good. Men lost their jobs, Boyd's beautiful bar was destroyed, and three men got shot. Duke was forced to kill a man because of my marches."

An icy feeling rushed through Faith. Duke was the sheriff. It shouldn't have surprised her that his job had forced him to kill a man. But it unnerved her to know he'd taken a life, and terrified her that he might be forced to face his own death in the line of duty. He was rock solid, though, and she could depend on him to make the hard choice if he ever faced Judge Stone.

"Men who beat women should be castrated," Dahlia said. "I commend you for facing down those men, and I'd gladly join your marches if you were still doing it."

"The temperance union still marches, Dahlia, but Anna and I believe it's more helpful for us to offer a woman and her children a safe place to stay until she can make more suitable living arrangements."

"So do I," Dahlia said, her eyes lit with passion. "When I was seventeen, I saw a women beaten by her husband, begging a minister for help. He told her to be more obedient and sent her home. I vowed then and there to... to never marry."

Anna picked up two empty plates and held them near the pie Claire was cutting. "I don't blame you, Dahlia. If I ever get a divorce from Larry, I'll spend the rest of my life unmarried."

"Never say never." Claire scooped out a slice of pie and slid it onto a plate. "I swore I would never marry again, and I didn't think I could have children," she said. "But here I am with a husband and two boys I love and adore. I couldn't be happier."

"Why wouldn't you be happy?" Dahlia looked across the room to where Boyd was working, hammer in hand, his shirtsleeves rolled up muscled forearms, his dark, handsome profile too perfect for words. "If a man like your husband ever knocks on my door, I'll marry him before he can ask for directions."

Claire and Anna laughed, their warmth and kindness soothing the rawness in Faith's heart.

An echo of laughter came from the other side of the room, and they turned to see Patrick dancing Iris through the studded wall of the bedroom he'd just finished framing. Faith sighed and decided to let Iris off the hook. Although she'd flirted with Patrick all week, she'd maintained acceptable behavior for Cora's and Adam's benefit. And for her own.

Iris wouldn't admit it, but she'd finally met her match. Patrick Lyons was outrageous enough to keep her off balance.

And Tansy certainly enjoyed flirting with Cyrus. Mr. Darling was a quiet man, and acted with utmost decorum, but his eyes followed Tansy like she was an exotic butterfly in a field of wildflowers. Tansy's airy southern sweetness charmed the man, and the dazed look on his face said he was a goner.

Faith was too. Duke was temptation itself. Every treatment on his shoulder put them alone together and thrust temptation in her path. Every charming half-smile, every teasing wink from his thick-lashed eyes, every scorching kiss and touch of his strong hands drew her closer to his flame. And that heat built between them the following week as he and the men finished framing up her house.

But Faith wasn't the only one craving Duke's attention. Adam hung on Duke's every word, trying his hand at carpentry, beaming when Duke praised him, letting Duke teach him skills a father should teach his son.

Faith wanted Duke to be the one who guided Adam into manhood—and for him to guide her into becoming a wife and mother to their children.

Chapter Eighteen

Adam left his kicking-stone by the greenhouse and hurried out onto Liberty Street. Sheriff Grayson had a rowboat stashed in the gorge behind the house he shared with his mother, and he'd told Adam they could take it out today—after Adam apologized to Faith. So Adam had told Faith he was sorry, and she'd forgiven him as she always did; but her forgiveness only made him feel worse. He would never lie to her, or to anyone, again.

As he walked past Rebecca's house, he saw her family in the front yard under the huge oak tree. Rebecca's father was on his knees straddling William, who was calling for help. A little boy ran across the yard with a wild whoop, and jumped on Mr. Grayson's back. "Got you, Daddy!" he cried.

Rebecca's dad gave a loud grunt and fell to his side.

Adam huffed out a quiet laugh. It would take a man the sheriff's size or bigger to knock over Mr. Grayson.

"Help us, Becca!" the little boy yelled, clamping his arms around his dad's neck.

Rebecca dashed across the yard, her pretty black hair bouncing across her back.

Adam's heart cartwheeled, and he stopped to watch. He hunched down and braced his elbows in the tumble of morning glory vines that flowed like a waterfall over the stone fence.

Rebecca planted her foot on her father's stomach. "Unhand my brothers, you ogre."

Her dad lunged upward and grabbed Rebecca's waist, making her screech as he pulled her into the fray.

"Get her, Dad!" William yelled.

Rebecca swatted at her brother. "You little turncoat," she said then burst into wild laughter as her father tickled her.

"What are the magic words?" Mr. Grayson asked.

"I love you," Rebecca gasped and giggled, kicking her feet.

"Are you sure?" he asked, not letting up.

"Yes!" She shrieked with laughter. "I love you, Daddy!"

Her father stopped tickling, and kissed her forehead. "I love you too, sprite."

Mrs. Grayson planted her hands on her hips and looked at her family sprawled on the lawn. "Who is going to scrub those grass stains out of your clothes?" she asked.

"Nobody. We'll wear them to clean the barn." Mr. Grayson caught his wife's hand and pulled her down beside him then promptly growled and bit her neck.

Her laughter filled the yard. "You need a shave."

"I need a kiss." He planted a big one right on her lips.

The boys both groaned and tried to save their father by tugging him away. Rebecca laughed and cuffed William in the head as she sprinted toward the tree.

That's when she saw Adam.

She gave him a cheerful wave, but Adam was too stunned to return her greeting. He didn't know a father wrestled with his sons and tickled his daughter and kissed his wife in the middle of the yard.

Rebecca trotted to the fence. "Thank you for the gift," she said, her face glowing with happiness.

Gift? Adam had tucked a note in the stone fence for her two days ago, but he hadn't been sure she would remember to look for one. She had suggested it the last time he'd walked her to school. But the note sure seemed to make her happy.

Rebecca's father was walking straight toward them with a look on his face that made Adam's stomach queasy. "I'd better go," he said, pushing off the fence. "I'll leave another note when I can."

"Mama made some sweet tea this morning. Can you stay for a glass?"

He shook his head. The cool look in her father's eyes told him that he wasn't welcome.

Mr. Grayson put his hand on Rebecca's shoulder. "Your mother needs help getting lunch on the table," he said.

Rebecca's brows pinched in confusion, but she could only cast a worried glance at Adam before dashing into the house.

Mr. Grayson sat on the fence, his manner friendly, his eyes suspicious. "Adam, you seem like a nice young man, but Rebecca is too young for courting."

"COURTing?" Adam cleared his throat. "We're just friends, sir."

"A friend doesn't leave an expensive parasol on the doorstep."

Adam shook his head. "Sir, I haven't given Rebecca any gifts."

"Did you not leave that parasol on our doorstep for her?"

"No, sir."

"You're certain?"

"Yes, sir."

Mr. Grayson nodded, but didn't seem convinced. "Rebecca is too young to keep company with you, Adam."

In other words, stay away from my daughter. Adam got the message. Mr. Grayson was judging him unfairly, assuming the worst, and it made Adam want to yell at the top of his lungs so the whole world would know he was *not* a bad person. But he clamped his teeth against his anger, gave Rebecca's judgmental father a curt nod, and walked away.

Nicholas Archer was coming down the road, and shouted to him, but Adam sprinted across the apple orchard to escape the boy. He didn't need two beatings today.

The sheriff's place was the next house up the road, and Adam was burning with anger when he banged on the door.

The sheriff answered, thrust a fishing rod into Adam's hand then lifted a wicker hamper off the floor. "Let's go hook some bass." He pulled the door closed behind him, and they headed across the back yard.

Adam trudged alongside the sheriff as they crossed a field of shin-high grass and sprawling maple trees with lime-green leaves. Birch, pine, oak, and ash trees hugged the path that cut down into the gorge. Robins and swallows swooped overhead, twittering and singing. Small animals rustled beneath the ferns and sumac bushes, and the burbling sound of water grew louder as they descended into the gorge.

"My boat is over here," the sheriff said, pointing to a cluster of towering pine trees. He set the basket on the grass, ducked beneath the low branches, and disappeared from sight. "Put the rod by the basket and come give me a hand."

Adam laid the rod aside and ducked beneath the drooping limbs of the pine tree. He found the sheriff standing in a small, shadowy cathedral in the center of the trees. Sunlight shot down in beams from the towering tops of the trees to the thick cushion of pine needles beneath his feet. The scent of pine was heavy and fragrant, and Adam knew he'd never been in a more magical place. "This is... I don't even know how to explain it," he whispered.

The sheriff grinned. "It keeps my boat hidden so it doesn't tempt anyone to paddle themselves into a dangerous situation."

"I could live here."

The sheriff laughed, but Adam was serious. It felt safe here.

They carried the boat twenty feet to the creek. Adam ran back for the basket and rod then gingerly stepped into the boat. The sheriff used the oars to push them away from the bank then worked the paddles with long, dragging strokes that propelled them north on Canadaway Creek.

Gliding through the water in a boat was a feeling Adam had never experienced, and he wanted to go faster, to race across the water like the wind. Trees that were perfect for climbing lined the shale and earth banks. A white, hairy dog stood with his front paws in the water, long, pink tongue lapping noisily from the creek. From the boat, everything along the banks seemed to tower above him.

The sheriff lifted his left oar and angled it toward shore. "There's the greenhouse," he said.

Adam viewed it from the back, seeing the little stone addition tucked against the huge white plank building. Faith was hanging laundry in the side yard, but from Adam's position on the water, she looked like she was on a stage.

"Faith!" Adam shouted, waving his hand. He wanted her to see him in the boat. "Down here," he said, rising up so she could see him. The boat rocked up on one side, and he gripped the edge, his heart thundering as he nearly fell overboard.

The sheriff grabbed his arm and pulled him back to the bench seat he'd been sitting on. "The first lesson is to never stand up in a boat."

"Sorry, sir."

The sheriff laughed. "You would have been more sorry if you had fallen in that water. It's cold."

"It's July."

"The water's not warm enough for me until August." He nodded toward shore. "Your sister has spotted us."

She had, and Faith was smiling. Adam waved, feeling proud.

When she curtsied to them, the sheriff laughed.

Adam knew Faith liked the sheriff, and that she would probably marry him if he asked her, but he didn't care about that today. He wanted to get his hands on the oars and row the boat. They followed the creek through Fredonia, hearing talking and shouting and carriages rattling along the rutted roads. A mile out of the village, water dragons and horseflies buzzed along the banks. Birds chirped, and a woodpecker hammered a tree high above his head.

The sheriff grimaced and paused to rub his shoulder. "I could use a rest," he said. "Think you could row for a bit?"

"Yes, sir!" Adam's heart leapt as the sheriff pushed the oars into his hands. His first uneven stroke caused the boat to swing sideways. Sweat prickled beneath his shirt, but after a few awkward strokes, he got the boat heading north.

"Now, pull evenly with both oars," the sheriff instructed.

It sounded easy, but Adam struggled to plunge in both oars at the same time and at the same depth. His left oar skimmed the surface and flung water across the sheriff's face and shirt. The right oar sank deep and spun the boat sideways again. Adam waited for the sheriff to cuff him in the head for soaking him, but the man just laughed and wiped his face.

"I did the same thing to my dad the first time he let me row his boat."

"REAlly?"

"REAlly," the sheriff said, in a squawking imitation that made Adam laugh. Grinning, he said, "It takes some practice to. get a good, even pull with both oars."

"I didn't think it would be so hard," Adam admitted, looking behind him occasionally so he wouldn't paddle them into a bank.

"You're doing fine, son."

A strange warmth filled Adam's chest. If the sheriff married Faith, he would be sort of like a father. Adam didn't like the sheriff's lectures, but it was nice having someone to show him how to frame in a room or row a boat.

"We're about to enter Lake Erie," the sheriff said.

Adam peered over his shoulder to see a vast blue-green lake of water. His stomach soared with excitement then dove in terror. The lake was huge.

They didn't go far from shore, but Adam rowed until sweat rolled down his back and his muscles burned. When the sheriff told him to stop, he almost sighed aloud.

Their boat drifted and bobbed on small waves while they ate delicious slabs of ham and thick slices of bread that the sheriff's mother had packed in the wicker hamper. They shared a quart of water then the sheriff baited the fishing hook with a fat night crawler. He cast the line three times to show Adam how to do it. But when Adam tried it, he failed miserably. The third time his distance was better, but he snagged the hook on the lake bottom and lost it.

The sheriff didn't seem to care at all. He just repaired the line and handed the rod back.

Adam wouldn't take it. "I'll ruin it," he said.

"Adam, I've lost more hooks than I can count. That's part of fishing. The first time I tried casting, I threw my father's best fishing rod right into the lake. Sank like an anchor. I dove in after it, but the water was too deep to retrieve the rod. That's one reason I fish close to shore."

"Is that true?"

"I always tell the truth, Adam."

Of course he did. He was the sheriff. And he was a Grayson.

Adam took the rod, but his mind was on Rebecca's father when he cast the line. The hook and sinker shot over the water and landed with a soft blip six boat lengths away.

"Nice cast," the sheriff said, but Adam's jaw was clenched. He didn't know anything about a stupid parasol.

"A fish is going to need a steam engine strapped to his tail to catch that hook you're reeling in. Go slow and steady."

"Yes, sir."

Adam drew the rod up and cast the line again.

"Something eating at you today?"

"No, sir." He reeled slowly, but his heart hammered. The sheriff wouldn't be happy to learn that Adam hated his brother.

"You remember the talk we just had about speaking honestly, don't you?"

"Yes, sir." And Adam had just vowed not to lie to anyone ever again. "I'm angry, sir, but believe me, you don't want to know why."

"Is that a polite way of telling me it's none of my business?"

A sick feeling rippled through his stomach, but he'd made a promise not to lie. "Your brother thinks I gave a parasol to Rebecca because I'm trying to court her."

The sheriff's eyebrows lowered, but he seemed confused instead of angry. "Did you tell Rebecca you wanted to court her?"

"No, sir."

"Did you give her a parasol?"

"No."

"Are you being truthful with me?"

"Yes," Adam said, clenching his teeth so hard his jaw ached.

"All right then." The sheriff gave him a nod as if to say Adam shouldn't worry about this. "I'll talk to Radford."

"You believe me?" he asked, shocked.

"Yes, Adam. I'm trusting you to be truthful with me. Now go on and cast that line. I'd like some fish for my supper."

Stunned, mind reeling, Adam obeyed, but his hook had barely hit the water when the rod dipped.

The sheriff gripped the pole and gave it a quick upward thrust. "You got him."

"A fish?"

"Either that or a mermaid."

Adam winced at his stupid question. "Should I reel him in?"

The sheriff released the rod and shook his head. "This fella wants to run. We'll have to tire him out before we net him."

The fish was pulling so hard he was towing the boat! Adam panicked. "I don't know what to do." His heart pounded and he tried to hand the rod to the sheriff, who wouldn't take it.

"Just keep your grip firm and don't let him run the line out." He looked at the reel then at Adam. "When the line slackens, reel it in. If he fights hard, give him a bit of line to run with. He'll get tired before you do."

The reel spun as the fish fought the hook. Adam locked his fingers around the rod, reeling when the sheriff said to reel, holding steady when the sheriff warned him to hold the line. Sweat burned his eyes, and his heart banged wildly in his chest, but he didn't let go of the rod. The sun glared on the water and made his eyes tear, and half the time he couldn't tell whether the fish was zigging or zagging.

"I'll bet it's a bass," the sheriff said.

More like a whale, but Adam knew there were no whales in Lake Erie.

Whatever it was, it wanted loose. Adam kept a firm grip on the rod, sweating and reeling and praying, until finally, he landed the fish.

The sheriff let out a low whistle as he lifted the net and plopped the biggest fish Adam had ever seen into the bottom of the boat. "Looks like you'll be bringing home supper tonight."

He propped his elbow on his knee and grinned at Adam. "Good job, son."

Sweat stung Adam's eyes and his arms ached like they'd been wrenched from his shoulder sockets, but he felt ten feet tall.

Chapter Nineteen

Wayne Archer thumped his fist on his counter. "I'm telling you, Sheriff Grayson, the parasol was stolen. We displayed it in that stand right by the door, and Miss Richards has had her eye on it for two weeks. It was our fanciest sunshade, and I can assure you I would remember selling it."

Duke rolled his shoulder to ease the tension that was climbing his neck. "Could Mrs. Archer have sold the parasol?"

"Certainly. That's why I checked with her. My wife didn't sell it."

"Did you sell it, Nicholas?" Duke asked Archer's son, the boy involved in the incident at school with Adam and Rebecca.

"No, sir."

Wayne scowled. "I've asked all the necessary questions, Sheriff. We conducted a thorough search of our store and could not locate it. The parasol was stolen."

"All right." Duke sighed, wondering if he'd been wrong to trust Adam. He didn't want to be wrong about the boy. "I'll need a list of everyone who has been in your store since Saturday."

Wayne's chin dropped. "That's impossible. Nearly everyone in Fredonia frequents my apothecary."

"It's only Monday, Wayne. Surely you can remember who came in on Saturday and today?"

"Maybe. Maybe not," he said belligerently.

"As a candidate for sheriff, you must know how important it is to have a good memory. If you can't name the people who have been in your store—"

"I can name every one of them."

"Good. I'll come by in the morning for your list."

"I'll have it ready. Not that it will do any good."

Archer had publicly condemned Duke for allowing two swindles to take place in town. After the unfortunate incident with Henry Oakley, the farmer, Duke had warned the residents not to sign notes for anybody, but Ernie Lorenzo did it anyhow and got swindled. Now Archer would add petty theft to the list of crimes Duke hadn't stopped. The man was as relentless as a mosquito, and Duke had to walk out of the apothecary before he squashed the annoying man.

The man who'd swindled Oakley and Lorenzo was probably several towns away by now, working his cons on other unsuspecting farmers. Duke had sent a telegram with the man's description and crime to every township in the county, and one to Buffalo, and another to Erie, Pennsylvania. That was all he could do unless the man came back to town. The parasol incident was an altogether different issue, though, and one that nagged him as he walked to his family's sawmill in Laona.

Who, other than Adam, would give Rebecca a stolen parasol?

When Duke got to the mill, Radford was howling with laughter. Boyd's hands were lifted as if proclaiming his innocence, but the look in his eye said he was guilty. That's when Duke noticed the soaked front of Kyle's shirt.

Kyle set an empty water jar on a drag of maple logs then stalked Boyd. "If you ever again stick a board up my ass when I'm drinking, I'll beat you with it."

Boyd gave him a lopsided grin. "I gave you a goose to see if you were awake."

"I'll show you how awake I am."

Boyd danced away from Kyle's swinging fists. Radford braced his axe on the ground, laughing himself to tears. Duke stood outside their circle, chuckling at Boyd's shenanigans, but feeling removed from their horseplay. He had been missing too many of their conversations and jokes to fit in. He watched with envy as Boyd and Kyle laughed and wrestled in the sawdust pile.

Radford went back to chopping bark off a maple tree, but stopped when Duke approached him. "You need something?"

Duke shook his head. Radford would give him money, a warm place to stay, even his own body to protect his back, but Duke didn't need any of those things. He needed to fit in here, and to be connected with his brothers. "I just wanted to thank you for helping me frame up Faith's house."

"You'd do it for me."

Duke would do anything for his brothers. That's how it was with them; they shared the load. Always had. Always would.

"I'm courting her, you know."

Radford grinned. "Is that what all that drooling was about last week?"

As brothers, they had smart-mouthed each other all their lives, but Duke couldn't join in today. The situation with Adam bothered him too much.

"If I marry her, Adam Dearborn will become part of our family."

"Whoa!" The humor fled Radford's eyes. "You've known this woman a month maybe? You're falling a little fast, aren't you?"

He was. He knew that. But he also knew Faith was the woman he wanted to marry, and that he'd lose the chance if he didn't move fast. Faith and her aunts were the talk of the town, and any eligible man would jump at the chance to make Faith his wife. Her financial situation wouldn't allow her a lengthy courtship. She needed a husband and provider now, and would be forced to marry soon. She wouldn't have to wait or look elsewhere because Duke was eager to marry her. He wanted her companionship, her passion, her love. He wanted what his brothers had with their wives.

"Marriage will bring you more than a full-time bed-partner, Duke. You'll be responsible for her aunts and her children. That's a heavy load to carry, although I suspect Adam could benefit from a little guidance. That boy has a worldly, troubled look in his eyes that concerns me. And it should concern you too, if you're really planning on marrying his sister."

Duke's sheriff's pay, added to a generous income from the mill, would allow him to support all of them. Radford, who got an equal cut of the mill profits, would know that; he was just jumping to unfair conclusions about Adam and couching his bias in concern for Duke's financial welfare. "Faith is his guardian. The boy's mother died two months ago."

Radford's shoulders lowered and compassion replaced the wariness in his eyes. "That's a shame. I feel for the boy."

"Then let him be friends with Rebecca. He just moved to town, and she's the only person who has been friendly to him."

"He's being too friendly. He's giving Rebecca gifts."

"Adam said he didn't give her the parasol."

"Rebecca thinks he did."

"Did she see him leave it? Or did he tell her he left it?"

"No."

"Then it's unfair to assume he's guilty. The parasol was stolen from Archer's Apothecary."

Radford blew out a breath. "Which makes this situation even worse."

"Which means it could have been left by anyone. Or perhaps Rebecca got it for herself."

Radford's eyes sparked with insult and outrage. "If you're insinuating that my daughter would—"

"Of course not. I'm just pointing out that other possibilities exist."

"Well, I don't like any of them. And I'm sorry for Adam, but I don't want him around Rebecca. He needs to find a boy his age who can be his friend."

"What's so threatening about him befriending Rebecca?"

"He's leading her astray. She never was in trouble at school until she met Adam. And now she has a stolen parasol in her possession."

The irritation in Radford's voice brought Kyle and Boyd over. Kyle brushed sawdust off his clothes. "What's going on over here?"

"I invited Faith and the children to the mill this evening," Duke said, but kept his eyes on Radford. "If you can't be cordial, stay away from them."

"I never said I disliked the boy. I dislike his pursuit of Rebecca. I'm only guilty of being a father."

"Wrong, Radford. You're being narrow-minded and overprotective as always."

Radford's face reddened. "Maybe so, but at least my thinking isn't clouded by lust."

"You think this is about lust?"

"I think you and the lady should spend some time alone before you put your neck in a noose."

Duke took a menacing step forward. His feelings for Faith went far beyond lust, and he felt insulted on her behalf.

Boyd stepped between them, clapping his hands over their shoulders. "If your bickering is going to lead to a fight, you two are leaving me in a real quandary here. I would wager on Radford winning, but then our good sheriff puffs up like a boiler ready to burst a seam and makes me reconsider. How's a man to make a good wager when you're both such hotheads?"

"No one is going to fight," Radford said, turning back to work as if nothing had happened.

Kyle nudged Duke's sore shoulder. "Before you overheat, I can use some of that steam to help move this timber."

And so they went to work. Duke fumed silently, irritated with Radford, irritated with himself. Faith was deserving of more respect. She and the children would hopefully become part of his family soon, and Radford needed to lose his attitude.

Adam did need a guiding hand, but what thirteen-year-old boy didn't? Adam wouldn't compromise Rebecca. Even if he tried, Rebecca was smart enough to walk away. Radford wasn't giving her enough credit, and that annoyed Duke too.

Pain sawed at his shoulder while he pounded grappling hooks into a drag of pine logs. He liked owning and working the mill, but his shoulder resented the hard effort tonight. He couldn't afford to lose the generous stream of income it brought him, but more important, he couldn't lose the connection it gave him with his brothers. And that's why his argument with Radford grated on him.

He wanted his family to approve of Faith. She was a beautiful, smart woman running a decent business. Anna Levens had assured him that Faith and her aunts were honest women, and that nothing untoward was going on at the greenhouse behind his back. He was proud of Faith's gardening abilities and her talent with healing. And he wanted to marry her.

Kyle nudged Duke's thigh with his hand maul then pointed it toward the road. "You have visitors."

The instant Duke saw Faith, his anger drained away. Cora ran across the yard to meet him. "Can I ride the horses?" she asked, her eyes fixed on the team of Percherons that were pulling a drag of timber to the sawmill.

He chucked her under the chin. "Sorry, princess. You can't ride these beasts, but I know something you'll like even better." He walked her to a mountain of sawdust. "You can climb all the way to the top if you want to." His boyhood experience proved it unlikely she would get halfway up; climbing the pile of pea-sized wood chips was like climbing an hourglass filled with sand.

Cora dove in hands first and gave the sawdust pile her full attention.

Faith and Adam walked up. "No wonder you wanted me to see this," Faith said, her pretty eyes taking in the buildings and mountains of stacked lumber and hewn trees in the yard.

He'd wanted her to see that he had plenty to offer, that he could support her and her family, but now that Radford had slapped him awake, it seemed like a dumb idea. He didn't want Faith, or any woman, to marry him for security any more than he wanted to marry because of lust. He would gladly support a wife, but he wanted the passion and love that burned between his brothers and their wives.

If Faith married him for security it wouldn't be enough for either of them.

Faith frowned. "Is something wrong?"

"No," he said, but everything was wrong because all he could think about was kissing her. Was this intense need just lust?

He could slug Radford for planting doubt in his head.

"The heat in your eyes could ignite your lumberyard," she whispered, continuing the flirtatious game they'd been playing for two weeks.

He wanted to touch her and kiss her and make love to her every night for the rest of his life. He'd never felt more sure of anything.

His gut insisted Faith was the one. And Radford could stay away if he didn't approve.

Sighing, he knelt down and had Adam lift Cora onto his shoulders. She didn't weigh more than a full picnic basket, but his sore shoulder wouldn't allow him to lift her above his head. He walked her and the others past towering pallets of stacked lumber and piles of hewn timber being readied for the saw.

Cora waved at the horses as Kyle drove their team of Percherons to the barn for the night. Adam was so busy exclaiming over the size of the mill when they entered the office, he walked into the statue of Duke's father.

"Sorry sir," he said, before he realized he'd just apologized to a huge wooden carving. "Gosh, it looks just like a real person."

Duke chuckled at the boy's surprise. "Don't be embarrassed. That statue surprises everybody. My brother Boyd is a master carver. He made the statue in my father's likeness to honor him. My dad started this mill thirty-five years ago with an axe and a band saw?"

"That's your dad?" Cora asked from her perch on Duke's shoulders.

Faith reached up and straightened Cora's stocking. "It's a statue that looks like his dad, sweetheart."

"What's all this stuff on the walls?" Adam asked, inspecting a circular saw blade hanging from a metal hook.

"We keep our parts here so we can find them when we need them."

He let Adam inspect the tools and saws and grapple hooks that lined the wall, understanding the boy's keen interest. One of Duke's earliest memories was gaping at all the strange, exciting items displayed like a wall of toys. They weren't playthings of course, but as a boy, anything that could cut, shoot, or pound made his hands itch to use it.

"Come on. I'll show you how those blades work." He took them into the mill building, and they clapped their hands over their ears. Adam watched the huge circular blade in awe, Faith gaped in fear, and Cora rocked her legs as if telling Duke to giddy-up and get out of there.

They stayed long enough to watch the head sawyer slab a maple then hurried outside away from the screaming noise.

Adam turned in a slow circle to survey the mill. "I want to work here." He faced Duke, his expression enthralled. "I'll do anything. I'll shovel sawdust, or carry lumber, or anything at all."

Faith shook her head. "It's too dangerous for you."

"My brothers and I worked here as soon as we could fetch and carry," Duke told her. He took Cora back to the sawdust pile where she dove in with childish delight. "I started learning how to run the saw when I was Adam's age."

Faith pointed at the mill. "That big saw? In there?"

He nodded.

"Good heavens." She pressed her hand to her stomach as if the thought alone made her nauseous.

"I wouldn't let Adam near the blade," he said, causing both Faith and Adam to react—Faith with horror, Adam with wild optimism in his eyes.

Faith shook her head. "This is no place for a boy"

Adam's expression fell, but he kept quiet, his eyes begging Duke to convince her otherwise.

"I have to talk to my brothers first, but we have plenty of safe jobs for a boy Adam's age." And Radford couldn't deny they needed an intelligent boy with a strong back around the mill.

Faith surveyed the lumberyard as if seeking evidence of a safe job. Adam looked for Duke's brothers, who were in the yard finishing up for the day. Duke could tell when Adam spotted Radford; the optimism drained from the boy's face and he hung his head.

"Never mind," Adam said. "I have a job at the store, and Faith needs me at the greenhouse."

But Duke knew Adam needed to be at the mill with other men he could watch and learn from. He needed a chance to become a man he could be proud of.

Chapter Twenty

Faith made room for Iris on the scratchy wool blanket that she'd spread in the lumber wagon. Duke had filled the box with straw, and was taking all of them to Dunkirk to watch the Independence Day parade.

"It's not a coach and four," Iris said, "but it'll get us there."

"I like it." Adam moved to the front to sit with Dahlia, who was spinning a tale for Cora about turning straw to gold. Tansy and Aster were in the back sharing Faith's blanket.

"I couldn't allow Duke to pay for the street rail for all of us," Faith explained.

Iris lifted her eyebrows. "'Duke' is it? Hmmm, sounds like you two are getting friendly."

Faith lifted her chin. "That was the plan, wasn't it?"

Tansy patted Faith's arm. "Ignore her, dahlin'. She's jealous of your youth and beauty."

"Of course she is. Our seven-month age difference has always come between us."

Tansy's mouth gaped. "Did I just hear sarcasm from you, child? Lord! You must stay away from Iris. She'll turn you into a sarcastic, jealous viper like herself."

Cyrus, who was up front with Duke and Patrick, clicked his tongue and started their wagon toward Dunkirk and the fireworks. Iris gripped the edge of the box and arched a black eyebrow at Tansy

"No wonder you're all aflutter. I didn't realize Mr. Daaaahlin' would be joining us."

"Neither did I," Tansy whispered.

"It must make you breathless to see him handle those massive horses."

"God, yes." Tansy pressed her palm to her heart. "I can't keep my eyes off the man."

Faith laughed with Aster and Iris.

"What?" Tansy glared at them with feigned innocence. "What is so humorous about a woman appreciating a man while he works?"

"Not a thing," Iris said, "I've always enjoyed watching my male friends work."

Tansy pursed her lips. "You have a filthy mouth, lady"

"No, dahlin', it's your filthy mind that twisted my words. And I'm not a lady."

Tansy lowered her voice. "If I didn't love you so much, I'd fill your feminine syringe bottle with peppermint tea."

"Ooh, it sounds exhilarating."

Faith hid her smile, but Aster howled from the belly, openly appreciating the bawdy humor that had kept them sane at the brothel.

"Mama, what are you all laughing about?" Cora asked.

"Yeah, what are you ladies doing back there?" Patrick hollered.

Faith felt like she'd been caught peeing in the straw. Two weeks ago she'd been furious with Iris for risking their reputation by acting too outrageous with Patrick, and here she was sharing brothel humor within earshot of the sheriff!

"Tansy almost fell off the wagon," Iris said, lounging against the side of the wagon. "Don't worry, Mr. Dahlin', she's still with us."

Tansy leaned over and pinched Iris's thigh. "I'm going to use an infusion made from poison ivy instead!"

Faith clapped her hand over her mouth to hide her laugh, loving her aunts despite, or maybe because of, their irreverent humor.

They left the wagon at Duke's friend's house on Seventh Street then they walked to Central Avenue to watch the parade. Crowds of people lined both sides of the street, and the crush pressed Faith against Duke's hard body.

He stood behind her, but she could feel his torso shift as he leaned down to speak to her. "Best parade I've ever been to," he said near her ear.

"The parade hasn't started yet, Sheriff."

"I hadn't noticed."

His warm breath on her neck made her shiver in the July heat. If Cora and Adam weren't standing beside her, she would risk a playful retort, but they were trapped in an endless crowd of people cheering as the first fire company marched toward them, their hose cart proudly leading the way as the marching band followed behind playing the national anthem.

Faith watched the long procession of fire companies pass. Then carriages with prominent citizens rolled by, followed by a cluster of bicycles that delighted Adam, and Cora, who had charmed her way onto Duke's shoulders. When the last cyclist waved, the crowd followed the parade to Washington Square to hear a local reverend invoke a blessing on the nation, and the mayor read the Declaration of Independence.

Every surge and shift of the crowd brought Duke's body against Faith's. He touched her back with wide splayed fingers, making her skin tingle in five places. His thigh brushed hers when they strolled arm in arm. When he stood behind her, his groin occasionally nudged her bottom, warning that he was close enough to devour her. And God forgive her wanton ways, but she wished he would.

She was relieved when he took Cora and went to buy beverages for them. His flirting and teasing and hot kisses were making her crazy.

And so was Iris. The blasted woman was flaunting her desire for Patrick and not watching a word she said. Faith whispered to her to behave, but Iris was preoccupied with Patrick.

"Why aren't you married, Patrick?"

"I've never had the urge."

"I think you enjoy women too much to settle for just one."

Faith nearly choked. Discreet flirting was one thing. But to have this reckless conversation in the middle of a crowded park was just begging for trouble. Especially when Iris and her exotic looks drew as much attention as the parade.

"It's not the one-woman part that's kept me a bachelor, sweetheart. I was waiting for the right woman." He fit his palm to her waist and pulled her against him. "I was waiting for you," he said in a sinfully husky voice.

To Faith's utter shock, he pulled Iris into an alley as if she were a dockside hussy.

By dusk, every nerve in Faith's body was tense. Iris and Patrick had only slipped away for a minute, but it was long enough for Duke to notice their absence and raise an eyebrow at Patrick when the group rejoined and walked to the lake. The crowd gasped and sighed at the colorful display in the dark sky but all Faith could see was her future shattering like the fireworks and burning out one hope at a time.

How would she and her aunts build a respectable life here if they all behaved as if they still lived in a brothel?

Chapter Twenty-one

Faith opened the doors and windows to air the smell of paint out of the house. Now that the walls were plastered, Tansy was painting like she was possessed. She was in Faith's bedchamber talking to Cora when Faith entered the room.

"Look at that bland wall for the last time Tansy waved her hand in a grand arc. "I'm going to paint rolling hills of green grass, with buttercups and purple clover and lavender, and a little gray pony grazing by a crystal clear stream."

Cora's eyes widened. "We're going to have a pony in our room?"

Tansy tittered. "Not a real one, dahlin', but if it's all right with your mother, I'll paint a picture of one on your wall."

"Wouldn't it be easier to leave it blue?" Faith asked.

Tansy's expression fell. "I haven't sketched or painted in fifteen years, but this big empty wall has inspired me to try. I thought a pony would make Cora happy. But if you'd rather leave it blue—"

"No. Go ahead. Cora will love it," Faith said, remembering the half-finished drawing Tansy had left on their kitchen table years ago. Tansy had later tossed the beautiful sketch into the cookstove and declared her talent dead. Her talent wasn't dead. Tansy was. Inside. But it warmed Faith's heart to see that she was corning back to life and finding her desire to paint again.

While Cora was occupied watching Tansy, Faith slipped out of the bedchamber and found Iris painting the room she shared with Dahlia.

"Blue does not suit me," Iris said, scowling at the wall. "I'd prefer something more dramatic, like red."

"I'm not surprised. I think you'd choose the boldest, most outlandish of anything to get attention," Faith said, unable to hide her irritation.

Iris gaped, her paintbrush suspended in mid-air.

"Don't look at me like I have three heads. You know why I'm upset with you."

"I'm afraid I don't, but I think you're going to tell me."

Exasperated, Faith pushed the newly hung door shut to keep their conversation private. "Your behavior with Patrick last night was abominable."

Iris sighed and lowered her paintbrush to her side. "The second that man smiles at me, I forget everything but him."

"Then don't see him in public."

"Was I that bad?"

"You went into an alley with him, Aunt Iris! I can't believe I was the only one in the crowd who noticed."

"I won't see him anymore." She sighed, her contrition melting Faith's anger. "I was going to stop anyhow."

"Are you in love with him?"

"I don't know. All I know is I'm in trouble." She tossed her brush into the pail of paint. "I'll tell him not to call anymore."

"That's not necessary. I'm just asking you to show some restraint in public and act like a respectable lady."

"I'll never be respectable, Faith. Two months ago I was a prostitute. How am I supposed to go from being a whore to a lady?"

"By *trying*." Iris was making excuses because she was afraid. She was a fish out of water in this pretty little village. Patrick had hooked her, and she was fighting the tug of her heart. And for the first time, Faith understood how difficult this move was for her aunts. For her, it was a new beginning filled with hope; for them, it had to be a constant trial to shed their old ways and make themselves over into women they could barely recognize. But Iris's struggle was greater, because her true personality bubbled and surged like a geyser, throwing forth intermittent jets of the irreverent, outrageous and loving woman she was inside.

"Iris, you're not a prostitute anymore," Faith said softly, feeling a new sympathy and understanding for all her aunts. Her previous annoyance fell by the wayside.

"Then who am I?"

"Anyone you want to be."

Iris scoffed. "Not when you've lived my life. You know what you are every time a man ogles you."

"Maybe you should ask Patrick what he sees when he looks at you. If you're not afraid of his answer," she added as she left the room.

Chapter Twenty-two

On Wednesday afternoon Faith was watering herbs with Iris when Aster rushed into the greenhouse. "The sheriff left this for you," she said, handing Faith a large cloth-wrapped bundle.

Faith's heart skipped, and she set her watering can aside. This had to be her new dress for the lawn party Duke was taking her to this evening. He had invited her during the Fourth of July parade, but she'd declined because she didn't own an appropriate dress. When he offered to purchase her a gown, Aster had poked her in the ribs and told her to accept the man's offer.

So she had. But he'd insisted on choosing the dress for her, which terrified her. Would he know that a day dress wouldn't be suitable for the party? Or that a ball gown would be too fancy?

Iris set her watering can in a flat of horehound, and crowded in to watch the unveiling.

Faith's hands shook as she unpinned the silk wrapper and lifted out the dress she would wear. The bodice and skirt were made of light-brown french silk layered over a froth of creamy lace. Duke had included a silk parasol, and a brown hat trimmed with poppies, and had wrapped the gifts in a gorgeous matching shawl. The dress suited her coloring, and was perfectly appropriate for a lawn party, making her wonder if he'd chosen the outfit on his own. Even the size looked perfect.

"You better try the shoes," Iris said. "You can't dance on sore feet."

Faith handed the skirt to Aster, and let Iris help her on with one shoe. It fit perfectly. "Duke must have slipped into our house and taken my measurements while I was sleeping," she said with an amazed laugh.

A mischievous sparkle lit Iris's eyes. "I think he didn't have to sneak. What have you two been doing in the bathhouse every night?"

Things that turned her body to warm clay, that made her ache to be molded by Duke's large, thrilling hands.

"Too naughty to divulge?" Iris asked. She rose to her feet. "Make the most of that pretty dress he gave you, and drive the man wild tonight. Get him on his knee, begging you to marry him," she advised.

"I'm trying," Faith admitted. She felt no embarrassment; brothel life had killed their need for modesty with each other.

"Good girl." Iris turned her toward the bathhouse. "Now, hurry with your bath so I can style your hair. I can hardly wait to see the sheriff's face when he sees you this evening."

Aster scooped up the bundle of clothing. "I'll lay out your wardrobe in your bedchamber," she said.

Faith spent the next two hours being scrubbed, rubbed with herb-scented oils, and dressed and polished by four experts in the art of seduction. It felt sinfully luxurious to be dressing for her first outing with a suitor, and she wished she could tell Duke about her aunts and how hard they were trying to help.

"Ooh... beautiful," Iris cooed, patting Faith's hair. She'd pulled it up and left a waterfall of ringlets down the back of Faith's head, and a long, dangling curl by each ear. She added the hat, tilted it at a slightly jaunty angle, and stepped back with a satisfied smile. "I wish we had a mirror so you could see yourself."

Faith stood and gazed down at her dress. The skirt was pleated with two panels that opened in a wide vee down the front to reveal a drapery of creamy silk that rippled like a frothy waterfall to her toes. The breast and cuffs were trimmed with matching silk and set off with poppy-red ribbons. She had never owned a dress she hadn't made for herself. Her sewing skills were passable, but at the brothel she'd only needed her plain, serviceable day gowns. She had to add yards of lace and several ribbons to transform her best dress into a worthy church outfit.

She stroked her palms over the luxuriant material with sinful affection. "Tell me I'm not dreaming all of this."

"You're not, but the sheriff's going to think he is the second he lays eyes on you. Come on. Everyone's waiting."

Faith followed Iris out of the bedchamber and into the dining room where Dahlia, Aster, and Tansy were playing a game of Draw dominoes with Cora and Adam at the table. The instant they spotted her, the room fell silent. Giddy with pleasure, Faith opened her parasol, angled it like a sunshade, and turned in a slow circle.

Cora's eyes goggled. "You look like a princess, Mama."

Faith felt like a princess.

Iris beamed like a proud mother, while Aster, Tansy, and Dahlia gave her a rousing round of applause.

Adam gawked, and looked worried. "Do men have to know how to choose a lady's wardrobe?"

Faith leaned down and kissed his cheek. "I don't think it's required for courting," she said, "but the sheriff's knowledge sure impressed this lady."

"You should let him buy all your dresses."

"That's not a bad idea, Adam." She gave Iris a playful wink then kissed Cora good-bye.

The knock at the door sent her stomach flutter-birds into a wild flurry of flapping and swooping that left her breathless. With a hopeful heart, she greeted her handsome suitor, praying she was greeting her future husband.

⊷⊶

Duke stood in the warm July night, staring in stunned appreciation. He'd known the hue of the dress would complement Faith's whiskey-colored eyes and dark hair, and had imagined how beautiful she would look in it, but he hadn't come close to the vision standing before him.

"It's a perfect fit," she said, stepping outside to show off the garment. She turned one full circle then faced him, her skin glowing, her eyes shining. "I've never owned such a beautiful thing. Thank you, Duke."

"It was made for you," he said, truthfully. He'd paid a local seamstress a handsome fee to make the dress in five days. The woman had suggested green or yellow silk for the gown. He knew very little about female wardrobe, but he knew what he liked about Faith, and he was glad he'd chosen the brown silk.

Faith poked her shoe from beneath the hem of her dress. "How did you know my shoe size?"

"I measured the print you left in the sawdust at my mill."

A slow, appreciative smile broke across her face. "How clever you are. No wonder you make such a good sheriff."

He couldn't keep his eyes off her lips. They were lush and shiny, as if she'd just moistened them with her tongue, and all he could think about was tasting her sweet mouth.

The evening was warm with a light breeze, and he'd been comfortable in his suit until now, until Faith's sparkling eyes and inviting smile made him burn to make love to her. He tugged his collar away from his hot neck, and lifted the cloth sack in his hand. "I brought licorice sticks for Adam and Cora since I'm stealing you away for the evening."

Her smile softened, making her more beautiful, more desirable. "For a man who carries a gun, you sure have a kind heart."

The tender look she gave him shook his willpower. He touched his thumb to her bottom lip, so tempted. Her lips parted and her chin lifted, her willingness giving him deep pleasure, but he forced himself to step inside before he shocked her neighbors who were strolling by.

The licorice sticks thrilled Cora and commanded her attention, allowing him to quickly return to Faith. She held his arm as they started for the party, but he sensed she was nervous. "You'll know some of the guests," he said. "My brothers and sisters-in-law will be there."

"It'll be lovely to see them and your mother again," she said, clinging to his arm.

"Mother is home with Rebecca watching all the grandchildren." He wanted Faith's closeness, but not her fear. "What are you nervous about?"

"I'm not nervous." She huffed out a laugh. "Yes, I am. I've never been to a lawn party."

"It's the social event of the season for this village. The money profits the church society. It's festive, but not as fancy or formal as a wedding."

"I've never been to a wedding, either."

Alarm bells went off in his head and he glanced at her, confused. "What about your own wedding?"

An odd, almost panicked expression crossed her face and she lowered her lashes. "Um... we married at home with just my family there. I meant I'd never been to anyone else's wedding. My mother didn't go to social events," she admitted quietly. "I'm dreadfully inexperienced. I've read books on social etiquette, but if you think I'll embarrass you, please take me back home."

He squeezed her arm against his side, not knowing what to think of her odd life. All he knew was that he was proud to have her on his arm. "You'll be the most beautiful woman there," he said, knowing it was true. In his eyes, she would always be the most beautiful woman.

All Faith knew was she would be the most terrified woman at the lawn party. "I see someone bought the Colburn house," she said, changing the subject and trying not to sound like her heart was breaking. She couldn't afford the house, but she loved it, and as long as it remained empty, she could dream of owning it someday.

"I'm surprised it sat empty this long," Duke replied. He stopped abruptly and faced her. "Faith, I talked to my brothers about having Adam work at the mill. If you'll let him, he can work with me on Saturdays."

Her stomach plummeted. She'd hoped the conversation would turn more personal, that he would ask if she cared for him, if she could love him, if she would marry him. He only wanted to talk about his business.

"I won't let anything happen to him."

Her first inclination was to say no, absolutely not, but Duke looked so pleased that she couldn't refuse him outright. "It's kind of you to offer, but I need him at the greenhouse—and he has a job at the store two days a week. That's enough for a boy his age."

"He would like working the mill—"

"No." Her face burned for cutting him off, but the mill was too dangerous. They had too much peril in their lives already without adding that huge whirling blade to the mix. "I appreciate your kindness, but I need Adam at home."

"All right. I understand." Duke brushed his knuckles across her cheek. "Maybe when he gets a little older you won't need his help in the greenhouse."

She looked away from the disappointment in his eyes, feeling she'd failed both him and Adam. "I'm sorry."

"Don't apologize for caring about the boy. He's lucky to have you looking out for him." He took her arm and started walking. "I hope your shoes are comfortable, because Damon's band is playing tonight and everyone will be dancing."

"They fit like they were made for me."

"They were." He gave her a wink that made her heart skip. "Relax, Faith. You'll enjoy the party."

She heard the gathering before she saw it, and when the judge's house came into view, she gasped in astonishment. Chinese lanterns lit the whole vast lawn and the people promenading the grounds. Tables were set under awnings and on a large front porch that Faith's mother would have coveted. Off to one side was a carriage house, strung with lights and filled with music from the string quartet.

Duke ushered her onto the lawn, tall, composed and sure of himself. She clung to his arm, scared stiff that she would be exposed as an imposter.

Judge Barker and his wife greeted them. Faith assured the judge, who had witnessed her scare at the circus, that her back was good as new. He encouraged her to enjoy the evening then took his well-dressed wife off to the dance floor where Faith saw several men, including Kyle and Radford Grayson, dancing with their wives.

Everyone in the village seemed to be there, talking and laughing, milling around and filling the grounds so completely, Faith felt a frisson of panic. Judge Stone could be lurking in this crowd and she wouldn't even know it. Already she'd seen four men with full white beards and snowy hair straying from beneath their hats, and it scared her witless that she couldn't be sure it wasn't Stone until the man was within feet of her.

She moved in a stupor, too scared to let go of Duke's arm. Maybe it was just the party and the crush of people that upset her. Maybe Stone would never find her. She'd been careful not to leave a trail he could follow, but the man was as sly as a fox.

Duke poured her a glass of strawberry punch and took a glass of wine for himself. "I'd prefer ale," he said, "but I think the church society would frown if I rolled in a keg for the boys."

"Wine will do nicely," she said then pulled the glass from his fingers and swallowed the contents. With a wobbly smile, she gave him back the empty glass. "I'll try the punch now."

"You're a surprise a minute," he said, giving her a warm, flirtatious grin.

"Just trying to keep your interest, Sheriff." And keep herself from panicking. She didn't belong with these people. How could she court and possibly marry Duke when she didn't fit into his world?

He set his empty glass on a tray, the move bringing his mouth near her ear. "If you arouse my interest any more, we'll have to leave the party."

Her breath sailed out and heat rose to her face in a volcanic rush. "I need another glass of wine."

His low, seductive laugh sent a tingle of awareness down her neck and spine and caused longing to pool within her. Did he know what he did with that suggestive, intimate voice of his?

He pressed his palm to her waist. "Dance with me."

"My legs are shaking too much."

"If we don't move, I'm going to kiss you."

"Oh, my. Bring the wine."

His wonderful, rich laughter turned all eyes on him—on them—and Faith wanted to duck under the lace skirt of the beverage table. But Duke's long fingers circled her hand and he led her to the floor.

With a confidence she envied, he slipped his arm around her waist and fit his hand to hers. A half-smile touched his lips as he took a step and drew her into a waltz. Faith's mother and aunts had taught her to dance, but this was Faith's first waltz with a man. Duke's hard shoulder and firm hand held her steady, his muscles flexing with every step he took. Warmth filled his eyes, and something more passionate and intense showed in his gaze as he drew her closer, moving his tall, hard body in perfect rhythm to the music.

The sweet sound of violins and the darker strains of a cello washed over her. With each turn he pulled her closer until his long legs brushed her skirt, and the crowd around them slowly disappeared. Faith was floating in a dream, living in a world she'd scarcely dared to imagine, anchored in the strong arms of a man who stood for truth and justice and everything honest and good in life.

Hints of his cologne and soap teased her nose, and she wanted to move closer, to press her lips to his neck and taste his warm skin. The lanterns cast a soft glow across the taut, freshly shaved skin of his strong jaw. He was all muscles and angles, tall and rock solid, beautiful and majestic like a mountain.

He drew her closer on their next turn and brushed his lips to her ear. "This song is 'Kissing in the Dark' by Foster and Cooper. I sent Damon's bandleader a note earlier and asked him to play it when I brought my lady to the dance floor."

His lady? She was his lady? "It's... beautiful," she said, enjoying the song and the seductive mix of intimacy Duke brought to it.

"So are you." The look in his eyes made her feel beautiful. "I'm glad you like it."

"The song? Or kissing in the dark?"

His laugh drew so many curious looks that Faith lowered her chin and used his wide chest to shield her burning face. As soon as the song ended, she nudged him off the dance floor. She couldn't remain in his arms a moment longer. He made her dreams seem possible, and she couldn't bear to believe, only to have her hopes crushed in the end. Because he could walk away.

But she couldn't let him walk away, even knowing she didn't belong in his world, that this decent, honorable man deserved a better woman than she, because Adam and Cora needed him and the life he could give them.

And who was she fooling but herself? She was falling bonnet over boot tops for Duke Grayson.

He stopped by the beverage table and handed her a glass of punch. While she was quenching her thirst, a rugged-looking man with auburn hair and bushy sideburns spoke to Duke. "Taylor's making a hard push this year, but he'll have to sway a lot of voters to win the election, Sheriff. A big campaign don't mean beans compared to your eight years of service."

"Taylor's a good man, Sam, and so are most of the other candidates. If the vote falls his way, I'll support him." Duke paused to introduce Faith to his deputy, Sam Wade then turned back to his conversation.

"But you're the man who keeps the ruffians and scalawags out of our county," Sam said.

While the men talked, Faith slipped a glass of wine off the table, angled her back to Duke, and poured it into her punch.

Another man joined the conversation and started the long line of introductions to Duke's friends. Duke cast an apologetic look at her, as if he wanted to be with her but couldn't neglect his supporters. Smiling away his concern, Faith finished her wine punch and discreetly made herself another. Only when his brothers stopped by with Evelyn, Claire, and Amelia did Faith feel a measure of comfort. But they were soon swallowed in a crowd of friends and neighbors who displayed enormous respect for the Graysons and for Duke as their sheriff.

Duke finally excused himself from his conversation and drew her away from the table where they'd been trapped for half an hour. Her glass was halfway to her mouth when he said, "Don't drink too much of that wine. I have plans for later."

Wine punch sloshed over the edge of her glass and dribbled down her knuckles, and a roguish grin tipped his mouth. "If we were alone I would lick that off your fingers," he said quietly.

Her breath whooshed out. "You... you don't miss anything, do you?"

"Maybe because I can't keep my eyes off you."

His attention thrilled and excited her, and filled her with guilt. He was better at flirting than she was, but he was baiting his own trap with every intimate innuendo. Because when he finally captured her, he would trap himself into marriage—and perhaps a lifetime of despising his wife.

Would he hate her if he found out the truth about her past? She couldn't bear his hatred. Would it make a difference to him that she hadn't been a prostitute?

She was in over her head. Why hadn't she sought a man with less rigid values? Why did she have to choose one of the most respected men in town? But she hadn't chosen him. He'd chosen her, and most of what she'd told him had been the truth. But everything she'd left unsaid was worse than a lie.

Her mind seesawed, arguing one way then the other until she admitted she couldn't settle anything tonight. The wine was making her head light. All she could do was straighten her spine and play out the evening.

Minutes later, Duke escorted her inside the most opulent house she'd ever seen. Glittering chandeliers hung from the ceilings, velvet draperies dressed large windows and complemented the paisley and floral wallpaper. Plush carpets covered the floors, and a grand staircase climbed from a spacious foyer to a candlelit second-floor landing.

But it was massive golden oak hall tree, that snared her attention. The seven-foot beveled mirror reflected her image, allowing her to see the beauty of her dress, and the man at her side. They were a handsome, well-dressed couple, suited in looks, suited to the surroundings. Hope surged through her, and she met Duke's questioning gaze in the mirror. Physically she could blend into his world. Maybe that would be enough. If she hid her fears, maybe no one would ever know she didn't belong here.

The jaunty angle of her hat made her smile, and Faith silently thanked Iris for giving her a touch of attitude with which to face the evening.

They filled their plates at the buffet table then found seats at a table on the porch. Faith nodded to their tablemate, Dr. Milton, the man who'd advised Duke to abstain from using his arm then later came to her greenhouse to warn her not to prescribe harmful treatments to the women visiting her. She gave the snob a cordial nod then turned to her supper.

Another man joined them, and Faith looked up to see Wayne Archer sit opposite Duke. She felt the tension inch higher. He nodded to Faith then Duke.

"Archer," Duke said, greeting the man with a brief nod before returning to his meal.

Not only Duke's doctor to deal with, but Duke's rival, and her nemesis, as well? Her appetite fled.

Dr. Milton laid his napkin over his partially eaten meal. "How is your Evergreen House coming along, Mrs. Wilkins?"

"Quite well, thank you." She wasn't offering the doctor or apothecary any information.

"Mrs. Guthrey has been raving about some sort of hot bath and massage you're giving her," Dr. Milton said. "She claims you're restoring her health."

"I'm sure you know that Mrs. Guthrey's discomfort comes from working too hard. The bath eases her aches and gives her a chance to rest. The massage and balm soothe her muscles. The treatment would rejuvenate anybody with her ailment."

"She claims you give her an herbal tea remedy and a balm to rub onto her skin. It distresses me to have an uneducated woman treating my patients. Are you not afraid of injuring someone with your concoctions?"

Duke set his fork on his plate, but Faith slid her foot over and tapped his. She could handle the doctor's arrogance. She didn't want Duke making enemies on her behalf.

"I know my herbs, doctor. It's true I haven't the benefit of your formal education, but I've read numerous medical texts like the pharmacopoeia, and studied anatomy, botany, herbal medicine, and Eastern healing techniques. The tea I give Mrs. Guthrey contains chamomile and willow bark to relax her and ease her pain. The balm is a topical treatment for the same purpose. Mrs. Guthrey is likely suffering pain in her gluteus maximus and biceps femoris muscles because of a pinched sciatic nerve."

His eyebrows lifted before he could hide his surprise. "Impressive, Mrs. Wilkins, but what is causing this situation?"

"I suspect she twisted her hips and strained her back by doing work that's too heavy and strenuous for her."

"Reading a few books cannot compare to years of study and practice. I learned alongside a knowledgeable, well-respected doctor."

"Then I'm surprised you advised Sheriff Grayson not to use his arm until his shoulder injury healed. Surely you could see that his deltoid, triceps, and biceps muscles were shrinking and growing stiff. By the time the sheriff asked for my help, he could barely lift his arm as high as his shoulder."

"Are you suggesting that your treatment has improved his condition?"

"She doesn't have to suggest, Doc. See for yourself," Duke said, lifting his fist above his head.

They had made progress in the five weeks she'd been treating him, but his range of motion was still restricted by shrunken, tender muscles, and it would take several more weeks to completely free up his arm. For him to lift his arm like that had to be unbearably painful. His jaw was clenched, but he stared at the surprised doctor and lowered his arm without a single grunt of pain.

"There's your proof. Her business is a nice addition to the healing arts in this town."

The doctor was silenced, but Archer scoffed. "Sheriff, I realize Mrs. Wilkins is your companion, but you go too far defending someone who dallies in medicine without proper education."

Faith feared Duke was going to throttle Archer, but he shocked her by grinning. "Are you threatened, Archer?"

"Only by the trouble we've been having with those swindlers and thieves you've been letting run loose."

The doctor pushed away from the table. "Excuse me, gentlemen... Mrs. Wilkins, I'm in need of a cheroot and a cup of coffee."

"I'll join you," Archer said, stepping away from the table. He stopped and scowled at Faith. "Your brother bought some glass vials from my store the other day. I would prefer that you come for the items yourself, as I've had some things come up missing of late."

Duke shoved to his feet, but Faith caught his hand. "I'd like another dance if you don't mind?" She stepped around the table then faced Archer. "Rest assured no one in my family will visit your business again."

Duke leaned close to the man, his voice low and controlled. "One rumor, Wayne, even one negative comment about Mrs. Wilkins or her family, and I'll be knocking on your door. And it won't be to make a purchase."

He stepped around Archer and guided Faith down the steps. "I'm sorry," she said as they crossed the yard. "I should have kept quiet."

Duke looked at her with clear admiration. "You were amazing with the doctor."

Relief washed through her, followed by a giddy sense of victory. "So were you," she said. "How did you manage to raise your arm so high without screaming?"

"I knew it was the only way to keep my fist out of Milton's arrogant mouth."

"The doctor *was* rather arrogant."

"He was an ass."

She smiled. "So was Archer. No wonder you don't like the man."

"I don't dislike him or Doc Milton. They've both done good things for the community. Archer's hoping that by discrediting me, it will get him the job as sheriff."

"Why does he even want to be sheriff when he has his apothecary?"

Duke shrugged. "I don't know. And I don't care, as long as Taylor, Phelps, or I win. Archer would ruin our community."

"I'm glad you didn't hit him. I would never want to cause you to fight." And she prayed he would never have to. But Syracuse wasn't that far away, and Judge Stone would never stop looking for her.

"It was Archer's mouth that boiled my blood, not your comments. He glanced at the carriage house where the band was tuning up. "Did you want to dance?"

She shook her head. "Truthfully, I'd rather leave, but I suppose it would look bad."

"Not if we slip away." He guided her through the crowd of people scattered across the lawn, nodding to several guests but not stopping to speak them. When they reached the beverage table, he picked up two glasses of wine. "I'll return the glasses tomorrow."

"Are those for you?" she asked, wondering if this was a side of him he kept hidden. Iris said no one was perfect. What if he had a taste for alcohol?

"They're for us."

"You just warned me not to drink any more."

"Because you were drinking it like punch." He handed a glass to her. "Sip this one."

Before she had a chance to taste it, Duke led her across the side lawn then pulled her behind the carriage house. He hurried them to a side street then walked her to Main. Gas streetlamps cast circles of hazy yellow light across the dusty street.

"That was exhilarating," she said, sipping her wine to calm her racing heart.

He chuckled and slipped his arm around her waist. "I had hoped to have a few more dances with you."

"And I had hoped to use the dance floor to show off this gorgeous dress," she said, watching the play of light and shadow across the silk fabric of her skirt.

"Here I'd thought you wanted to dance so you could get your hands on me."

She laughed. "That too."

"Really?" He stopped and faced her. "Do you enjoy being with me?"

"I would think it's obvious, but yes," she said, her face warming as she spoke aloud the truth in her heart. "I enjoy it very much."

"I want to talk with you in private," he said, leading her down Eagle Street. "Do you have a blanket or towels and a lantern in the greenhouse?"

"Yes, but my anxiety is as strong as my curiosity. Why do you want those things?"

He linked his fingers with hers. "I'm taking you to a swimming hole not far from your place. Colburn dammed a section of the creek behind that building so he could manage his water supply to the gristmill. My brothers and I have been swimming there since we were boys. The mill pond makes a good spot to cool off in the summer."

They stopped at the greenhouse then headed across her backyard Duke carried the towels and a lantern. Faith carried their half-full wineglasses in one hand and lifted her skirt with the other. They followed the bank of the burbling feeder stream that cut through a rutted field clotted with bushy maple trees.

"If I don't break my neck it will be a miracle," she said.

"Just don't spill the wine if you fall," he replied.

She laughed and stumbled, bumping his shoulder. "Oh! I'm sorry. Did I hurt you?"

"No."

Of course not. He wouldn't admit it if she had.

She stepped cautiously, but her ankles wobbled over every ridge and crevice in the rutted ground. "If I ruin my new shoes—"

"I'll buy you another pair." He clamped the towels under his elbow and transferred the lantern to that hand, allowing him to slip his free arm around her waist. "We're almost there, but I'll carry you if you'd like."

"And ruin all my work on your shoulder? Not a chance. Besides, you would break your back if you tried to lift me. I'm wrapped in yards of material."

"Careful, you're tempting me to unwrap you."

"And you're tempting me to run back to my safe little greenhouse."

They laughed quietly in the dark, the two of them sneaking away from a world that judged too harshly and asked too much. The night air was soft against her face and smelled earthy fresh in her nostrils. She liked this place already, and knew she would find her way back as soon as possible. The sound of night peepers filled the night, and she could hear the plop of a toad or frog jumping into the water as they approached a large pond.

The lantern shimmered across the water and gilded the leaves of a maple tree growing at the edge of the pond. Duke set the lantern beneath the tree and spread the towels on the grass. He dimmed the lantern until it illuminated a small circle around it.

"Look up, Faith."

Standing, she lifted her face to a vast night sky peppered with bright glowing stars. Her tension flowed out with her breath. "I haven't looked at the stars or watched the sunset in two months."

Sadness filled her. "How do we forget so quickly? How do we allow ourselves to get too busy to appreciate such simple things as a night sky?"

He didn't answer. Because there wasn't an answer. You either looked for the stars or missed them.

He stood behind her and slipped his arms around her waist, holding her loosely. "My dad could clap his hand on my shoulder and make me feel ten feet tall. A small gesture, but one I'll never forget."

In life, those were the things that mattered most—a night sky, a touch of affection, a smile of approval, all without cost but of immense value to a person's soul. Faith finished her wine in silence, looking at the stars, listening to the rhythm of the night peepers, wishing she could enjoy this without memories and guilt weighing her down.

"My mother visited Fredonia one fall when the leaves were turning, and the smell of ripe grapes filled the air. She told me the church bells sounded like angels singing."

Duke's arms tightened in a gentle hug, as if he understood her heartache, and that words would never console her.

"She wanted to live here in a small house with a big porch and a rose garden, but she never came back."

"Why not?" he asked softly, echoing Faith's own relentless question. Why not? Why hadn't she dared what Faith and her aunts were doing? What had stopped her?

"I don't know." Faith sighed. "Maybe it's best. She would have been disappointed to know there are horse thieves and men like Archer living here."

"Weeds grow in every garden, Faith."

She laughed at his analogy. "You've been spending too much time in my greenhouse."

He nuzzled her neck. "I like spending time with you."

What she felt for him went far beyond *like*. Hot desire, deep admiration, and an embarrassing fondness for his kisses could only begin to describe her feelings for him. Her body was tingling in a so many places, she would sound like the peepers if her nerve endings could emit sound. She wanted to make his body sing like hers, to give him one good reason to marry her. Wasn't that what mattered most to a man? To have a submissive and pleasing wife?

"Faith, why don't you ever talk about your late husband?" He may as well have shoved her into the cold pond. "Doesn't Cora ask about him?"

Her heart clamored, but she warned herself to stay calm. "I don't want her to know the caliber of man who fathered her."

Duke turned her to face him. "Did he hurt you?"

"Not the way you think," she said, trying to find an explanation that would allow them to permanently bury the subject. "Her father was corrupt. I was relieved when he was no longer part of our lives." Her conscience barely balked, because every word was the truth.

And she was done talking about her life for the night. She wanted to head toward her future, not linger in her past. For her own sake. For Cora's and Adam's sakes.

She frowned and upended her empty glass. "We should have brought more wine."

"Are you thirsty?"

"No."

"Nervous then?"

"Yes. I'm not used to standing in the dark with a shadow man."

His mouth quirked. "This shadow man would like to kiss you."

"Permission granted," she whispered, and lifted her mouth to his, giving him her trust and her passion.

His arms slipped around her waist, his empty glass dangling from his long fingers, hers resting against her thigh as their bodies met. She thrilled to his touch, and her wishful heart beat hard, begging him to hear her prayer, to marry her and make her dreams come true. And she would give him the one thing she'd never been able to give another: her heart.

His mouth grew more eager and she fit herself against body, making him groan. He kissed her hard and fast, like he was starving and couldn't control his greed. But maybe she was greedy. She felt desperate and needy. He ground his hips against hers, his hard thigh riding high between her legs as he kissed her like she'd never been kissed in her life.

Because none of the men before Duke had cared about her. She was a whore's daughter unworthy of them.

Her body trembled as she broke the kiss. "Have you ever been in love?" she whispered.

He braced his chin against her forehead, his breathing ragged. "Once," he said. "When I was ten."

She smiled at his honesty, and at the thought of him as a dark-haired, wide-eyed boy.

"She was my teacher, and she had the nerve to marry a man her own age and move away."

Touched by his mix of humor and sincerity, Faith caressed his warm cheek, loving the prickle of new whiskers breaking through his recent shave. "You are so charming. I don't know how any woman could walk away from you."

He leaned back, revealing the sculpted shadows of his face. "Don't walk away, Faith."

"I won't."

"I mean ever." He broke away to kneel by the lantern. He raised the wick, illuminating his handsome face and the hand he held out to her. "Will you marry me?"

Her breath whooshed out. She stared at him, so golden and beautiful kneeling beneath the gilded maple tree, offering the life she'd prayed for.

"I've seen how happy my brothers and their wives are with each other. I didn't think I'd ever find that with anyone until I met you. My head, my heart, and my gut say you're the one for me, and that we can share that same joy and passion. Say you'll be my wife, that we can create a good, happy life together."

To see him on his knee, his gorgeous gaze filled with trust and desire, made her eyes fill with tears.

"Say yes, Faith. Say you'll meet me right here beneath this tree three weeks from now and take your vows with me."

"Oh, Duke..." She linked her fingers with his, wishing she could be more for him, tortured by her conscience, torn by her need for truth and her need for security. She knelt in front of him. "I'd be honored to be your wife."

"I'll make you happy," he promised then sealed the vow with a tender kiss.

"You already have." She cradled his face, the face she would kiss each night and wake to each morning, and vowed in her heart to be perfect for him, to bring him joy and laughter if not truth. Starting now, right here beneath these beautiful stars, she would put her past behind her and think only of their future, of pleasing him, of making sure he never regretted marrying her.

Chapter Twenty-three

Radford dropped his hand maul in the lumberyard and gaped at Duke. "You're what?"

"I'm marrying Faith on August second."

Boyd and Kyle exchanged a shocked glance.

"Stop looking like someone died, fellas. I'm not new at this. I've been courting women since I was sixteen. I don't need months to decide if Faith is the right woman for me. She is, and I'm going to marry her in three weeks. Radford, I'd like you to be my best man."

Radford's jaw dropped farther.

"I stepped in so Evelyn had someone to give her away when she married you. I was hoping you'd stand for my wedding, too." Duke had considered asking Patrick or Boyd, but he wanted Radford to stand beside him and give his blessing, to witness their vows, and to accept Faith and Adam and Cora as part of their family. "I'd like you to do it."

Radford gave him a half nod. "All right. I will." He shook Duke's hand. "Congratulations," he said, but sounded like he was offering his condolences.

Kyle gave Duke's shoulder a hard squeeze. "Does Mother know yet?"

"I told her this morning, and she was pleased. She wants to help Faith plan the wedding."

Boyd whacked Duke upside the head. "You just cost me a two-hour body rub. Claire said you'd propose before summer ended. I said you'd hold out until Christmas."

"So you'll have to rub your wife's body for two hours? What a hardship."

A wicked grin lit Boyd's face. "I'll hate every minute of it." He caught Duke's hand in a firm clasp. "Congratulations. Where's the party?"

"I'm not sure yet."

"We can have it at our house," Radford said.

His offer surprised Duke, and it meant a lot that Radford was trying to be supportive despite his reservations. "Thanks, Rad. I'd like that."

"What can we do to help?" Boyd asked.

"Welcome Faith and Adam and Cora to our family." he said, swelling with pride that his beautiful Faith, his soon-to-be wife, would take her place alongside his lovely sisters-in-laws.

⊷ ⊶

On Tuesday afternoon Dr. Paul Milton limped into the greenhouse. He was the last person Faith wanted to see while feeling so disheartened. The new owners of the Colburn house were beginning to move in. She'd seen men carrying furniture inside all week, and this morning, Nancy Grayson had delivered a housewarming gift.

Aster puffed up like an angry bulldog as she faced the doctor. "If you've come to give us another lecture, Dr. Milton, you just limp your sorry self right back out the door."

Faith gawked at her aunt. Aster had always been blunt, but never intentionally rude. When they'd heard that the doctor had had a buggy accident on Saturday, Aster said he'd needed to be taken down a peg. Faith sent a note wishing him well, and apologizing for her unladylike outburst at the lawn party. She wasn't sorry at all, but she didn't want to antagonize any of Duke's acquaintances, especially when he might need their vote in the election.

"I'd like to speak with Mrs. Wilkins," the doctor said, but Aster blocked his way to the counter where Faith was showing Cora how to use a mortar and pestle to crush peppermint leaves.

"My niece is planning her wedding to the sheriff, and I won't let you rain on her happiness."

Iris and Tansy were a row away clipping herbs for two customers. All four women turned their attention to Aster and the doctor.

His face flushed. "I have no intention of raining on anything, Miss Wilde. I'm seeking a turn in this bath I've been hearing about."

Aster arched a white eyebrow. "Are you referring to the herbal bath we're using as a means to 'swindle money from the innocent ladies in town'? Isn't that what you accused us of?"

"I'm willing to try the bath myself and change my opinion."

Aster shook her head. "Sorry. Doctor, but the bath isn't available to men."

"Sheriff Grayson comes here for treatment, does he not?"

"The sheriff is using our services to assure you kind citizens we're running a respectable business."

"Those of us in the healing profession would like that same assurance."

"Rubbish, Doctor. You're here because your own medicine won't relieve your pain, and you're desperate enough to try our bath. I should boot your arrogant carcass right out the door— but proving you wrong is going to be much more satisfying." She ignored the gasps and titters from Iris and the ladies, and headed toward the bathhouse. "Come along, Doctor. You have the pleasure of being my patient for the morning."

The doctor limped along behind Aster, looking a bit bewildered and browbeaten, which Faith found immensely satisfying. Her aunts gave her constant lessons in handling men. She just wished they could help her silence her conscience. It was killing her to let Duke walk into their marriage blind.

Three days had passed since she'd accepted his proposal, and she could barely think of anything but their upcoming marriage. Their commitment to each other had eased her anxiety about the future and allowed her to return his warmth and affection. Each night after stretching his arm and shoulder, they kissed passionately. She trusted Duke to keep them from going too far because his honor was solid, and because she had no willpower when his hands were on her. But she felt deceitful and undeserving of him, and that wouldn't change as long as her black secrets were between them.

"Is this squished enough?" Cora asked, peering into the mortar bowl at the greenish paste.

"Yes, sweetie. We'll add some lavender after lunch." She kissed the top of Cora's head and reminded herself that marrying Duke was the right thing to do.

Faith fed Cora then put her down for a nap in the pasture, as Cora now referred to their pretty bedchamber. Tansy's talent was impressive, and Faith felt a sense of peace and wonder as she gazed at the pony and the expansive view Tansy had painted on her wall.

She found Tansy whisking her brush across the parlor wall, creating a green and cranberry paisley pattern. "I'll finish the rest tomorrow," the woman said, her eyes lit with excitement.

"It's going to look gorgeous," Faith said. "We'll be the envy of every woman in town."

"Wouldn't that be ironic?"

Faith laughed. "It surely would be." She helped Tansy carry the pails and paint brushes to the greenhouse where they found Aster, Dahlia, and Iris at the counter howling with laughter.

"Dr. Milton shucked his arrogance right along with his clothes," Aster was saying.

"What are you old hens cackling about?" Tansy asked, plunking her pail and brushes on the counter. Faith followed and set her bucket beside Tansy's.

"Aster's telling us about Doc Milton's visit," Dahlia said, her bosoms bouncing from her chuckles.

Faith scanned the greenhouse and was relieved to see it empty.

"Well, you should have seen that man," Aster said, her cheeks more flushed than Faith had ever seen them. "When I dug my fingers into his sore left buttock, he squeaked like a frightened mouse. He says, 'Miss Wilde! What are you doing down there?'" She cackled and pressed her hand to her stomach. "I said, 'Surely, Doctor, you're intelligent enough to realize I'm massaging your ass.'"

"Oh!" Tansy squealed with laughter. "I wish I could have witnessed that."

"Doc says, 'Woman, you do have a foul mouth on you, but I could surely get used to those hands of yours?'" Aster slapped the counter and laughed until she coughed. "You know, I actually liked the man."

Faith's laughter mingled with their howls. She loved these bawdy women and their honest revelations.

"Did you ladies scare away our customers?" she asked. Two women had come earlier for a mix of chamomile and bee balm to make a tea to ease their monthly discomfort. One woman stopped for rosemary and mint oil to help her sleep better. But Faith's busy greenhouse was empty of customers for the first time all week.

"It's been quiet all day," Dahlia leaned her elbows on the counter, resting her ample bosoms on the surface. "I may as well go help Anna and her houseguest Millie with a quilt they're working on."

Dahlia and Anna had become fast friends, and Faith was glad her aunt was settling in to their new life. They all were in small ways, and it pleased Faith, but she was worried about their income. If the customers stopped coming in, so would their money. She couldn't expect Duke to provide for all of them.

"I can't imagine our hot bath has much appeal in mid-July," she said, hoping it was just the weather keeping the women away. "Maybe we should offer a cold bath instead."

"That would have seriously shrunk the doctor's arrogance," Aster said, setting everyone off again.

When the door opened, their laughter ceased, and they turned to see a boy Adam's age carrying a large package in his arms. "I'm looking for Mrs. Wilkins," he said.

Faith identified herself, and the boy brought the package to the counter. She gave him a nickel she had in her skirt pocket, and he scooted outside with it clutched in his fist.

"What is it?" Tansy whispered.

"I don't know. I didn't order anything."

Iris, who had behaved herself all week, poked at the package. "I'll bet it's from the sheriff."

It was. He'd sent a dress in sky-blue silk patterned with tiny white dewdrop flowers and decorated with blue satin ribbons. He'd included matching shoes and a shawl as he had for her other dress. Faith had planned to wear that dress again to the theater performance tomorrow evening, but he clearly had a better idea.

Iris heaved a dramatic sigh. "Now I regret not trying to steal him away from you."

"You couldn't have," Tansy said. "The sheriff wanted Faith the minute he set eyes on her. But I think Mr. Lyons will buy you lots of dresses if you marry him."

"What I want from that man doesn't involve wearing a dress."

Tansy whacked Iris's arm. "You are utterly crude."

"Don't play innocent with me. I'm sure Mr. Dahlin' has found his way under your petticoats by now."

Tansy lifted her chin. "That man can barely find his way to my mouth without a map."

"So he's kissed you!" Iris clapped her hands together. "With you and Faith getting married soon, we won't have to worry about our income. He'll ask soon, Tansy"

"Won't matter. I can't marry a Yankee."

"Why not?" Aster asked, her voice booming across the greenhouse.

Tansy pulled back as if Aster had slapped her. "Because Yankees killed my husband."

Faith dropped her dress onto the counter and gaped with the rest of them.

"You were married?" Iris asked softly. "You never told us."

Tansy released a trembly sigh. "I married Leroy when I was nineteen. I was two months pregnant when he went to war in 'sixty-one. I lost the baby shortly afterward, and Leroy was killed three years later."

"Oh, honey..." Iris stroked Tansy's narrow back. "That's heartbreaking."

"It destroyed me," she agreed, the sadness in her voice making Faith's eyes tear. "When they gave me the news about Leroy, I thought of Mama and Daddy and all the people I loved and would someday lose, and I wanted to die right there. Everything in the South was destroyed by then, and I walked out the door hoping to find my own death, but I wasn't that lucky. I became a prostitute, and y'all know the rest."

Aster patted Tansy's shoulder. "Why didn't you ever share this with us?"

"Because it hurt too much to remember. And it never mattered until now" She hung her head. "Cyrus sings like an angel."

Dahlia released a sad laugh and hugged Tansy. "No wonder we love you."

"We surely do." Iris hooked her arms around Dahlia and Tansy. "Maybe Cyrus wasn't even in the war, hon. You should ask him."

Aster looked on like a mother hen, and Faith felt a deep sadness for all of them, for their lost innocence, for their lost dreams, for the love they were worthy of but didn't have.

⚑ ⚑

After supper, Cora rushed into the house with a note clutched in her hand. "A man said to give this to you."

Faith had her hands in dishwater, so Aster read the note to her.

"'Time for us to settle this matter'," she said, a scowl drawing her white eyebrows down. "'Meet me in the greenhouse tonight at ten o'clock. Come alone. I won't take no for an answer.'"

Faith's blood turned to ice and she froze with her hands in the water.

Aster's face turned as white as her hair.

Tansy dropped the pan she was drying. It landed on the floor with a *bong* and rolled into the wall. "God in heaven, who sent that?"

"It doesn't say."

Iris and Dahlia rushed from their bedchambers. "What happened?"

Fingers trembling, Aster passed the note to Iris. "I think Judge Stone has found us."

Iris and Dahlia read the note, and Dahlia slammed her hand on the table. "I swear I'll kill that man."

Cora cast a frightened look at Faith.

"Come here, honey" Faith wiped her hands on her apron then opened her arms. "Who gave you the note?"

"A man did," Cora said, rushing into Faith's protective embrace.

"What did he look like?"

"A bear with white hair."

Faith had seen several white-haired men in the village, but the only man who would write a note like that was Judge Stone. Her stomach clutched with fear, knowing he had approached Cora and could have easily taken her, and would have done so deliberately to remind her of his power. She looked for Adam and panicked.

"Where's Adam?"

"Under the bridge with Rebecca," Cora said. "He told me not to come down there by the water."

Faith trembled with fury and fear. Adam was supposed to be watching Cora while Faith was cleaning up. Instead he was flirting! Was that all boys and men could think about?

She handed Cora to Dahlia. "We need to make a plan. I'll be right back with Adam."

She stormed to the bridge that crossed Canadaway Creek at Water Street, and saw him sitting on the bank with Rebecca. "Adam Steven Dearborn! Get up here this instant!"

His head snapped up, and he stared in shock.

She had never screamed at him, but she was terrified. "Judge Stone just gave Cora a note while you were down here playing. He could have taken her!"

Adam's eyes widened, and he clawed his way up the bank. "Is he here?"

"Somewhere, yes. And he's coming back."

"I got to go," Adam yelled to Rebecca then ran for the house.

Faith followed him, not caring if the neighbors saw her mad flight. She wanted to get inside and bar the door. She wished she could run for Duke, but how could she ask for his help without confessing everything? What a mess she'd made for herself. What a grave she'd dug when she cheated Stone of the prize he wanted.

Faith gathered at the table with her aunts and slowly formed a plan. At nine-thirty that night, she slipped out to the greenhouse with Aster and Iris, leaving Tansy and Dahlia behind to guard Adam and Cora. She lit a lantern on the counter then lowered the wick to keep the interior deeply shadowed. They armed themselves with clubs and a strong rope then crouched between flats of plants to wait for the judge.

A few minutes after ten o'clock, the door swung open. Iris leapt forward with a grating growl and beaned the man on the head with a three foot piece of leftover lumber. He clutched his head and fell into a flat of wintergreen. Aster leapt at him with her club, and Faith rushed forward with the rope.

"Stop!" Patrick Lyons thrust his hand up to block Aster's swing. "Are you women daft?"

"Patrick?" Iris dropped to her knees beside him. "What are you doing here?"

"Getting killed by crazy women." He rubbed his head and pushed to his elbow. "What did you hit me with? I'm bleeding like a stuck pig."

Faith rushed to the counter and raised the lantern wick. The right side of Patrick's forehead was covered in blood. "Good grief," she said, grabbing a clean linen off the shelf. She rushed it to Iris, who pressed it to Patrick's head. "You stupid man. Don't you ever sneak in here again."

"Sneak?" He winced. "I sent a note."

They all gaped at him.

"You idiot!" Iris punched his shoulder. "I didn't get the note. Some white-haired man gave it to Cora, and it scared us half to death."

"I had one of the men I work with deliver it." He groaned and sat up. "I told him to give it to the pretty lady with black hair."

"Well, he forgot that part because he gave it to a four-year-old girl and told her to give it to her mother."

Faith's legs gave out and she sank to her knees. "Patrick, if I had any strength left, I'd wallop you again. You just scared ten years off my life."

"Mine too," Aster said, "and I don't have any to spare." She nodded to Iris. "Finish him off."

"Don't tempt me." Iris pinched his arm. "Are you insane?"

"I'm injured, and my ass is planted in six inches of wet soil. I'm about to sprout mushrooms in places I can't mention."

She stood and tugged him to his feet. "Come over to the counter so I can patch you up."

Faith's legs quaked as she got up, but she needed to make sure Patrick was all right, and that he wouldn't tell Duke what happened out here.

Iris dabbed the blood off his forehead and Faith was relieved to see only a small gash in his hairline.

Iris scowled. "You're going to have a goose egg and a sore head for a while, but you'll survive. Now, what was that note all about?"

"This." He pulled a folded paper from his pocket. "I got your letter, but I'm not taking no for an answer, Iris. You care about me. I know you do. And I care enough to marry you."

Faith exchanged a surprised look with Aster. Patrick had teased Iris, but no one thought he was serious. At least, Faith hadn't.

Iris pushed the paper away. "Stand still so I can finish this."

Patrick scowled, and Faith wanted to leave them to their private conversation. "I would appreciate it if you wouldn't tell anyone about what happened here tonight," she said, praying he wouldn't ask for an explanation.

He braced his elbow on the counter. "No one would believe me anyhow." He tipped his head so Iris could clean the gash with iodine. "What are you afraid of, Iris?" he asked quietly.

"Nothing. This gash on your head should prove that."

But Faith could see Iris was afraid: She wouldn't meet Patrick's eyes, and her fingers trembled as she taped a thick pad of gauze over the bleeding wound.

"Done." Iris stepped away. "Go home, farm boy."

He sighed and asked, "Are you afraid you won't live up to my expectations?"

"I'm afraid you won't live up to mine." She threw the towel at his chest then stormed outside, letting the door bang shut behind her.

Faith's jaw dropped, but Aster caught her hand. "Come on, honey, let's go back to the house and figure out how you're going to get rid of that property."

Chapter Twenty-four

F aith had Iris wrap her hair into a pretty twist in back of her head then added a sprig of forget-me-nots to match her new blue dress. The outfit was so beautiful and gay, Faith wished she could sneak into the Barkers' foyer and peek in their big beveled mirror.

To celebrate Duke's thirty-first birthday, they were going to Union Hall to see Ashton's theater company present *Rip Van Winkle*. She heard him knock at the door then Cora's feet pounding across the floor. The little girl couldn't wait to give Duke his birthday gift.

Faith picked up her reticule and left the room. Cyrus was in the parlor with Tansy, building a window seat she wanted. They all greeted Duke, but Cora was too excited to mind her manners. "We made a present for you," she said, interrupting.

"Is that so?" Duke knelt and tweaked the child's belly "Whoa! Are you getting fat, princess?"

Cora giggled. "I got your present under my shirt."

"Is that why you're all lumpy?" He tickled her side, and she danced away.

Faith watched her handsome suitor tease her daughter. He wore a navy blue suit and a starched white shirt that made his smile seem wider and brighter. He raised his eyes to hers, and she wanted to rush into his arms, into his passion.

"This will make your shoulder better," Cora said, interrupting their private exchange.

WENDY LINDSTROM

Adam looked up from the wing chair where he was reading. "Well, give it to him before you bust a seam."

"Surprise!" Cora pulled a drawstring bag filled with field corn from beneath her shirt and thrust it at Duke.

His expression made Faith laugh. He had no idea what he was holding.

"It's a heating bag," she said. "Heat the corn in the oven then pour it back into the bag and pull the draw cord tight to close it. The corn will stay hot for about half an hour, and the heat will feel good on your shoulder."

He bounced the bag in his palm a couple of times then grinned at Cora. "I'll bet this was your idea."

"Nope." She shook her head and pointed at Adam.

Duke's eyebrow lifted, and he looked at Adam, who slouched down in the chair.

"It's just a bag of corn," the boy said.

"Well, it's a smart idea and a perfect gift. My shoulder says thanks for being such an intelligent young man."

Adam rolled his eyes, but Faith noticed his pleased look. "Mama sewed the bag, and I put the cord in by myself," Cora said.

As was becoming his habit, Duke spoiled the children, and even Faith's aunts, with licorice sticks before he whisked her outside.

"Seventeen days, and you'll be Mrs. Grayson," he said, pulling her behind a tree for a kiss.

A reckless thrill rushed through her, as if she were standing on the roof of her three-story greenhouse.

She would be his wife.

His lover.

The mother of his children.

And the one who deceived him each day of their lives.

She couldn't do it.

She *had* to do it.

Once they jumped, there would be no turning back. Somewhere, someday, the truth would come out and they would crash to the hard, rock-strewn earth below.

Duke leaned back and rubbed her arms. "Why are you trembling?"

"I've never seen a theater performance."

"You'll love it. No arrogant doctor to battle, no nasty competitor to attack you, just an evening of entertainment for you to enjoy."

"Speaking of the doctor, he visited my bathhouse yesterday." She recounted Aster's story about massaging the doctor's posterior, and Duke was howling with laughter when they reached Union Hall on Main Street.

The second floor was jammed with people. Heavy velvet draperies covered tall windows on the north and south ends of the spacious room, and a huge crystal chandelier hung in the center of the ceiling.

"Impressive," she said then moved her gaze to Duke who was stunningly handsome in his crisp white shirt and gabardine suit with his shiny dark hair combed back and dipping slightly over his forehead. "Very impressive."

He grinned. "Likewise."

With immense pride, she took his arm, honored to be this man's choice. Of all the women vying for his attention, he'd chosen her. She smiled with pleasure as he escorted her to the front row where Claire and Boyd were sitting.

"You're going to love the performance," Claire said, greeting her with warmth. "Ashton's troop is the best."

"That's what I told her," Duke said, giving Boyd a nod then settling himself in the chair beside Faith. She liked the feel of his shoulder against hers, and the way he linked her nervous fingers with his. Maybe his actions were too familiar for polite society, but she couldn't give up his solid, steadying hand.

They would be married soon, and his strong hands would touch more than her fingers. Faith's stomach dipped and she pressed her palm against it to settle herself. Duke would be considerate. He would keep his big hands gentle and not overpower her. He would control his strong, muscled body and make love to her. Soon she would know him intimately. And he would know her, and her lack of experience.

Anxiety flooded her as Duke rubbed his thumb over her hand and pointed out friends in the audience. Then Ashton's troop came out and the performance began. In minutes the drama captured her attention so completely, she lost track of time. When the artists gave their final bow to a roaring applause, her chest expanded with joy. Never had she been so enthralled in her life. She wanted Adam and Cora to experience this wonder. She wanted her aunts to find decent, honorable men who would bring them to lawn parties and heartwarming performances. And she wanted to spend her life at Duke's side, sharing these occasions without a heart full of guilt.

Chapter Twenty-five

Flutter-birds beat their wings in Faith's stomach, but she spoke her wedding vows with assurance. She stood beneath the leafy maple tree with Duke where he had proposed, her emotions fluctuating between joy that she was marrying a man she was falling in love with, and terror that Duke would someday hate her for the colossal crime she was committing against him.

Their families were there to witness and celebrate their marriage on the balmy August afternoon. Adam gave her away, looking so grown-up in his new suit it made Faith's heart swell with pride. Iris stood with Faith wearing a satisfied smile on her face, but Radford stood beside his brother looking concerned.

Holding Duke's strong hand, Faith looked into his handsome face and promised to love and honor him.

"Forever," she mouthed silently, and the affirmation she saw in his eyes made her heart turn over in her chest. She'd accepted his proposal in the shadowy night, misrepresenting herself. Now she would commit her heart, body, and soul in the light of day and pray it would be enough. Together they would sink their roots into their marriage garden and grow strong enough to weather any storms. She would be diligent in keeping the weeds of life from choking them. She would bloom for him and bring sunshine and nourishment to his life.

"I, Duke Halford Grayson, take Faith Celia Wilkins to be my wife... to have and to hold from this day forward..." He looked deep into her eyes while promising to stand beside her through all troubles, to honor and protect her, and to love her. "I promise," he mouthed.

A tear rolled over her lashes and streaked down her cheek. He brushed it away with his thumb as he leaned down to seal their vows with a kiss.

An instant later, Iris gave Faith an exuberant hug then passed her to Radford, who welcomed her into the family with a more reserved, gentlemanly embrace.

Duke hugged his mother, but before she turned him loose, she caught Faith's hand and pulled her to Duke's side. She held their hands, and spoke to them both. "I never realized how hard it would be to see my last son marry and leave home, but I couldn't be happier for you two." Her eyes sparkled with moisture and sincerity. "Love requires you to be patient, strong, and wise. Be faithful, share your troubles, and never lie to each other. Be kind and respectful and forgiving. And when it rains, think about this glorious sunny day when you promised to love each other."

"We will," Duke said, promising for both of them.

"Enjoy each moment together as if it were your last because you just... you never..." She bit her lip, and tears appeared. "Oh, honey, I wish your father were here. He'd be so proud of you." She broke down and buried her face against Duke's chest.

The onslaught of Nancy's tears was like a purge to those around her. Everyone standing in that pretty field of wildflowers had once lost someone they loved. The ladies sought handkerchiefs to wipe their eyes. The men stood silent and stiff, chins tucked to hold back their emotions. And Faith no longer felt embarrassed about her own wobbly feelings.

Nancy lifted her head and gasped when she saw everyone weeping. "Dear God, what have I started here?"

"An intense craving for a glass of wine," Aster said drolly, causing watery laughs in the group.

Nancy straightened her pretty green shirtwaist. "Amen to that, Aster. And amen to this marriage." She caught Faith's hand and pulled her into a warm, motherly hug. "Welcome to the family, sweetheart. Now I promise to quit raining on this joyful, sunny day and help you and my son celebrate."

Her announcement brought a deep sense of homecoming and warmth to Faith, who needed Nancy's motherly welcome. She'd barely begun to imagine what it might mean to her to have such a woman for a mother-in-law.

They hugged and laughed beneath the maple tree then walked to Radford and Evelyn's house for a small celebration.

With her husband beside her, Faith met the rest of her guests. Duke and his mother invited both mill crews and their families. Amelia's mother, Victoria, had come with her new husband Jeb. Agatha Brown and Duke's mother were doting on the children, including Adam and Cora, like two contented grandmothers.

Agatha slipped her arm around Adam, but spoke to Duke. "You're getting a fine young man here."

Duke gave her a nod. "I agree, Mrs. Brown."

"Did you see those beautiful flower boxes Adam built for me? They're chock full of pink impatiens. Why, my store has never looked so nice."

"Looks like a new place," Duke said.

Adam's cheeks flushed, but Faith could see how pleased he was by Agatha's praise, and how manly he was becoming as he escorted Agatha to a chair on the porch.

She felt Duke's arms slip around her waist, and she leaned into his embrace. "What a lovely group of friends and family you have."

"Got everyone's names memorized?" he teased.

"Ask me that on our twentieth anniversary."

He laughed and nuzzled her neck. "Speaking of friends, looks like Aster and the doctor are getting friendly over there."

Faith's heart jolted then shuddered with relief when she saw them standing near the porch, a proper distance apart. They were squabbling over something, but Faith noticed a softer and warmer side to Aster, and the doctor seemed less arrogant than usual.

Throughout the evening, Faith kept an eye on her aunts, but they were too busy serving food and cake to misbehave. Faith's body hummed with an intense awareness of Duke. Each touch of his hand against her back thrilled her. Every private glance from his dark eyes was filled with heat and longing. Despite her nerves, she yearned to be skin-to-skin with him and consummate their vows.

In the early evening, he slipped his arms around her and pulled her against his muscled body. "Let's sneak away right now," he said, his voice husky.

"To your brother's hayloft?"

His low chuckle poured over her like warm rain after a long dry summer, and she basked in his hug. "Don't tempt me." His lips and teeth nibbled her ear. "I have a place you'll like better."

"Then let's say good-bye."

"Let's sneak away. Your aunts will see the children home and keep them entertained for the night." He linked fingers with her. "It's time for us to celebrate alone."

Her thudding heart made it difficult to act casual as she strolled across the yard on Duke's arm. But when he ducked behind the house and pulled her out of sight, she was breathless and giggling. "I like this business of sneaking away together."

He had the most pleased smile on his face she'd ever seen. "Gather your skirt," he said. She clutched the silk fabric in her fists, and he lifted her over the fence. A second later, he braced his hands on the pile of fieldstones and swung his feet over like a young boy. "We've escaped," he said, his eyes alight. "Onward."

She laughed and took his arm. "Where are we going?"

"It's a surprise."

He had been teasing her for three weeks, but she suspected they would stay at the Taylor Hotel by the Common.

"I need to stop home to get my bag," she said, but when they turned down Mill Street, he surprised her by stopping in front of the greenhouse. "My bag is at the——"

He put his finger over her lips. "Close your eyes."

"What?"

"I'm going to give you your surprise."

She shut her eyes. "What are you up to?"

"No peeking."

She gasped as he lifted her in his arms. "You're going to hurt your shoulder and ruin all our progress."

He started walking. "We aren't going far. Just keep your eyes closed."

"You could make this more fun by kissing me."

He laughed and gave her a light kiss on the lips. Seconds later he stopped. "You can open your eyes now." The instant her lashes lifted, he turned her to face the Colburn house she had wanted to buy. "I hope you like our new home."

She stared in disbelief.

"It's ours."

It couldn't be. She looked at her husband. "You bought the house?"

"I did."

"*You* bought it?"

He nodded, his grin saying he was mighty pleased with himself and proud of his gift to her.

"You rat!" She thumped her fist against his chest. "You knew this whole time and let me suffer, watching people move in furniture, knowing I would never have a chance—"

"It was a surprise," he said gently.

"My heart's been breaking for three weeks because... oh, Duke, I love it." She hugged his neck. "Thank you."

"Well, that's better than getting punched."

Her face heated and she rubbed his chest where she'd hit him. "Thank you for the wonderful surprise."

He carried her up the steps onto the front porch. "You didn't think we were going to live with my mother or your aunts, did you?"

With only three weeks between his proposal and their wedding, she hadn't known what to think about their living arrangements, and had uneasily left the decision to him. It was his town, his money, his choice. But she hadn't expected him to buy a house, and certainly not the one she dreamed of owning.

He feigned a gasp. "Open the door so I can carry you inside before my arms fall off."

She laughed and hugged his neck. "I'm glad you chose me to be your wife."

A pleased grin tipped his lips. "So am I, Faith. Now open the door and let me carry you over the threshold before I collapse."

She turned the doorknob and pushed it open.

He groaned and staggered inside, making her laughter the first sound to fill their house. With sure steps, he strode through a spacious foyer and into a large parlor where he twirled her in a circle. "What do you think?"

He stood her beside him, and Faith could only stare. When she'd seen the house three months earlier, it had been bare to the floor.

"I didn't want to bring you into an empty house. My mother and the girls outfitted the parlor for us, and chose necessities for the other rooms, but if you don't like the furnishings we can replace them."

For the first time that day Duke looked uncertain. She turned a slow circle, drinking in the garden setting, the deep green parlor furniture, the plush rug of browns, golds, and greens. Tiny green-stemmed wildflowers of aster, bee balm, forget-me-nots, and pink pasture roses patterned the cream-colored walls. She crossed the carpet and touched a bouquet, feeling the dried paint beneath her fingers. Tansy had given her this gift by painting these delicate flowers for her.

"It's beautiful," she said. Sateen drapes of tan and buff with brown tassel tie-backs covered three large windows that were partially open to let in the evening light and fresh air. The room was gorgeous. "I can't believe this is our home." She looped her arms around Duke's warm neck. "I'm going to love being your wife."

Relief filled his eyes as he lowered his head to kiss her. They shared their first passionate kiss as husband and wife in their parlor.

He held her against him, his arm banding her back as they swayed together, moving to the slow, seductive rhythm of his delving, stroking tongue. Heat burned through her, and she basked in the sound of his low groan. They would consummate their vows in this house tonight.

"I never got my bag," she whispered against his mouth.

"Tansy put it in our bedchamber."

"So my aunts knew about this too."

"We were all plotting against you, darling."

She sighed and rubbed her palm over his chest. "Thank you for the best day of my life."

"I want it to be the best night of your life, too."

By the look in his eyes, they would be sharing their new bed soon. She knew what was required of her, and was more than willing to lie with her husband. But what if he sensed her inexperience and asked questions she couldn't answer?

"Can I see the house before we...before I change?"

"That's what I'd planned to do before you distracted me." He grinned and took her hand. "Kitchen first." A bottle of red wine sat on the counter with two glasses that he promptly filled. "Do you think we can navigate while carrying these?"

She accepted the glass with a smile. "If I can cross a rutted field in the dark without spilling a drop of wine, I think I can manage a hardwood floor and a few doorways."

He tapped his glass to hers. "Welcome to your new home, Mrs. Grayson."

"Our home." She lifted her glass to toast him. "I wish I had something to give you in return."

He linked his fingers with hers. "You're all I want."

"I hope that never changes," she whispered, paralyzed with fear to think, to *know* that this sweet bliss could shatter at any moment.

He lit a lantern then led her through the dining room, a small music room, and a large water closet downstairs. Upstairs, they passed four partially furnished bedrooms, two of which Cora and Adam would use, and at the back of the house a small nursery connected to a master bedchamber as big as their parlor.

Faith trailed her fingers across a tall chiffonier and matching dresser in a lustrous cherrywood that brought a rich warmth to the room. Awed by luxury she never thought to enjoy, she admired the dressing table with a beveled oval mirror—and was shocked by the reflection of a bride in her finest dress standing beside her husband.

A huge canopy bed loomed behind them, with a bouquet of herbs and wildflowers lying on the white linen pillowcase.

Their eyes met in the mirror, his dark and too compelling. Faith's breath locked in her chest, and she waited for him, for whatever he might expect of his wife.

"Somebody left a salad on our bed," he said, nodding toward the herbs.

Her breath shuddered out and she brought her glass to her mouth and finished the last drops of her wine. She set the empty glass on the bed stand then picked up the bouquet. "It's a tussie-mussie," she said. The stems were tucked into a white lace doily and tied bouquet fashion with a pink ribbon. "It's from my aunts. Tansy must have left it when she brought my bag."

Duke leaned his shoulder against the carved cherry bedpost, and finished his wine. "What exactly is a tussie-mussie?"

"It can be a gift. Or a curse. It depends on what herbs you put in it." She skirted the bed to show him the herbs. "Basil is for love and good wishes, peppermint-scented geranium for happiness, and lavender for devotion." She brushed her finger over a daisy-like white flower with a deep yellow center. "Chamomile is for wisdom and fortitude." Which she would surely need to get through her wedding night. "This blue, star-shaped flower is borage for bravery." A virtue she could use more of right now. "And this wild rose is for love."

"You forgot that one," he said, pointing to a green stalk with tiny leaves and miniature pink flowers.

"Thyme. For daring."

He chuckled. "Thyme for daring. That must be from Iris."

Her face flushed. Only Iris would have thought to add the thyme, knowing Faith would find the tussie-mussie on her marriage bed. Today, on her wedding day when she needed it most, her aunts had brought love and encouragement and a bouquet of heartfelt wishes.

"Now you know why I love those women," she said, sniffing the green, reviving herbs to hide her discomfort.

"I'm glad you have them." Duke was watching her play with the herbs, but she sensed his thoughts were elsewhere.

With a sigh, she laid the tussie-mussie on the dressing table, looked at her handsome, patient husband, and swallowed hard. It all hinged on this, her wedding night, and making him believe she was an experienced woman. One rushed intimate involvement was hardly enough knowledge to get her through the consummation, but she wasn't a virgin, and for that she could finally be thankful.

Duke lowered his wine glass. "Why don't you change now?"

The heat in his eyes seared her. "I'll need your help with my corset." She could manage her dress, but not the white lacy corset Iris had given her. The corset, chemise, and drawers were an expensive gift from one of Iris's former johns, but Iris, who disdained corsets and pristine white underclothes, had never worn them.

Faith's fingers trembled and she fumbled with the buttons on the bodice of her dress. She heard the rough slide of her husband's gabardine suit as he crossed the room, felt his hard body beside her even though he didn't touch her. He set his empty wineglass on dressing table then gently lifted her chin.

"I'm not going to rush you. There's no hurry"

He was so beautiful, so tender, giving her his trust, his faith, his passion—a perfect wedding night—while she was holding back, keeping secrets.

He brought his mouth to hers in a tender, wine-flavored kiss that sent a rush of heat through her. She braced her hands on the dressing table to steady herself. He kept the kiss light and nibbled her lips, slipping her buttons free from the bottom up. When he freed the last button at her throat, he pushed the fabric over her shoulders and exposed her lacy undergarments that suddenly felt too seductive and revealing.

Passion flared in his eyes and he dipped his dark gaze to her breasts, returning slowly to her mouth and at last to her eyes. "Let's get this off you."

Chapter Twenty-six

Obeying Duke's gentle command, Faith turned her back to him. He slid the bodice of her dress off her shoulders and down her arms, tugged the sleeves over her hands then draped the soft fabric across the dressing table. Then his warm lips touched the nape of her neck, and flutter-birds circled her stomach like dandelion puffs caught on a hard swirl of wind.

"Don't move," he whispered, his breath soft and warm against her bare skin.

She felt a gentle tug in her hair, as he removed the spray of wildflowers she'd worn. When he laid the tiny cluster of white and orange trillium and yellow snapdragons down, his eyes met hers in the mirror. Pin by pin, he freed her upswept locks, dropping the pins onto the table until she felt her mass of hair tumble down her back.

"Do you have a brush in your bag?"

She nodded.

He stepped away to retrieve her bag from beside the chamber door. When he set it down, she reached inside the small, worn valise and found the brush Adam had stolen.

"Sit," he said, taking the brush from her. "I'd like to do this."

She sat with her back to him, watching his reflection in the mirror. He pulled the brush through her curls, over and again, placing the bristles at the peak of her forehead and lightly dragging them back across her skull and down the length of her hair, which ended above her waist.

A sigh of pleasure slipped from her mouth and she closed her eyes.

"You like this?"

"Mmm...yes. My mother used to brush my hair for me." And she'd craved those precious minutes of affection. "Mama owned a beautiful brush with stiff bristles and a porcelain back painted with roses. It was a gift to her, and my mother treasured it." A sharp sense of loss filled Faith. She opened her eyes, needing to see Duke, needing to know she wasn't alone anymore. "I wanted to keep the brush forever, but I left it behind when we moved."

"Have you sent a letter to your old address?" he asked, drawing the bristles across her scalp in a soothing motion. "You could ask the new residents to look for the brush and forward it to you."

She shook her head, disrupting his brush stroke. "No...I...the landlord probably tossed it out or gave it away." She lowered her lashes, realizing she'd been foolish to mention her mother and open a conversation about her past, especially on her wedding night.

"I'm sorry you lost something so treasured. Now I understand why Adam wanted to give you a brush."

She nodded, but dared not say another word about the brush or her mother lest she slip and mention the brothel she still owned. "Would you unlace my corset?"

He laid the brush on the dressing table then untied the drawing ribbon on her corset and unlaced it for her.

As she pulled the stifling garment off her body and laid it on the bench beside her, Duke's strong, warm hands slipped over her shoulders. Their eyes met in the mirror, but he gently tilted her head back until she was looking up at him.

He leaned down to kiss her.

Their mouths met upside down in an awkward but sensual kiss. He slowly moved his hands down over her collar bone, and slipped them beneath her chemise, easing his fingers over her breasts. She gasped against his mouth.

His tongue and teeth made small swipes and nibbles across her lips, making her crave a deeper kiss. She arched her back to lift her aching breasts into his warm palms. He captured her hard nipples between his thumb and finger, shaping and tugging them to aching peaks.

"I've wanted to do this from the minute I first saw you."

But he hadn't done it. He'd been a gentleman, even during their most passionate kisses.

His warm lips caressed her neck, her shoulder, and then he was kneeling on the floor behind her, turning her to face him. Her nose brushed his thick, shiny hair as he freed the buttons at the waist of her skirt, and she pressed her face into the silky soft strands to inhale the scent of him, soap and cologne and man.

He pulled her into his arms, kissing her deeply as he brought them both to their feet. His hands roamed her back, dipped inside her skirt to caress her bottom through layers of fabric then moved back to her breasts. A moan of pleasure escaped her, and she slipped her fingers into his hair, deepening the kiss. His low, shuddering groan excited her, and a wild desperation edged their kiss.

Suddenly, he broke away. "I need to get out of this suit."

"I'll help you," she whispered, wanting to please him, to be his wonderful willing wife, feeling as desperate and inflamed as he looked. She pushed the suit coat over his wide shoulders and down his muscled arms. He tugged his hands out of the sleeves, but his wince reminded her of his tender shoulder. She unbuttoned his shirt while he removed his tie. Then he wrested the gold links off his cuffs and shrugged out of his shirt, exposing his broad, bare chest.

When he stepped back to remove his trousers, her skirt that he'd unbuttoned fell to her ankles in a cloud of puffy silk, leaving her standing in her white chemise, drawers, and petticoats. His hands stilled at the waist of his trousers, a look of wonder and amazement filling his eyes. "You are so beautiful..."

His sincerity touched her. Maybe her experience with lovemaking was limited, but her knowledge of the human body was vast. If she watched and listened, her husband would show her how to please him.

An unexpected sense of daring filled her, and she untied the waist ribbon on her petticoat. Slowly, she pushed it down her legs to lie in the heap of silk at her ankles.

His dark gaze melted down her body like warm wax, molding her breasts, skimming her waist, caressing her hips, lingering on her lacy drawers and stocking-clad legs. That pleased him. She smiled and opened her arms to her husband.

He embraced her and lifted her out of the mound of fabric. Breast to chest, she felt his heart hammering, and her own answering. Somehow, someway, she would make this strong, handsome, trembling man in her arms want her as his friend and lover for life.

⊷⊱ ⊰⊶

Duke pressed his face to his wife's temple, physically shaken by his desire for her. "I've wanted you in my arms like this since the first time I saw you. I want to give you romance and fireworks." He brushed a thick wave of hair away from her forehead, needing to see her eyes. "I hope you don't view our marriage bed as a duty."

She sighed and caressed his cheek with her warm fingertips. "What we share privately is our gift to each other. I'm nervous, though, that I'll disappoint you."

"You could never disappoint me."

"Remember that the first time I irritate you."

He smiled, relieved by her playful words. "I promise."

"Show me those fireworks." She nipped his chin with her pretty white teeth. "Make me your wife."

A surge of lust tightened his groin, and he pulled her against him, kissing her urgently, deeply, hard. Because he couldn't hold back. He couldn't wait any longer. Her peaked breasts pressed through her chemise and flattened against his chest, making him wild for her. He rocked his hips against hers, demanding, insisting he satisfy the instinctive urges of his body.

Gasping, he broke away to pull her chemise over her head. The garment lifted her long, gorgeous hair up for a brief second then let it fall like a silky cape around her shoulders. Her skin was lightly bronzed, and her breasts round and full. He let the chemise fall at her feet. He circled her waist with his palms, sliding them up to cup her breasts. Drunk by her beauty, he leaned down and swirled his tongue around the tan aureole of her breast then sucked her peaked nipple into his hot, hungry mouth.

She clutched his shoulders and arched against his lips, her breathy moan sending a jolt of heat straight to his groin.

He hissed with pain and broke away, needing to shuck his trousers before they crippled him. He toed off his shoes, wrangled out of his painfully tight trousers then shoved his drawers down, freeing his turgid shaft.

He looked at Faith as he tugged off his socks. She was staring at him, at his lusting body, with parted lips and uncertainty in her eyes. If she asked him to slow down now, he may as well get his revolver and shoot himself. Because he couldn't stop. And if he dallied much longer, he was going to embarrass himself and disappoint her, something he hadn't done since his introduction to the act of lovemaking.

"You're magnificent," she whispered, her gaze filled with desire.

That was all the invitation he needed. He yanked off his last sock and went to her. With shaking hands, he untied her drawers, taking deep breaths that did nothing to calm him. His body wanted and needed release. But he needed more. He needed to make their lovemaking special for her, for both of them and the vows they'd exchanged.

As Faith slid her lacy drawers off her slender hips and down her long legs, he knew he was a goner. He lifted her in his arms and carried her to the bed, not daring to kiss her. But when he sat her on the bed, she looped her arms around his neck and gave him a sweet smile.

"It might be more civilized if you take off my shoes first."

He winced. "You've got me so wound up I can't think straight."

She laughed, a light, happy sound he hoped to hear every night for the rest of his life.

She sat nude on the bed, her hair streaming over one breast and down her back, looking up at him, smiling with that lush, kissable mouth, her whiskey-colored eyes promising him forever—and his heart knew love.

Radford had been wrong. This wasn't just lust. This was the beginning of the rest of his life. Finally, after sharing a mill with his brothers and a home with his mother and a job with a whole county, he had something to call his own. He had someone to take in his arms and love.

He removed Faith's shoes and fancy stockings then lowered the lantern wick, the golden light revealing every curve of her breasts and waist and hips. His breath jammed in his chest.

She turned back the covers to welcome him into bed, and his groin tightened yet again. It was all he could do not to lay her back and push between her long, slender thighs. His urges pounded through him, making his body shudder as he joined his bride in their marriage bed. He took her in his arms and kissed her, vowing to make this perfect.

For all his fear of losing control, Duke found himself taking his time exploring his wife's body. She was slender-boned and soft. Everywhere. And hot. She was ready for him, arching her hips up to his hand, gasping in his ear, but he wanted more—for her.

She moaned into his mouth, raising his temperature, but he held back, moving his hand to her breasts to give her body time to level off before he took her higher.

But she was writhing, her hands clutching him, her boldness surprising and pleasing. She suckled his neck and splayed her soft hands across his back, rubbing them down his body in a sweeping massage. Then she brought her hand forward to his stomach, and lower, her warm fingers circling him.

Heat surged into his groin and he groaned, wanting to grip her hand around him and rock his hips. He deepened his kiss and moved his hand to her hot center, stoking her fire, making her whimper until she broke their kiss.

"This is magical," she said, her voice trembling, wonder filling her eyes.

She met his mouth with an ardor that shook his control, and he sensed she was ready to soar. He fit himself between her legs and, finally, thankfully, joined them as man and wife.

Nothing had ever felt as right or as good as joining his body and his life with Faith's. He took her to her peak with a slow rolling and thrusting of his hips, her cry of release washing over him, making him want to stay forever, but in the tight heat of her body, her gasps and shudders pushed him into his own soaring climax.

Aftershocks of pleasure shuddered through Faith as she lay beneath her husband, breathing in ragged gasps, her mind and body stunned. Iris had told her the difference between intercourse and making love, but now Faith knew for herself. She wasn't a virgin, but she'd just made love for the first time in her life.

With her husband, her lover.

She kissed Duke's neck, loving the smell of his skin and light cologne. "I didn't see fireworks," she whispered in his ear. "I *felt* them."

He pushed to his elbows and looked down at her, his hair mussed and adorable. "I wanted to take it slow for you, but seeing you like this, so beautiful, so willing to please me"—he brushed his knuckles over her jaw—"it just bowled me over."

"I love this part of being your wife."

A pleased look lit his eyes. "Am I too heavy for you?"

"No." She smiled and stroked her hands up his back. "I like you in my arms."

"Good, because I'm not going to be able to keep my hands or body off you."

He kissed her tenderly then rolled to her side and pulled her into his arms, holding her against his warm body.

But she felt her secrets lying between them.

The peepers outside their window serenaded them, and nothing could be more perfect than being held in her husband's arms, hearing the strong, steady beat of his heart assuring her she wasn't alone, that she was desired, and possibly even loved. They had so much... to lose.

She shuddered as warm night air drifted across her skin, scenting the room with cut grass and a hint of their lovemaking. She stroked her husband's shoulder, wanting to remember everything about this night—his smooth skin and flexing muscles, the sound of his ragged breathing when he'd consummated their vows, the taste of wine on his tongue, and the contented look in his eyes.

"Are you tired?" she asked, needing his arms and the assurance that he was real, that this was real.

"Not with you beside me."

"I want more," she whispered. Heat shimmered in his eyes and leaned to kiss her, but she drew back. "I want to learn how to please you."

"You please me by being here."

"I can do better." She *would* do better. "Lie on your stomach."

"I don't think I can."

She looked down and gasped.

A naughty chuckle rumbled in his chest. "There's the hard evidence that you please me."

She stared at him, surprised but deeply pleased they would share bawdy humor in their marriage bed. Maybe they could share more someday. Maybe when she was assured of his love, when she knew he could understand and accept the truth, she could tell him.

The admiring look in his eyes made her yearn to touch him. She splayed her hands over his broad chest and urged him onto his back, taking her first good look at her husband, the man behind the badge and the clothes. On her knees beside him, she smoothed her palms over his wide shoulders and dark-haired chest then down the hard ridges of his abdominal muscles. "You're like bronzed steel... strong... beautiful, a handsome warrior," she said, pleased that her touch was making his body react and his breathing grow ragged. His thighs were rock hard and feathered with hair, tensing beneath her touch, and inviting her to explore his glorious maleness.

He groaned low in his throat and pulled her down beside him. Their mouths fused with urgency, and they explored each other with tender wonder and intense ardor. And when he pulled her beneath him, she sighed with pleasure and a fulfillment she'd never known. In her moment of soaring passion, she knew she would tell him the truth—when he was ready, when their future would be more important to him than her past.

Chapter Twenty-seven

"When do they go to bed?" Duke mouthed to Faith, who was sitting on the sofa with Cora, inventing a story about a moose with one antler. Adam sprawled on the floor with his chin propped on the heel of one hand, studying a book.

"Soon," she mouthed back with an intimate, heart-stopping smile that brought his body roaring to life.

He folded his newspaper and put it on the coffee table. After thirty-one years of living in his parents' home, it felt deeply satisfying to be sitting in his own house with his own family; but he was more than ready to take his wife to bed.

"Daddy, do you know a story about a moose?"

From the minute he and Faith were married yesterday, Cora called him daddy, but each time he heard the word from her sweet little mouth, it melted him.

"No, princess."

"What about a dog?"

Adam lifted his head as if someone had just handed him a silver dollar. "Are we getting a dog?"

Faith laughed. "No, Adam. And before you ask, we don't need a dog."

His expression fell and he turned back to his book.

Duke thought of Boyd's crazy dog Sailor and knew Adam would love a mutt like that. But he wasn't talking about pets on his first night of being a family man.

Cora slid off the sofa and leaned against his knee. "Will you tell me a story?"

He glanced at Faith, but her smile said she wasn't about to bail him out of his new duty "Sorry, Cora, I don't know any."

"Just make up something," Adam said, his eyes glued to his book. "She won't care."

Make up something? Duke had spent so many years teaching himself to be precise, accurate, and truthful, he couldn't begin to concoct a tale. But Cora's hopeful stare melted him. Gads, he couldn't fail at his first test as a father. "All right," he began, summoning his nerve. He would tell her a true story. "One winter when I was a boy we had a huge storm that buried everything in snow."

"What kind of snow?"

"Um, the white, fluffy kind," he said, seeing Faith hide a smile behind her hand. "My brothers and I spent the morning shoveling out the entrance to the barn. When we finished, we decided we could slide off the roof and land in the huge snow bank we built."

Cora's eyes goggled. "Was it scary on the roof?"

"Not really," he said. "My brothers and I climbed trees much higher than our barn."

Adam closed his book and sat up to listen. "Did you go off the roof?"

"All afternoon. We hit that pile so many times it half crumbled. Kyle gouged a path through it, and before long, we had a long, icy slide. My brother Boyd got this crazy idea about riding our toboggan off the roof. He said we'd slide down the shingles, hit the snow bank, shoot through the grooved path, and sail clear across the yard."

Adam's eyes lit with excitement. "Did you do it?"

"Unfortunately, yes."

Faith winced. "You didn't."

"Radford warned us not to. Kyle said we were crazy. But Boyd made it sound like such an adventure, I had to try. We got the sled clear to the roof peak, but when I jumped on, my weight jerked the sled out of Boyd's hands. He was supposed to ride with me, but I streaked down the roof alone and shot into the air like a lightning bolt."

"Dang! How far did you get?" Adam asked.

"Too far. I overshot the snow bank and landed in the shoveled driveway. I broke my arm, and when my parents found out what we were up to, we all got a strap laid across our backsides."

Faith arched an eyebrow at Adam. "So the moral, young man, is that you don't climb onto the roof."

"Sorry, wrong story," Duke said. This job as father was more complicated than he thought.

"You're fine," Faith said, "but I know a certain young man who might be impressed and tempted to try something like that."

He's a boy, Duke wanted to say. Boys climb trees. They swing from wild grape vines to drop twenty feet into the gorge. It was the adventure and the thrill that drove them to be daring—or dumb. Duke didn't know about girls, but Evelyn had done many of those same daring, albeit dumb, things with them. That wild sense of adventure, to him at least, had been the best part of his childhood.

Not that he wanted Adam jumping off a roof. But a boy was entitled to some adventure in life.

Faith chased the children upstairs to put on their nightclothes. Alone for the first time all evening, Duke stole a kiss from her, and she was so warm and willing, he wanted to carry her straight to their big bed and make love to her.

But that had to wait, because for the first time in his life, Duke helped his wife tuck their children in bed. Adam suffered Faith's hug then dove onto his new mattress. He sat on the coverlet in his nightshirt looking suddenly uncomfortable. "Um, I don't know what to call you, Sir."

Duke didn't know either. It would have been easier if Adam, like Cora, was Faith's child. But he wasn't, even though she treated him as such. So that left Duke feeling like a father, but relegated to brother-in-law and guardian. "You're nearly a man, Adam. Why not call me Duke?" He hoped the acknowledgment would allow them to be friends, and still give Adam someone he could depend on.

"Sure, Duke." Adam sat up a little straighter on the mattress. "You and your brothers sure did some crazy things when you were boys."

"You will too, Adam. I just hope you'll be smarter and more careful than we were."

Adam grinned. "I promise I won't ride a sled off the barn roof."

"Thank you for that small blessing." Faith kissed his boyish cheek. "Enjoy your new bed and sleep well."

"I will." He flopped to his side and bunched a thick feather pillow beneath his head.

Duke extinguished Adam's lantern then they went to Cora's room. She was sprawled sideways across her bed, lightly bumping her heels against the wall and singing to herself.

"Time to tuck you in," Faith said, turning back the coverlet. She swept Cora into a tight hug and kissed her cheek. "Sweet dreams, honey"

Cora kissed Faith's cheek then reached so naturally for Duke, he felt his heart do a crazy little somersault. "Goodnight, Daddy" she said. She squeezed his neck with her skinny arms, and kissed his cheek with her puckered lips.

Being a sheriff for eight years had numbed Duke in some ways, making him able to handle life-threatening situations with a cool head, but nothing had prepared him for the rush of tenderness he felt for Cora. He'd tucked his nieces and nephews into bed many times when his mother kept them overnight, and though he loved those children with all his heart, they belonged to his brothers. This little rose-scented girl with her bright eyes and blabby mouth was his—the daughter he would love and protect and rescue from being fatherless.

"Goodnight, princess." He barely squeezed the words from his thick throat. Another few seconds of holding her, and he wouldn't be able to breathe. "Don't let the bedbugs bite," he added, tweaking her side.

She giggled and squirmed away. Faith caught her and guided her into bed, following with a smacking kiss on Cora's forehead. "No playing. It's late." She pulled the sheet and blanket over the child. "See you in the morning."

They extinguished her lantern, left the door open, and hurried to their bedchamber.

Duke closed the door then started to unbutton his shirt. "Last one to undress has to shut out the lantern."

"No fair," Faith protested. "I'm wearing twice the clothing you are."

"Ah... but you'll have twice the help undressing." Burning with desire for his beautiful new wife, he gathered her soft, slender body against him and covered her mouth with his, feeling that his arms and heart were full at last.

Chapter Twenty-eight

When Adam got to the swimming hole in the gorge, Rebecca was in the water. He hadn't seen her since Faith and Duke's wedding three weeks ago, and it was making him crazy. Did she considered him her cousin now? Could they still be friends?

"Set this in the shade," Faith said, handing him the huge basket of food she'd brought for the picnic with Duke's mother and brothers. Everyone from Adam's family was there, and Doc Milton and Patrick and Cyrus were tagging along too. It seemed like the men were always around now, but Adam liked listening in on their naughty jokes.

The stones on the creek bank burned his bare feet, and he hurried to water. Submerged to his shins, Adam watched Boyd swing over the creek on a wild grape vine and drop into the water with a splash.

Boyd's four-year-old son Colter grabbed the vine. "I want to do it!"

"All right, but hold on until I tell you to let go." Boyd treaded water in the middle of a deep pooled area of the creek, fanning his muscular arms to stay afloat.

On the bank, Kyle lifted the boy, made sure he had a firm hold on the vine then gave him an easy push over the water.

"Let go!" Boyd shouted.

Colter released the vine and fell. As soon as he surfaced from the water, Boyd grabbed him and swam ashore with his dripping, grinning, dark-haired son clinging to his strong back.

Teaching courage and daring, and giving rescue, was something fathers did that Adam hadn't known about.

Rebecca's dad went in next then waited for his sons. William swam ashore on his own, but Joshua needed some help. After a while, the fathers and sons got all mixed up, and Adam learned that fathers take care of their brothers' children. Another slice in his heart. Why didn't his own father want him?

"Adam!" Rebecca waved to him. "Come try the swing."

Anything was better than standing on the bank thinking about a man he hated. The swing was exciting, but it would have been more thrilling if the drop was longer.

His aunts and Rebecca's grandmother each took a ride on the swing, hooting and laughing so loudly it embarrassed him. Tansy blew a kiss to Cyrus then dropped into the pool and pretended she was drowning. When he swam out to rescue her, he stole a kiss. Iris hooted like the boys, and kicked her feet so high when she rode the swing, her red drawers showed. It made Patrick whistle like a fool. And Duke wouldn't stay away from Faith for a minute. She blushed and laughed and pretended to push him away, but she liked Duke's teasing. Only Aster and Doc Milton behaved themselves while everyone else acted foolish.

Adam swam downstream where the water rushed over rocks. Alone, he dug up stones and piled them in different shapes, liking the way it changed the sound of the burbling water.

"What are you doing?" Rebecca asked, from behind him.

Startled, he dropped a rock against his knee, but refused to wince at the bloody scrape. He glanced upstream where everyone was still splashing and hollering. "My family is embarrassing."

"So is mine," Rebecca admitted. "They're all playing charades and laughing like they've had too much wine."

"Are they drinking?"

"No, just acting silly." Rebecca dug up a rock and stacked it on the pile. "My dad says we're cousins now."

They were not cousins.

"I don't think we are," she said. "But maybe my dad will let us be friends now."

The ache in his chest lightened. "Did you find my note last week?" he asked, fussing with the rock pile.

"Joshua found it, but I got it away from him before he could show my father."

Adam's gut rolled. "I won't leave any more."

"There's a better place," she said, looking upstream to make sure they weren't overheard. "You know the creek that cuts through our apple orchard?" At his nod, she continued. "Under the little wooden bridge there's an old bird's nest on the side nearest my house. I'll check there for notes."

He remembered the bridge from when he'd chased Rebecca through the orchard at Faith's wedding. His stomach was all tight and odd feeling that day. And when he'd caught Rebecca around the waist and she'd brushed against his thighs it made him ache in an embarrassing place. He didn't touch her after that, but thinking about the way she felt against him made his body start feeling odd and achy again.

He sank lower in the water. "You better go before your dad gets angry."

But it wasn't her father's voice that boomed down the gorge. It was Duke's. "You two get up here where we can see you. I don't want you floating into Lake Erie."

Adam rolled his eyes, and Rebecca laughed then they made their way back toward their noisy, embarrassing families.

After a month of marriage, Faith still had to pinch herself to know she wasn't dreaming. She never knew life could be filled with so much joy and laughter, or that she—a prostitute's daughter—would be blessed with a beautiful home and loving husband.

Each evening after chores, she and Duke and the children, and sometimes her aunts or his family, would share a filling supper then retire to the parlor to read and play games. After tucking the children in bed, she and Duke would seek their own bed with an eagerness that both thrilled and shamed her—because she still wasn't going to tell him the truth.

She couldn't. He'd been wearing his sheriff's badge on his leather vest for eight years with pride and devotion. Each morning, he strapped on his gun belt, pulled on his vest, and whistled his way out the door, sure of himself and sure of Faith. He was so content with his new family, and so proud of his new wife, the truth would crush him.

So now when she ached to confess, she kept her silence to protect her husband.

In early September, Adam went back to school with a firm warning from Duke to behave himself and stay put in the schoolroom. Adam grumbled, but did as he was told, and Faith was grateful for Duke's help.

Although Duke was busy with his job as sheriff and working the mill with his brothers, he asked again if Faith would let Adam work at the mill with him on Saturdays. It scared her too much to let him go, so Adam continued to work at the store and help in the greenhouse when not in school.

Faith only gave massages to Duke now, and his shoulder was steadily improving. With fewer demands on her time, she was becoming the sort of wife and mother she'd dreamed of being, and she thanked Duke each night in bed for his generosity.

Her aunts seemed to be settling in, too. Dahlia spent most of her evenings at Anna's house, helping the women who sought refuge there. Despite Tansy's objection to Cyrus being a Yankee, she was clearly falling in love with the man. Iris and Patrick were a mystery: They obviously cared for each other, but they were at some sort of standoff that Faith didn't understand and couldn't ask about.

In late September, Cora got sick to her stomach, keeping Faith at her bedside for four exhausting nights. The fifth evening Cora was better, but Faith wasn't feeling well.

The next day all was right again, and that evening, after the children were sleeping, she stole across the street in the early autumn night with her husband. Inside the greenhouse, she felt her way along the counter. "Will you light the lantern while I get some linens?" she asked.

He struck a match, illuminating his handsome face and intense, dark eyes. "Bring some of that smelly oil you like."

She raised an eyebrow in surprise, but his attention shifted to lighting the lantern. She grabbed an armful of linens and snatched a jar of almond oil off the shelf then followed him to the bathhouse.

"Finally." He shut the door behind them, sealing them in, and the world out. "This has been the longest, most miserable week of my life."

"Mine too." She deposited her towels and the oil on the table at the end nearest the tub, and he set the lantern at the other end. "And tomorrow I need to drain and clean the tub."

"I'll help you," he said, drawing her into his arms. "I've missed you in our bed. But if you're still feeling poorly, we can wait another night."

"I don't want to wait."

"Are you sure? Your eyes are dark."

"I'm fine. I'm just worn out from sitting up with Cora."

"I'll make you feel better." He held her against his chest and rubbed his hands over her back, kneading her tight muscles with his warm fingers.

"Mmm... I like your doctoring."

"I'll take care of you," he said, massaging her neck.

"My muscles thank you."

He chuckled and worked his fingers along her shoulders, in the way she'd done to him so many times. "What made you want to learn about the body and herbs and all those concoctions you make?" he asked.

Desperation. Loneliness. "I tended my mother's roses with her and discovered I liked growing things. When I realized that some medicines were made from plants and trees, I wanted to learn about them, and that fed my curiosity about anatomy."

"I've developed a curiosity about anatomy too." He palmed her stomach. "I don't know what muscles I'm feeling, but I like when they tense up like they're doing now."

"That's my abdominis muscle, which will probably be stretched six ways from Sunday when I carry our first child."

"You'll be beautiful, but let's hold off a while. I like sneaking away with you in the middle of the night."

"I like it too."

He reached around behind her and filled his hands with her backside. "I'm particularly fond of these muscles."

"My gluteus maximus is flattered."

He wrinkled his nose. "That's an awful name for something so lovely." She laughed, and he lowered his mouth to nibble her neck. "Last chance to escape if you're not feeling up to this, because if you don't run from the room right now, I'm going to kiss you and make love to you all night."

"I'm not leaving."

"You're sure then?"

"More than sure. But I could use some help with my dress. There are thirty buttons on this thing."

"I'm in no rush." Slowly, he slipped open the long line of buttons down the front of her dress then pushed it off her shoulders. "You know what I thought the first time I saw you?"

"Nothing. Your mind was blank because you were stunned by my beauty"

He pulled back, eyes wide in mock surprise. "You knew?"

She laughed and nudged his ribs. "What did you think?"

"That you shouldn't be sad. That your whiskey-colored eyes should shine with happiness, that your beautiful lips should always wear a smile."

He'd thought all that? She smoothed her palms over his broad chest, touched by his tenderness. "I'm the happiest I've ever been. Being with you is... it's I don't know, I just feel complete in a way I've never known."

"You won't want for anything if I can help it."

"Neither will you. If I could give you your heart's desire, I would."

"You have, Faith. Your gorgeous body. Your smile. You. My heart's desire. Simple as that."

"That's all you want?"

"It's everything I need." He hooked his hands around her hips and pulled her against him. "I'll always want you." He kissed her neck. "I'll always crave you."

"Mmm..."

"I want to devour you." He rocked his hard loins against her. "Let's get in the tub."

"So soon? I was enjoying your doctoring."

"I'm just getting started." He gave her a playful whack on her backside. "Off with your clothes, woman. Doctor's orders."

He helped her take off her shoes then took off his own while she slipped out of her petticoats and stockings. The room was warm from the bath and boiler, but she shivered, missing his arms. He stripped off his shirt then shucked his trousers. Then his drawers.

Arms at his side, back straight, he planted his bare feet on the stone floor and faced her, all bold and glorious, unmindful of his nakedness and warrior-like pose.

"You sure don't look like a doctor," she said, unable to take her eyes off her husband's virile body.

A crooked grin tipped his mouth. "Looks deceive, sweetheart. But you'll like what I prescribe." He tugged the ribbon at her waist and pushed her drawers over her hips and down her legs, kissing her thighs as he slid her undergarment to her ankles. He nibbled his way back up to her neck. Her legs were quaking when he pulled the chemise over her head. Naked, breathing in short, excited gasps, she stepped out of her drawers.

He lifted her into the tub then climbed in behind her. "I've been aching all week for you," he said, drawing her against his hot, slick body.

"You can stop aching." She hooked her arms around his neck and pressed her breasts to his wet chest. With a growl, he took possession of her mouth.

Water lapped at their bodies as he kissed her, his firm lips and delving tongue stoking the fire in her body. He took it deeper, slower, rubbing his water-slick skin against hers. "I need to get the oil, sweetheart," he said, his hot breath caressing her ear.

"What oil?" she asked, drugged by his kiss.

"The oil I'm going to rub all over your body"

Oh..."I didn't bring any."

A low chuckle rumbled in his chest. "It's on the table."

She remembered then that she'd brought almond oil. "Don't leave me. I don't care about the oil." She tightened her arms around his neck and fit their bodies closer together.

"I'll never leave you." He nipped her chin then rose until her arms slipped from his neck and he stood in the tub, rivulets of water streaming down his bronze, muscled body like tiny rivers cutting down a craggy mountainside.

Mesmerized, she stroked her palm up his rock-hard thigh to the sinewy, rippling muscles in his abdomen, awed and intrigued with his reacting body, with him, with this man who was revealing himself one layer at a time with each look, each caress, each word he spoke. His breath sailed out and he jerked his hips back as if her touch scalded him. He clutched the edge of the tub, leaned over and grabbed the jar of oil off the table then submerged himself to his chest in the bath.

"Back off, woman."

She smiled at his playfulness.

He blew out a shuddering breath, uncapped the jar and filled his palm with oil. "Sit on the stool and give me your foot."

"What?" She laughed. "I'm not concerned with my feet right now, darling husband."

He pointed to the end of the tub. "Humor me."

She sat on the stool and lifted her foot out of the water.

He knelt in front of her and slathered the oil over her foot. "Gads, what is this stuff?"

The scent of lavender rose from the water. "I must have I picked up the wrong jar."

He wrinkled his nose. "Wonderful. I'll smell like a flower tomorrow. Just give me a dress and I'll be able to sashay up and cuff the bad guys before they suspect a thing."

Her laugh sailed through the room. "Want me to run out and get the other oil?"

"No. I want you right here with me," he said, kneading her foot.

She leaned her head back against the edge of the tub, enjoying the massage and the feel of his hands stroking up her calves. "You know what I thought when I first met you?" she asked.

"That I was a hard-nosed, inconsiderate lawman who was trying to take advantage of you."

"No, I thought you were a hard-nosed, very handsome lawman who could easily seduce me."

A crooked grin slanted across his mouth. "Believe me, you weren't easy to seduce."

She lifted her foot from his hands and trailed her big toe down his chest to his stomach. "I wouldn't have resisted if I'd known how tender and loving and playful you are."

He released an exaggerated sigh. "And here I'd thought my big, bad sheriff act attracted you."

"That tough, commanding side of you is a bit titillating."

"Then stand up, sweetheart."

"As you wish, Sheriff." She rose to her feet, waiting for his instruction, willing to give him anything—everything. She would be the perfect wife, the perfect playmate, the perfect lover.

He moved to sit on the stool then poured more oil into his hands and rubbed his palms together. Gently, he circled her waist with his hands and pulled her onto his lap. His body was hot and hard beneath her legs, against her bottom, everywhere. He pushed the pads of his thumbs on either side of her spine and slid them up to her shoulders, soothing her, exciting her, making her body surge forward and fall back into the cradle of his thighs with every delicious stroke. Over and over again he swept his hands across her shoulders and down her back, slipping around her ribs to caress her breasts then back again and down and around and oh... everything in her melted.

"You have magical hands," she said, sighing with pleasure. "I noticed them the first time I met you."

"Ah... another confession. I think I'll keep rubbing your body until you divulge all your secrets."

She wished she could divulge everything, to ease her conscience, to be truthful with her husband, to rid their marriage bed of the lie that slept between them. But she could only give him love.

She pushed off his lap and knelt in front of him. "Let me rinse this oil off." She slipped under the water, but two large hands clamped around her waist and lifted her back to the surface.

"Leave it," he said, his voice hoarse with passion. He kissed the side of her jaw and she sought his mouth, hungry for him. Slowly, he moved his palms down her back and over her bottom then up and around to her breasts. She moaned and arched toward him, but he continued that languorous rubbing down her back and over her buttocks, driving her crazy with longing.

Finally, his large, work-roughened hands cupped her bottom and lifted her onto his lap. She embraced his neck and twined her legs around his waist, sighing as he filled her. He moaned low in his throat, and her head fell back in ecstasy.

Could something this beautiful really last? This man in her arms was so good and steady, and she was lying to him every minute of every day with every word, every kiss, every caress.

Water sloshed around them, lapping at their bodies as they clutched each other breast to chest, their mouths fused, hot and urgent as they brought each other to that blissful, soaring release Faith had come to know so well. Shattered, she lowered her forehead to her husband's shoulder, loving the man who had claimed her heart, who trusted her with his friendship, with the intimacy of his most private self. She bit her lip, but tears of mortification leaked past her defenses because she didn't know how to protect him without betraying him.

Chapter Twenty-nine

The urgent pounding on the front door brought Duke to full attention. He tossed aside the newspaper, and headed to the foyer. "Adam, stay in the parlor, and keep Cora with you."

"Yes, sir."

Duke opened the door to find a woman he didn't know standing on his porch, white-faced and trembling. "I'm Millie, and I'm staying with Anna. Her husband b-broke in and he has a gun."

Shock and fury rushed through Duke. Larry Levens was in prison for life. He had killed two men, one of them a deputy sheriff. He'd beaten Anna half to death five years ago and could only be out for revenge now. "Wait here with my wife."

The terrified woman stepped inside as Faith hurried into the foyer.

Duke opened the closet. "Anna's husband broke out of prison," he said, wondering why he hadn't been notified of the man's escape. He took his gun belt off the top shelf and strapped it on. He opened the chamber, made sure the revolver was loaded, and asked Millie if anyone else was at Anna's house. It would be safest if it was only Anna and Larry, but Duke half-hoped someone like Boyd, who lived across the street, was there to distract Levens until he could get his hands on the mean son of a bitch.

"Dahlia's there," Millie said, "but Larry hit her with his gun. I ran out the back door like Anna told me to do."

Faith gasped and caught Duke's hand. "Anna and Dahlia could already be dead."

"Stay put, sweetheart. I'll get Dahlia home safely."

He gave Faith a quick kiss then bolted outside, cutting across lots behind several buildings. He came out on Main Street and jogged up West Hill. Slowing his pace, he crept close to the old Pemberton Inn that had once housed his brother's saloon. He crouched beneath the windows and stayed close to the building, hoping to get into Anna's home through the small storeroom in the back. Anna's pained cry, and Dahlia's vivid, angry curse, bled through the plank walls.

With light steps, Duke eased inside and crossed the storeroom. He inched open the door that led into Anna's community room.

Levens had Anna bent backward over her sofa, with his hand pressed to her throat and his gun barrel planted between her eyes. Dahlia sat frozen at the piano, her face contorted with horror.

"Please," she croaked. "She's your *wife*."

"Shut up, bitch, or I'll put a bullet between your eyes, too."

"Don't do this," Dahlia begged.

Duke drew his revolver. He needed to be fast and accurate. Because Levens would shoot; he had nothing left to lose.

Gun cocked, breath even, Duke slipped inside, one silent step at a time.

"Five miserable years I sat in that hole because of you," Levens said, his nose an inch from Anna's face.

Duke raised his revolver and locked his elbow.

The flash of surprise in Anna's eyes gave him away: Levens swung his pistol and fired, shattering the plaster behind Duke's head. Duke ducked into the storeroom. A second shot splintered the pine door. Finger on the trigger, he leapt back into the room, but the coward was shielding himself with Anna.

Levens fired again, and the bullet whizzed by Duke's right ear. The man's aim was getting hotter.

Duke angled for a clear shot that could bring Levens down, but before he could squeeze the trigger, a wild screech filled the room, and Dahlia swung the piano bench into the back of Levens's head. The wood cracked on impact, and the man stumbled forward but didn't fall. He grabbed Dahlia and slammed her to the floor so hard the windows rattled.

Now, Duke fired.

The bullet hit Levens in the shoulder and spun him sideways. Lunging like a tiger, Duke dove into the man's side, taking him to the floor and knocking the gun from his hand.

Levens scrabbled for his pistol, but Anna kicked it away. With a howl of outrage, he lunged at her, fist raised. "You traitorous bitch!"

Duke hauled him back before the man could slam his fist into his wife's already-bloody face. Pain screamed through his shoulder as he forced Levens's arm up and snapped a handcuff around his wrist.

The monster's enraged howl filled the room, and he tore away, lunging at Anna with a vicious growl. Duke grabbed the cuff dangling from Larry's wrist, but before he could haul him down, the crack of a pistol sent Levens to his knees. Blood stained the thigh of his trousers where Dahlia had shot him.

The man growled like a rabid dog and tried to get to his feet, but his injured leg collapsed and he fell to his knee. Duke slapped the other cuff around Larry's wrist, binding the man's hands behind his back.

"I'm not going back to prison!" With an enraged growl, Levens lunged at Dahlia, yanking the cuffs on his bound wrists, and wrenching Duke's shoulder.

"Neither is Anna," Dahlia said. And she pulled the trigger.

The bullet knocked Levens backward over his boot heels, and yanked the metal chain linking the cuffs from Duke's raw hand. Larry's head cracked on the coffee table as he crashed to the floor.

The front door flew open, and Duke reached for his revolver, but it was Boyd who stormed inside. His brother gave the room a sweeping glance and rushed to where Duke crouched beside Levens.

"What's going on?"

Duke's breath shuddered out. "Anna's husband paid her a visit."

"What's he doing out of prison?"

"Getting himself killed."

Boyd had met Levens five years ago when the man tracked Anna to Claire's house and threatened both women. Shortly after jailing the man, Duke had taken Anna to Pittsburgh to testify against her husband.

Levens lay in a pool of blood. Duke checked for a pulse, knowing he wouldn't find one; Dahlia had shot straight into Levens's black heart. Levens had fought too hard and pushed too far. Maybe he'd known Dahlia would pull the trigger and end his miserable life. The abusive wretch deserved the bullet in his chest, but Duke felt a crushing weight settle on his shoulders. Dahlia had knowingly and willingly killed a man.

<hr />

Faith put the children to bed then waited in the silent parlor with Millie. They were too tense and scared to talk. Duke had been gone for an hour, and Dahlia hadn't arrived yet.

Someone knocked on the door at nine-thirty, and Faith's heart nearly stopped when she found Doc Milton on her porch.

"Larry Levens is dead."

Faith pressed trembling fingers to her dry throat. "Is Duke... is he all right?"

The doctor nodded. "Anna and Dahlia are at Boyd's house. You'll have to ask Duke what happened," he said then offered to walk Millie to Boyd's to be with Anna.

Shaken and shivering, Faith grabbed a lantern and followed them outside. Alone with her worry, she buttoned her sweater against the chill then sat on the porch swing, listening to dry leaves scuttle across the ground and praying for Duke and Dahlia to hurry home.

When they finally approached the house, Duke's stride was shorter, his shoulders stiff. He wore a deep scowl and had his thumb hooked in the front of his gun belt, a sign that his shoulder was hurting. Dahlia was limping, and she pressed her hand to her hip as she slowly climbed the steps ahead of Duke.

"Thank goodness you're all right!" Faith leapt from the porch swing and threw her arms around her aunt. "I was worried sick about you two."

"I'm not all right." Dahlia stared across the porch, her face ravaged by grief or pain or both. "I killed a man."

Faith's heart stopped, and then she saw the anguish in Duke's eyes and the strain around his compressed lips. Something awful had happened.

"I had to." Dahlia clamped her lips together, but couldn't hold back her tears. "He wouldn't have stopped," she cried. "They never stop."

Faith pulled Dahlia onto the swing and sat beside her. "What happened?"

Breathy sobs shook the woman's shoulders. "I begged Daddy to let me come home. He said, 'Obey your husband.'"

Faith frowned, confused by Dahlia's rambling.

"I tried, God help me I did. But Carl wouldn't stop."

As understanding dawned, sickness washed through Faith. Dahlia was telling her own story. She said she'd witnessed a woman being beaten by her husband, and that a minister refused to give her refuge. But that beaten woman was Dahlia, and the minister was her own father.

"Oh, Dahlia...." At a loss for words, Faith rocked her aunt.

"I didn't want any man to touch me ever again."

"I don't blame you."

"Your mother let me stay in her house anyhow, and it was a whole year b-before I could work upstairs."

Faith's heart contracted, and she pulled Dahlia close. "Shhh..." she whispered, comforting her and warning her not to divulge any more in front of Duke, whose bleak expression had changed to a sickly, suspicious scowl.

Dahlia stiffened and sat up by degrees, as if she knew she'd said too much. "I want go home." She wiped her palms across her cheeks and looked at Duke. "Unless you're taking me to jail."

"What? Why would he?" Faith pressed her hand to her churning stomach. "Are you arresting her, Duke?"

His somber look terrified her.

"You can't... that man *killed* people."

"I know, Faith, but..." He released a hard, shuddering breath. "Go home and rest, Dahlia."

The torment in his eyes killed any relief Faith expected to feel. Whatever had happened at Anna's was torturing him.

Dahlia got to her feet. "I'm sorry about everything," she said, but Faith didn't know if she was apologizing for saying too much, or for what she had done at Anna's.

She walked Dahlia across the street. Tansy was out with Cyrus, but Aster fixed Dahlia a cup of tea, and Iris rubbed balm on her sore back. When Faith returned home, Duke was waiting on the porch. She gave him a hard, thankful hug, needing to touch him to know that he was okay.

"I was so worried about you," she said. She sensed he wouldn't talk about what happened at Anna's, so she simply held him and listened to the peepers.

"Faith, what kind of work did Dahlia do upstairs at your mother's house?"

Fear drizzled down her body like a freezing rain, coating her with ice. She couldn't move. She couldn't speak.

"Who are those women you call your aunts?" he asked, his voice flat, controlled, cold.

This was the moment she would crash to the hard unforgiving ground, and everything would shatter: her body, her heart, her life.

"They're my aunts, like Rebecca is Evelyn's daughter," she said, wanting him to understand her love for them.

His nod acknowledged her right to claim the women as family, but she could see the truth dawning in his eyes.

"Your mother didn't just sell roses, did she?"

She shook her head.

"Did all your aunts work upstairs at your mother's house?"

She nodded because she couldn't speak past the shame clogging her throat.

He inhaled sharply, as if the truth had speared him in the chest, and his appalled expression broke her heart.

"I knew you would look at me with disgust."

"How would you expect me to look?"

"I don't know," she whispered.

"For God's sake, your mother ran a brothel!" He stared at her as if seeing an unwelcome stranger on his porch. "Did you...

were you..." His breath rushed out as if he couldn't bear to ask the question.

"No." She shook her head. "I only gave massages."

—+—+—

"Stop!" Duke raised his hand, unable to listen to his wife any longer. He couldn't stomach the thought of her hands on another man. To know she'd massaged their bare bodies twisted his heart into a painful knot. This was why his gut had kept insisting there was something she was hiding. And he suspected she was hiding more.

"I had to think of Adam and Cora," she said, tears brimming her eyes.

Two hours ago her quavering voice would have wrenched his heart with sympathy. Now it left him cold.

"Duke, I needed to get them away from the brothel. How could I do that by announcing where we came from?"

She couldn't have. He understood that. If anyone had known Faith's mother ran a brothel and her aunts were prostitutes, Faith and her family would have been run out of town. If anyone discovered the truth now, their lives would be ruined. Her life. His life. His mother's and brothers' lives.

And she'd married him knowing this.

Her betrayal sliced through him. One slip of the tongue, and Faith's reputation, and his own, would be ruined. His family's reputation would be shattered, and the sawmill business would suffer as well as Radford and Evelyn's livery. All because he'd been a blind, lust-deceived fool.

"Who else knows about this?" he asked.

"My aunts and Adam. We lived behind the brothel."

"How could any mother—" He pinched the bridge of his nose, furious that any child was exposed to such a life. No wonder Adam had a worldly look in his eyes. God only knew what the boy had seen, and what he'd shared with Rebecca.

"I don't know how she stayed," Faith said, her soft voice wringing his emotions. "I couldn't bear raising Adam and Cora there. That's why I changed my name and came here, to give us all a decent life."

"You what?"

"My last name is Dearborn."

He pinched the bridge of his nose, willing away the headache throbbing behind his eyes. He understood her need to protect the children, but to lie and change her name and let him walk into their marriage blind.

Radford had been right to be concerned, and he himself had been a fool.

He felt deflated and cold and sick inside. And stupid. She had brought this mess to his doorstep, and he, being the lust-struck fool Radford had accused him of being, had opened the door and welcomed her into his life.

"I had to do it, Duke. I couldn't take a chance of having my name being traced back to that brothel."

"Then why didn't you change Adam's name?"

"I would have, but..." She huffed out a breath. "He's a boy. He wasn't thinking when he told you his name."

It sickened Duke that the boy would even have to lie about something like that. "I married a woman named Faith Wilkins, not Faith Dearborn. Do you realize I could annul our marriage on those grounds?"

Her lips parted, but no words came out. Her eyes flooded and she shook her head. "You can't... Duke, no." She clutched his hands.

"If you annul it... oh, God, think of Cora." Tears spilled over her lashes. "Please, Duke, you can't do that. You can't tell anyone about this or we'll be driven away in shame."

Her tears gouged his heart. His anger choked him.

"Don't punish them because of me," she pleaded. "I'm the guilty one. Don't cast out two innocent children."

"Those innocent children are my responsibility now. How could I cast them out?"

"Because you hate me."

"I don't hate you. I hate lies. I hate being stupid. I hate being deceived." He slammed his hand on the porch column. "I hate this burden you've put on my conscience!"

"I had to," she whispered, killing him with those sorrow-filled eyes. "I'll get rid of the brothel as soon as I can."

His blood ran cold. "You *own* that place?"

Her sheepish nod heated his neck and doubled his heartbeat. What she owned, *he* owned.

Fury turned his voice to ice. "Do you know what will happen to my job and my family if anyone discovers that my wife, that *I*, own a brothel?"

She shivered and clutched her sweater tighter. "I want to sell it, but I can't find the deed. My mother had no will, and I haven't been able to talk to a lawyer about this."

He gritted his teeth and faced the chill breeze, struggling to control his outrage. "Who was your mother's lawyer?"

"I don't know. None of us knew anything about her affairs. She may not have even had a lawyer."

His fists clenched and his shoulder ached deep in the socket. "Where are her papers? Surely she had some?"

"Just a key and a guestbook."

He faced his deceitful wife. "A what?"

"Mama recorded the guests and their fees in a book. I don't know what the key is for. It didn't fit her jewelry box or any locks in the house."

Guests? The euphemism repulsed him, and he suddenly hated Faith's mother. "Get the book."

"The deed isn't there."

"Get it." He didn't want to talk. Not tonight. He was too outraged, too ready to smash his fists into a wall until he beat the frustration out of his system. In all his life, he'd never been so naive or made such a stupid, drastic mistake.

Worse yet, he'd compromised his integrity tonight by not charging Dahlia for killing Levens. Her deadly shot had probably saved several lives, including her own, which Levens would have snuffed out in his rampage to punish and kill Anna; Levens had hurt both women, and probably would have killed them, but Duke had stopped him. He'd cuffed the man and would have taken him back to prison. Dahlia had known that, and she'd still pulled the trigger.

Duke didn't blame her, but his job was to uphold the law, not decide a person's guilt. That job was for a jury. Once a person bent the truth—or the law—to suit himself, he would bend it a hundred times. Faith was proof of that. Her life was a web of lies.

He didn't lie, and he'd never supported or approved of prostitution in his life. But now he owned a brothel. His father would roll in his grave.

Chapter Thirty

Adam took Rebecca's hand and crept up the greenhouse stairs to the second floor where Faith dried herbs. It was closed on Sunday, which made it a perfect hideaway for him and Rebecca. But the sound of voices made him freeze near the top of the stairs. He brought his finger to his lips to warn Rebecca they weren't alone.

Patrick had Iris trapped in his arms and backed against the plank wall. "You'll never get away from me," he said.

Dang it all! Adam had hoped he and Rebecca could sneak in here and talk, and maybe even kiss, but now everything was ruined because Patrick and Iris had gotten here first.

"I wasn't trying to get away," Iris said, breathless. "I planned to bring you up here and seduce you."

Gads! Adam hoped Rebecca didn't know he'd brought her here to steal a kiss.

"You won't respect me if I submit," Patrick said.

Iris laughed then got a strange look on her face. "I wish I'd met you before I... many years ago."

Adam ducked lower on the stairs, worried she'd seen him. Rebecca sidled closer, and he knew they should leave, but spying was too exciting.

"You would have hated me then. I was afraid of spirited girls like you." Patrick began unbuttoning Iris's shirtwaist. "Are you wearing a corset?"

"I never wear a corset." She ran her hands down his stomach to the top of his trousers. "Until I was thirteen, I was so sweet and naive, I would have bored you to sleep."

Patrick pushed her shirtwaist open, showing off her lacy red chemise that Adam had seen drying on a rack in the house. "And you are definitely not boring, Iris Wilde."

"Being outrageous is more exciting," she said.

"I like outrageous." Patrick buried his face in her breasts. "I like exciting."

So did Adam. But he clutched Rebecca's hand and nodded toward the foot of the stairs. If he were alone, he might peek a little longer, but he had to get her out of here.

Rebecca shook her head and grinned like she wanted to stay.

Adam hesitated then saw Patrick put his whole hand over Iris's breast. "I want you. Right here. Right now. Forever."

"I don't need forever. Right here, right now, is enough." Iris straddled his thigh, and Patrick ground his body against hers.

Rebecca clenched Adam's hand.

"Marry me, Iris."

Iris gripped Patrick's face, looking angry. "Don't you dare fall in love with me."

"Too late. I fell the first time I saw you." He kissed her neck and she got all breathless.

"I'll break your heart, farm boy"

"I won't let you." He put his hand on the front of Iris's skirt then pushed the fabric between her legs, making her gasp and causing Adam's stomach to go light.

"Men have been paying me to do that for twelve years," she said.

Adam gulped. Rebecca shouldn't know this.

"Do you understand what I'm saying, Patrick?"

"Yes." He pulled his groping hand away to lift her chin up so she had to look at him. "And now I understand why you've never met a man you wanted to marry."

Adam's mouth fell open. Patrick didn't care that Iris used to be a prostitute? Is that what he was saying? Because if he didn't care, maybe Duke wouldn't care that they'd lived behind the brothel. Maybe Rebecca wouldn't care either.

"My sweet, wild Iris." Patrick kissed her very gently and looked sad, like he was dying or something. "I'm a plain, honest man who loves you. Is that enough for you?"

Iris looked like she was going to cry. "You deserve better."

"I couldn't find better."

"Do you know how many men I've known?"

"Too many," he said, gently. "But now you know me, and I'll take good care of you. Marry me. Let me love you."

And with that, he tugged her chemise down and put his mouth over her bare breast like he was starving.

Rebecca's gasp was so loud it startled Patrick and Iris apart. Adam grabbed Rebecca's hand and pulled her down the stairs and outside into the windy afternoon. They raced down the bank and followed the creek to a pool and small waterfall near Rebecca's home.

Adam stopped, chest heaving from their run. "I didn't know anybody would be there," he said, but was too ashamed to look at Rebecca.

"Were they... you know?"

How did she know about... Gosh, he'd thought she was innocent, but she knew what happened between boys and girls. "Yeah, they were," he said, heat scorching his ears. Did she think he'd taken her to the greenhouse to do what Patrick and Iris were doing? He'd just wanted a kiss.

"I've seen our horses when they... a couple of times."

"I didn't mean for you to SEE that," he said, his voice squawking, which made his whole face hot.

Rebecca didn't even blink.

"Will your aunt tell on us?" she asked.

He hadn't considered that, but if Iris blabbed, he was dead. Rebecca was supposed to be at a neighbor's house, and he was supposed to be fishing in the pond behind the greenhouse. If Duke or Rebecca's father learned they were together, especially in the greenhouse where they would have been alone if not for Patrick and Iris, they would string Adam up by his heels.

Duke had been scowling all week, and Faith was crying a lot for some reason. This wasn't the time to get in trouble with either one of them. But if Iris told, he was dead.

"No one can know about this," he said.

Rebecca flushed, but she didn't look away. "They're grownups. Why would they get in trouble?"

"They're not married. It would ruin Iris's reputation, and maybe Faith's." Adam sighed and sat on a rock beside her. "I'm going to tell you something, but you have to promise to keep it a secret."

"Cross my heart," she said. The soft look in her eyes warmed him. He'd never had a friend like Rebecca. He could trust her.

"My aunts used to be prostitutes."

She squinted at him. "I don't know what that is."

"They did what Iris was doing with Patrick."

"Is that bad? I'm pretty sure my mother does it with my dad."

"My aunts did it with lots of men who paid them money."

"Oh..."

"So did my mother."

Rebecca was so quiet, Adam figured she would walk away and never talk to him again.

"She wasn't much of a mother," he said. It hurt to admit it, but it was the truth, and Adam wasn't going to lie about anything ever again. "That's why Faith has always been more like a mother to me."

"Does my Uncle Duke know about your aunts?"

Adam shook his head. "Faith never did that stuff with men. We moved here so my aunts could stop being prostitutes, but I guess Iris missed it or something."

"Maybe that's what my mother was like. I never met her, but maybe she was like your aunts." Rebecca hooked her arms around her knees and stared at the rippling water. "Maybe that's why she didn't want me."

"Did your dad say she was a prostitute?"

"No, he said she was a ballerina."

"Gosh, that's a lot better than being a prostitute." Adam wished his own mother had been a dancer.

"I wonder what my mother looks like." Rebecca's eyes sparked. "Maybe I look like her. Maybe if she saw me now, she'd wish she hadn't abandoned me. That's what my dad says she did."

"You're real pretty. I'll bet she'd be sorry she gave you away"

A small smile touched Rebecca's lips and she ducked her head.

"Do you miss her?" he asked.

"No." She lifted a flat rock with the toe of her shoe and flipped it over so the wet, loamy side faced the gray sky. "I would never want a different mother than Evelyn. But sometimes I wonder about my first mother. You know, what she's like, what her voice sounds like."

"Yeah, I wonder about my dad too. Faith thinks he's in prison or something, but he could be dead for all we know."

"Do you think he is?"

He shrugged. He had no idea.

They tossed rocks in the creek for a few minutes then started skipping the flat stones across the surface. For a girl, she was good at it, and he liked being her friend. He wanted to be more, but he couldn't ask.

"I noticed that Nicholas Archer hasn't been bothering you in school."

It was because Adam stayed away from him, and told everybody that Rebecca was his cousin now.

"I hope you're going to stay in school this year." She gave a flat rock a good ride across the creek then faced him. "I like walking to school with you."

She was so close he could see the gold flecks in her eyes. Heat burned through his body and he felt his stomach tighten. "I like it too," he said, his voice rough and shaky, but it didn't squawk.

"Do you think we'll ever do that... you know... what Iris and Patrick were doing?"

Strange things were happening to his body, and he was shaking so badly he was too afraid to answer.

"We could kiss, if you want to," she went on. Her voice was so soft he wanted to trap it in a jar and keep it with him forever. He wanted to keep Rebecca and her friendship forever.

"I want to," he said, and before he lost his nerve, he did the one thing he'd been aching to do since the day he met her in the store. He leaned forward and touched his lips to hers. They were warm and soft, and her brown eyes were filled with so many gold flecks it made him dizzy. His whole body went weak then got shaky and sweaty.

"That's the best feeling in the world," she said softly, her voice filled with pleasure and wonder, her mouth so near his he had to kiss her again.

Something wild and hot flooded through his stomach, and the feeling grew heavy and moved lower. Kissing Rebecca was the best feeling in the world for him too. He put his shaky hands on her arms to bring her closer to him, but the sound of a branch snapping jolted them apart. If her father caught them...

Rebecca stumbled backward over a small pile of rocks. Adam caught her arm and saved her a fall, but Rebecca glared at the trees along the bank. "Melissa Archer is spying on us again!"

"Why is she so stupid?" He scanned the bank but couldn't see the girl.

"She likes you."

"Well, I don't like her."

"Good." Rebecca brushed sand and bits of leaves off her skirt then gave him a warm smile. "I don't blame her for liking you. I sure do." She surprised him with a quick kiss then backed away. "I won't tell anyone about Iris and Patrick. Or about us."

"We'd get in big trouble if you did."

"You can trust me." She grabbed her skirt and lifted it to her shins. "I have to get home before I'm missed." Then she darted into the trees, tall and beautiful and as graceful as a deer, and Adam knew he would never love any girl but Rebecca Grayson.

Chapter Thirty-one

Friday afternoon was the first it hadn't rained in days, and Duke was stuck inside at the town meeting. The good news in an otherwise dismal week was that Arthur Covey had been convicted of horse theft and sent to prison.

Wayne Archer stood up and addressed the Board of Trustees. "I want to register a complaint against the sheriff of our county," he said. "It's becoming painfully obvious that Sheriff Grayson is biased in how he upholds the law in our village."

"In what way?" Duke asked, growing weary of Archer's constant attacks. He had returned the fancy parasol to Archer weeks ago, but hadn't told Archer where he'd found it, because it would have only confirmed the man's suspicion that Adam was the thief.

Duke didn't know who'd taken the parasol, but since it was returned, and both Adam and Rebecca claimed no knowledge of how the item got to her house, Duke had let the incident rest.

"Not only have two swindles taken place under your nose," Archer accused, "but there is a thief in town who is living in your home."

Duke shot to his feet, but he kept himself from planting his fist in Archer's face. "Until you can provide a witness who saw Adam take your parasol then you'd best not cast accusations, Wayne."

"I'm not referring to the parasol. My best fishing rod was stolen out of my barn last Sunday afternoon. My daughter saw Adam take it."

Duke's gut twisted. Archer was playing dirty to bring this up at the town meeting days after the alleged theft, but the man had never before been a liar. "I'll talk to your daughter," he suggested. "Let's get this business taken care of right now."

"That's just the beginning of my concerns." Archer turned back to the board members, his chest puffed up, his fingers tugging on his vest. "I have reason to believe Sheriff Grayson's wife is running a house of ill repute right here in our village."

"What?" Duke grabbed Archer's arm and spun the man to face him. "On what grounds are you making this ridiculous accusation?"

"Dr. Milton claims he's been getting private massages from Aster Wilde on the second floor of the greenhouse."

Maybe he was. Aster and the doctor had grown quite friendly, and Duke suspected they were past courting, but it wasn't his business to chaperone a grown man and woman.

The board members stared, mouths open, eyebrows raised.

Duke released Archer's elbow and faced them. "As you probably know, Dr. Milton suffered a carriage accident in early July. He was skeptical of my wife's business, so he limped into her greenhouse after his accident and tried the herbal bath and massage to test her claim that it would help him. Since the doctor is still taking treatments, I assume it's because he's finding them beneficial to his health."

"But the doctor isn't the only man who's enjoying those private treatments," Archer said. "My wife stopped there to buy cooking herbs and saw Cyrus Darling at the top of the stairs kissing a blond woman quite passionately."

President A. C. Cushing scowled at Duke. "Is this true?"

Who knew? Duke didn't. No doubt Archer had sent his wife to snoop, but if she had seen Cyrus kissing Tansy then anything was possible. He should have stopped those baths and massages when he married Faith. But he admired her skills and knew her treatments improved painful conditions like his shoulder injury.

"I'm unaware of any sordid activity," Duke said truthfully, but he was going to put a halt to the rumors immediately. Feigning calm, he nodded to Archer. "I'll look into it along with your claim that your fishing rod was stolen."

Archer spoke to the board president. "I would caution all of you that we are discussing the sheriff's family, and that it's very possible he will act with bias."

Duke grabbed two fistfuls of Archer's shirt and slammed him against the wall. "If you insult my integrity or my family again, Wayne, I'm going to take off this badge and answer your insults with my fists."

Board member Gideon Webster gripped Duke's shoulder. "Wayne not only underestimates your patience but our intelligence. We've depended on your integrity and judgment for eight years, and won't be swayed by anyone's petty rumors."

His confidence rubbed salt in Duke's festering conscience. He *had* been biased when he didn't charge Dahlia with murder. And knowing Faith's aunts, there probably was something tawdry going on in the greenhouse. For all he knew, Adam could be the thief Archer accused him of being.

He shoved Archer away from him. "Let's go talk to your daughter about that missing fishing rod of yours."

Duke excused himself from the meeting and strode alongside Archer to his house, feeling more like a criminal than a law enforcer for the first time in his term as sheriff. Archer was a pain in the ass, but he wasn't all wrong.

Melissa Archer swore she'd seen Adam sneaking out of their barn with her father's fishing rod last Sunday afternoon. She claimed it was half past two when she finished her piano practice and headed outside to play. And she described Adam perfectly, even mentioning the shirt he had been wearing that afternoon.

Duke expected Archer to act smug, but the man gave him a look of pity. "I don't envy you your position, Sheriff."

Who would? What man wanted to discover that his son was a thief? Melissa's detailed account made her a convincing witness.

Duke left and walked out Liberty Street then cut through the field behind his mother's house and followed the path down into the gorge where he kept his boat. He needed time to think before going home. His dad had always worked out his problems while fishing in the gorge or running the saw at the mill; Duke needed to do the same. But when he reached into his boat to get his fishing pole, his problems grew by one expensive fishing rod.

"Son of a bitch," he said, lifting out the rod Archer claimed was stolen. Only Adam and Duke's brothers knew where Duke kept his boat. Did Adam think he could stash the rod here and make Duke believe it was one of his own? Did the boy think Duke would be that gullible? Why not? Duke huffed in self-disgust. He'd never suspected Faith's lies. Why shouldn't Adam try to hoodwink the blind sheriff too? Faith would try to protect the boy, but it was time for Adam to face the consequences of his actions.

And for Duke to face reality.

He gripped Archer's fishing rod and walked home with it. He found Adam helping Faith and Cora rake leaves. A smile covered Cora's face as she ran to greet him with a hug. He tweaked her side, and set her back on her feet. "I need to talk to your mother and Adam alone," he said. "Go play on the swing for a few minutes."

"Will you push me?" she asked.

"I can't, princess. I'm working." He gave her a pat on the head, and she scampered off.

"What's the matter?" Faith asked, tugging a pair of worn gloves off her hands. She approached him warily, like a snarling dog she was unsure of.

He couldn't blame her. He'd snapped at her a dozen times since learning about the brothel. Her attempts to stroke his hackles back into place only antagonized him. He needed to work out his anger alone, and figure out how to get them out of this mess without losing everything he and his family had worked for.

A worried look creased Adam's forehead as he dropped the rake, but when he saw the fishing rod, his eyes lit up. "Did you get a new rod?" he asked, stopping in front of Duke.

The genuine excitement in his face unbalanced Duke. He'd expected to see fear or feigned innocence, not boyish enthusiasm.

"Where were you last Sunday afternoon, Adam?"

The boy's gaze shifted slightly and became guarded. "In the gorge."

"Did you at any time go into Wayne Archer's barn and remove this fishing rod?" he asked, finding that a direct question could sometimes shake loose an honest answer.

"No, sir," Adam said, his scowl deepening. "I don't even know where Mr. Archer lives."

"Melissa Archer said she saw you leaving her father's barn with this fishing rod Sunday afternoon at two-thirty."

Anger flashed in his eyes. "She's lying."

"Then you're saying you were in the gorge?"

Adam's jaw clenched. "Yes."

"What were you doing in the gorge?"

"Skipping stones."

"You told me you were going fishing."

"I changed my mind."

"Did you put my rod back in my boat?"

"I didn't take it out. I just stayed in the gorge and skipped stones."

"Then you never went to my boat?"

"No, sir. I haven't been there since the day you took me fishing."

"If you're telling me you didn't take this rod from his barn then I want to know how it got on my boat."

Adam clenched his jaw and said nothing, his stubborn silence increasing Duke's ire.

"Adam..." Faith rubbed his shoulder, coddling him, which made Duke madder. "Do you know anything about this?"

The boy shook his head.

"All right then." She glanced at Duke. "I believe him."

She would. It irritated Duke that she accepted Adam's word without considering the facts. "How did this rod end up on my boat if Adam didn't put it there?"

"I don't know," she said, "but I know when Adam isn't telling the truth."

"Do you? Then why couldn't you tell he was lying when he was skipping out of school?"

"Because I didn't ask him where he was going."

Furious, Duke planted the pole on the ground. "How do you suppose this rod got on my boat, Adam?"

The boy glared at him. "You're the sheriff, you figure it out."

Duke's chest felt close to exploding. Tangling with Archer at the meeting had gotten his blood warm, but finding the fishing rod on his own boat then getting wise-mouthed from Adam pushed his temperature to boiling.

"All right, Adam, I will. I'll do my job without your help. But you stay in the yard. No wandering in the gorge. No going anywhere but to school. I want Faith to know where you are every minute of the day."

"Why? I didn't do anything wrong."

"I'm your guardian, and your actions reflect on me. Don't challenge me on this, Adam, or I'll put you in jail and keep an eye on you myself."

Faith gasped, her eyes wide with disbelief and disappointment.

"How come nobody ever believes me?" Adam demanded.

"Because you've lied to both of us," Duke said. "This is what happens when you break a person's trust."

"I didn't take that stupid fishing rod!"

Before Adam could bolt, Duke clamped a hand on the boy's shoulder. "I told you to stay in the yard."

"You aren't my father."

The boy's words hit Duke like a bucket of ice water, hurting and startling then infuriating him.

"Maybe not, Adam, but I'm the sheriff in this town and I can confine you to the yard if I see fit. Since you don't like that idea, I'll see if a jail cell suits you better."

He marched Adam across the yard.

"Duke!" Faith hurried after them. "You can't take him to jail. He's only a boy!"

"Age has nothing to do with it, Faith. Adam has been caught stealing and lying, and he's being charged with another theft. I can't turn a blind eye to the boy's shenanigans and expect to keep my job. It's time Adam faced the consequences of his actions. You lie, nobody trusts you. You steal, you go to jail. You mislead people, you risk losing everything."

"You're trying to punish *me*, Duke. I'm the one you're angry with. I'm the one who lied. I'm the one who misled you. And you'll never forgive me for burdening your lily white conscience, will you?"

She was crying now, tearing him apart with her tears and words. He turned away, unable to look at her, not wanting to believe she was right, or that he was allowing his anger make him cruel.

Adam tried and failed to jerk his elbow free. "Faith hasn't hurt anybody!"

Duke kept his grip firm and propelled Adam down the street. "You'd better get all the facts before you pass judgment, Adam."

"Maybe you should take your own advice. I didn't steal anything but that brush. And Faith wouldn't hurt anybody for any reason."

Duke blocked out Adam's angry denial, and Faith's tears, and marched the boy straight to his empty jail cell. He left his deputy to watch the boy then took a walk to cool off.

He strode up West Hill and turned left on Chestnut Street, trying to burn off his anger. All he'd wanted was a truthful and loving wife. Supporting Faith and her large family was a job he'd accepted without complaint or resentment. Being a father to Cora and Adam was as rewarding as it was challenging. And he could understand why Faith hid the truth from him.

But he'd earned her trust. All those nights in the bathhouse, when he'd ached to make love to her, he'd protected her from his lust and waited until they were married to consummate their attraction. He'd bought her the house she loved. On their wedding night, he nearly crippled himself trying to take things slow, to give her as much pleasure as possible in their marriage bed. Like an open book, he shared his life and his memories with her, but never pressed her to talk about her own life because he sensed it brought her pain. He gave her his heart and his passion.

She gave him lies.

Damn right, he was angry. With himself. In his efforts to protect Faith and her aunts, he was becoming a man he couldn't respect.

His brothers had accused him of being rigid to a fault, but laws were black and white, and meant to be rigidly adhered to, and enforced with diligence. He should have pursued the parasol theft until he found the thief. He should have charged Dahlia with killing Levens and let a jury decide her guilt. And he should have listened to Radford when his brother warned him to slow down. Because if he'd suspected Faith's past, he'd have done things differently. He'd have done them right. He'd have shut down the bathhouse, married off those crazy aunts of hers, and sold the brothel.

Then he would have married Faith—because he loved her.

And that's why her lack of trust wounded him so deeply. From the minute he met her, he'd wanted her. He'd opened his heart and his life and left himself open to her betrayal. To realize she knowingly misled him was like expecting a kiss only to get slammed in the gut with a hand maul.

It was his own fault for being too sure of himself. He'd known Faith was hiding something behind her smile, but he ignored the feeling because he wanted her, and because he knew she was the one, the woman he would love for the rest of his life.

His anger burned away, and his pace slowed, but he continued to walk. He headed out of town on Water Street then cut over to Liberty Street where the whining sound of the saw at the mill echoed along the gorge and beckoned him closer.

There was commotion in the yard when he got there. His brothers were talking with Patrick and Cyrus, but they looked pissed off, especially Radford, who swore and slammed his hand axe into a pile of maple logs.

"What's going on?" Duke asked, closing in on their gathering.

They all looked at him, but Radford got right in his face. "I was just going to come find you," he said, all tensed up like he was ready to throttle somebody.

"Why?" Everyone was looking at him, but he spoke to Radford. "What's going on here?"

"You have a brothel operating under your nose, that's what's wrong! My daughter walked into that greenhouse you own and saw Patrick fondling Iris's bare breast."

"What?" Duke's gaze shot to Patrick. "Is that true?"

Patrick gave a shamefaced nod.

Duke's gut twisted and he felt nauseated. To think an innocent like Rebecca had witnessed something so base and intimate made him want to slug Patrick—and kick himself for being so blind.

"The greenhouse was closed for the day. We thought we'd be alone," Patrick said. "We didn't know Adam and Rebecca would be tromping upstairs." Pat's shoulders sagged. "I feel awful, Radford. I thought you should know so you could talk to her. She's got to be shocked and confused by what she saw."

"At the least. She should have never witnessed something like that." Radford's nostrils flared. "Whatever is going on at that greenhouse had better stop right now, Duke. If anyone hears about this, it could shred our reputation. You may not mind, but I do."

"So do I," Boyd said. "We've each got a wife and children to think about."

"And Mother," Kyle added. "If she gets dragged into this, Duke, I'll tear that greenhouse apart board by board and get rid of the problem."

They had every right to be angry, but he was unable to believe what he was hearing. Archer wasn't just trying to undermine Duke's bid for election; the man had genuine cause for concern.

"Were you there too, Cyrus?" he asked, figuring he may as well hear the whole disgusting truth.

"Not that day."

"Not *that* day. What does that mean?" he asked. "Archer's wife said she saw you and Tansy kissing at the top of the stairs in the greenhouse. Was Tansy servicing you upstairs, too?"

Shock flashed across the man's face then his expression hardened with anger. "Tansy was accepting my marriage proposal."

The announcement surprised Duke and left him momentarily speechless. He'd figured Cyrus would remain a bachelor for life. And knowing Tansy's past profession, Duke assumed none of those bawdy women would ever marry. Did Cyrus know about Tansy's past? Or was he an unsuspecting fool like Duke had been?

"We're going to marry tomorrow afternoon."

So soon? Was there a reason for haste? It wasn't Duke's place to share the information with Cyrus. All he could do was try to keep everything from collapsing and burying his family in a mess they had nothing to do with. His mind spun, groping for a way to undo the damage Faith's aunts and Cyrus and Patrick had caused with their fooling around. Then it struck him. "I want you to marry Tansy in the Common," he said, an idea forming in his mind.

Cyrus scowled. "We were going to do it quick and quiet."

"You could have if you hadn't been so careless in kissing Tansy in the greenhouse. You two are the cause of this rumor, Cyrus. If you and Tansy marry in the park, people will think you were just an eager fiancé who was stealing a kiss from your intended. That should silence any rumors the Archers may have started, and it will keep suspicion from being cast on my family."

"All right." Cyrus gave him a nod. "I accept the responsibility for that, and I'm sorry for it. I'll let Tansy know."

Duke faced his brothers and had never felt so cut off from them in his life. In all their spats, there was never a time when they all stood against him as they were doing now. Duke was the peacekeeper in the family. He was the one who calmed them down and made them see reason. But not today. Because they all had everything to lose. And it was Duke's poor judgment that had put them in this position. "I'll shut down the bathhouse and stop the massages," he said. "But it'll break Faith's heart if I make her close the greenhouse."

"The greenhouse isn't my only concern here." Radford's scowl darkened, his temper escalating. "It's that boy Rebecca's been sneaking around with. She wouldn't have been there if not for Adam. You keep him away from her, or *I'm* going to have a talk with him."

Under the circumstances, Duke didn't blame his brother for being angry and protective, but it galled him that Radford was dumping the blame on Adam's shoulders. Rebecca had a mind of her own and was with Adam because she wanted to be.

This wasn't the time or the place to argue about it, though.

He gave Radford a nod then turned and jabbed his finger against Patrick's chest. "I suspect the only reason Radford hasn't throttled you for being such an idiot is because you're a good friend. But if you and Iris want to get naked, do it on your own property or I'll beat you myself."

He walked away before he slugged Patrick for being so careless and stupid, and before he started an argument with Radford over the children.

No one ever told him that being a husband and father would be a continuous exercise in control. Only an hour ago he'd wanted to shake Adam until the boy confessed the truth about the fishing rod. But now he knew Adam was with Rebecca last Sunday afternoon when the rod was supposedly taken, and he didn't know what to think about the theft. Adam couldn't have been in two places at the same time.

But if Adam didn't take the rod, how did it get on Duke's boat? The dinghy was too well hidden for someone to stumble upon it. So

Adam, or someone who knew where Duke kept his boat, put the rod there. Rebecca knew where he kept it, but she wouldn't steal a piece of bread if she were starving.

His mind spun, gathering facts and sorting details as he walked to the greenhouse. Somehow he would figure out this mess, but his first order of business was to nail some female asses to the wall and put a stop to the rumors threatening his family.

Chapter Thirty-two

The slam of the greenhouse door startled Faith, and she nearly dropped a jar of balm she'd been scenting with herbs. She looked up to see Duke standing inside the door, his face a mask of fury.

"Do you know what people are saying about you, Faith?" The indignant look on his face assured her it wasn't good.

Her stomach plummeted and she clutched her fist to her belly, crushing the dried herbs in her hand. "What's wrong?"

"Are your aunts here?" he asked.

"Everyone except Dahlia. She took Cora to the store with her."

"Do you have any customers?"

"Not at the moment."

"Good." He lifted his chin and his voice cracked through the greenhouse. "Iris Wilde, get your ass out here! Aster and Tansy! Wherever you are, get out here."

Faith gasped, fearing what was coming.

Tansy flitted out from behind a large cluster of Saint-John's-wort, her eyes wide. Aster stepped in from the bathhouse, wiping her hands on her apron and scowling like a mother.

"What are you yelling about?" she asked, pushing her way through the plants.

"Where's Iris?" he asked.

"Right here," Iris said, descending the stairs with pinched lips and an arched eyebrow. "What are you riled about?"

"I'll give you a list." Duke lifted his fist and raised his thumb. "First, Wayne Archer says Doc Milton is bragging about the private treatments Aster is giving him on the second floor."

"He is?" Aster's lips tilted in a pleased smile.

Duke's scowl darkened.

"Second..." He glared at Tansy. "Archer says his wife saw you and Cyrus out here kissing like two overheated lovers."

"We *are* lovers," she said meekly.

"I don't care!" Duke swatted the bush of lemongrass in front of him. "Do you women realize that you've jeopardized my family's reputation?" He strode five paces then slammed his fist on the counter. Faith dropped the jar she held, and it shattered on the floor.

"My mother and my sisters-in-law put their reputations on the line when they promoted this business to their friends. My brothers spent two weeks pounding nails in that building next door so you women could have a decent place to live. And what do they get for their kindness?" he asked, his voice cracking with righteous anger. "They get put in the middle of a nasty rumor that could shred their reputations. My brother's daughter saw something no child should see. And I get the pleasure of being responsible for all of this."

Iris braced her hand on the railing. "You're overwrought, Sheriff—"

"You bet I am!" He jabbed his finger toward her. "You're the worst offender, Iris! My niece, an innocent little girl, saw you and Patrick... fondling each other upstairs last Sunday. *No* child should see that!" He slammed his fist on the counter again. "I'm fighting the urge to send you packing."

The smell of the resinous balm that was splattered on the floor and across Faith's feet rose to her nose and made her nauseated. She looked at her aunts, and not one of them would meet her eyes. They were guilty of every sin Duke accused them of. Duke knew, and they were ruined. It was over with him, and over for them, and there was nothing she could do to stop it.

"I'll leave." Iris descended the last few steps and crossed to the counter. "You're right to despise me for what happened with your niece. My carelessness and inconsideration are unforgivable. I should never have come here."

"You can't leave." Faith reached across the counter and grasped her aunt's hand. "You're my family. Adam and Cora love you. You can't leave us."

"She's not going anywhere." Anger etched deep grooves in Duke's face. "But all this bathing and massaging and philandering upstairs stops, and it stops right now. Not one more person outside this family uses that bathtub. Not one man climbs those stairs or enters the bathhouse." He looked at Aster. "That includes the doctor."

Aster nodded. "I presume that will change when the doctor becomes my husband?"

Faith was as surprised by Aster's announcement as Duke seemed to be, but his eyes narrowed as if Aster said something extremely important. "Are you marrying the doctor?"

The woman nodded. "Paul asked. I said yes." She whacked dirt off her apron as if they were discussing plants and not her future, but Faith saw a happy spark in her aunt's eyes.

"Would you marry him tomorrow?"

They all gaped at his odd request.

Duke looked at Tansy. "I asked Cyrus to marry you in the Common tomorrow. A public wedding should silence the rumors about why you two were kissing in the greenhouse." He pinned Aster with his stony stare. "I'd like you and Doc Milton to do the same."

"Makes no difference to me when or where I marry the man," Aster said. "I didn't realize his visits were causing trouble or I'd have stopped them myself. I'm sorry. I'll go talk to Paul now."

"I'm sorry, too," Tansy said, plucking at her apron. "I was so overcome when Cyrus said he hadn't been in the war and asked me to marry him, I kissed him like a darn fool." She lowered her lashes. "I didn't mean to start any nasty rumors."

"I don't fault your intentions, but I am holding each of you responsible for your actions." He turned to Iris. "As long as you and Patrick conduct your romance in private and away from this business, you can stay"

And with that, he blew out the door like strong wind, leaving everything in his path trembling.

And that was that. Faith's fist was still pressed against her stomach, where nausea returned full force. Her husband had just walked out, without a word, without a tender glance, without a single assurance that he would ever forgive her. She'd ruined everything for him and for their marriage. She'd married a tender, considerate, passionate man, and she'd single-handedly killed those parts of him, the best parts of him.

She'd shattered their marriage as swiftly and completely as she'd crushed the dried herbs in her hand.

⚊◁┼ ┼▷⚊

Duke unlocked the door to his holding cell, regretting his harshness with Adam and with Faith and her aunts. Faith would never forgive him if Iris left. Adam probably wouldn't forgive him either.

"Come on out," he said, swinging the door wide.

Adam stalked out, chin high, eyes blazing with anger.

"Why didn't you tell me you were with Rebecca last Sunday afternoon?"

"It wasn't your business."

"Maybe not, but there's more at stake than solving the mystery of the stolen fishing rod, Adam. Rebecca is a beautiful young lady, and I can see why you would like her," he said, "but there are consequences for giving your heart away when you're too young. Ask my brother Kyle. What if Rebecca changes her mind about you someday?"

"We haven't made any promises," Adam said.

"Good." Duke closed the door and leaned against it. "I'm not condemning you for caring about Rebecca, but you're causing trouble between her and her father. Radford has forbidden her to see you, Adam. You either respect his wishes and stay clear of Rebecca, or I'll put a stop to it myself."

Adam's scowl deepened. "Is this lecture over, Sheriff Grayson?"

Duke's breath shuddered out and he nodded. The lecture was over because he was out of energy. He was out of answers.

Adam stormed out, and Duke went to his office. He sat at his desk, head in hand, missing the time in his life when he didn't question his character or actions. He'd strayed so far from his ideals, he no longer knew what was right or wrong, or what he stood for.

Exhausted, he rubbed his aching shoulder and read through the list of names and comments in Faith's mother's guest book that spanned three decades. It was only a list of names, dates, and amounts, but Duke knew each name represented a man that his wife's mother had sold her body to, and it disgusted him.

Two names stood out because they appeared frequently. Lawyer Steven Cuvier's name was noted many times in the early years then so infrequently Duke would have missed its next occurrence if he hadn't been looking for the name. It disappeared altogether six years ago.

At that time, Judge Franklin Stone's name started appearing regularly then became the only name noted in Rose's guest book for the last five years of her life. No amounts were noted with Stone's entries, which was odd. Was Stone Rose's lover? Is that why she didn't charge him? If so then who was Steven Cuvier, and why had Rose's lipstick kiss decorated two of the early entries for Cuvier?

Had she loved both men?

If so, why had Cuvier paid for Rose's services when Stone got the goods for free?

Duke rubbed the heels of his hands against his gritty eyes. God only knew what Rose's life was all about. All he could gather from her book was that Stone and Cuvier knew her well. They were both in a position to help Rose with any legal work she may have needed. Maybe that's why Stone was getting free visits to Rose's bed. Maybe she owed him for legal work.

Maybe not, but Stone and Cuvier were the only leads worth tracking down. Even if neither man had done any legal work for Rose, one of them might know something about her that could head Duke in the right direction. Anything that could help him dump that miserable brothel would be welcome. He'd already sent a letter to three banks in Syracuse, asking if they had any information about the deed to Rose's property, but no one had yet responded.

He would try Stone and Cuvier too.

After forming his query in his head, Duke penned a letter to Stone then wrote a similar letter to Cuvier. When he finished writing, he folded the pages into envelopes and used his official wax seal to keep his correspondence confidential. He would post the letters before he headed to Mayville.

Chapter Thirty-three

Tansy and Aster's double ceremony in the park was simple but touching despite the dreary mid-October day. Faith stood among family and friends who sheltered themselves beneath umbrellas, but anyone walking through the park was welcome to watch the couples take their vows.

Intermittent wind gusts tugged the red and gold leaves off the maple trees and carried them through the air like small vessels. Faith wanted to sail away like the leaves and go back to the warmer, happy days of summer when she and Duke spent their days laughing and their nights making love; but she stood in the cold wind, shivering beside her distant husband. He hadn't left her, but would be leaving for Mayville after the ceremony. He said he'd return in a week. Maybe he wouldn't be so angry then. Maybe he would miss her. Maybe someday he would forgive her and welcome her back into his arms. Because he hadn't touched her since the night he learned about the brothel, and she was losing hope.

She didn't blame him for being upset, especially on behalf of his family. Faith hadn't considered that she would be putting his family in jeopardy when she married him. All she'd thought about was giving Cora and Adam security—and herself a respectable life with a man she cared about.

She hadn't counted on Dahlia killing a man, or her aunts having affairs in the greenhouse. She'd begun to believe that it was kinder not to tell Duke, that her past might not matter at all unless he learned the truth. Now it was all that mattered.

"You have a leaf in your hair, Mama."

Cora was happily perched in her daddy's arms. Despite Duke's anger with Faith, and his earlier harshness with Adam, he'd been loving and affectionate with the child. He'd admitted to Adam he'd been too hasty in judging, but there was a rift between the two that worried her. Adam needed Duke more than ever, and she blamed herself for the distance between them. Duke was disappointed in her, not in Adam.

They walked home together after the ceremony, but instead of joining the small gathering in their parlor, Duke packed a bag, changed his clothes, and strapped on his gun belt.

Faith followed him outside onto the porch where he shrugged on his coat. He would walk to Radford and Evelyn's livery to rent a horse for his trip. "How long will you be gone?" she asked.

"A week or so."

She nodded, not wanting him to leave with this chasm between them, but having no idea how to bridge it.

"Sam Wade will know how to reach me if you need anything."

Again, she nodded. "I'm sorry, Duke. I wanted so much for us..." she whispered, too choked by her emotions to go on.

He sighed and brushed his knuckles across her cheek. "So did I."

She caught his hand and pressed it to her face, missing him desperately. "I'll do anything to make you happy again."

He embraced her and gave her a hug, the first affection he'd shown her in a week. "I don't hate you, and I'm not even sure I blame you for anything. I'm just... I need to sort this out."

She lifted her face, aching for his kiss. "Will you do that while you're gone?"

"I'll try."

"Try real hard. For Cora and Adam. For us."

He lowered his head and kissed her, and the day seemed to fill with sunshine. Faith clutched his wide shoulders, returning his kiss with passion, hoping he would find forgiveness on his journey and a reason to return and reclaim the joy in their marriage.

He backed out of her embrace. "I've got to go." He grabbed his bag and descended the steps. "Wire if you need anything," he said, but he walked away without looking back.

Eight days later, Faith raked leaves into a big pile, assailed by doubts and worries. Where was he? Why hadn't Duke wired to let her know when he'd be returning home?

In the yard, Cora crawled through the leaves searching for Adam. When Adam lunged out of the pile, she shrieked with glee. They played all afternoon, raking the leaves into a pile then scattering them across the lawn, before raking them up again.

Faith went inside to make supper, but she could hear Adam's roars and Cora's shrieks of laughter. They were happy sounds. They were happy children. She'd done the right thing for them. Maybe not for Duke or for herself, but she had made the right decision for Adam and Cora. Surely Duke would see that her choice was the *only* choice, right or wrong, good or bad. Maybe he would realize that there was no right or wrong involved, that she'd based her decision on what was useful, and perhaps then he could forgive her. Maybe then he would find his way back to being the tender man she married.

Cora's scream, and Adam's yell, pierced Faith's thoughts so violently she dropped the potato she was peeling and ran for the door.

The instant she stepped outside, her insides turned liquid, drenching her in fear. Cold eyes stared down at her, like a bird of prey stalking its next meal. Judge Stone sat on a big, prancing horse, holding Cora, who was as limp as a wilted flower.

"Hello, Faith."

She would never forget those predatory eyes or that gritty, commanding voice.

"What have you done to her?" she asked, her fear for Cora so acute she could barely breathe. The child's eyes were closed as if she was sleeping, but she wasn't sleeping. Had the judge knocked her out?

"Nothing to damage her."

"I'll do anything you ask, just... let her go."

"Too late to negotiate, Mrs. Grayson. Now that your husband owns the brothel, my business is with him. You can thank him for sending me this letter. It helped me find you." The judge tossed the folded parchment at her feet. "Tell him to bring the deed to the brothel and meet me in Syracuse. If he tries any tricks, his esteemed family will pay for his arrogance."

He kicked the horse and bolted from the yard.

"No! Wait!" Faith leapt forward, but the horse raced down the street. "We don't have the deed!" she yelled.

Panic exploded in her chest and she raced after the judge and Cora, but Stone turned the horse onto Eagle Street and disappeared. Faith slammed to a stop at the edge of her yard. She couldn't scream for help. And that manipulative crook had known that when he rode up as bold as brass and took Cora. Faith couldn't tell anyone who he was or what happened without putting herself, and Duke and his family and their own children, at risk.

But she needed help.

She had to get Cora back.

Her heart pounded and she wrung her hands, feeling useless and frantic and...if it took until her last breath, she'd find Stone and kill him for this. She'd slip foxglove or aconite into his food. No longer would she let him threaten her and her family or put Duke's family at risk. No longer would she live looking over her shoulder for that greedy parasite.

Leaves rustled and the sound of Adam's groan terrified her. She rushed across the yard and fell to her knees beside him.

"Are you hurt?" she asked, not daring to touch him.

He curled forward then rolled to his knees. His face was pinched and he clutched his chest, gulping as if he couldn't get air.

"Just point to where you're hurt."

He shook his head then sucked in a gulp of air. Then another. Then he began to sob. "I tried to stop him." He groaned and rocked on his knees. "He kicked me in the chest."

"Oh, honey." Faith pulled him into her arms, terrified and furious and sick to her soul. The children she was trying to protect were in more danger than ever.

Somehow, she would make Stone pay for this.

The neighbor lady stepped onto her porch and peered in their direction. "I heard a scream. Is everything all right?"

"Yes, Mrs. Brooks." Faith kept her chin down so the woman wouldn't notice her wet cheeks. "My brother just took a hard spill in the leaves, but everything's fine."

"All right then." To Faith's relief, the woman went back inside.

Adam pulled away and struggled to his feet. "I got to get help."

"Wait." She put her hand on his shoulder. "We need to get a message to Duke without letting anyone know what happened."

Chapter Thirty-four

Duke road his weary mount out of Westfield, tired but certain he would win the election next week. Every township and village he'd visited had shown their support, and his under-sheriff and deputies stood solidly behind him. But of all the trips he'd made on sheriff's business, none had ever been so tedious or unfulfilling.

Where was his sense of purpose?

Where was the conviction he always felt during these visits? Where was the man who wouldn't compromise his integrity? Or his badge?

He was losing his moral compass. Decisions that used to be black and white were all tangled up with Faith's idea of useful or not useful. Nothing was clear anymore. Laws felt too harsh, and rules seemed too rigid in judging some cases fairly. Like Dahlia's situation. Duke had seen her aim the gun and pull the trigger. But there was truth in what she said: Levens would have killed Dahlia without a second thought, and he would have come back to kill Anna the first chance he got. It was so mixed up in Duke's head, he couldn't think about it without tying his gut in a knot.

Eight days of traveling had taken its toll on his shoulder and his mind. All he wanted was a good soak in the bathhouse and a few hours alone with Faith.

He missed her. He'd left too much unsaid between them because he'd been shocked into a state of outrage he'd never before known. From the minute he met Faith, each step that should have taken him due north had been a few degrees off course. Now, without true direction, he couldn't navigate his way through the day, much less his life.

Everything was in shambles with his brothers because of his lack of attention. He'd strayed off course with them as well.

The thunder of horse hooves racing up behind him made Duke reach for his gun. He was traveling alone, moving through towns like a drifter, crossing paths with all sorts of characters. If anything happened to him out here before he could apologize to his brothers for putting their reputations at risk, and offer Faith the forgiveness she sought, they would never know how deeply he regretted his actions.

He slowed his mare and drew his revolver.

"Sheriff Grayson!" He turned to see a man on horseback waving his arm. "A message for you!" he shouted.

Duke holstered his revolver and reined in his horse. There was trouble, but not from the man stopping beside him.

"Sam Wade said we'd find you heading out of Westfield."

Duke had wired Wade shortly before leaving to tell him he was heading home, but the wire was from Faith.

Cora missing.
Hurry!

Missing? All Duke could think about was the creek running high and hard from two weeks of heavy rain.

"Any return message, Sheriff?"

"No." With a tug on the reins, Duke wheeled his horse away, and kicked the big mare into a run. It didn't matter how or where or why his daughter was missing, it only mattered that she was.

His heart pounded with each mile he covered. The mare was sleek and fit, and Duke wanted to push her harder and faster, to eat up the miles between him and home. But he reined in his panic and alternated the mare's pace between a trot and a gallop.

Each minute that ticked by drove his anxiety higher, and when an hour passed, his chest was so tight it hurt. Another twenty minutes saw him trotting past the Common and down Water Street. When he finally dismounted in his front yard, he was praying Cora had been found and was safe in the house with Faith.

But Faith met him in the foyer, her face ashen. "Judge Stone took Cora."

Stone? "The man listed in your mother's guestbook?" The man Duke had sent a letter to? "Do you know him?"

"Yes."

"Why would he take Cora?"

"Because you sent him a letter! You told him where to find us!"

She was acting crazy, and it was making him crazy. "What are you talking about? Why would my letter make Stone come and take Cora?"

"Because he's Cora's father."

As if a boulder struck his chest, Duke's breath whooshed out and he stumbled back a step. "How can that be?" Stone had visited Rose. Faith said she didn't work upstairs. Nothing was making sense. "Did you and Stone... You said you were a widow"

The desolate look in her eyes scared him. "I'm not a widow," she whispered.

Duke stood perfectly still, his world crumbling around him.

"The judge was my mother's guest. And Cora was my mother's last child."

His mind spun with the horrifying reality of their situation. If the judge was Cora's father then he was entitled to take his child. Duke couldn't do anything legally to get back the little girl who'd stolen his heart.

Worse yet, he himself had sent the letter that brought the man to their doorstep. He wouldn't have sent the letter if Faith had told him about Stone. "How could you let me marry you without telling me this?"

"How *could* I tell you something like this?"

"How could you not?" he countered, pierced by another betrayal, this one unforgivable. "You lied about everything, Faith."

"What would you have done in my place?"

"I would have... I don't know." He scraped his hair out of his eyes. "I wouldn't have lied."

"Of course not," she said, her voice laced with sarcasm. "It's easy to be honorable when your belly is full, when you have a family to lean on, when you're a man who can fight your own battles. But no one helps a whore or her children. My mother made me ring a bell to get her attention! And I could only ring it if I had an emergency!" He expected tears, but she faced him with cold resolve. "When you live in a brothel, nothing is 'good' or 'bad'. Right or wrong don't exist. The only way I got through each day was to choose what was useful and ignore the rest. I'm asking for your compassion, not your approval."

"I'm your husband. You should have trusted me."

"I couldn't! Did you hear a word of what I just said?"

"I heard you, Faith. You don't trust me. Cora isn't your daughter. And you aren't a widow. So... why weren't you a virgin?" he asked, his heart bleeding.

"Because I was a fool. I believed Jarvis loved me, and that he was going to marry me."

"Who is Jarvis?"

"He was a guest at the brothel. When he saw me and learned I didn't work upstairs, he hired me to give him massages."

Duke ground his teeth. He was going to stand in the foyer until he learned every sordid detail once and for all. "No more lies, Faith. No more secrets. Tell me all of it."

She lifted bleak, swollen eyes. "Jarvis was the son of a wealthy planter from Kentucky. He stopped at the brothel each time he passed through Syracuse."

So she'd never been married. Another lie. It hardly mattered at this point.

"Jarvis bought a small house for us and gave me money to furnish it while he was away. He said he would return in two weeks to move me in. I thought we were getting married, so I gave in and... but after... when my mother found us, she made Jarvis confess the truth. He wanted a mistress, not a wife."

Duke could imagine how manipulated and hurt she felt, because he was experiencing that same painful betrayal. Everything he'd believed about Faith was in ashes. She wasn't a grieving widow from Saratoga. She'd grown up in a brothel in Syracuse and massaged men's bodies for money.

But the worst blow of all was that Cora wasn't legally Faith's daughter. It made him sick and more afraid than he'd ever been in his life.

"Why didn't you tell me about this the night I found out about the brothel?"

"Because the truth was too unbearable for you to hear all at once. And I was trying to protect Cora."

"Keeping secrets didn't protect her! That judge has every legal right to keep our daughter!" In hopeless rage, he slammed his fist against the wall.

Her chin shot up and her eyes flashed with anger. "Well, he can't have her! I'm going to Syracuse to get her. And I'll bleed, beg, or kill to get her back."

"How, Faith? He's legally entitled to his child."

"He doesn't want her. He wants the brothel. He caused my mother's death trying to get it."

Duke's blood ran cold knowing Cora was in that man's hands. Maybe Duke had no legal right to the girl, but when he'd married Faith, he'd bound his heart to the precious, precocious youth and vowed to protect her. That vow had brought him joy, a sweetness and light that he had never known. Like Faith, he would go anywhere, and do anything to find Cora and bring her back.

"Where's Adam?" he asked, his decision made completely and irrevocably.

"Next door with Dahlia."

"I'll take him to Boyd's house where he'll be safe. Pack a bag for us. When I get back, we're going to Syracuse."

⊶⊷

Duke left Adam with Boyd then sent a telegram to Steven Cuvier, hoping the man knew something about Stone or Faith's mother that would help them. But when Duke reached his office, his brisk manner deserted him. Despair settled in his gut, slowly hardening into a solid, unbreakable resolve.

He climbed the steps of the Academy building, aching to the bone from eight days of traveling. All he'd wanted was to get home, but now he wished he'd taken more time to thank each of his deputies for their service. They were good men, and he was honored to work with them.

But his life as sheriff was over.

He crossed the hall, unlocked his door, and entered his office. Everything was painfully familiar—the heavy oak desk, the rickety chair, the old metal safe—but no longer his. Another man would soon rest his elbows on the scarred desktop. Another man would carry the keys to the safe. Another man would wear the badge that Duke had worn with pride for eight years.

He'd known the day would come when he stepped down of his own accord, or when the vote supported another man. At each election he was prepared to pass the position to a man who could do the job. But he'd never imagined giving up his badge because he wasn't fit to wear it.

It was only a piece of metal, but when he unpinned the silver star from his leather vest, it felt like he tore out his heart. He closed his fingers around the medallion, missing the weight of it on his chest. He'd worn the badge so long, it had left an impression in the leather, a painful reminder of a position he could no longer live up to. Because he was going to cross the line. He was going to break the law.

The outside door squeaked open and footsteps echoed in the hall. "Glad you're back," his deputy called.

"You alone, Sam?"

"I will be in a minute."

Duke sat at his beat up old desk to write a short note of resignation. He heard keys jangle in the hallway then the cell door opened and closed then more jangling as Sam locked it.

"Sleep it off, Morton." Sam's boot heels clunked across the wood floor then he appeared at the door, his auburn beard looking like it needed a good trim. "Did you get your telegram, Sheriff?"

"Yeah." Duke knelt by the safe to open it. This was the last time anyone would call him Sheriff. When he walked out of his office, it would be as a private citizen.

And a father.

The law said Cora belonged to Stone, but she belonged to Duke. Maybe Faith was correct, that right and wrong didn't exist.

But without those boundaries, how did one maintain a true course? Without knowing right or wrong, how could a man judge himself?

"I'm turning in my badge, Sam."

Sam's eyebrows pinched above his craggy nose. "I got water in my ears yesterday and I still can't hear right. What'd you say?"

"I have a shoulder that won't heal, so I'm withdrawing from the election."

"But you can't... you're sure to win."

Duke's hands shook as he put his badge inside the safe. "Maybe. Maybe not." Didn't matter. He unbuckled his gun belt and laid it beside the gleaming badge then stood and handed the keys to Sam. "You and the under-sheriff can manage for a week until our new sheriff is elected. I suspect Phelps will be the man. Maybe Taylor will surprise us with a win, but I'm confident that Archer is out of the running."

Sam gawked at the keys. "You're serious!"

Duke wished he wasn't, that he could confide in his friend, but his decision was made. "I've got a train to catch. Will you get this to the *Censor* for me so they can print my resignation in tomorrow's paper?"

Sam stared at the note. "Sheriff, is your shoulder that bad?"

His shoulder was improving each day and would probably heal completely, but his conscience was festering like a deadly wound.

"I'm not the sheriff anymore," he said.

Just Duke Grayson.

But who was *that* man?

Chapter Thirty-five

The rocking motion of the train would have soothed Faith, but she was too brokenhearted and scared to be comforted by anything. Cora must be terrified. Duke hadn't spoken a word other than to ask questions about the judge that she couldn't answer. So he sat in grim silence, studying her mother's guestbook with scowling intensity.

"Did you really quit?" she asked, afraid to disturb him, but needing to know the truth.

"Yes." He didn't look up from the book.

"Why? I don't understand, Duke. You were sure to win the election."

"Phelps will likely win now, and he's worthy of the job."

"But it was *your* job."

He sighed and lowered the book to his lap, his eyes cold. "I can't wear a badge and commit a crime, Faith."

"What crime? We're getting our daughter back." She hoped. She *prayed.*

"If Cora's in Syracuse, how do you suppose we'll get her away from Stone? I'll have to kidnap her from her father who has a legal right to keep her, and that's against the law."

"You're a sheriff. The *law.* Make the judge understand that he's tangling with a powerful man. My mother couldn't fight him, but you can."

"I'm not wearing a badge anymore. I'm a private citizen now."

"But he's a lying, blackmailing criminal!" she insisted quietly. "Can't you take back your badge and arrest him?"

"For what, Faith?"

"For taking Cora and..." She sighed, and her eyes welled up. Stone was protected, and there was no way to prove he'd committed any crime. "Maybe you could have used your badge to scare him off."

Duke scoffed. "A sheriff's badge is little threat to a big city judge."

"I don't understand why you couldn't get Cora back and still keep your job. She should be with us. The judge is corrupt and in the wrong here. Not us. You know that."

"That doesn't make it okay for an officer of the law to break the very rules he's supposed to enforce."

She saw the loss in his eyes, as if some part of him had died. "Why didn't you tell me you were going to quit?" she asked softly.

"There was nothing to discuss."

She knew it was because Duke was a black-and-white type of man. As soon as he'd realized he would have to break the law to get Cora back, he'd made his decision immediately and irrevocably. He hadn't needed to mull it over or talk about it with her, he'd just borne the pain and done what he had to do. To know that her lies had brought him to this point and caused him to sacrifice so much, shredded her heart.

As the train pulled into the Syracuse station, she fought back her tears, praying they would find Cora, and that Duke would someday forgive her.

She was physically and emotionally exhausted by the time they reached the courthouse where, according to Duke, Steven Cuvier and several other lawyers kept their offices. She both worried and prayed they would run into Judge Stone, who supposedly sat the bench here, but they crossed the lobby without seeing anyone. Duke scanned a sign on the wall then guided her across the marble floor to Mr. Cuvier's office.

The lawyer was a tall, lanky dark-skinned man, who looked familiar enough to have Faith searching her memory for where she might have seen him. Not at the brothel. Surely Iris would have raved about a handsome man like the lawyer. Not at the market. Maybe nowhere. Maybe she had never crossed paths with the man.

The lawyer was waiting with Duke's telegram in his hand. "Sheriff Grayson, what's the emergency?" he asked, but before Duke could answer, the lawyer's gaze fell on Faith. He stared as if seeing a ghost. "You must be Celia's sister Constance."

Hearing her mother's first name startled Faith as much as learning her mother had a sister. Her mother went by Rose at the brothel, but it made sense this man would know her full name if he was in fact her lawyer. "I'm her daughter Faith," she said, sensing kindness in him. "Did you handle my mother's legal work?"

"I did." Sadness filled his eyes as he clasped Faith's cold hands. "I didn't realize you were her daughter. I've been looking for you since I heard the sad news about your mother. I can't express how deeply her passing grieves me."

She felt her own razor-sharp grief that was always near the surface, and it made her eyes tear.

"Come. Sit." He pushed the door closed and turned the lock then directed her to a chair. The leather furniture and mahogany walls of the plush office suited his dark, good looks. He leaned his narrow hips against his desk, and looked at Duke, who continued to stand. "I have business with your wife, but first, tell me how I can help you."

As though Duke were presenting his case to a judge and jury, Faith listened to him state the crime of Cora's abduction and his suspicion about the judge then listed the facts and events of the case. "I need any information you may have on Faith's mother and Judge Stone, and where I might be able to find Cora," he said.

But the lawyer's dark-skinned face had turned a sickly gray. "Rose was telling the truth," he said, gazing trance like into the middle distance. "He duped me. Rose and I were nothing but pawns to him."

Faith exchanged a look with Duke, who was scowling at the lawyer's odd behavior.

"He was after the property" The lawyer's half-insane laugh unnerved Faith. "The dirty wretch orchestrated this whole thing!"

"What does this have to do with us?" Faith asked.

The man propelled himself off the desk and across the room then back to his desk, his dark eyes flashing with fury. "Stone cautioned me to think of my career, and warned that I would be ruined if anyone saw me in the badlands. It's a shoddy, nefarious side of the city that's referred to as the badlands," he said, clarifying the term for Duke. "But like a jealous dog, Stone was guarding his bone."

Duke's scowl deepened. "Cuvier, I don't know what you're talking about, but my daughter is missing, and I need any information I can use to get her back."

The lawyer stopped pacing. "Are you or Mrs. Grayson aware of a project by the city of Syracuse to change the badlands section into a theater district?"

"No." Duke looked at Faith, but she shook her head. Her mother hadn't bothered with the newspaper because she, and women like her, weren't welcome to participate in social events.

"I suspected as much." The lawyer began pacing again. "Judge Stone started a renewal project over twenty years ago. It evolved slowly, and was nearly lost on several occasions. But the judge pressed on for years, insisting our city needed to clean up the badlands and build an area that would attract investors and new business. I admired him for being so civic-minded, and even did the legal work for several properties he purchased in that area."

"Why would he want my mother's house if he owned so many properties?" Faith asked, suspecting the lawyer was unaware it was a brothel.

"Because your mother's property sits in the middle of the proposed theater district, and it's one of the last properties still owned by the resident."

"Which makes the property more valuable and of interest to Stone," Duke said.

"Exactly." The lawyer gave him a curt nod. "A bank or investor looking to build a business in the area would offer a good bit of money for the property."

"Are you saying my mother could have sold the broth—property for a lot of money?"

The lawyer nodded. "She could have made a small fortune. I assumed she was waiting to sell in order to gain an advantage."

"Are you in possession of the deed then?" Duke asked.

"Rose kept a safe deposit box at the bank and gave me a key," he said. "To my knowledge she kept the deed there."

Finally Faith new the location of the elusive deed and what the key in her mother's guestbook was for, but all she could think about was how close her mother had been to owning that little house with the porch and rose garden. Had she known about the city's renewal plan? Or had she died never realizing she was so close to gaining her freedom?

It sickened Faith, and it broke her heart that one powerful and corrupt man could hurt so many people.

"Give it to him," she said to the lawyer, wanting nothing more than to get Cora back. "I'll sign the deed over to him."

"No, you won't." Duke's fierce scowl made her heart trip.

"Duke, I want to get Cora back and go home."

"We're not giving in to that crook. I'll find Cora, and we'll sell the property, but not to the judge."

"But he'll come after us again."

"And he'll deal with me this time."

"He's heartless and conniving. My mother tried to stand up to him and it caused her death."

"What?" Shock and rage filled the lawyer's dark eyes. "Did you witness this?"

"My aunt Iris did. Mama was arguing with Stone over the brothel, and it enraged her when he threatened to take Cora. She attacked him. Maybe Stone didn't mean for her to go over the railing, but she did, and Iris said he didn't try to stop her fall."

The lawyer's throat worked, and he turned his back. The room was dead silent for several long seconds.

Without a word, Cuvier strode to a file cabinet and pulled out a large envelope. He spread the contents on his desk, and picked through several papers before finding what he was looking for. His eyes were misty when he handed the paper to Duke. "This is the address for Stone's mistress. I handled all his personal business, so I'm aware that he supports this woman. It's the only place I can think he'd be able to take your daughter without answering a lot of uncomfortable questions. His mistress could easily keep the girl for him. Stone has court this afternoon. I would suggest you pay a call now while I have a long overdue talk with your wife." His voice broke and he cleared his throat. "Faith, I think... I'm fairly certain you're my daughter."

His words sucked all the oxygen from the room, and Faith gripped the upholstered arms of her chair, fighting a dizzying rush of disbelief. She stared at Steven Cuvier, at his bronze skin and his almond shaped eyes and lanky body, and knew this man was her father. And the reason he looked familiar was because Adam resembled him.

A sudden pounding then the rattle of the doorknob broke the silence in the room and startled a gasp from Faith.

"Steven! Are you in there?"

Faith recognized Stone's grating voice, and was glad Cuvier had locked the door. "It's the judge," she whispered.

Rage flared in Duke's eyes and he started across the room.

Cuvier caught his arm. "Wait," he whispered.

Duke stopped and gave him curt nod.

Another knock. Another rattle of the knob. "Cuvier?" A second later, they heard the judge's heavy footfalls echoing through the lobby then up the stairs.

"The judge's chambers are at the front of the building, but he could be anywhere upstairs," Cuvier said. "Let's go out the back exit. I'll take Faith to my house then come back here and detain the judge as long as I can while you go for Cora."

"We have lodgings near the station," Duke said.

"You're registered under Grayson?" At Duke's nod, the lawyer shook his head. "Now that I know what the judge is up to, neither of you are safe. Keep the room, but don't stay there. I'll take Faith by to get your bags then drop her at my home. She'll be safest there." He scratched his address on a piece of paper and handed it to Duke. "Meet us there as soon as you can."

The lawyer peeked out his door then rushed them out a back exit and across a brown lawn raked clean of dried leaves. They crossed a brick street, and cut between Horton's Mercantile store and a bank. A block away from the courthouse, they parted company. Faith and her father headed toward the hotel near the train depot.

Duke jogged several blocks in the opposite direction, following the lawyer's hastily scribbled map, until he came to a row of brick houses near the canal. At house number forty-seven, he stopped to catch his breath. When all remained quiet outside, he casually peered in the windows, acting as if he were heading to the back entrance.

He spied Cora sitting on the floor beside a huge dining room table, playing with a book, and his heart jumped with relief then pounded with uncontrollable anger. He would kill the judge if he'd hurt her.

At the back door, Duke wrestled his anger under control then gave a sharp rap with the brass knocker. "Delivery!" he yelled in a disguised voice he hoped Cora wouldn't recognize. He didn't want her alerting the mistress, because it would be much easier to walk through an open door than to break through a solid slab of oak. And it would draw less attention from the neighbors.

"Who's delivering?" a male voice asked from the other side of the door.

He'd hoped the mistress was alone. Now it was a guessing game of how many people were inside guarding Cora. He scrambled for a name then remembered the store behind the courthouse. "Horton's Mercantile!" he hollered to whoever was on the other side of the door.

"What do you have?"

"Don't know, sir. The package is sealed."

A grumble came through the door then the rattle of a key, and twisting of the door knob.

The second the door started to open, Duke slammed his shoulder into the solid oak and shoved the man back several steps. The man was short, stocky, and half asleep by the look of his eyes, but Duke's abrupt entrance into the kitchen snapped him to attention.

He lunged for a cast iron frying pan on the stove, but left his jaw exposed to Duke's fist. The first blow spun him away from the stove and into the sink. The second blow rolled his eyes back in his head. He crashed to the floor, and Duke bolted into the next room.

A tall, striking woman spun to face him, her eyes filled with fear.

"Daddy!" Cora scrambled to her feet, but the woman caught Cora's arm and held her back. "Daddy!" Cora cried again, her fear slicing through him.

"Whoever you are, get out of my house," the woman said, pulling Cora toward a doorway that led to another room.

"I'm that little girl's father," Duke said, striding across the room. "And I'm taking her home."

He reached for Cora, but the woman screeched and raked his face with her fingernails. "Get out!" She pummeled him with her fists, as if she were fighting for her life. And maybe she was. Maybe Stone would punish the woman if she let Duke take Cora, but he didn't give a damn. Until now, he had never once considered hitting a female, but it was all he could do to hold himself back when this woman jerked Cora's arm and hauled her toward the open doorway.

He wrenched her crazed grip off Cora's elbow then swept Cora into his arms. The woman came at him again, but he used a straight arm to her chest to knock her back three steps. He headed for the door, feeling every blow she rained across his back, thanking God she hadn't picked up the candelabra from her table. Her friend was awake and waiting in the kitchen doorway with the frying pan clutched in his hand, bleeding from the mouth and huffing from his nostrils. With Cora in his arms, Duke was unable to push past without risking injury to her.

Pivoting on his heel, he grabbed the clawing, fist-swinging witch by her arm, and shoved her into her pan-wielding friend. The pair fell against the kitchen door, giving Duke the opportunity to dash for the front exit. He yanked open the door just as the frying pan bonged off the wall beside him. The crack of a gunshot, and sound of splintering wood, drove him out the door at a dead run.

With Cora clutched in his arms, he bolted between houses and across yards, over shrubs and through clusters of trees, until he was certain they weren't being followed. Gasping for breath, he leaned against a dilapidated building and hugged Cora to his pounding chest. Hard sobs shook her body and she gripped his neck.

"It's okay, princess. You're safe now. Daddy's got you."

He stroked her back and let her cry, knowing she needed the comfort, and that he needed the time to catch his breath. His shoulder was killing him, and he had no idea where he was.

"I don't want to go b-back there," she cried.

"You won't, princess. Not ever. Daddy's taking you home."

"Is Mama there?"

"No, she's waiting for you at a friend's house."

Cora's face was covered in tears. "Can we see her now?"

His throat closed and he could only nod, unable to bear the devastation in her eyes.

She looked at his cheek. "That woman s-scratched you."

"It doesn't hurt." Nothing hurt but his heart. He pulled out his handkerchief and cleaned her face, and helped her blow her nose. Then he pulled his coat around her and held her against his chest to keep her warm in the cold night.

"Ready to go?" he asked cheerfully, but inside he raged, wanting to wrap his fingers around Stone's neck and kill him.

Duke stayed to the alleys and backyards, trying to avoid walking the streets as he navigated in a northeasterly direction. The neighborhood could only be called dilapidated, the people destitute and desperate, and he wanted to get out of it as soon as possible.

But Cora's squeal brought him to a stop. "There's grandma's house!" she said, her face lit with wonder as she pointed at a big house on the corner. "Is Mama there?"

Shocked, Duke looked again at the enormous two-story house. It wasn't as shoddy as the surrounding homes, several of which were being torn down and the lots cleared, but it was far from what he would want to live in.

"Can we go there?" Cora asked.

He nodded, feeling a deep need to see the root of all his troubles.

They scared off two young boys who were playing on the front stoop. Duke forced the back door then went through the big house where Faith's mother and aunts had sold their bodies, and where Faith had used her beautiful hands to give other men pleasure.

"This is pretty," Cora said, ogling the gaudy parlor. "Grandma only let me and Adam come in the kitchen."

Thank God.

Other than the loud I, the house was unremarkable. Still, Duke couldn't help wondering which room Faith had worked in—and where she'd lost her virginity to Jarvis.

"Our house is out back," Cora said, tugging his hand as if she were giving him a tour.

She showed him a ramshackle greenhouse where Faith had grown her herbs, and where her mother had tended roses. Then Cora showed him the house where she, Adam, and Faith had lived.

It was a shack.

A one-room, one-bed, miserable little shack.

But Cora trotted to the bed like it was her favorite place in the world. "I slept here," she said importantly. "And Mama and Adam did too."

He'd suspected that. Their spare existence outraged him, but Cora seemed to think she'd had a fine house. With a cry of joy, she scrambled off the mattress and dove for something beside the bed. "My book!"

She lifted the book, and a brush fell to the floor with a clunk, but she was too absorbed with the book to notice. But Duke noticed. He knelt beside Cora, picked up the brush with the silver handle and painted porcelain back, and tucked it into his coat pocket.

How on earth had Faith survived this?

Knowing she had spent twenty-five years living in this barren little room sickened him. It must have been a prison. No wonder she had spent her time in the greenhouse. How easy it would have been for a well-traveled man like Jarvis to mislead a desperate girl into believing she was finally getting an opportunity to escape this life.

"We need to go, princess," he said.

"Can I take my book?"

"Of course. Take whatever you'd like."

She rooted between the wall and the mattress like a dog digging for a bone. She found another book and proudly hugged it to her chest as she headed for the door.

Duke lifted Cora and her two precious books into his arms. He peered out the window to make sure they hadn't been followed then stepped outside and closed the door on a place he never wanted Faith, Adam, or Cora to see again.

"Bye, Grandma." Cora's comment confused him, until he saw her waving at a small rosebush behind the shack. "Mama says grandma's sleeping beneath the rosebush now."

As much as he wanted to remain indifferent, or silently curse the woman who'd allowed her children to live in such sordid conditions, he couldn't bring himself to walk past the grave marker.

Faith, Adam, and Cora loved her. Even their crazy aunts loved the woman. She must have had some saving graces.

With Cora tucked inside his coat, Duke knelt by the bush. "I'll take care of your children for you," he said, speaking his first words to his mother-in-law.

Cora reached out and plucked a dried, withered rose from a thorny stem. "Mama will like this," she said, closing her fingers around the ugly brown flower.

It was nearly dark when Duke found the lawyer's house. And not a minute too soon. His shoulder throbbed, the scratch marks on his cheek stung, and he was starving.

Cuvier opened the door before Duke could knock. "I was preparing to come look for you," he said, hurrying them inside.

Faith rushed into the foyer, but when she saw Duke holding Cora, she burst into tears and threw her arms around them both.

"Thank God. Oh... thank you, Jesus."

"Mama, I got my books!" Cora said, but Faith sobbed too hard to respond. She pulled Cora into her arms and rocked her.

"Oh, baby, I missed you."

Cora buried her face in Faith's neck. "Daddy says I won't go back there no more."

"You won't, sweetie. Never again."

"I got this for you." Cora opened her hand to show her the crushed rose that was falling apart. "It was on Grandma's rosebush."

Faith frowned and raised wet eyes to Duke. He nodded to say that Cora wasn't confused, that they had been to the brothel and he finally understood.

"Oh, no." Her lashes swooped down to cover her eyes, but he'd seen the shame in them.

"Don't you like it?" Cora asked.

"Yes, baby. I like it very much."

As they clung to each other, Duke began to understand that they were never sisters. From the moment of Cora's birth, this little girl had been Faith's daughter.

And now she was Duke's daughter.

He felt small for having judged Faith, for condemning her for keeping secrets and marrying him to secure Adam's and Cora's future. She'd chosen that path out of necessity. He couldn't blame her for that. But still knowing she'd *had* to marry him, left a hollow hole in his chest.

⚬⚬⚬

Faith gave Cora a bath, read her books to her and rocked her to sleep. She put her in bed then went downstairs to her father's study where he and Duke were talking. She accepted a glass of wine from the lawyer then sat in a large leather chair.

Cuvier stood by the fireplace, deep in thought. Finally, he sighed and turned up his palms. "There's no easy way to explain this, so I'm going to state the bald truth. I was a young man just out of law school when I first visited your mother's brothel," he said. "My flower of choice was Rose. Every time. She told me it was foolish to care about her, but that didn't stop me from falling in love. I thought we could find a way to be together, but she insisted it was impossible...."

His subsequent silence unnerved Faith. If he left the story unfinished, she would never feel settled. "Did you know about me?"

"Not right away," he said, refilling his glass from the decanter on the wine cart. "My uncle offered me a job at his law firm in Chicago, and Rose insisted I take the opportunity to start my law career. I thought if I earned enough money, I could bring Rose to Chicago with me." He rested his wineglass on the stone mantel.

"I didn't make it back to see her until the second year, and it was only twice, but each time I asked her to come to Chicago with me, she refused. By the third year, I was miserable. I quit the firm and moved back to Syracuse." Sadness filled his eyes. "That's when your mother finally told me she had a daughter. But she insisted you weren't mine. I didn't know what to believe because she was always twisting her words and changing her mind about seeing me."

Faith nodded to let him know she understood, that his absence in her life wasn't completely his fault.

"It didn't matter to me. I wanted to marry your mother and move us to another city, but she refused. When I pushed, she called me a fool and said I was becoming bothersome, and that she didn't want me to visit her anymore. I stormed out, feeling like the fool she called me. It took me ten years to discover that my father had paid her a visit. He'd told her about my successful family and my achievements in law school, and explained that I would forfeit everything and ruin my life if I continued to visit her. So she made sure I didn't come back."

Of all the possible scenarios Faith had imagined about the man who fathered her, this wasn't one of them. He'd always been the one at fault. Her mother had always been the victim. But the truth was harsher, because they were all victims. Her mother had loved a man enough to save him from his own destructive love. Her father had loved a woman from the wrong side of town. And their children had suffered the shame of their sins.

"I loved Rose from the minute I first saw her, and I still wanted her, so I went to see her. She welcomed me as a lover, but refused to marry me. Being continually spurned and lied to finally wore me down, and one day I just decided not to go back."

Which explained why he didn't know about Adam. Because if he'd ever seen the boy, he would know Adam was his son.

"I thought by helping the judge push the theater project, it would raise property values and your mother could sell the brothel and buy that house she wanted."

Pain squeezed Faith's heart to know her mother had shared her dream with this man—and that he might have been able to make her dream come true.

"I didn't know Judge Stone was working against us. I thought he was an honorable man like his brother and father. He promised me great career rewards if I worked hard and kept my nose clean. So when he warned me to stay away from the badlands section of the city, I never suspected it was because of your mother. But now I see what a blind fool I've been. Your mother sent me a letter shortly before she died, but I thought..." He sighed, a deep sadness filling his eyes. "I didn't trust her. I suspected that my father was using her again to manipulate me. He wants me to go back to his brother's firm in Chicago."

"May I ask what was in her letter?" Faith asked.

"Rose said Stone was trying to strip her of her property. I did some digging while I was at the courthouse watching Stone this evening, and it appears she was right. Stone has recently filed papers with the city to list the property as abandoned and seize it for his theater project." Cuvier shook his head. "I feel like the world's biggest fool. Judge Stone was using me and your mother to protect his investment." He handed the letter to Faith. "I let your husband read it while you were tending Cora."

Faith's hands shook as she accepted the letter. Her mother's pretty script filled the page and brought an ache to Faith's heart.

My dearest Steven,

I need your help. Your father may have directed my actions years ago, but he was right. You would have regretted the sacrifices and losing your position of respect. To confess that Faith was your daughter would have tipped that first domino in your downfall—and perhaps your eventual hatred of me. I kept the truth from you, planning to take our baby away from this place and give her a decent life, but I didn't have the money and neither did you. I loved you, Steven, and couldn't stay away from you, but when I got pregnant with Adam, I knew you would recognize him as your own so I had to drive you away before we both did something foolish and ruined your career.

I thought Judge Stone with his big promises could help me and the children break away from this life. He promised to buy the brothel property for double its value if I became his mistress for a year. He talked of tearing down the brothel and building a grand theater right here on this very property. I thought it a noble and admirable plan. He promised to move me and the children to a nice house in a new town where we could build a respectable and happy life. Like a bird following a trail of bread crumbs, I was too busy gobbling up his promises to realize I'd walked myself into a cage.

Stone intends to strip me of my property and home, Steven. He swears he'll ruin you if I disappear. He is threatening to take Cora from me if I don't sign the deed over to him. I can't run and I can't stay. I have begged Faith to pose as a widow and take Adam and Cora to a safe place, but she fears we'll never see each other again.

I'm afraid to take a step in either direction for fear of causing more harm, but I refuse to let Judge Stone take away my only means of escaping this life. Please, Steven, go back to Chicago and take our children with you. I know I've sacrificed my chance at love and happiness but please help Faith, Adam, and Cora find the life they deserve.

Please accept my love and apology, and respond quickly.
Celia Rose

Faith lowered the letter to her lap. For the first time in her life, she understood her mother's deep sadness. Each time her mother had prodded her to move away, Faith wondered if they were too much of a burden to her. But her mother had just wanted them safe. She'd made awful choices, and there were many things she could have done better, many ways she could have made Faith, Adam, and Cora feel wanted, but for all her faults and failings, she was only guilty of being naive and thinking with her heart instead of her head.

"Can this letter be used as evidence against Stone?" Duke asked.

Cuvier nodded. "It might not do much good, but I'm willing to face the consequences."

"You can't do that." Faith lifted the letter. "My mother sacrificed her heart to protect you from ruin. To bring all this out now would make her sacrifice worthless."

Cuvier sighed. "It may not serve us anyhow. But Stone has undoubtedly swindled others. I'll look over the deals I did for him and see if I can track down any of those former homeowners."

"Don't let Stone know what you're doing before we have a noose around his neck," Duke said.

"No worry. Now that I know how corrupt he is, we all need to be careful."

"Why would he do this?" Faith folded the letter. "Why would he manipulate my mother and orchestrate a plan that took twenty years just to make money?"

Cuvier finished his wine and set his glass on the mantel. "I don't know that it's about money. But if I were to guess, I'd say he's trying to outshine his brother Gordon, who is the governor of New York."

Duke's mouth fell open. "Governor Stone is the judge's brother?"

Cuvier nodded. "They're twins, but they're as different as night and day. Before Gordon left Syracuse, he donated his money and intelligence to building the courthouse. The statue out front honors him and his work."

"So by turning the badlands into a thriving theater and business district," Duke said, "Stone not only gets rich but gets the fame and glory for instituting the project, and possibly upstages his brother."

"It makes sense. His brother is running for senator, a position once held by their father. Maybe the judge is feeling pressured to measure up to his brother's success." Cuvier shrugged. "I don't know what's driving him, but I'm going to make him answer for his crimes." Cuvier crossed to Faith. "I'm sorry I disregarded your mother's letter, but I never knew when she was being sincere. Every time I believed her, she would do something to tear my heart out. I thought she was lying about Stone because she knew I admired him, and that the letter was a ploy by my father to get me back to Chicago."

Faith sighed and handed the letter to him. She didn't blame Cuvier for being suspicious of her mother's motives; all her life, Faith herself hadn't known her mother's thoughts or feelings about anything.

"I'm sorry about all of this," her father said, his voice filled with remorse. "I let my pride and my pain blind me to a truth I didn't want to see. Despite your mother's coldness, I sensed her love, and I sensed you were my daughter. But I didn't want to know for sure, because with your mother's constant rejection, I couldn't bear to have a daughter in my life I wasn't free to love."

His honest confession didn't ease her pain or the years of heartache she'd suffered from being fatherless, but it finally satisfied her question of why he hadn't come to see her. Steven Cuvier was too easily controlled by others, but he seemed a decent and sincere man. That was far better than the man she'd imagined him to be. And she could forgive him.

"I know it's too late for me to be a proper father to you, but would you consider letting me come see you from time to time?" A mix of hope and fear filled his eyes. "I can understand if you object, but I hope you'll allow me the chance to get to know you."

Her whole life, she'd longed to hear those words from her father. To hear them now was both healing and wounding. It was too late for her to sit on her father's lap like Cora did with Duke, to feel secure and comforted in his arms. But it wasn't too late to befriend a man she'd been missing all her life.

She extended her hands to him. "I've always kept a place for you in my heart, and I can make a place for you in my life."

As Faith received her first hug from her father, Duke felt as choked by emotion as he had at his own father's funeral. It shamed him to think he'd taken so much for granted.

He thought about the times his dad had taken him fishing or swimming or hunting, or even when they cleaned the barn or worked the mill together. His dad had been always there, always taking care of him, until he grew too ill. Only now, as Duke witnessed Faith's pain, could he understand just how blessed he was—and how right she was. It was easy to choose between right and wrong when you had respectable and loving parents providing for you.

And maybe that's what his father meant when he said a man had to live with his actions and be able to face himself in the mirror. Maybe he wasn't talking about the laws and rules Duke had built his life on. Maybe he'd meant that a man should make choices he could live with, that each man had to decide for himself what was important, what was worth fighting for, and set his own standards. And the only true direction for Duke was to love and protect his family.

Chapter Thirty-six

At home in Fredonia the next evening, after an exhausting train ride from Syracuse, Faith put Cora to bed. Duke had gone to Boyd's house to get Adam, but only Adam returned, slamming through the door, his face pinched with worry.

"Is Cora all right?" he asked, huffing like he'd run all the way. "Duke said she was fine, but—"

"Yes, honey, she's fine." But Faith could see that Adam wasn't. She hugged him and kissed his temple. 'This wasn't your fault."

"Yes, it was." He wrenched away. "If I wasn't so weak, the judge wouldn't have taken her."

"The judge didn't give you a chance to fight, Adam. He kicked you in the chest. Believe me, even if I'd been outside, he probably still would have gotten her away from us. He's a smart, powerful man. He'd probably been watching and waiting for exactly the right time to make his move." She nudged the bottom of her brother's chin to make him look at her. "Cora's sleeping, but I need to run across the street to let Dahlia and Iris know we're back. Will you stay with her?"

His eyes widened. "You still trust me to protect her?" he asked in disbelief.

"Yes, Adam, I trust you. You can lock the door and let me in when I get back."

"What if Duke comes home first and has to knock?"

"Then he'll know what a smart young man you are."

She stepped outside, listened to the grating sound of the key turning in the lock then hurried across the street. She entered the house without knocking, and found Iris in the kitchen near their small cookstove.

"Duke got Cora back, and she's all right," she said, feeling relieved and thankful to have her baby back unharmed.

Iris whirled, her black-diamond eyes startled and full of tears. "Thank God," she said. "Did Duke kill him?"

In all the years Faith had known her, Iris had never cried. "N-no, I... we didn't see him."

"Well, I'll pay the judge a visit when I get to Syracuse." Her shoulders drooped and she faced the stove. "I'm leaving."

"What? Why? Aunt Iris, what's wrong?"

"I don't belong here."

"This is your home. You have honest work here, and a decent man who wants to marry you."

"I can't marry Patrick."

"Is that what's making you cry?"

Iris shook her head. "I can't drink this tea."

Confused, Faith glanced at the steaming liquid. "What's wrong with it?"

"It's a purgative."

Faith eyed her aunt. "Did you and Patrick... are you expecting?"

"I could be." Iris sloshed the brown liquid in her cup. "I've taken a small dose of tansy and pennyroyal oils in my tea once a month since I... since I started this life. I always drank it before my monthly was due so I wouldn't know if... I couldn't even consider having a baby."

"Of course not." Faith smoothed her hand over Iris's thin shoulders, beginning to understand the hard choices and sacrifices women like Iris made each day.

"Your mother wouldn't drink this." Iris shivered and huddled closer to the stove. "She said life belonged in God's hands, not ours."

Faith agreed, but she understood why her aunts, who had lain with several men a night, would cleanse their bodies each month to avoid pregnancy. Right or wrong, she couldn't condemn them for it.

"I'm going to move away, and if I'm... if I have to, I'll pretend to be a widow like you did."

"Nonsense. You'll stay here and marry Patrick."

"I can't. I don't have what it takes to be a wife and mother."

"Poppycock."

"It's true." Iris moved to lean against the counter. "All I needed at the brothel was a smile and a body men wanted to touch. They didn't care about me or the woman inside. But a husband would care. Patrick cares. Even knowing what I did before I came here, he wants me. And he wants to know about my life." She pulled a handkerchief from her house robe and blew her nose. "But how do you tell someone your own mother sold your virginity to the man who provided for you?"

Faith covered her mouth, horrified.

"She was a geisha, Faith."

"Is that a Japanese word for prostitute?"

"No. A geisha is a trained hostess. Geishas spend years learning dance and music and the art of conversation so they can entertain men in teahouses. Some entertain them privately. When a geisha reaches mizu-age, her virginity is sold to the highest bidder. My mother wanted to go back to Japan, so she sold my virginity to buy our passage."

"How awful."

"She didn't see it that way."

"But you did."

Iris nodded, tears pearling up on her lashes. "I hated her Japanese blood and everything about her. When I scrubbed that man's filth off my body, I scrubbed away as much of my Japanese appearance as I could then I left her house."

"Your Japanese features make you beautiful. Don't hate what you are."

"I don't," Iris said. "I've had twelve years to think about this, and I don't hate being Japanese. It's my mother I hate."

"Have you seen her since you left home?"

"No, and I don't want to. I assume she's still in New York City with that despicable man, since she couldn't find passage back to Japan, I guess the money did her no good anyhow." Iris sighed. "She said she loved me, but she sold me to a man I detested. She killed the love I had for her. At the brothel men loved my body, and some men thought they loved me, but I've never loved—not until Patrick. And because of him, I can't drink this tea." She banged the cup down on the counter and stared at the sloshing liquid. "I should drink it. I should leave here."

"You can't."

"If I stay, I'm afraid he'll tear my heart out like my mother did."

"Oh, Iris, you can't let that stop you from trying. I'm afraid I'll never measure up to the sort of woman Duke deserves, but I've got to try. If I don't, I'll only live a half-life. And you will, too, if you don't open your heart." She hooked her finger in the cup handle. "Let's pour this out, all right?"

Iris looked at the cup, obviously torn. "I'll be risking everything if I stay"

"You'll risk having nothing if you leave. You have to be brave like Aster and Tansy. They've found love and happiness. Dahlia has found her place here. She's made new friends and is happy being able to help Anna and the women who stay with her. Even Anna is making a new life for herself now. You need to find your place too, Aunt Iris, and I think that place is here with Patrick. Don't you?"

"I don't know. I honest to God don't know." Iris dumped the tea into the sink then fled.

⊷⊱ ⊰⊶

Adam was alone in his bed, scared about everything. Duke and Faith had been home a week, and whatever Duke did to get Cora back had got his face all scratched up. His shoulder was real sore so he'd probably had to fight somebody. Duke warned them all to be vigilant, to watch out for Stone. He even had his brothers and Pat, Cyrus, and Doc Milton keeping an eye on them.

If Adam had muscles like Duke, he would have beaten Judge Stone until he couldn't move, but the man had kicked him so hard and so fast, Adam's head exploded with black dots that swallowed him up. He was still having bad dreams about the judge coming to take Cora away.

A lawyer named Steven Cuvier had arrived this morning from Syracuse. He'd told Faith he got a big offer on the brothel property right away and just needed her and Duke to sign the deed so he could close the sale then he could transfer a lot of money to the bank for them. Adam thought Faith would be happy, but she'd cried real hard, like when their mother died. When the lawyer hugged her, Duke didn't say anything about the man being familiar with her. And the man was odd. He seemed too friendly, like he was family or something, and he kept giving Adam a sad look, like Adam was going to die or something. He was even staying the night in the guest room.

Everything was confusing. And scary.

Duke said the judge might try something sneaky. So he'd told his brothers the truth about Faith and their mother's brothel. Faith worried they would hate her, but Duke's mother had come the next evening and talked to her in the kitchen for a long time. Then she'd hugged Faith in the foyer and told her she was a strong woman. Adam didn't know why she said that, but it seemed to make Faith happy.

Adam wanted to learn how to use a gun, but Duke said no, that he was only supposed to run for help if Stone showed up. Duke didn't trust him. He didn't say that, but Adam knew it was true. He hadn't been able to stop the judge from taking Cora, so Duke didn't trust him to protect their family. Adam promised he could do better with a gun, but Duke had only yelled at him. Then later, he'd said he was sorry for yelling, and that he just wanted Adam to get help and keep himself safe if something happened.

But Duke was disappointed in him; Adam could tell. And it made his throat ache so bad he could hardly breathe. He buried his face in his pillow. He was weak and stupid. And scared of everything.

Morning light shone outside his window when he opened his eyes and heard people arguing. His bedroom was above the kitchen, and he could smell coffee and hear the rumble of tense voices.

A jolt of fear sat him up in bed. What if it was the judge!

He threw off the covers, pulled on his trousers then crept downstairs as fast as he could. They were in the kitchen, and he heard Duke's voice as he tiptoed across the foyer and through the dining room. If Duke was in there, maybe everything was all right.

"I think the boy should know, but I'll leave this up to you, Faith." The lawyer's voice made Adam pause outside the kitchen door.

"Since you can't step in now, I think it will hurt him, and just make matters worse," she said.

"The boy has a right to know." Duke sounded frustrated.

"I'm not denying his right." She sounded ready to cry. "But what purpose will it serve? It's been too long. This will just confuse him."

"I think it will answer some of his questions," Duke argued.

"What if it doesn't?" she demanded, her anger surprising Adam. Faith never got angry. "What if it just hurts him? What if it reminds him of all the years his father wasn't around for him? That's not useful, Duke. Even if he has a right to know, it won't serve him."

"If it were me," Duke said, "I'd want to know."

"Well, it's not you. It's Adam, and I've been caring for him since he was born. I'm not going to hurt him with this."

Adam was already shaking from jumping out of bed, but his stomach got real queasy. They were talking about him. And his father.

Duke huffed out a breath like he was mad. "It hurts him every day to not know who his father is."

"What makes you an authority?" she asked. "You never spent a day of your childhood wondering about a man who wasn't there. Adam has spent his whole life that way, and nothing's going to change. Is it?"

"I don't know," the lawyer said.

His answer confused Adam. Why would Faith ask the lawyer that question? Did the lawyer know who his father was?

"I'm willing to try, but I don't think I can be the kind of father Adam needs. I can't be here all the time, and he wouldn't want to leave you, so..."

Adam's stomach felt like it dropped to his ankles. That *lawyer man* was his father? That skinny, big-eyed, sharp-talking man with the fancy suit was his father? No wonder he'd been looking at Adam so strangely last night. Was he here to take Adam home with him?

He didn't want to go anywhere with the man. Is that what Duke was saying? That Adam had to go with his real father? Is that why Faith sounded like she was going to cry?

Well, he wasn't going. He shoved the kitchen door open and glared at the surprised lawyer. "I'm not going anywhere with you. I don't care who you are. I don't need a father!" Tears choked him and Adam ran to the foyer. He grabbed Duke's heavy hunting coat off the hall tree and his muddy boots by the door then bolted outside. If they couldn't find him, they couldn't make him go anywhere with that man.

He ran barefoot and bare-chested across the frost-covered yard then followed the creek. Sniffling and huffing, he stopped to stuff his freezing feet into the cold boots. He laced them tight, but they were still too big. Shivering, he pulled Duke's coat on and buttoned it clear to the collar. He backhanded his eyes, and trudged down the rocky gorge. Why didn't Duke want him around?

"Adam!"

He looked up and saw Rebecca standing on the creek bank with one of her horses. She smiled and waved at him, but he ducked his head and ran into the trees. He didn't want her to see him crying.

He walked until he was at the place Duke kept his boat then ducked beneath the branches of the pine trees. Duke's boat was still there, turned upside down to keep the rain and snow out.

He sat on the hull and looked up to the tree tops. No warming shafts of sunlight filled his private cathedral, just a cold gloomy darkness that made him cry.

He didn't lie anymore. And he'd only stolen that brush for Faith. He'd done everything Duke asked of him. Why did they want to send him away?

Cora called Duke Daddy.

Why couldn't Adam call him Dad?

Why didn't Duke want to be his father?

No matter how hard he tried to hold back his tears, they just flooded out of his eyes and made his nose run. He scrubbed the heels of his hands against his eyes.

It was stupid to cry. He was just a cry-baby. Maybe that's why Duke didn't want to be his dad. Maybe he thought Adam was too old to have a dad. Or maybe Duke was ashamed of him because Adam's mother was a prostitute. But Faith had the same mother, so that didn't make any sense.

Nothing made any sense.

Why would that lawyer man want to be his father *now*? Had Duke found him? How did the lawyer know about the brothel? But after a minute of thinking, Adam realized that if the lawyer really was his father, he must have been one of his mother's guests. So that's how he knew about the brothel. And the judge had been a guest, too, so maybe the men were friends. Or maybe they hated each other because they both had liked Adam's mother.

His mother was the cause of all of this. If she hadn't been a prostitute, none of this would have happened. And Adam wouldn't have met Duke Grayson.

A surge of tears burned his eyes, but Adam didn't care. It hurt not to be wanted.

It hadn't mattered so much before he met Duke, but now he liked having a man to show him how to build things, and to take him fishing in a boat, and to tell him about riding a sled off the barn roof. That stupid lawyer probably didn't know any of those things. And he wasn't half the man Duke was; Adam could tell just by looking at him.

"Adam?"

Rebecca's worried call jerked his head up. He scrubbed his face on Duke's coat sleeves, but didn't answer.

The tree limbs lifted and she stepped inside. "I found you," she said, but her smile died the instant she looked at his face. "What's wrong? Are you hurt?"

He was hurt worse than he'd ever been in his life, but he shook his head. It was on the tip of his tongue to tell her he got dirt in his eyes, but Duke's words about being truthful rang in his ears. "I can't see you anymore."

A sick look crossed her face. "Why?"

"Because you have a good father, and it's not right for me to cause problems between the two of you."

"My dad's too protective."

"You're lucky to have a dad like that."

"I know, but he's still too protective."

Maybe he was. Adam wouldn't know. His own father hadn't cared enough to even let him know his name.

"Did something happen to you?" she asked, sitting on the boat hull beside him.

"I met my father this morning."

Her eyes widened and she gave him a beaming smile that almost made him cry again, because this was the last time they would meet like this. "That's wonderful!"

"It's terrible. He's a lawyer from Syracuse."

"But you thought he was in prison. Isn't this good news?"

"If he was in prison, he wouldn't have been able to come see me. A lawyer could. If he wanted to."

"Oh..."

He watched her smile fade and knew she was starting to understand it was better not knowing, because then he could believe anything he wanted. He could make excuses for the man. But now, the only excuse was that the lawyer didn't care.

"Have you ever wondered what your life would be like without your dad?" he asked.

"Once. When I was thinking about my first mother, I wondered what it would have been like if she hadn't given me to my dad. But it made me sad, so I quit thinking about it."

"Well, all those hugs he gives you would be gone if you lived with your first mother. He wouldn't be there to catch you when you let go of the grape-vine swing in the gorge. You wouldn't clean the livery with him, or ride horses together. He wouldn't pull you into a wrestling match on the lawn with your brothers and tickle you." He shrugged. "All the things he says to you, and all the things he does for you would be gone. You might not even know his name or what his voice sounds like."

"That would be awful." She pressed her hands to her stomach as if she felt sick. "Oh, Adam, I never really understood what it was like for you."

"I didn't know what it was like for you either," he admitted. "That's why I can't see you like this anymore. It's causing trouble for you. Your dad is the kind of father I wish I had, and you're lucky to have him."

"Why does that mean we can't see each other?"

"I want Duke to be my dad, but he won't want to be if I'm betraying his brother and sneaking off to see his niece."

"But... we aren't doing anything wrong."

"Yes, we are. Just being here together goes against your father's wishes. An honorable man wouldn't do that. I don't want to be like those men who came to my mom's brothel. But when we're alone like this. I want to do things like Patrick and Iris were doing." He felt stupid confessing something so personal, but Duke wouldn't take advantage of a girl or sneak around. Neither would Rebecca's father. Adam wanted to be like them. He wanted to make Duke proud, and make him want to be his father. "I'm not going to do those things to you. I'm going to stay away like your dad asked."

"You aren't going to meet me anymore?"

He shook his head. "I'm not going to walk you to school either." He couldn't, because it would just tempt him to sneak off with her again.

Tears filled her eyes and she stared at him as if he'd just slapped her. "I thought you liked me."

His feelings went way beyond liking, and that's why he wouldn't see her anymore and cause problems for her and her father. Rebecca needed her dad more than she needed Adam. "We're cousins now. Rebecca."

"No, we're not!" she said. "We aren't even related. You said that yourself."

He wanted to hug her and tell her he was sorry, but it would just hurt her more because he had to honor Duke and her father. "We can still be friends."

She was crying as she slid off the boat. "I have friends, Adam. I don't need another one." She ducked beneath the limbs and out of sight, but he heard her crying as she ran up the path that led out of the gorge.

He knew he'd done the right thing, but it felt wrong.

Shivering, and feeling as miserable as he'd ever felt, Adam crawled under the boat. He wasn't going home until the lawyer left tomorrow. The boat smelled of wood and fish and winter air, but it kept the wind off Adam's neck. His stomach growled, but he burrowed in Duke's too-big coat and closed his eyes. If he slept, he wouldn't feel hungry. He wouldn't feel cold. He wouldn't hurt.

Minutes or hours passed; he didn't know how long he huddled beneath the boat, but someone or something startled him awake.

Maybe it was Duke, who cared enough to come looking for him. Maybe it was Rebecca coming to tempt him to change his mind.

Adam braced his shoulders against the hull and lifted the boat, but when he came face-to-face with Nicholas Archer, he knew he was in trouble.

Chapter Thirty-seven

Duke knew Adam was upset, but when the boy didn't return by lunchtime, he went looking for him. His first stop was Radford's house, because Rebecca was Adam's only friend. But when Radford realized Rebecca was missing, he jumped to conclusions and blamed Adam.

Duke helped Radford scour the gorge. They found Rebecca's gelding tied to a tree, but they couldn't find her anywhere.

"Where could she be?" A sick look washed through Radford's face, leaving him gray and drawn.

"We haven't checked Mother's house yet."

Radford bolted for the trees. Duke sprinted behind him, his gut twisted with worry. Fueled by panic, they threw open the door and raced into their mother's house, breathing hard, praying harder.

Rebecca sat on the sofa, sobbing her heart out on her grandmother's shoulder.

"Thank God!" Radford knelt by the sofa. "Are you hurt, Rebecca?"

"She's nursing a broken heart," their mother said, stroking Rebecca's disheveled hair.

"A what?" Radford looked as confused as Duke felt. "Where have you been, Rebecca?"

She cowered in her grandmother's arms. "In the g-gorge."

"Doing what?"

"Riding."

"How? You left the gelding tied to a tree. You've been gone for hours!"

"I n-needed to talk to grandma."

"Why didn't you bring the gelding with you?"

"I don't know." Rebecca buried her face in her hands and sobbed.

Radford scraped his hair back with both hands and looked at their mother. "What is going on here?"

"Your daughter is suffering her first broken heart, Radford. And you're not helping."

"A broken heart from what?" he demanded.

Rebecca didn't answer.

Duke still didn't know where Adam was, and it worried him. The boy had been gone all day. He was half-dressed, and probably starving by now. "Rebecca, have you seen Adam?"

She nodded and cast a worried look at her father.

Radford gaped at her. "Were you with him today?"

"Y-yes."

Radford rose to his feet, fire burning in his eyes. "If that boy did anything to my daughter, I'll wring his neck."

"That boy is practically my son, Radford. You're the one who's hurting Rebecca, not Adam."

Radford grabbed the front of Duke's jacket and jerked him toward Rebecca. "Look at her. I didn't cause those tears. Now you keep Adam away from her!"

Furious at being manhandled, Duke shoved Radford back a step, but Radford didn't let go. "Your daughter is growing up, and you'd better accept it."

"This has nothing to do with her growing up. It's her sneaking around with Adam I can't accept. And I'm telling you for the last time, I won't stand for it."

Duke clamped his hands over Radford's fists. "Well, I won't stand for your unwarranted accusations. Adam has suffered enough unjust treatment, and I won't stand aside and let anyone, be it some crazy judge or my own brother, do any more harm to that boy. Now take your hands off me."

"Stop this!" Their mother shot to her feet. "Both of you!"

Duke faced Radford glare for glare. "I'm sick of you pointing the finger at Adam every time you lose track of your daughter."

Radford's eyes flashed. "Until Adam came around, Rebecca didn't run off. She was hurt once because I wasn't vigilant enough. If that makes me overprotective, too bad. She's my first concern. And if your *son* hurts her again, I'll go through you and anybody else to put a stop to it."

"Radford!" Nancy Grayson clutched her son's arm and gave it a hard shake. "What has gotten into you?"

"I've had enough," he said, and Duke knew he meant it.

But Duke had reached his own limit. Adam would never hurt Rebecca, and the boy shouldn't get blamed because Rebecca was showing some backbone. He wrenched Radford's hands off his jacket then knelt in front of the girl. "I'm sorry about what just happened here," he said, wishing he would have controlled his temper for her sake. "Where did you see Adam?"

"By your b-boat," she said, her face awash in tears.

"Thanks, Sprite." He hugged her then stood and faced his brother. "What are you going to do when some father tells you that your son isn't good enough for his daughter?"

⊷⊶

The sound of Adam crying pierced Duke's heart. He lifted the branches out of his way and ducked into the small clearing.

Pine needles stuck out of Adam's hair and his head was bleeding. Duke knelt beside the boy.

"What happened here?"

"I hit my head on the boat when Nicholas shoved me."

"Nicholas Archer?" Duke saw scuffle marks in the pine needles. "What was he doing here?"

Adam held up a jewelry box. "This was in the boat. I think he wanted it, but when he saw me, he shoved me hard and ran off." Adam's eyes filled with tears and he hung his head. "I tried to stop him, but I blacked out a little when my head hit the boat."

"It's okay, Adam. I'll go see Nicholas about this."

"I'm sorry I wasn't strong enough to stop the judge from taking Cora," he said.

"It wasn't your job to stop him. He's a grown man, Adam, and more than twice your size."

"I'll learn how to fight better. I promise. Just p-please don't make me go with that lawyer." He knuckled his tears away. "I'm pretty sure I could make a good son if you could teach me to fight and stuff."

Duke had held back tears under some of the most difficult times of his life, but seeing a young boy begging to be loved shredded his control. Choked by emotion, he pulled the skinny, shivering youth into his arms.

"I'm the one who needs to apologize," he said, forcing the words from his tight throat. "I've pushed too hard and expected too much. You're a good boy, Adam. The only one here who needs to prove himself is me."

⊷⊰⊹⊱⊶

After Adam changed and ate two bowls of soup, he went with Duke, Judge Barker, and Sheriff Phelps to Wayne Archer's house. Even with so many men on his side, Adam felt nervous.

Wayne Archer denied any knowledge of the stolen ring. But Nicholas Archer shocked everyone by saying his sister Melissa was behind the theft.

His father gaped at him. "What are you talking about?"

"Melissa's been following Adam and Rebecca around since he moved to town."

Adam knew that, and he hated it, but he'd figured it was a dumb girl thing to spy on people.

"That has nothing to do with stealing a diamond ring," his dad said. "Nor does it explain why you're getting blamed for hitting this young man."

Nicholas winced and looked at Adam. "I'm sorry about that. I just wanted to get the ring back and return it so nobody got in trouble. I didn't know you'd get hurt when I shoved you."

Duke looked like he wanted to question Nicholas, but he let Sheriff Phelps do it.

"How did you know the ring was there if you didn't take it?" Sheriff Phelps asked.

"I read Melissa's diary." He glanced at his father. "The way she followed Adam around made me wonder what she was up to. I thought maybe... I was just trying to look out for her. I didn't know she was being an idiot until I read her diary. She took the parasol from the apothecary and left it at Rebecca's house, hoping Rebecca would get blamed for stealing it. She was jealous that Adam liked Rebecca."

All the men looked at Adam, making his face burn. Girls were so stupid.

"Did she take the fishing rod?" Duke asked, apparently wanting to clear up the whole mess.

Nicholas nodded. "When she found out Adam got blamed for taking the parasol, she took Dad's fishing rod and hid it in your boat.

She knew where you kept it because she'd been following Adam around."

"How long have you known about this?" Sheriff Phelps asked.

"Since right after she took the parasol. But my dad was trying to get elected sheriff, and I knew it would be bad for him if anyone found out. I didn't know Melissa would do something stupid like steal an expensive ring from the jeweler. I thought if I got it back and returned it to the store owner, he might not say anything to anyone."

Mr. Archer sank down onto the parlor sofa as if the air leaked out of him. "All this time I've been pointing a righteous finger at others, and my own children have been at the root of the trouble."

Adam almost felt sorry for Archer. The man looked gray and stunned, like someone had knocked him on the head with a rock.

Sheriff Phelps hooked his thumb in his gun belt like Duke used to do. "Where's your daughter, Mr. Archer?"

Archer shook his head, but it was hard to tell if he was saying he didn't know, or if he was just shaking his head because he couldn't believe what was happening.

"I'll get her." Nicholas jogged up the stairs then returned a few minutes later with Melissa, who looked scared to death when she saw the sheriff and the other men in her living room.

Serves her right for spying and stealing, Adam thought, but after the sheriff questioned her, and her father berated her for being a foolish, inconsiderate chit, Adam felt sorry for her. She was crying so hard it brought her mother rushing into the room. And when her mother learned the truth, her disappointment made Melissa howl all the more.

"You owe this young man an apology," her father said sternly.

"I'm s-sorry" she blubbered, barely able to look at Adam. "I just wanted you to like me."

Her crying made her face all blotchy and his head ache worse. All he wanted to do was go home and crawl into his warm bed.

She sniffed, and it made his stomach kind of sick. "Am I going to be put in jail?"

Sheriff Phelps rubbed the back of his neck as if he didn't know what to tell her. "You're in pretty big trouble, missy."

Another gush of water fell from her eyes, and Adam couldn't stand it. "Why don't you do what Sheriff Gray—my—Mr. Grayson did with me," he said, confused about how he should refer to Duke. "Let Melissa work for the jeweler until she makes up for what she did."

Sheriff Phelps lifted an eyebrow. "That's mighty kind from the young man who's been accused of taking these items."

"But you know the truth now, so it doesn't matter." He rubbed the throbbing lump on his head and looked at Duke. "Can we go home?"

At his nod, Adam shot out the door intending to run home, but Duke hooked an arm around his shoulders and walked him across the yard. Then he said something to make Adam feel ten feet tall. "You're a special young man, Adam, and I was very proud of you in there."

⚎ ⚎

Duke donned a nightshirt while Faith tucked Cora in their bed. "I thought you were putting her in her own bed tonight," he said.

"I tried, but she woke up crying. She's afraid."

Of course she was. Duke looked at his sleeping little girl and didn't blame her for being scared. But he longed to be alone with Faith, to have their bed to themselves again.

His wife stood uncertainly beside the bed, brushing Cora's curls off her cheek. "I wish you hadn't seen the brothel," she said quietly.

He drew her warm body against his, missing her, needing her. "It helped me understand."

She rested her forehead against his shoulder. "I thought I'd be escaping with Jarvis, and that everything would be all right because he knew the truth. Instead of being my salvation, he was my first mistake. Lying to you was my worst one."

"Did you love him?"

She was silent for a long time, but Duke didn't rush her. He wanted the truth. "Jarvis was the first man who made me feel special, but I didn't even know him."

Then she couldn't have loved him.

"Tell me about the bell."

Faith lifted her head, confusion in her eyes.

"Why did your mother make you ring a bell?"

A sigh escaped her and she stepped away to fiddle with the hand mirror on her dressing table. "Mama couldn't have me around while she was working, so she rigged up a bell as a way of checking on me."

While Duke wrestled his urge to pull her into his arms, she told him about the bells and being left alone while her mother and aunts worked, and how she'd welcomed Adam and Cora as her own babies because she needed them in her life.

"I've loved them from the minute they were born," she said. "I regret hurting you with my lies, but I don't regret protecting them."

Duke could see Faith as a little girl like Cora, missing her mother, needing a daddy and wondering why she didn't have one. How easy it had been to take his parents and the good life they'd given him for granted.

"Do you hate her?" he asked, knowing she had a right to, but hoping for her sake that she didn't.

"I did. Sometimes. Mama didn't share herself with anyone. Not with my aunts. Not with her children. Until I read her letter, I didn't know if she loved me or loathed me." Her voice broke and she lowered her chin. "I hated her as much as I loved her. I didn't know she was trapped and couldn't leave. I thought she was a coward, and that she didn't love us enough to give us a better life."

Duke wanted to embrace her, but he held back, sensing she had more to say.

Sorrow and regret filled her eyes. She pressed her palm to the spot on his chest where his badge used to rest. "What are you going to do now?" she asked quietly. "You've been the sheriff for so long..."

"I'm content working the mill," he said. And despite the tension with Radford, he enjoyed being there and working with his brothers.

"That's not the same as being sheriff."

No, it wasn't. But it wasn't less of a job, and it didn't make him less of a man.

Tears brimmed in her eyes. "I'll never forgive myself for causing you to lose something you were so proud of."

"I'm proud of the mill."

"You were proud to be a lawman, a *sheriff*."

He was, and he would miss the purpose and direction that had come with the demanding position, but his new disorderly and messy life was just as challenging and rewarding.

He'd always followed rules and enforced laws and never seen himself as separate from his badge. He'd never really made up his own mind about life or even what mattered to him. He'd chosen his path as a way to shine in his father's eyes. Boyd shared their father's wood-carving talent and had always made their father laugh. Kyle was a businessman to the bone, smart and rock solid with a good head for investments and expanding their business. Radford went to war and became a decorated hero. Duke was a third son unworthy of notice or any particular distinction until he'd pinned on his badge. Then he was Deputy Grayson, and later sheriff, a man his father could be proud of.

But now he was more than a lawman.

He was a family man.

"I have a more important position now," he said, drawing Faith into his arms. "Because of you I'm a husband." He looked toward the bed where Cora lay curled on her side. "And a father."

"Is that enough?"

"Yes," he said with conviction. It was enough because it was everything that mattered. He lowered his mouth to hers and took their first honest step toward their future.

Chapter Thirty-eight

Faith crossed the yard by the greenhouse where Adam and Cora were building a snowman. "These will make perfect eyes," she said, pushing two big black buttons into the snowman's head then adding a bulbous red button for a nose.

Cora giggled, the sound a balm to Faith. Her little girl was healing. And so was Faith's relationship with Duke. With each day and each conversation, he was learning to understand and forgive her. And she was learning how much he loved her and the children.

Even now, he was across the street on their porch talking with her father about Adam, while watching over the children, ever vigilant.

"Mama, he needs arms," Cora said, scowling at the snowman. She dug up a handful of snow with her mismatched mittens and stuck it on the snowman.

Faith would knit them warmer sweaters and matching mittens, but Cora didn't care about her clothes any more than Adam did. Duke said he would buy them boots, and get Adam a gun so they could go hunting, but Adam didn't need a gun. He just needed to know he could stay here with his family.

"There," Cora said, eyeing the arm she'd made for the snowman.

Adam laughed. "It looks like a white pickle sticking out of his shoulder."

Cora giggled, sending little puffs of frosty air from her mouth.

"A couple of small twigs will make fine arms," Faith suggested.

Cora trudged through the snow to get a small branch that was lying beneath their maple tree. The snow nearly reached her knees, but she merrily plowed through it. Adam could have jogged over and back in the time it took her to reach the branch, but Faith was proud of him for letting Cora get it. She liked doing difficult things on her own; it made her feel grown up.

Instead of picking up the branch, Cora gasped and backed away as if she'd seen a snake. But snakes didn't come out in winter.

A man stepped from behind the building, his cold gaze spearing Faith's heart like a blade of ice. She'd known he would come, but thought he'd sneak up like a thief in the night, not waltz into her yard in broad daylight.

Before Faith could yell or lift her skirt to run, Stone grabbed Cora by her blue knit scarf and pulled her against him. Cora's terrified cry drove Faith forward in panic. She reached for Cora's arm to pull her free of Stone's grip, but he raised a revolver and swatted Faith away like an annoying dog.

Lights exploded in her head as the gun struck her, and she felt herself falling.

"Unhand her!" Duke's fierce command cracked across the yard, and the sound of boots thundered across the road.

Head ringing, forehead bleeding, Faith pushed to her knees and looked into Adam's terrified eyes. "Get help, Adam."

A rush of wind hit her as Duke raced past and lunged for the Judge. The loud, echoing crack of a gunshot filled the neighborhood, and Duke stumbled back three steps.

Adam bolted from the yard.

Duke staggered forward, swinging his fist upward to try and knock the gun from Stone's hand, accepting this was going to be a bloody, perhaps deadly day.

The judge angled away and pressed the revolver against Cora's temple.

"I don't want to hurt her, so stay back," he said, his voice tense and grating.

Duke's legs turned to rubber. One careless move by the man and that gun could fire. Duke couldn't even think about the result. Burning with outrage and pain, he clutched his bleeding left shoulder and stared intently into Cora's eyes.

"Don't move, princess. Be like your snowman. Be very quiet and very still."

"You're b-bleeding, Daddy." Tears streamed from her eyes, and her nose ran.

"It's only a scratch."

"That's your sore sh-shoulder."

"I'm all right, sweetheart. You just stay real still." She stared at him, tears streaking her face, but she stood still like he'd asked. "Good girl," he said gently, praying to God he could get her out of this safely. "Don't move at all, honey." He met Stone's ice blue eyes. "Take the gun off her."

"I underestimated you once, Grayson. I won't make that mistake again." Stone kept his eyes on Duke then spoke to Cuvier, who appeared behind Faith. "Get that woman away from me."

Cuvier helped Faith to her feet, his lips drawing back in a snarl. "I'll bury you for this, Franklin."

"You'll bury yourself too, Cuvier. Your name is on all those deals you handled for me. Did you really think you could sell that property out from under me?"

"We don't care about the property," Faith said, her voice frigid and trembling. "You're holding a gun to your own... you could hurt her, you fool!"

"Shut up, woman!" Stone's angry voice lashed like a whip crack and made Cora cry. "This is your fault for running off on me."

"I didn't have the deed!" she cried. "I had no choice but to run."

From the corner of his eye, Duke saw Iris run into the yard wide-eyed and out of breath. "What's going on?" she called then her gaze fell on Stone. "Dear God!" She whirled away and rushed down the street.

Her appearance riled Stone, but he remained vigilant and focused on Duke, as if he knew who was his biggest threat. "I want the deed to the brothel property," he snarled.

"I'll get it for you right now. Just let her go." Duke would do whatever it took to get the man to release Cora. Cuvier was about to expose the corrupt bastard anyhow, and they would take the judge down before his peers.

Stone's eyes narrowed. "A man like you doesn't give in so easily."

"A man whose daughter has a loaded gun to her head does. Cuvier brought the deed to us. Let's go in the house and I'll sign it over to you," Duke said.

Stone's laugh made his hand twitch, and Duke's breath locked in his chest. "We'll just go inside like two old friends, eh, Grayson? I suppose you'll want to seal the deal with a whiskey in your parlor afterward," the man taunted.

A curl of hair from beneath Cora's pink hat twisted around the steel barrel of the revolver, causing a volcanic fury to rise up in Duke. His hands shook, and he curled them into fists to keep from lunging for Stone's throat. One opening, just one—that's all he needed. Just one distraction and he would jump the bastard.

"I'll give you what you want, Stone. I swear it." He'd get on his knees right here in the blood-covered snow and beg the man if it would free Cora.

"I have a better plan," Stone said. "I'll take this little girl back to Syracuse with me, since I have a legal right to do so and—"

"No!" Faith tried to wrench her arms free, but Cuvier kept his arms strapped around her waist. "Judge, please, she's a little girl. She doesn't understand this. I'll go with you. Duke will sign the deed. You can have the property, just let her go!" Duke sensed Faith's growing panic and was afraid she'd break completely or push Stone too far.

But Stone ignored her. "Have Faith take the morning train to Syracuse. Alone. When I receive the signed deed, I'll leave Cora with my mistress. You already know the address, apparently, so you can retrieve her there."

"No." Duke shook his head. "Leave Cora here, and we'll take care of this matter now. No tricks. No trouble. You have my word."

"Your word means nothing to me, Grayson. We do this my way, not yours."

"You'll get what you want. Right now. Just take the gun away from her head."

A slick smile lifted the judge's chapped lips. "I won't hurt this precious little girl unless you do something stupid."

That precious little girl was *his* little girl, and that deranged man was playing with her life. Molten fury rose up in Duke, bubbling and surging, seeking a way out. He longed to slam his fists into Stone's face and pummel the man to death, but he checked his rage for Cora's sake.

From the corner of his eye, he saw Radford sprint into the yard with a rifle. Had Adam run for his brothers instead of the sheriff? His chest cramped and pain ravaged his shoulder. He didn't want his brothers in danger, too. Radford had a gun but couldn't shoot; not only was his position bad, but he hadn't used a gun since the war. Did he think he could simply use the weapon to negotiate the situation? It wouldn't work. The gun would increase Stone's desperation. Duke wanted to wave Radford away before the situation got worse, but his brother stopped on his own, crouched beside the greenhouse, observing and waiting, ready to step in if needed.

Faith was seething, her expression outraged as she edged closer to Stone despite Cuvier's grip on her shoulder. "You're a judge, for pity's sake! You're supposed to uphold the law and help people, not rob and threaten them."

Stone ignored her, tightened his hold on Cora's scarf and nudged her forward.

Duke's desperation almost choked him, and he sidestepped to block Stone's way. "Is it money you want?"

"Stand aside."

"I'll give you money. I'll sign the deed. Anything you want." He widened his stance, trying to keep his legs from quaking and to counter the woozy feeling that was creeping over him. He was losing too much blood. He had to force Stone to shift that gun away from Cora's head.

Stone smirked. "It always amazes me what a desperate man will do when his back is to the wall."

"Me too," Cuvier said, his lip curled in disgust. "And I'm thinking your brother's new position as senator is making you a little desperate."

"Shut up, Cuvier! You're nothing but a weak, stupid man."

Cora started crying again.

A neighbor across the street stuck his head out the door and looked in their direction. He'd likely heard the shot, but all he would see was a cluster of people outside. From his distance, he'd likely assume they were visiting, helping a little girl build a snowman.

Faith's head was bleeding and she was starting to break down. The situation was escalating out of control, and if Duke didn't move soon, he wouldn't have the strength to wrestle the revolver away from Stone.

"I'm c-cold, Daddy," Cora said.

"I'm going with you, Stone." Duke would push a confrontation. He would force the son of a bitch to turn the gun on him, and give Faith or Cuvier an opening to grab Cora. "I'll get the deed and see you safely back to Syracuse."

"Forget it." Stone started forward again, but the sound of thundering horse hooves made him pause. The horse raced up the street then into the yard, and stopped abruptly twenty feet away.

Boyd leapt off Evelyn's mare, and Duke groaned. Adam *had* gone for Radford instead of the sheriff, and likely Evelyn had raced to the mill on her horse to get Boyd and Kyle.

"Hey, fellas, why didn't you tell me you were having a party?" Boyd asked, swaggering toward them as if they were all old friends.

Stone's shoulders tensed. "Stay back or I'll pull this trigger," he snarled, making Cora sob harder. Her little mouth was wide open, her desperate eyes fixed on Duke, tearing him apart that he couldn't save and comfort her.

And Boyd was walking into the situation blind. Duke's heart thundered in his chest.

Boyd froze when he spotted the gun against Cora's temple, and the look in his eyes turned deadly. "I guess this is invitation only." He raised his palms as if fending off Stone's glare, but Duke knew his brother. Boyd understood the situation now and was telling Kyle, who was climbing the creek bank, and Radford, who was still crouched by the greenhouse, that they were all defenseless against Stone's position. "No need to get cranky over a small breach of etiquette," he said, taking another casual step toward the judge.

A nauseated, drained feeling washed through Duke, and he knew a bone-deep fear he'd never experienced. If Stone realized he was surrounded and had a gun trained on his back, he'd know things were as bad as they could get. Without Cora to get him out of Fredonia, he was a dead man. And Cora might lose either way.

"What's a man got to do to get an invitation to the party?" Boyd continued.

"Just take one more step," Stone growled.

Boyd took the step, and Duke realized what his brother was after. The idiot was trying to provoke Stone into shooting at him, because the man would have to shift the revolver away from Cora to do it. He was willing to risk a bullet to turn the situation to their advantage. And Duke had to let him do it.

Duke watched Stone's gun hand, searching for a twitch or tick or shift in his protruding veins that would reveal his intentions. If Stone pulled that trigger and harmed Cora or Boyd, he was a dead man. Duke would use his last breath to rip the man's heart out.

Stone narrowed his eyes at Boyd. "Either you're an incredibly stupid man, or a very intelligent one."

"What a coincidence," Boyd said. "I was thinking the same about you."

Stone's lips lifted in a snarl. "Don't push me. Get on your horse and leave or I'll make you wish you had."

"Your argument is with me," Cuvier called, his voice echoing across the yard. "I'm the one who used your connections to get an offer on the brothel."

Boyd grinned. "You got hoodwinked?" he asked, blocking Stone's attempt to move forward. "You let this two-bit lawyer get one over on you?" Boyd's laughter boomed across the yard. "Not too smart of you, eh, Judge? Talk about stupid."

It worked; Stone growled and swung the revolver toward Boyd's chest.

Duke leapt forward, arms extended, hands open. With his right hand, he palmed Cora's tear-stained face and shoved her backwards.

In the same instant, he hooked the bloody half- numb fingers of his left hand over the gun and pulled the revolver down and back, risking a bullet in his legs.

The blast echoed through the neighborhood, followed by another loud, deadly crack that sent Duke reeling backward.

Screams filled the yard, and Duke fell. He tried to twist his body and gain an advantage, but he didn't have the strength to out-muscle Stone. They hit the ground together, Stone on top.

Duke gripped the man's neck with his good arm and held him, refusing to let him fire another shot, even if it meant his own death. Everything was turning gray, but Duke held on, praying he'd been fast enough to shove his daughter out of harm's way, and that his brothers would hurry up and pull Stone off his shoulder that was screaming with pain.

Stone won their battle and tore himself away.

"Stop him," Duke yelled, but the words were a croak. He grabbed for Stone's arm, but other hands pulled him clear.

Radford was there, crouched beside him, yanking open Duke's coat. "Where are you hit?"

Duke batted his hands away. "Get Stone. He'll take Cora."

"She's okay. Faith has her."

"Get him, please..."

"We did." Boyd pointed to the judge, who was lying face down in the snow.

Kyle lifted his fingers from Stone's throat. "He's dead."

A huge stain covered the back and side of Stone's coat, but Duke's pain-dazed mind struggled to comprehend what happened. Stone was dead.

Shot.

By Radford. Who wouldn't touch a gun. But today he had killed a man to save Duke and his family.

"You shot him..."

"And the bullet might have hit you, too," Radford said, pushing Duke's coat over his shoulder.

"Rad, you shot him. You couldn't... you shot him..."

"Hold still, damn it!"

Radford had killed men in the war and it had torn his life apart. A deep, cutting sorrow pushed a sob from Duke's throat. "Rad, I'm sorry..."

"The man didn't leave us a choice." Radford's jaw locked and he yanked Duke's shirt open. Buttons flew, and Radford grimaced at the sight of Duke's shoulder. "You're a mess."

"Feels that way. Will you—"

"No!" Radford gripped Duke's jaw and stared him in the eye. "I killed a man so you could live, and damn it, you're going to."

Boyd and Kyle brought Duke to his feet, and that was the first time since jumping Stone that Duke noticed what was going on around him. Cuvier was carrying Cora and helping Faith into the house. Iris was jogging down the street with Aster and Doc Milton hurrying behind her. Sheriff Phelps was racing toward them from the other direction, with Adam a few paces ahead, his boyish face filled with fear and anguish.

Everything receded in a black haze, and Duke's body grew heavy.

"Put him down," Radford said.

His brothers lowered him to the snowy ground then knelt on either side of him.

"It'll torture him if we lift under his arms," Boyd said. Duke wanted to agree, but his tongue felt too thick to move.

"We won't need to. Remember those chair races we used to have when we were boys?" Duke couldn't answer Radford, because his head was reeling. "We're going to give you a ride and see how fast we can get you to the house."

He felt Kyle and Radford reach beneath his legs to lock their hands on each other's arms and form a sling chair. Boyd moved behind him, locking his hands on Radford's and Kyle's forearms to provide a back support, which Duke needed because everything was moving in a nauseating, dizzying swirl that made it impossible to sit up.

Radford, being the eldest and the one who always gave the count when the four of them combined their strength to do the impossible, gave the nod to move.

Duke's last conscious moment was feeling his brothers lift him in their arms.

Chapter Thirty-nine

Stabbing pain jolted Duke from the black nothingness he'd been drifting in. He groaned and squirmed away from whatever was digging in his shoulder.

"It's almost over," his mother said.

He felt her fingers smoothing his hair back then a cool cloth wiping his forehead. He forced his eyes open and saw Doc Milton and Aster bending over him, working on his shoulder, and his brothers standing near the bed. His mother was seated beside him.

"Is Cora all right?" he asked, but the black swamp sucked him under before he heard his mother answer. It seemed like a second later that another sharp pain jerked him back the surface, but it was Aster, bandaging his shoulder.

Faith was at his side wiping his face with a cold cloth. She tried to smile, but her lips quivered and tears slipped down her cheeks.

"It's bad?" he asked, his voice gravelly and slow, his mind so groggy he fought to keep his eyes open.

"Doc got the bullet out, but you've lost so much blood." Her jaw trembled. "Oh, darling..."

He understood the fear in her eyes. He himself had seen strong, healthy men die from festering gunshot wounds.

Faith's cool hands felt good on his face, but he was slipping away.

"I love you, Duke," she said.

Her tremulous voice lifted his heart, but the heavy black swamp swallowed him again.

When he woke, Faith was gone.

His brothers stood around the bed, and his mother sat beside him, holding his hand. "It would please me immensely, Duke Halford, if you would stay with us a while longer this time. A mother can only take so much worrying, you know?" She looked drawn and ashen, sitting there with fear etching grooves between her eyes.

"You shouldn't worry," he said, his voice hoarse. "It makes you look old."

She laughed and sobbed at the same time. "You always were too honest."

"Promised Dad I'd always tell the truth."

She felt his forehead like she'd done hundreds of times before, but he'd never seen fear in her eyes. Worry, yes. Fear, no. His injury was bad, and the strain on his mother's face confirmed it.

"How long have I been out?"

"About four hours."

He turned his fingers up and grasped her hand. "I'm sorry Radford and I upset you with our argument."

"That is nothing for you to worry about now." She smoothed her palm over his knuckles. "You've been so little trouble, always my helper then my keeper then the town protector. You're a good man, Duke, and a good son. You deserve a long, happy life. Your wife and children need you. *I* need you." Her voice broke and her chin trembled. "And your brothers... it's always been the four of you." She kissed his cheek. "They need you too," she whispered then hurried from the room.

Duke felt woozy, but he needed to talk to his brothers before he got sucked under again. A spear of pain shot through his shoulder, and he struggled to ignore it. "You could have gotten yourself killed, Boyd," he croaked.

Boyd arched his eyebrow. "Did you have a better idea?"

"No. Not one. Thanks for being there." He directed his thanks to all of them, forcing himself to confront the truth. "Will you look out for Faith and the children if I... if this turns bad?"

One by one his brothers nodded, gravely silent.

Radford gripped his hand. "Damn it, Duke, I saw men get their legs and arms blown off in the war, and they survived. If they can pull through that, and I can fight my way back from being half-insane, you can fight your way through this."

"This may be bigger than me," Duke half-whispered.

"Bullshit." Boyd laid his hand over his brothers' clasped hands. "You've always said nothing is impossible if the four of us tackle it together."

"That's right." Kyle covered their hands with his. We're here, Duke, and none of us is quitting. Got that?"

Duke got it—their strength, their commitment, and their love. His brothers would be there for him, no matter what.

Chapter Forty

A dam stood outside Duke's bedchamber door, unable to stop shaking. He'd gotten to Radford, he'd brought the sheriff, but he didn't know if he'd gotten them in time to save Duke.

Duke's brothers and mother were in the room with him now. Aster and the doctor had taken the bullet out of his shoulder. Faith slipped in and out of the room, but Cora whimpered the whole time she was away. No matter how many times Faith told Cora the judge was dead, Cora insisted he would come back and get her. She was terrified of the man. And like Adam, the thing the little girl feared most was that her new daddy would die.

Nobody was telling Adam anything, and that's why he couldn't move away from the door. No matter how many people came and went, he didn't budge. Not even when Duke's brothers Kyle and Boyd brought their mother out to wait with the others in the parlor. Not even when Duke groaned, and Radford's low murmur responded; Adam didn't move, because if he left that spot then his silent plea to Duke might not be strong enough to reach him.

The door opened again, and Radford Grayson came out, his face drawn, a fat tear streaking down his left cheek. He wouldn't cry unless Duke was going to die.

Adam's heart cramped, and a big, ugly sob burst from his mouth. He hung his head, not even caring that his nose was starting to run. Nothing mattered now. Duke was the only man he'd ever looked up to. Ever loved. The only man who'd ever been nice to him.

"Come here, son." Rebecca's father pulled him into a hug, and Adam sobbed like a five-year-old against the man's hard chest. All Adam knew of having brothers was from the memories Duke had shared with him. Without Duke's stories and his advice, Adam would have to guess how to become a decent, honorable man—like the sheriff, his father, his friend.

"He'll pull through, Adam. I know my brother, and he won't let us down."

Adam stepped away and wiped his nose on his sleeve, ashamed of his tears. "Sorry I messed up your shirt."

Mr. Grayson pulled a handkerchief from his pocket, and handed it to him. "I owe you an apology, Adam. Your interest in Rebecca was no reason for me to suspect you of bad intentions."

Adam dried his face on the soft cloth. "I should have stayed away like you said, sir."

"Rebecca told me what happened when you two met in the gorge."

"I didn't know she would be there."

"I know. I judged you unfairly. You're an intelligent, courageous young man, and today your quick thinking protected your family."

Adam shook his head. "You did that, sir."

"No, Adam. If you hadn't done what you did, my brother could be dead." Mr. Grayson gripped Adam's shoulders and looked him square in the eye. "Thank you."

⊷⊶ ⊷⊶

As soon as Faith got Cora put to bed, she hurried to her bedchamber to check on Duke. Adam was sitting in the hall with his head against the wall, sound asleep. He hadn't budged from the spot since Duke was carried into the bedchamber twelve hours earlier.

Faith squelched her urge to kiss her brother's forehead as she'd done so many times when he was a round-cheeked baby, but Adam was more man than boy now, and her fussing would embarrass him. She would wake him so he could see Duke, but first, she needed to see her husband alone.

Duke was sleeping when she entered the room. Dr. Milton said he was doing as well as could be expected, but Faith understood too much about wounds to feel comforted. Duke's face was drawn and white as the pillowcase. The sheet and blankets were drawn up to his chest, leaving his shoulders exposed. A bulky bandage covered his left shoulder, and she gave thanks that the bullet hadn't hit his chest and struck his loving, forgiving heart. His mother and Kyle were with him in the room, but they stepped outside with the doctor as Faith entered.

She laid her palm on her husband's hot forehead. He had a long struggle ahead of him. He'd lost a lot of blood and was subject to infection and fever and a host of other things. Her stomach twisted in a knot of worry.

He opened his eyes, but they were glassy and didn't focus.

"You know what I noticed about you the night of the lawn party when we were dancing?" she asked, clasping his right hand with both of hers. "That your voice was as deep and smooth as that cello in Damon's band, that every word you speak is music to my ears." She brought his hand to her chest, hugging it, wishing she could hug him. "I would love it if you'd talk to me."

She waited for the musical sound of his voice, but only his lashes twitched. The doctor had given him a large dose of laudanum to blunt his pain.

"I want to grow old with you, Duke. I want to spend my life loving you." She kissed his lips and stroked his cheek, willing his glazed eyes to see her. "My husband, my lover, my friend—I love you."

She lowered her cheek to his chest, listening to his heartbeat, praying it would grow stronger each hour. She hoped his sigh meant he heard her. If this was their final exchange, she wanted the last words he heard to be "I love you."

An hour later, she was bathing his face when he woke, groaning in pain. The doctor tried to give him more laudanum, but Duke turned away. "I need to see Adam," he said, his voice grating and weak.

Faith hurried to the hall and woke her brother with a gentle shake. He jerked awake and stared at her with round, fearful eyes. "Duke wants to see you," she said.

His eyes lit with hope. "He's awake?"

She nodded, and he scrambled to his feet and slipped into the bedroom. Faith stood aside with the doctor while Adam made his way to the bed.

Duke grimaced in pain as he manipulated his good arm from beneath the covers. He gripped Adam's hand and tugged until Adam was sitting on the mattress beside him. "I understand you've been waiting to see me," he said, sounding more alert but also in more pain.

"Yes, sir." Adam lowered his chin, but Faith could see his throat working, and she knew he was crying. "I saw the gun in Stone's hand, and I wanted to warn you, but I couldn't get the words out."

Duke hooked his hand behind Adam's neck and pulled the boy into a one-armed hug. Emotion clogged Faith's throat. So that's why Adam had needed to see Duke; he needed Duke's manly shoulder and his forgiveness.

"I saw the gun too, son."

Adam sat up, his face wet. "You knew Stone had it?"

"Yes. And I knew he'd try to shoot me, but I wanted to get that revolver away from him before he could hurt someone else. I knew the risk, and I took it. You did everything right, Adam. Without your help, Cora and I might not be here. You did exactly what I told you to do, and that means a lot."

"I wish I could have got Cora away before Stone grabbed her."

"And I wish I could have wrestled that revolver away from Stone before he shot me or pointed it at your sister's head. We both did the best we could." Duke sighed then winced, and Faith could see the effort it took him just to talk. "I need a favor," he said.

"Yes, sir. Anything you want."

"Stop sleeping in the hall." Duke gave him a man-to-man wink. "Sleep with Cora, so she won't be so afraid, and help Faith take care of things while I'm healing this shoulder."

"Yes, sir." Adam slid off the bed. "Your brother, Mr. Grayson, I mean, Rebecca's father, asked me to help out at the mill while you're healing. But don't worry, I'll chop our firewood and take care of everything here, too."

Surprise crossed Duke's face, and he looked at Faith.

She shrugged. "Radford was persuasive." And kind.

"Good." Duke's jaw clamped, and Faith nodded for Adam to leave the room. She sensed they were all at peace now, that whatever weight Adam had been carrying on his shoulders was relieved by Duke's hug.

After Adam left, the doctor moved to the bed where Duke lay with his jaw clenched and his eyes closed. "How about that laudanum now?" the doctor suggested.

"Make it a double," Duke said without opening his eyes. Perspiration beaded on his forehead, and a deep scowl drew his dark eyebrows low.

Dr. Milton gave Duke the laudanum then went home to get some rest after a long afternoon and evening of doctoring.

And Faith's fear mounted. For all her early complaints about the doctor's arrogance, he knew far more about surgery and infection than Faith did, and she longed for his steadying presence.

Duke's mother was a pillar of strength—and also fear and doubt. She helped Faith straighten the room and carry in fresh water then she sat on the bed and wiped a cold cloth over Duke's hot forehead. Her hand shook and her jaw trembled, and she crumbled like a mud wall in a rainstorm. "Oh, honey... I can't lose you." She buried her face against her son's chest and wept, clutching his blood-speckled nightshirt in her fist.

Faith clamped her hand over her mouth to hold back her emphatic sob. She couldn't bear to lose him either. After all the true and honest things she'd failed to do, Duke had given her and her family everything.

Possibly his life.

And if he died, how could she live without him, without his love and passion that illuminated her life? She would live in darkness. But she would owe it to him to go on.

She choked back her tears and tightened her resolve. She would nurse him back to health. She would apply everything she'd ever learned in those books she'd read. She would not give up.

She spent frantic hours mixing herbal remedies to keep Duke's temperature down. Her aunts helped and offered advice, but his body grew warmer through the night and was burning by morning.

"What does the fever mean?" Boyd asked, his voice hoarse from talking all night. He'd sat at Duke's side, rambling about their childhood, and the mill, and anything that might allow Duke to hear his voice.

"I don't know," Faith said. It could mean anything, including the onset of infection, but it was too soon to tell.

Radford came later that morning to take his turn at Duke's bedside, and Faith learned about the brothers and their lives as mischievous boys and struggling young men. She saw them as Duke's friends and his strength. And she saw that without him they were incomplete.

Duke's mother pulled herself together and stayed at Faith's side, lending her strength as they nursed Duke through another day and night of a fever that wasn't breaking.

Another night passed, and this time Kyle kept Duke and Faith company, his low voice soothing and reassuring as he talked into the wee hours of the morning.

And Faith lost track of time.

Evelyn and Claire and Amelia took turns stopping to see Duke and to offer Faith and their mother-in-law a helping hand. Even Anna and Millie stopped to offer their help. The house was full of people cleaning and cooking and lending a hand when needed, but there was nothing they could do for Duke but add their prayers to Faith's.

Cora had settled down and was sleeping in her own bed now that Adam was staying with her. It allowed Faith more time with Duke, but nothing seemed to be helping him. Dr. Milton stayed nearly around the clock, wearing a worried scowl that filled her stomach with dread. They cleaned Duke's wound and sponged his body and did everything possible to give him comfort and help him survive. His brothers pushed him to fight, cajoling then demanding then one by one they would break down and bury their face in their hands and beg him to wake up.

As the days turned into a week then stretched toward two, an ominous hush filled the house. The only sounds were whispered prayers and the unceasing murmur of his brothers' hoarse, exhausted voices as they sat at his bedside.

Duke mumbled and groaned and thrashed in restless fits, his big brawny body struggling against the fevers but shrinking with their heat. Then he would lie so still that Faith's heart would stop and she would check to see if he was still breathing. By the end of the twelfth night, the whole family was hollow-eyed and exhausted.

Faith sat in a chair with her head and arms resting on the bed beside Duke. Radford sat on the other side of him talking to Duke about some sort of dungeon they had dug in the field when they were boys.

"Boyd was our robber-prisoner, and you were the guard," he said.

Faith smiled. Of course Duke was the lawman. He would never be the bad guy.

She fell asleep to the sound of Radford's hoarse voice, and woke to the feel of someone's hand stroking her hair. Thinking it was one of her aunts, Faith wearily lifted her head and found herself looking into Duke's dark eyes.

"I'm starving," he said.

She blinked, thinking her sleep-deprived brain was playing tricks on her, but it really was Duke stroking her hair.

"I want a dozen eggs. A loaf of toasted bread..." He paused, out of breath, his poor body ravaged and weak.

Shock silenced her, but Radford laughed with relief and shot to his feet. "It's about time you woke up. I was running out of stories."

"Skip the stories. I want food."

"I'll go raid the kitchen for you," Radford said, wearing a wide smile as he left the room.

Stunned, almost afraid to move for fear she'd wake up and find she'd been dreaming, Faith clasped her husband's hand, her gaze roving his face, looking into the dark eyes that she'd feared she would never see again. "I've been worried sick about you."

He glanced at the window where weak winter daylight touched the pane. "How long have I been in bed?"

"Nearly two weeks."

He closed his eyes. "I thought I would do better."

She laughed at his absurd comment. "Only a man would say something so foolish." She sat beside him and cradled his drawn, whisker-covered face in her palms. "I missed you."

He slid his right hand up her forearm, his eyes dark and questioning. "Did I dream that you said you love me?"

"I said it, and I mean it." She kissed his forehead, thankful it was only warm and not burning hot. "I love you for treating Adam with fairness. I love you for being kind to Cora, and giving her the daddy she needs. I love you for showing me a world I've never known. I love you for forgiving my lies, for defending my family, and for surviving that nasty gunshot."

Her throat jammed with emotion, and she buried her face in the crook of his neck. He smelled of balm and the herbs she'd used to ease his discomfort and bring his fever down.

"I was afraid I dreamed that," he said hoarsely.

"You weren't dreaming. I love you."

"Then feed me. My belly button is touching my spine."

She smiled and sat up. "I'm afraid you'll have to start with chicken broth instead of eggs."

He made a face. "Skip it then. Lock our door, and climb in beside me."

She didn't lock the door, and she didn't climb into bed beside him, but she did lean down and kiss him. His lips were chapped, but their light, warm touch against her mouth comforted her. He was alive. Their nightmare was over. And he knew she loved him.

He turned his face away. "I must stink."

"Not at all. We've taken good care of you." She sat back. "You've had a sponge bath every day."

"Not from Iris, I hope."

"Only twice. We all took turns. Even Patrick and Cyrus helped."

His laugh was weak but so encouraging. "I can imagine the rumors going around the mill."

"Your reputation is shot."

"I don't mind. Trying to be faultless doesn't... leave much time for living... and loving."

"Then get better so we can do that." She linked her fingers with his. "Our house is full of people waiting to see you."

"Let 'em wait." He tugged her hand, and in the sweetness of his chaste, tender kiss, her heart turned over with love and gratitude that he had held on. For Cora and Adam, for his family, and most of all, for her.

Chapter Forty-one

Duke was standing up gripping the bedpost when Faith walked into the room carrying a steaming bowl of who-knew-what in her arms. She stopped and gaped at him.

"What are you doing out of bed?"

"I'm escaping."

She arched her shapely eyebrow. "You're going to fall and undo all my hard work."

"I can't take any more of your torture," he said, only half-joking. "I'll do anything if you'll let me out of here."

She smiled and set the bowl on the bed stand. "Get back in bed, darling, or I'll send for your brothers."

"They're traitors. They've deserted me."

"They come to see you every evening after they finish work."

"I'm going mad lying in bed around the clock. I need to get back on my feet."

"You will. When you've healed a little more and your strength returns. Now get in bed."

He eyed the green and brown stuff floating in the bowl with suspicion. "I'm not drinking that."

Her laugh rang through the room and she embraced him. "You don't have to. I'm making a poultice from birch leaves and bark to put on your shoulder."

"I don't need it. You're my best medicine." He kissed her, liking the way her eyes sparkled with concern.

"Please get in bed."

Her soft plea, and his quaking legs, drove him back to the bed he'd been living in for three weeks. Faith sat beside him and dunked a cheesecloth in the bowl of steaming water.

"Adam and your brothers are taking care of all the chores, so you can relax." She unbuttoned the nightshirt he'd come to loathe, and pulled it over his shoulder. "This might hurt a bit."

It all hurt. The concoctions she put on him; shuffling to the water closet; it even hurt to breathe.

She gently wrung the cloth, filled it with leaves, and folded it into a dripping square pad. "Your wound is turning a nice healthy pink," she said, laying the warm cloth over his shoulder.

He sucked in his breath, knowing her concoctions were helping, but hating the constant assault on his shoulder. Exhausted, he flopped his head back against the pillow, as annoyed as he was reassured by her constant tending. "You're turning me into an invalid."

"The gunshot to your shoulder did that." She dried her hands on her apron. "If you don't stay in bed and rest, who will Cora play with?"

While Duke had seen little of Adam, because the boy was happily filling in as the man of the house, little Cora had been his constant companion, sitting on his bed "reading" to him from her favorite books.

"Just promise me you'll share our bed again soon," he said.

"I will." She kissed him, killing him with tenderness. "As soon as you're well enough."

⟜⟊ ⟋⟞

Duke was so relieved to be out of the bedroom, he wasn't about to tell Faith how weak he felt, or how the wrenching pain in his shoulder drove him half mad, or how the constant stream of callers exhausted him. Family and friends came and went, helping his wife with chores, bringing meals, and teasing Duke that he was purposely loafing to avoid work. Faith seemed reassured by their presence, but she kept a watchful eye on him, feeding him herbal teas he hated, and coaching him to move his arm a little farther each day to keep his shoulder muscles from growing stiff.

Her strength and her love had drawn him like a magnet from death. During his twelve days of oblivion, she'd sat with him, nursed him with her balms and herbs, fought for him as hard as his brothers had, and their combined love and will and skill had brought him back.

And now that he was back, she was guarding him with the protective instinct of a mother. Even his own mother was willing to let him step onto the porch for fresh air, but Faith wouldn't hear of it. She was worried he'd slip on the ice and fall.

But as the days wore on, Duke worried he'd lose his mind if he didn't get out of the house.

Her boisterous aunts and their outrageous stories saved his sanity. They made him laugh so hard it drove spikes of pain through his shoulder, but the crazy women lifted his spirits. Between them and his own family, they eased the load on Faith's shoulders. Tansy even painted Cora's room with a speckled pony and a knight in armor to watch over her, which convinced Cora to try sleeping alone again like a big girl.

Sheriff Phelps stopped by, to reassure Duke that no charges would be brought against Radford for killing Stone. The *Censure* hailed Radford as a hero who'd saved a former sheriff's life. The article went on to name Stone as a corrupt judge whose involvement with a theater project in Syracuse was being investigated.

Cuvier had made sure no one would look for a connection between Duke and Stone, and possibly uncover Faith's tie to the brothel, by claiming the judge had come after him for discovering the man's criminal dealings. Then Cuvier had returned to Syracuse to dig up the truth on Stone. He was coming back today.

Duke was going to get his father-in-law's help in making his escape. After four weeks on his back and two more of being housebound, he was staging a revolt. Faith had him settled on the sofa and gussied up with a footstool and an afghan, for Pete's sake!

When Cuvier strolled into the parlor and caught him bundled up like an infant, Duke flung off the afghan then ground his teeth from pain. His shoulder was healing, but was still extremely tender.

"Glad to see you up and about," Cuvier said, tossing a copy of a Syracuse newspaper on the coffee table. "It appears Stone worked alone, I suspect to guard his reputation."

"A man like Stone would work alone just so no one had the power to manipulate him."

"I agree," Cuvier said. "I visited Stone's father, and the old man is shaken up over his son's death but sincerely shocked by the news of Franklin's scheming. He told me about the lifelong competition between Franklin and his twin brother Gordon. He said the boys fought from birth, first for their mother's nurturing, and later for his attention. When Gordon started following in the old man's footsteps and pursuing a political career, Franklin pursued law. According to their father, Gordon was the smarter of the two boys, and his early success drove Franklin into a rage on several occasions. It got so the old man wouldn't speak to the two about each other."

"Why did Franklin begrudge his brother success?" Duke asked, baffled. Sure, he'd envied his brothers at times, but he'd always celebrated their achievements with complete and sincere happiness.

Cuvier shrugged. "I went to Washington to ask Gordon that very question. He thinks Franklin's animosity stemmed from their competition over a gal they were both smitten with. As soon as Gordon married the girl, his brother seemed driven to outdo any success Gordon had. Gordon suspects that's why Franklin started the theater project. But his plans collapsed so many times, both Gordon and their father pushed him to give it up. He refused, of course, and vowed he would build that theater, name it after the old man, and renew the city his father was born in."

"For what? Recognition?"

"That's what Gordon thinks. And after talking with their father, it's the only motive that makes any sense to me. Franklin reveled in his power as judge, and I know he liked being recognized for any achievement, no matter how small."

"Pathetic."

"But true." Cuvier took a cheroot from his breast pocket. "I called on his mistress, and learned the judge was planning to have the woman's brother—the man you clobbered— anonymously deliver Cora to a family who wanted a girl child."

Duke's gut twisted. "Then he had no intention of returning her to us even if we had given him the property?"

"No. If anyone learned he had a bastard child by a prostitute from the very brothel he was tearing down, it would have ruined his reputation and lowered him another notch in his father's regard."

"But Faith and I could have publicized the truth either way."

"How could you prove it without having the child to back up your accusation?"

"That crafty, corrupt son of a bitch." Duke shook his head. "I think Franklin Stone was far smarter than his father thought."

"He manipulated all of us to some extent. The place he was sending Cora appeared to be a good home with people who would care for her.

That's what makes me think he was bluffing when he put that gun to her head."

Duke huffed out a breath, both shocked and infuriated by the news. "I thought he was greedy and too driven to care about his own child. I feared he'd pull the trigger if I pushed him."

"He might have. No one can know. His actions were desperate and his mind frighteningly unstable that day. He was so obsessed with finishing his theater project, he might have snapped completely if you'd pushed him."

Maybe. Whatever Stone's motives, the man's half-crazed mental state could have easily gotten Duke and Cora killed. Duke picked up the paper and angled it toward the window to read the article. After Stone's death, several homeowners came forward to testify they'd been coerced into selling him their property Stone had extorted every one of them. The article went on to say that Stone's brother was making amends by negotiating handsome contracts on the properties and giving the money to the homeowners. And while Faith's father brought most of Stone's corrupt deeds to light, incurring several tough questions from authorities about his part in Stone's scheme, there was no mention of Faith's mother or the brothel. And an audit and investigation cleared Cuvier of any wrongdoing.

Justice was served. Duke laid aside the paper, feeling proud of Cuvier. "Well done."

"And well deserved." Cuvier reached inside his suit coat and pulled out an envelope. "I've taken care of the papers you asked for."

Duke accepted the envelope, knowing what it contained, and that they had both said all there was to say on the subject. "Care to take a walk?" he asked, wincing as he pushed to his feet.

Cuvier stood. "I could use the air."

"Then sneak me out, because it's the only way Faith is going to let me leave the house."

His father-in-law was a good sport and distracted Faith while Duke slipped outside. They walked to the livery together, and found Evelyn outside talking with Anna and Dahlia.

The women greeted them with smiles, but Dahlia broke away to speak to them. "I vowed if you ever crossed my path again," she said to Cuvier, "I'd cut your heart out for hurting Rose. But I understand the situation now, and can only thank you for exposing Stone as a corrupt scoundrel."

Cuvier's lips twitched. "Hello, Dahlia."

A softer, friendlier look stole into her eyes. "Where have you been living these past thirteen years?"

"I haven't been living."

"Then Rose didn't suffer alone." With that she walked away and took up her conversation with Evelyn and Anna.

Cuvier chuckled and lit a cheroot. "I see why Rose loved those women."

Duke nodded. "They have a way of growing on a person."

"Go in and see your brother. I'm going to smoke and watch the horses for a bit."

He left Cuvier to his thoughts and entered the livery.

Pitchfork in hand, Radford was cleaning a stall, whisking the soiled straw into a nearby wheelbarrow. He arched his eyebrow at Duke. "I'm surprised Faith let you out of the house."

"She didn't. I tunneled through the parlor wall."

Radford laughed and scraped up another forkful of straw. "Kyle and Boyd were cooking up a plan to break you out. They'll be glad to know they don't have to cross Faith."

"I don't blame them. I'm hoping her father can sneak me back inside."

"By the looks of you, I'd put my money on Faith."

"Me too. That's why I'm laying low." Duke rested his arms on the pine boards of the stall, glad for the support, but irritated he needed it. He hated being so weak.

Radford tossed another forkful of straw into the wheelbarrow. "I've been wanting to apologize. Just haven't found the right time."

"How could you, when my house is overrun with women who won't stop fussing over me?"

"Could be worse." Radford smiled, and Duke regretted the harsh words he'd had with his brother.

"I'm sorry I condemned you for protecting Rebecca," he said. "That's what a father is supposed to do."

"A father is supposed to protect and guide his children," Radford said, continuing to work, "not smother them and make all their decisions for them." He rested the pitchfork tines in the straw and hung his hand over the top of the handle. "I misjudged Adam. He's worthy of your praise, and you were right to defend his character. You've got a fine young man for a son."

"Thank you." Radford's acknowledgment and acceptance of Adam soothed the wound in Duke's heart. "I wish you hadn't needed to shoot Stone," he said. His words were few, but Radford would understand all the things he wasn't saying: He was sorry to resurrect the demons that had nearly driven Radford insane after the war, he was sorry to burden Radford's conscience with another killing.

Radford sighed and leaned against the pine slats. "You know, after Kyle and I got in that fight here, I walked out of the livery wondering if I could ever pull myself together. I felt shaky and half-crazy like I was back in the war."

"You'd gone through hell. No one blamed you for losing control."

"I was a mess, Duke. I couldn't even hold a gun at William's funeral. Everything was exploding in my head like I was in the middle of Gettysburg. I couldn't have protected anyone that day, and I've wondered ever since if I'd fall apart when my family needed me." His shoulders lowered on a hard sigh. "Now I know. Right or wrong, shooting Stone was the only choice. I regret having to do it, but I don't regret my decision to save my brother."

Peace flowed into Duke's chest. Radford had finally escaped the war. Killing men had imprisoned Radford, but saving Duke had freed him.

No, neither of them would have chosen this situation, but circumstances had forced them to cross the line, to commit acts they would never willingly perform. Duke had kidnapped a child who needed him. Radford had killed a man to save his brother. And Faith had lied to protect her family. Right or wrong, good or bad, they'd all done what they'd had to do.

And Duke could live with that.

Chapter Forty-two

I t was a cold, snowy Christmas Eve, but Duke sat in the sleigh and inhaled the fresh air, feeling alive and somewhat healthy for the first time since he had been shot. He couldn't wait to work the mill again. He'd thought he would feel incomplete without his sheriff's badge, but he knew a wholeness and happiness he'd never before experienced. He knew who he was: a Grayson.

Radford had tried being a soldier. Kyle had once wanted to be a lawyer. Boyd had been a bar owner. Duke spent years as a sheriff. But those occupations had only defined a small part of who they were as men. They were brothers, sons, fathers, and husbands. They would defend their families as fiercely as they would defend their country. They would disagree at times, but they would always stand united when it counted.

They were Graysons. Men who argued and laughed and made mistakes sometimes. Men with families. Men with wives they loved and honored.

"Why so quiet?" Faith asked, brushing her warm lips across his jaw. She smiled up at him, her cheeks rosy, a tender expression in her whiskey-colored eyes.

"I was just thinking about you," he said, glad she looked happy. They snuggled beneath the lap robe, and she didn't express any curiosity about their destination until they stopped in the middle of Forest Hill Cemetery.

Adam leapt from the front seat of the sleigh with a youthful agility Duke envied. With painful slowness, he got himself out, but Cuvier assisted Faith and Cora.

"Is your father buried here?" Faith asked, standing beside him with her new hat and scarf, looking so beautiful he wanted to rush her straight home to their big bed that had been agonizingly empty while he'd healed. He would not wait one more night to love her.

"No, your mother is. She's in Fredonia now." Duke gestured to the engraved stone that marked Celia Rose's new resting place. "We can plant roses in the spring."

Faith stared at the stone and her lips parted. "Is she really... did you move her here?"

"Your father saw to it while I was laid up."

"Oh, Duke..." Faith knelt in the snow and smoothed her knit gloves over the stone. He was afraid she would cry, and that her tears would upset Cora, who was still easily frightened. But Faith looked up at him with the most radiant smile he'd ever seen. "Thank you." She shifted her beautiful joyful eyes to her father. "There's nothing you could have ever given me to equal this."

And there was nothing Faith could have given her father that would have equaled her unsolicited forgiveness. With one sentence she had freed Steven Cuvier of a lifetime of guilt.

"Let's decorate the stone and then get home," Duke said. "I have some gifts for the three of you."

"How can you have gifts for us when you haven't been out of the house?" Faith asked, giving him a suspicious squint. "Have you been sneaking out while I've been sleeping?"

"Of course not!"

She laughed and gave his ribs a playful nudge. "I have a surprise for you, too. We have an outing this evening."

They would go to his mother's house, where everyone gathered for holidays and celebrations. As always, it would be cramped and noisy, but Duke was looking forward to getting back to all the things he'd taken for granted.

He stood by as Faith, Adam, and Cora decorated Rose's grave with a pine wreath and a festive red bow, their faces illuminated with joy instead of the grief so often witnessed in a cemetery.

He joined them in singing carols on the way home, laughing at their off-key harmony When Faith tried to hurry them inside, he led them to the small barn near the greenhouse. "Let's give Cora her present first," he said, opening the doors.

When Cora saw Evelyn's dapple-gray gelding happily munching hay, her eyes grew as round as the buttons on her Sunday go-to-meeting coat. "There's a pony in our barn!"

"He's yours, princess."

Both Faith and Cora gawked at him. "This is too much," Faith said, but Cuvier looked pleased to see Rose's children being loved and taken care of.

"It's a special Christmas this year." Duke gave Adam a wink because Adam had been party to the surprise. The boy had gotten the pony for Duke and sneaked it into the barn.

They followed Cora inside to welcome Dandelion to the family. The gelding would go back to the livery in the morning until Evelyn and Rebecca taught Cora how to ride safely and care for him.

A squeaky little bark came from the back of the barn, and Adam's eyes lit up. "I think there's a dog in here."

Duke grinned. "I think you're right, and if you can find the little rascal, he belongs to you."

Adam found the beagle pup in a nest of straw.

"He'll make a good hunting dog," Duke said.

"Can he sleep in my room?"

Faith gave Duke a look of horror, but Duke could tell she was mostly happy for the boy.

By the time they went inside for hot chocolate, they were all half-frozen. Adam brought the puppy with him, and Cora wanted to know why she couldn't bring the pony too. She was easily distracted with a new doll and a bag of licorice sticks.

Adam could barely put his dog down long enough to open the box under the pine tree. He liked his new boots and coat and gloves, but his eyes widened when he saw the rifle. "I never got so many gifts in my life," he said, stroking the gun barrel with awe.

"We'll keep the rifle put up until I can teach you how to clean it and use it safely"

"Yes, sir."

Faith admired her new dresses, fussing over the lace and ribbons. But when she opened the package containing a new pharmacopoeia book, she let out a shriek that sent the puppy scrambling under the sofa. "Oh, Duke! How did you get this?"

The book had been hard to come by, but with Doc Milton's help and a good bit of money, Duke had acquired it.

She hugged the book to her chest. "It's the best gift in the world."

He knew better. *She* was the best gift in the world. She planted a sizzling kiss on his mouth, her sparkling, love-filled gaze locked with his.

———

Faith gazed into her husband's shining eyes, clutching the book to her chest, unable to believe it was hers, and that he was hers. "Thank you."

He winked then pulled a rolled paper from his coat pocket and handed it to Adam. "I'd like to make you a Grayson," he said. "If you sign this adoption paper then Faith and I can legally adopt you."

Adam's mouth gaped open as he stared at the paper.

Astonishment and love surged through Faith's chest, and she bit her lip, moved to tears.

A broad smile broke across Adam's face, and he leaned down to speak to his puppy. "I'm going to be a Grayson," he whispered.

Faith understood what being a Grayson meant to Adam. He would carry a name that was respected and valued in this community. And he would belong; he would have a father who would love and guide him into manhood with all the values Adam respected and admired.

Looking over at Steven Cuvier, the sad acceptance she saw made her heart squeeze. Her father would have been there for them if he'd had the opportunity, if Rose had been truthful. He was happy to become a father to Faith, but Adam needed and loved Duke, and considered him his father. Steven gave a solemn, kindly nod to acknowledge his understanding. "You have my blessing in this," he said to Adam.

Faith laid her book on the coffee table and got the ink stand and quill for Adam. Her father looked on while Adam signed a document that made him another man's son.

When they finished, Adam frowned at Faith. "If Duke's my dad, what does this make you?"

"Exactly what I've always been, Adam, your motherly sister." And her son by possession. The darling little boy she'd loved and raised from birth.

His nose wrinkled. "Does this make you my grandfather, Mr. Cuvier?"

Warmth filled his eyes and he smiled at Adam. "I'd be honored to be your grandfather."

Chapter Forty-three

Adam marveled that Faith and his aunts, with the help of Duke's family and Anna, had made the second floor of the greenhouse into a festive hall. He'd carried up chairs and coffee tables that Faith had grouped around the edges of the room, leaving the middle of the hardwood floor open. But the best part of helping was watching Duke's brothers and Patrick haul a piano upstairs. When they finally set it down, they were panting and sweating, and Adam was staring with awe. Someday he was going to be strong enough to lift a piano.

"It's so pretty in here," Cora said, her eyes wide as she stared at the pine wreaths and ribbons and candles that decorated every wall and table.

It looked kind of bright and girlish to Adam, but he and Cora had sure been enjoying the food table in the back. It was loaded with cookies and pies and food they had never tasted before.

Someone touched his shoulder, and he wheeled around to see if Faith was fussing with his shirt collar again. But it was Rebecca, looking pretty in a green dress and shiny green hair ribbon.

Her eyes were almost as sad as the day he'd told her he couldn't see her anymore. "Are you mad at me?" she asked.

"No," he said, glad his voice wasn't croaking as often. "I thought you were mad at me."

"I was just... I've missed skipping stones and walking to school with you."

He'd missed it too. Nicholas Archer had been coming around, but it wasn't the same as being friends with Rebecca.

Cora skipped across the floor to see Amelia's new baby, leaving him alone with Rebecca.

"Want to go raid the cookie trays together?" she asked with a smile.

He was going to say no, that he'd eaten more than his share, but the hopeful spark in her eyes wouldn't let him disappoint her. "If you're allowed to be around me."

"I'm allowed. Daddy said we can be friends."

Friends. It was less than he wanted in his heart, but he'd thought he'd lost everything. "Do you want to be friends?" he asked.

"Yes, Adam. But only until I'm sixteen."

Confused, he wrinkled his nose. "Girls are so odd."

"When I'm sixteen you can kiss me again."

His mouth fell open.

"If you want to," she said.

"Yeah. I mean, sure." He wanted to kiss her now! "If your dad will let me court you."

"He will. And when I'm eighteen we can—"

"Gads, Rebecca! Don't even say it."

"Why not?"

"Because you might be overheard, and... gosh, it's all I'll be able to think about now."

She laughed. "Is that bad?"

"It'll be torture. I've got three years to wait before I can even kiss you."

"Two and a half. I'm thirteen and one-half years old," she said, spelling it out for him. She stuck out her hand with those pretty long fingers that could skip stones better than Adam sometimes. "Friends?"

He closed his hand over her soft, warm skin, his heart lifting. She was worth waiting for, and someday he would make her his wife. "For now," he said, feeling shaky and eager. "But I can't WAIT until you're sixteen."

"I can't WAIT either," Rebecca squawked, and they both laughed, their smiles fading slowly as they held hands.

"Will you hate me if I steal a kiss now and then?" he asked, knowing he would, that despite his effort to be good and honorable and live up to the Grayson name, Rebecca's sweetness and warmth would be too tempting to resist.

"I'd be disappointed if you didn't."

He smiled, knowing he wouldn't disappoint her desire for a kiss. He just hoped he could keep his urges under control and not disappoint himself.

"Maybe we should go get some cookies," he said, because he couldn't stand there and look at her without wanting to kiss her. She tucked her hand into the crook of his elbow, and he guided her to the food table, proud to have her at his side.

Adam wove through the crowd and greeted everyone who'd been at Duke and Faith's wedding. Duke's younger brother Boyd caught him as he passed by, and clapped a strong hand over Adam's shoulder. "I hear you're a Grayson now," he said, clowning like he did at the sawmill.

"Yes, sir."

"That's yes, Uncle Boyd," he said, scrubbing his knuckles on the top of Adam's head.

Adam laughed and elbowed him away, but it was the best night of his life. He had a dog, a dad, and Rebecca's friendship. And later, maybe more.

Duke watched Boyd joke with Adam and his heart flooded with warmth. He linked hands with Faith and drew her to his side.

The joyous sound of bells filled the room and drew their attention to the front of the room. Bells in hand, Iris stood with Patrick beside the huge pine tree that Tansy, Claire, and Anna had strung with red and gold ribbons. "Welcome to our first annual family soiree," she said, giving the bells a jolly shake that made everyone clap.

Everyone except Duke. He wasn't chancing any activity that would make his shoulder ache, because he was making love to his wife tonight.

Iris winked at him. "This year we have much to be thankful for. I'll start listing our blessings by giving thanks for each one of you with your loving, forgiving, accepting hearts that have allowed me and my family to find a real home."

Duke lifted his glass of ale. "Here's to you, Iris, and your outrageous family, who has taught me not to take what I have for granted." A loud cheer shook the rafters then everyone fell quiet, waiting for him to go on, but he was so choked by emotion he could barely speak through the gratitude and love filling him. He moved his glass in an arc to encompass and salute his friends, his brothers and mother, his wife and children, and the Wilde women he'd come to love. "To each of you, for being too stubborn and noisy to let me die in peace."

His comment made them laugh, and one by one each person in the room added to the long list of their blessings. Rebecca said she was thankful to have a mother and father who loved her.

"I'm thankful to be a Grayson," Adam said, casting a half-grin at Duke that made his chest tighten with pride. "And to have a bunch of uncles who are as crazy as my aunts."

"Crazy?" Boyd lunged at Adam, and the boy danced away with a laugh.

"I got a pony!" Cora shouted.

When the laughter died down, Duke's brothers joked that he would have to carry the piano downstairs by himself, and teased him about taking so long to get back to work at the mill, but they all gave thanks that he had survived his injury.

"Amen." His mother raised her glass. "I'm eternally grateful to Faith and Doc Milton and this big, crazy family for nursing my son back to health."

Faith's arms slipped around Duke's waist, and she smiled at him with those lush lips. "I miss you," she whispered, making him want to ravish her on the spot. Her smile faded and tears glistened in her eyes. "I love you, Duke. I'm so grateful for you and for what we share. I feel so much love and... Oh, darling, there just aren't words—" She broke off and pressed her lips to his jaw. He drew her close, agreeing that what they were feeling was too big, too deep, and too powerful for words.

He pulled her closer, tighter, longing to make love with her. "Tonight's the night," he whispered near her ear.

"I know." She looped her arms around his neck and smiled up at him.

"Whoa you two!" Boyd lifted his palms. "Before you start a fire, I'll go play Faith's special request." He swept Claire into his arms and danced her across the floor to the piano. They sat and began playing "Kissing in the Dark."

The rich sound of the piano filled the room and Duke gathered his wife in his arms and kissed her in front of everyone. "I love you," he whispered. He would kiss her in the light of day and in the dark of night and every chance he got.

He opened the dance floor right where they were standing, holding his wife in his arms, sharing their deep and true love. He longed for Faith and the privacy to love her, but he savored the moment and the blessing of having this big, loving family gathered around him.

The dance floor filled, and Patrick and Iris twirled past, their bodies close, their eyes sparking with desire and fixed on each other's face. "She'll marry him," Duke said, resting his hand against the curve of Faith's waist.

"I hope so." She looked at Iris and sighed. "But you don't know my aunt like I do. She's stubborn and independent and terrified of giving her heart to a man."

"Well, I know Patrick, and my money is on him. He won't quit until Iris speaks her wedding vows with him."

"Good." Faith smiled. "She needs a strong man who isn't afraid of a challenge."

"Then Patrick is her man."

"And you're mine," she said, drawing him closer, making him tremble with the need to love her.

He felt the unmistakable tug of Cora's small hand on his suit-coat. She looked up with bright eyes and a chocolate-smudged cheek that wrung his heart. "Will you dance with me, Daddy?"

He wanted to, but he couldn't hold her in his arms yet. Faith reached down and lifted Cora onto her hip. "We'll both dance with Daddy," she said, and Duke gladly, joyfully drew his girls into his arms.

Chapter Forty-four

A fter a long night of celebration, Faith reached for her husband, missing him, eager for his loving touch. But he stepped away from her and set the lantern on the table in the bathhouse.

"I want to give this to you first," he said, pulling something from his coat pocket.

To her surprise, he placed her mother's silver-handled hair brush in her hand. Her breath sighed out and she held the brush in her palms. "You found it!"

"I'd forgotten about it until I put my coat on tonight."

"Oh, Duke, this is... it reminds me of the times Mama brushed my hair." She stroked her fingers over the painted roses on the porcelain back, remembering those brief but warm moments with her mother. "She loved me." The truth flowed into her heart, washing away the ache, leaving behind peace and love and forgiveness. "I was loved," she whispered.

"You were. And you are."

She drew the brush through her hair, feeling the delicious tug against her scalp and hearing the raspy sound of the bristles slipping through her hair. Her mother had loved her.

"I'll brush your hair if you like," Duke offered.

She raised her eyes to her husband, touched by his tender consideration, but she shook her head. She didn't need her hair brushed anymore; she needed to be in her husband's arms. She laid the brush on the table, at peace. "I want you to love me."

"I do," he said, his voice filled with sincerity and conviction. He embraced her.

"Even after all I've cost you?"

"You've brought me riches I never dreamed of."

"Would you have chosen me if you'd known the truth?"

"The only truth that matters is that I met and fell in love with a brave, compassionate and loyal woman, and I chose with my head and my heart when I asked you to marry me."

She cradled his firm jaw in her palms, loving the textures of his body and the smoldering heat in his eyes. "I could have been a wealthy princess with a kingdom of men to choose from, and I would have chosen you as the love of my life." He would always be her friend, her lover, the man of her dreams.

A sense of homecoming filled Duke, and he kissed his wife. "I wanted to sneak you down here hours ago."

"I'd have come willingly." She kissed his neck. "I'll always welcome your touch." She nibbled his earlobe. "And your love." She slid her hands down his sides. "And your passion."

His groin tightened and his breath hissed out.

She stroked her hands up his chest. "I don't want to hurt you," she whispered, driving him mad with her fondling and teasing. "But I can't stay away from you any longer. You might have to take a little discomfort with your pleasure."

"Gladly." He shook with a need to consume her, and yet he held back and kept the kiss tender. Love wasn't for the fainthearted. But it was worth the wounds. It was worth every moment of doubt and pain. Because to live and love, one had to be willing to bleed.

"It's been forever since you've kissed me," she whispered against his mouth.

"I couldn't kiss you and not make love to you."

"You can do both now."

"I will." He trailed his tongue across her lips and filled his palm with her breast. 'All night," he said, loving how she smelled of blooming flowers and scented oils and the good rich earth that filled her greenhouse.

She gazed up at him, her eyes sparkling in the lantern light. "It could be a long night. I brought some oil."

"Gads! Not the smelly lavender, I hope."

"Better than lavender," she said, in a warm, sexy tone he'd not heard her use before, a tone of openness and confidence and trust. "I mixed up a special combination, just for us."

"This better not be your sneaky way of treating my shoulder with another one of your concoctions."

She smiled, the glow of happiness on her face a feast for his eyes, her lush lips a temptation to his mouth. "You know what I thought of the first time you kissed me?" she asked.

"That I was taking advantage of you."

She shook her head. "I thought I'd kissed the sun. I didn't want to leave the warmth of your arms or lose the thrilling heat of your mouth on mine." She stroked his jaw. "I need your light, Duke. I need your love."

"You have my heart and my soul, sweetheart."

Her eyes sparkled with mischief. "Can I have your body too?"

"Only if you promise to stop your doctoring."

"Well, I thought I'd stretch your muscles before we—"

He growled and playfully bit her neck. "I can put your lovely hands to better use, sweetheart."

Her arms circled his waist in invitation, her soft laugh echoing off the stones and into his heart, and love was no longer a mystery out of reach, beyond his wildest dream. *Faith* was love. She brought companionship and passion and meaning to his life. All the struggles and sacrifices and lessons were worthwhile. Their future would be an amazing journey filled with family, laughter, passion. Giving his heart to Faith had changed him, altered his too-rigid way of seeing the world, and taught him what it meant to love, to be a husband, a father, and a better man—a complete man.

And their journey was just beginning.

⇒ THE END ⇐

Dear Reader,

Thank you for taking the time to read *Kissing in the Dark*. I've received so many requests for Adam and Rebecca's story that I wrote *Sleigh of Hope*, which is a special Grayson Christmas story with Adam and Rebecca and is the prequel to their adult love story (for release date please visit www.wendylindstrom.com). I hope you'll enjoy this special holiday story. If you would like to spend more time with the Grayson family, receive a notice when the next book is coming out, or learn more about the books in this series, please visit www. wendylindstrom.com and sign up for New Book Alert!

I sincerely hope you enjoyed *Kissing in the Dark* and consider it a 5-star keeper that brought you many enjoyable hours of reading. If so, and you would be willing to share your enthusiasm with other readers, I'd be very grateful. Telling your friends about my books and posting online reviews is extremely helpful and instrumental in elevating this series. It not only helps other readers find my books more easily but enables me to publish books more frequently. I have many wonderful stories to share with you, so please continue to spread the word.

Even with many layers of editing, mistakes can slip through. If you encounter typos or errors in this book, please send them to me at www.wendylindstrom.com (use Contact link).

Thanks again for your enthusiastic support. I'm wishing you many blissful hours of reading.

Peace and warmest wishes,
Wendy

About the Author

Wendy Lindstrom is a RITA Award-winning author of "beautifully poignant, wonderfully emotional" historical romances. *Romantic Times* has dubbed her "one of romance's finest writers," and readers rave about her enthralling characters and the riveting emotional power of her work. For more information about Wendy Lindstrom's other books, excerpts, and sneak previews, please visit www.wendylindstrom.com.

Please remember to sign up for New Book Alert! and post your online review!

CPSIA information can be obtained at www.ICGtesting.com
Printed in the USA
LVOW08s1714130614

389977LV00001B/130/P

[15]